Captured by Love

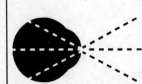

This Large Print Book carries the
Seal of Approval of N.A.V.H.

CAPTURED BY LOVE

JODY HEDLUND

THORNDIKE PRESS
A part of Gale, Cengage Learning

GALE
CENGAGE Learning

Farmington Hills, Mich • San Francisco • New York • Waterville, Maine
Meriden, Conn • Mason, Ohio • Chicago

GALE
CENGAGE Learning·

Copyright © 2014 by Jody Hedlund.
Scripture quotations are from the King James Version of the Bible.
Thorndike Press, a part of Gale, Cengage Learning.

ALL RIGHTS RESERVED
This is a work of historical reconstruction; the appearance of certain historical figures is therefore inevitable. All other characters, however, are products of the author's imagination, and any resemblance to actual persons, living or dead, is coincidental.

Thorndike Press® Large Print Christian Romance.
The text of this Large Print edition is unabridged.
Other aspects of the book may vary from the original edition.
Set in 16 pt. Plantin.

LIBRARY OF CONGRESS CATALOGING-IN-PUBLICATION DATA

Hedlund, Jody.
   Captured by love / by Jody Hedlund. — Large print edition.
      pages ; cm. — (Thorndike Press large print Christian romance)
   ISBN 978-1-4104-7316-5 (hardcover) — ISBN 1-4104-7316-3 (hardcover)
   1. Explorers—Fiction. 2. Mackinac Island (Mich.)—Fiction. 3. Michigan—
History—To 1837—Fiction. 4. Large type books. I. Title.
PS3608.E333C37 2014b
813'.6—dc23   2014026300

Published in 2014 by arrangement with Bethany House Publishers, a division of Baker Publishing Group

Printed in Mexico
1 2 3 4 5 6 7 18 17 16 15 14

To my wonderful mother

Your solution to every problem has
always been prayer and plenty of it.

Thank you for praying without ceasing
for me and for all your family.

We couldn't ask for a greater gift.

CHAPTER 1

Michilimackinac Island, Michigan Territory
May 1814

The dawn mist swirled around Angelique MacKenzie and shrouded the forest trail. She didn't need the light of day to guide her. She knew every path of her beloved island and could run them blindfolded if need be.

Even so, something in the damp foggy air sent a shiver up the back of her neck and forced her bare feet to move faster. The cold mud oozed between her toes, squishing and squelching with each step. She glanced at the dark tangle of bramble surrounding her as if a *loup-garou* would leap out at her and bare his sharp wolf's teeth.

She knew nothing of the sort could happen. Werewolves belonged only in tales, like the one she'd overheard the *raconteur* tell the night before. But she couldn't keep from seeing the hairy hunched back, long tail,

7

and pointed ears in every flitting shadow.

Her heart raced, its pounding rivaling one of the duty calls of the fort drummer.

Her secret early-morning deliveries were becoming riskier with every passing day. Especially now that nearly all the islanders were on the brink of starvation. The British soldiers living in the fort were faring even worse. Over the long winter they'd butchered all their horses. And now they were growing desperate.

And dangerous.

But danger or not, she had to make her delivery. Her dear friend depended on the meager food gifts she brought every morning.

With one hand Angelique pressed against the threadbare linen of her skirt and steadied the delicate lumps in her pocket. And with the other she dangled two of the trout she'd caught.

A crack of a branch and a low, raspy call pierced the silence, startling her.

She halted and sucked in a breath of the cool May air that hinted of newly bloomed spring beauties and trailing arbutus. She cocked her head to listen, peering through the mist.

Another raspy call came from overhead, and this time she recognized the sound. It belonged to a red-winged blackbird.

A breeze of relief whispered through her. The migratory birds were returning now. And if the birds had made it to the remote northern island, then maybe the supply ships would be able to reach Michilimackinac Island too. At least she would pray the ships would arrive soon, and put an end to their misery.

A twig snapped, and her gaze jumped back to the path. At the sight ahead, she froze.

There stood a loup-garou — the werewolf — half hidden by the mist, blocking her way, feet spread apart, tail poking out behind, and one ear pointing high.

Her blood turned as frigid as the lake water she'd waded in earlier when she climbed out of her birchbark canoe.

The loup-garou growled with a hacking cough. And then he took a swaying step toward her. "Give me your food."

Everything within her screamed to retreat, to disappear into the forest. With her knowledge of the woods, she could easily escape the beast. But fear planted her feet in the mud and refused to release them.

The werewolf lurched forward. With each step he took, his tail strangely changed into a long sword and his ear into an officer's hat that sat at an odd angle, as if he'd put it on backward.

"I know you have food." The words came out slurred. "And I command you to hand it over." He staggered nearer, and the mist seemed to evaporate, revealing an all-too familiar red coat.

This was no loup-garou. This was a menace even worse.

It was one of the British soldiers. The enemy. The *starving* enemy.

In fact, he was Lieutenant Steele, the quartermaster. And he was exactly the kind of danger she'd hoped to avoid.

She lifted her hand away from the two eggs in her pocket, not wanting to bring attention to her hidden treasure. And she resisted the urge to lay her hand protectively against the thin slice of ashcake and the few acorn shells tucked into her bodice. She could give him the fish if she must, but the eggs and the bread were her prized hoarding of the day.

His hollow gaze fixed hungrily on the trout. In the fog his gaunt face was more like that of a skeleton rising from the grave rather than the werewolf she'd first imagined. "The fish, lass."

"Yes?"

"What would Ebenezer Whiley say if he

discovered you were withholding some of your catch for yourself?" The question held a threat.

Everyone knew how stingy her stepfather was. Even the British soldiers who came to his tavern and store had learned he dealt a hard bargain. If Ebenezer found out that Angelique was holding back even a few small fish out of her morning deliveries, he'd do his best to stop her, and punish her harshly. Then what would become of Miriam?

Lieutenant Steele's lips twisted into a grin. "Ah, I see you don't want Mr. Whiley to learn about your cheating."

The soldier took another unsteady step. "As quartermaster I've been instructed by the general to help the commissary collect more food for the garrison this morning."

She didn't believe him for a second. With his bloodshot eyes and untidy appearance, she guessed he'd spent the night drinking and was on his way to the North Sally Port, hoping to sneak into the fort undetected.

She'd play along with his game. "Oh, I beg your pardon. In all my hard work this morning, I must have missed the sounding of reveille."

She knew for a fact the drummer and fifer hadn't woken the troops yet. She always listened for reveille. Even though it was played within the fort, the islanders used it as their clock. Ebenezer would expect her back shortly after the sounding.

But if Lieutenant Steele wanted to threaten her, then she'd do the same to him.

They both knew she could report him for being outside the fort. All the soldiers were restricted to their quarters once the fort musicians played tap-too in the evening until reveille the next morning. Breaking the curfew could result in severe punishment.

Only the week before, a soldier had been caught outside the fort after hours. His sentence had been one hundred lashes with the cat-o'-nine-tails. The captain had reduced the lashes to seventy-five when the soldier had pleaded that hunger had driven him out to look for food.

"If you give me the fish," the quartermaster said more soberly, as if he too remembered the recent whipping, "then we can pretend I never saw you and that you never saw me."

She loosened her grip on the string of fish, hesitated only a moment, and then tossed them at his feet. Every muscle in her thin body tensed with the need to escape the moment he bent over to retrieve the fish.

But instead of going after the trout, he lunged at her with a quickness that belied his vulnerable state. His bony fingers circled her arm, and he yanked her against his emaciated frame with surprising strength.

She was too stunned to react.

"I think you're hiding more food." His sour breath fanned her cheek, making her want to retch. The hard bones of his ribs pressed against the thinly wrapped ashcake in her bodice.

She pushed at his chest. His red coat had become threadbare after the harsh winter. His hair was overlong, his face scruffy, and his eyes sunken into what at one time had been a handsome face. He was a sorry sight now.

After two years on the island, *all* the soldiers were a sorry sight. The winters on Michilimackinac were hard on even the most seasoned islander, much less a thin-skinned, poorly clad British regular.

"We're all hungry," she said quietly. "Please take the fish as my gift. Then let me be on my way."

His grip wavered, but only for a second before tightening again. "Give me the rest of what you have. Now."

"I can't do that."

He grunted and slipped his hand around

her neck. His fingers coiled, cutting off her breath.

With a burst of panicked energy she kicked at him and plucked at his hand, trying to free her neck from his choking hold. But in his hunger-induced delirium, his strength was unshakable.

Her throat began to burn, and desperation dragged at her lungs. She needed a fresh breath, but no amount of twisting or grasping would loosen his clutch and allow the air through.

She could feel her eyes loll back into her head, and a wave of blackness crashed over her.

Was this how she was destined to die? On her beloved island, while fighting over the food she was determined to deliver to her starving friend?

A loud thwack came from behind the lieutenant, and instantly the deathly chain around her neck fell away.

Lieutenant Steele stared ahead blankly and then crumpled to the ground at her feet, sprawling into the mud with a splat.

She stumbled backward and gasped for air, wheezing through her bruised airway and staring at the motionless form.

At a sudden flash in the early morning mist, she ceased breathing.

There behind the lieutenant stood an even bigger apparition, another loup-garou, this one looming fiercer than the last. His long cloak swirled around deerskin leggings and a loose leather shirt. He held an Ojibway Indian club that he'd obviously used on the quartermaster. A single strike with the dangerous round ball on its top often proved lethal.

The apparition toed the lieutenant with his moccasin boot.

Lieutenant Steele groaned, yet he didn't move.

Her rescuer stuffed the club into a belt tied around his waist. It was no ordinary belt, but the special woven sash belonging only to a voyageur.

Angelique's heart gave a rapid burst of excitement. Besides the sash, he also wore weather-worn buckskin, a red worsted cap, and a cloak that was really more of a capote — an Indian blanket coat.

He *was* a voyageur. There was no doubt about it.

But if he was one of the canoe-paddling fur traders, why was he here now? So early in the morning?

She glanced around the woods that lined the path. Usually when the voyageurs arrived back on the island every spring, they came in great numbers with laughter and singing.

But she saw no evidence of anyone else. The island hadn't had any communication with the outside world since the end of last fall and the onset of winter, when the ice had isolated them as it did every year.

The voyageur started to retreat as silently as he'd approached.

"Thank you for saving my life," she said, unwilling to let him leave just yet.

He nodded but continued to move away.

She had to know where he came from and whether the rest of the voyageurs were on the way. "Wait." She started after him, forcing her feet to move finally.

He held out a hand to stop her from coming any nearer.

"Who are you?" she asked.

He put a finger to his lips. As he did so, for the first time, he faced her directly and the shadows fell away.

She stifled a gasp.

It was Pierre Durant.

Even with the heavy layer of winter scruff that covered his chin and cheeks, she had no trouble recognizing the face beneath. His features hadn't changed much in the five years he'd been gone from the island.

He still had the same dashing good looks

he'd always had. The deep, rich brown eyes that had always done funny things to her pulse, the unruly wavy dark hair, and the swarthy skin he'd inherited from his French father.

His legs were long, his shoulders broad. And beneath his Indian coat, his muscles bulged against the seams of his shirt.

Wonder tangled her tongue and made her shy and speechless. She waited for recognition to dawn, for his face to light up at the sight of her as it had so many times in the past.

But his eyes darted to the quartermaster lying prone in the mud and then to the woods that led to the west shore. A flicker of urgency crossed his face. When he glanced at her again, there was nothing in his eyes but irritation, as if she were an interruption he hadn't anticipated.

"I'm sorry, *mademoiselle*," he whispered tersely, "but I must ask that you speak to no one about our encounter."

Didn't he recognize her? She hadn't changed that much in five years, had she? Her fingers fluttered to her face. She rarely took the time to wash the grime away. She dressed plainly. And she always wore her long auburn hair tucked under her cap, the way Ebenezer required.

But couldn't Pierre see who she was anyway? She was still the same Angelique who had raced him along this very path more times than she could count. The same friend who had climbed trees, and fished together with her, and gathered wild strawberries, and swum in the pond.

The quartermaster gave a groan and stirred.

Without breaking his stare on the soldier, Pierre began creeping backward through the dense foliage, climbing over windfall and tangles of branches.

"Where are you going?" She couldn't possibly let him leave. Not yet. Not without knowing where he'd been, and why he'd come back to the island after so many years.

Once again he held out his hand to stop her from advancing. "Please, mademoiselle. You must pretend you never saw me."

At the coldness in his voice, she halted. So he really didn't know who she was? She fought back a wave of disappointment.

Part of her wanted to blurt out her name, to inform him that she was his childhood friend, that she hadn't ever stopped thinking about him in all the years he'd been gone. And part of her wanted to tell him that since Jean had been forced off the island, she was the one keeping Miriam alive

— that if it weren't for her sacrifice and help, his mother would have died by now.

But Pierre was already disappearing into the mist. From the furtive glances he was casting, she had the suspicion something wasn't right, that perhaps he was in some kind of trouble. Why else would someone come to the island before dawn and then attempt to slink away undetected?

She strained to see him and the red of his cap, but the fog swallowed him completely until he was gone. She had the urge to shout his name, but behind her the quartermaster moaned again. She spun and ran from the soldier, hastening down the path, needing to put as much distance between herself and Lieutenant Steele as possible.

In spite of the danger that lurked everywhere, she loved early mornings on the island, when everyone was still asleep, when she could pretend all was well and they weren't in the middle of a war, that they weren't slowly starving to death.

And she loved the spring, with the sweet cool air that came after the ruthless winter, the warmer temperatures that finally melted away the layers of snow and nurtured the island back to life.

If only she had time to linger and enjoy the beauty as she'd done so many times with

Pierre and Jean when they'd been younger. But she couldn't dally or Ebenezer would suspect that she did more than fish every morning.

By the time she reached the clearing, the misty meadow, and Miriam's log cabin beyond, Angelique was breathing heavy. Pink tinted the fog, indicating the sun was rising and would soon chase away the mist.

Angelique took a deep breath and tried to steady herself before entering the small home that belonged to her friend.

"Good morning, Miriam," Angelique said, slipping through the doorway of the one-room home.

"You've been running." Through the darkness of the interior, Miriam's reply came from near the hearth. "Is everything all right?"

"Everything's fine." She prayed Miriam would believe her.

From the rustle of straw, Angelique knew that Miriam was already hard at work weaving the hats she would sell to the visitors that came to the island during the summer. Thankfully, hat weaving was one thing Miriam could still do in spite of her failing eyesight.

Angelique loosened the string of her pocket, holding her breath, willing Miriam to share the news, to tell her she'd seen Pierre.

The rustling stilled, and silence filled the room.

"Something happened," Miriam finally said quietly.

Angelique slipped the eggs from her pocket and placed them on the table. If only the dear woman weren't so perceptive. "Did you have any visitors this morning?"

"Was I supposed to?"

Angelique reached into her bodice and pulled out the ashcake she'd wrapped in a rag. She laid it on the table next to the eggs, then crossed the room and knelt before the dying embers.

Pierre was a louse. Why hadn't he taken a few minutes out of his busy life to visit his mother? That wasn't too much to ask of anyone, was it?

"You can tell me the truth, Angel," Miriam said.

Angelique grasped a scant handful of the shavings and crumbles of bark that covered the bottom of the woodbox. "You're almost out of wood. It's a good thing the nights aren't so cold anymore."

"Who did you see this morning?" Miriam persisted.

Angelique sighed. She should have known

she wouldn't be able to avoid Miriam's probing.

What should she reveal? That she'd been attacked by the fort's quartermaster? Or that she'd seen Pierre? Which would cause Miriam less distress?

Telling her about Pierre would be much too cruel. What mother could bear the news that her long-lost son had returned but neglected to visit her?

"It's nothing to worry about." Angelique added the pieces of wood chips to the embers. "I ran into one of the soldiers on my way here this morning, and he demanded that I give him my catch of fish."

Miriam's chair scraped against the wooden floor. Through the dim light beginning to filter in through the east window past the faded yellow calico curtains, Angelique could see her rise. "Did he hurt you?" Miriam's voice was breathless.

Angelique pushed herself up and started across the room toward Miriam, wiping her dusty hands against her skirt. "Please don't worry."

Miriam grasped for Angelique. Her trembling fingers skimmed Angelique's face, sliding over her cheeks, her nose, her eyes. In spite of her near blindness, Miriam found the chafed skin on her neck where Lieutenant Steele had nearly choked her. "He hurt you, didn't he?"

"Only a little." Angelique lifted her hand to Miriam's cheek and caressed it with all the love she had for the woman who was more of a mother to her than her own had ever been.

In spite of Miriam's age, her cheeks were still smooth and unlined beneath Angelique's fingers, which were as scratchy as the sandstone cliffs along the shore.

Angelique blamed her rough skin on the daily ice fishing and the exposure to the frigid temperatures and icy water that often left the skin on her fingers cracked and bleeding.

"You must stop coming to me," Miriam whispered, gently tracing the swollen skin around Angelique's neck. "It's too dangerous for you."

"I'll be more careful tomorrow."

Miriam's fingers fell away, and Angelique helped guide her friend to the table, to the eggs and the ashcake. "Have you given me your own breakfast again?"

"No. It's for you." The sight of the food gnawed at the lining of Angelique's stomach. But she turned away from Miriam before the woman could sense the truth — that she had indeed given up her meager fare of coveted bread, part of her dinner from the previous evening.

"At least eat half of it, Angel," Miriam said.

"I'll have my breakfast once I return to the inn." Angelique crossed the room and knelt in front of the hearth again. "Betty will have fried fish."

At least she hoped Ebenezer's new wife would give her something for her breakfast.

"Please eat it, Miriam." Angelique bent near the embers, blew on them, and was rewarded with a glow of orange, a few sparks, and a waft of smoke.

Miriam never complained about her hunger or the scanty rationing. But the thin shoulders, bony arms, and loose bodice were testament to the constant struggle with starvation.

"I have a few acorn shells too," Angelique said. "I'll start the fire and then you can steep them for tea." She hated to leave Miriam alone with the fire and any form of cooking. The blisters from the last burn on the back of Miriam's hand had only recently healed.

"God is with us, Angel," Miriam said. "Whatever problems may come, He's our unchanging, solid rock. If we're standing on Him, nothing will shake us."

Angelique wanted to believe Miriam. But *unchanging* and *solid* were foreign words to her. There had never been anything even remotely solid about her life.

"We'll just keep praying the war will be over this summer and that Jean will be able to return to us soon. That you'll be able to marry him finally. And be safe."

Jean — kind, considerate, steady Jean. He might be Pierre's brother, but he was nothing like him. And even if Jean was away fighting with the Americans, they knew without a doubt he would return when he could.

A renewed stab of frustration sliced through Angelique. Why hadn't Pierre stopped to visit his mother? If he had, he would have seen how poor she'd become, how little she had without Jean there to take care of her, and how desperately she needed help.

But as much as she wanted to believe that Pierre would have stayed to help his mother if only he were aware of her hardships, she also knew Pierre was wild at heart and forever dreaming of adventure.

He would never be the steady source of help either of them needed.

Yes, it was for the best that Pierre had not visited Miriam, that he'd not gotten their hopes up.

In fact, it was probably better for all of their sakes if Pierre didn't come back at all.

CHAPTER 2

Pierre squinted at his reflection in the clear puddle and scraped the long razor across his cheek again.

"Ah, looking good, *monsieur.*" He sat up straighter and flashed himself a grin so that he could see the full effect of his personal ministrations. "Looking real good."

He'd spent more time taking care of his appearance in the past two hours than he had all winter. Like the rest of his brigade, he'd scrubbed the bear grease from his face and had lathered himself with soap to rid himself of all the dirt and vermin he'd accumulated during the past months of travel. He'd even attempted to launder his clothes, although the first chance he had, he was trading for a pair of corduroy trousers and a cotton shirt.

Red Fox watched him with his steady, serious eyes.

"What do you think?" Pierre rubbed his

hand across his chin, the smooth skin strange under his callused fingers. "I'll bet you've never seen anyone quite as handsome, have you?"

"I think you want to make a feast for black flies and mosquitoes."

Pierre knew the young brave thought he was foolish for shaving the heavy beard and washing away the bear grease that kept them from being eaten to the bones by vicious swarms of insects that came to life every spring.

"It's a small price to pay to get the attention of the pretty ladies." Pierre bent toward the pool of recent rainwater, cupped his hands, and splashed his face. "Where I come from, the smell and sight of bear grease isn't exactly going to endear me to anyone."

"You do not need those ladies." Red Fox's ever-watchful eyes scanned the lakeshore, where the rest of the voyageurs were washing and making themselves presentable before they forayed into civilized society. "Not when you could have a good woman from among my tribe."

Pierre rinsed his razor. Many *coureur de bois* like himself took Indian women as their wives. The native women knew how to paddle and patch a canoe and make bearskin robes, and they could ice fish in the harshest of winter temperatures. As the headman of a fur brigade, an Indian wife could be a great asset. Many of his fellow traders married Indian women, not only for their knowledge of the land and ability to survive in the wilderness but because the unions helped solidify trading relationships within tribes.

Maybe marriage to an Indian woman was his best option. Even so, he wanted to put it off for as long as possible. "I'm not ready to get married."

"Then you do not need the attention of ladies."

Pierre tossed Red Fox a grin. "There are some of us who get attention no matter what we do."

He dried the razor blade on the grass and then returned it to the leather case he only used in the spring and summer when he returned to civilization.

The wide open shoreline that made up the south side of the Straits spread before him. It had been cleared of all its timber in bygone years. In fact, the treeless terrain stretched back for at least three miles from the shore, evidence of the old fort and community that had once thrived there.

Now all that remained were a few charred

picket walls buried in drifting sand. Long before he'd been born, the old buildings had been dragged across the ice of the Straits and reconstructed on Michilimackinac Island, which was a more strategic location for a fort than the wide, exposed mainland.

Too bad the Americans hadn't been able to make use of that strategy and hold the fort at the beginning of the war.

He peered across the choppy water. In the distance he could see the rising hump of the island, the Great Turtle, as the Ottawa called it — the place where the waters of both Lake Michigan and Lake Huron flowed together around the island's shoreline.

Home.

He dragged in a breath of the damp, cool air, letting the familiar lakeshore breeze caress his bare skin. His predawn trip onto the island yesterday morning had made him realize how much he'd missed his childhood home in the years he'd been gone.

He'd never thought he would miss it, had always expected that once he left he'd never want to return.

But thankfully God had whacked him hard across the head and brought him to his knees.

And as much as he loved the wilderness and couldn't imagine living anywhere else, an urgent need to return to the island had haunted him these past months, ever since he'd learned that Michilimackinac had fallen to the British.

"We must go. The Great Spirit Git-chi Man-i-tou is waiting." Red Fox rose from the rock where he'd perched. His necklace of beads and metal disks clinked together and bumped against his shirtless chest. He'd already painted his face, one half blue and the other half red with the vermillion Pierre had provided the Chippewa in preparation for their return to the island.

Red Fox's tribe would be paddling to the island today too, arriving to receive their yearly gifts from the British, a system that provided provisions to the Indians in exchange for their friendship.

"We have waited too many sleeps to go to the Great Turtle," Red Fox said, his young face thin with worry. "We must not anger the Great Spirit by waiting any longer."

Pierre crossed his arms and assessed his crew among the throngs. "We'll leave soon. When the men are ready." His men were laughing and singing and excited about the stop on Michilimackinac.

Even though he was anxious to return, he

was nervous too. His parting with his family hadn't exactly been a happy occasion.

His foolishness weighed heavily upon him whenever he thought about the final heated argument he'd had with his papa. He may have made peace with God, but he'd never be able to make peace with Papa. Now he'd have to live the rest of his life with the regret of not being able to look Papa in the eyes, shake his hand, and ask for his forgiveness.

At least soon he'd be able to stand before his *maman,* hug her, and tell her he was sorry.

Of course, during his early morning mission to the island the previous day, he hadn't been able to resist swinging by his home and peeking in on her. He'd had to wrench himself away, even though his heart had swelled with longing to feel her gentle fingers comb his hair as she'd always done. He knew speaking with her would have put his entire mission in jeopardy. As it was, he'd stayed too long.

He hadn't planned to let *anyone* see him. But on his way back to his canoe, he'd come across a soldier strangling a young woman. Thankfully he'd knocked the soldier out before he knew what was coming. When the soldier woke up, he wouldn't have any clue what had happened. Which was a good thing, because the British liked him and thought he was their friend. If any of them suspected he was communicating with the Americans, they'd arrest him and lock him away for the duration of the war, if they didn't kill him first.

Unfortunately, the woman had seen his face, had been too curious, and dare he say — recognized him? And even though he'd pleaded with her to remain silent, he had the feeling she'd already spread word about his arrival to everyone on the island.

He couldn't really blame her. He remembered what it was like after the long winter, waiting for the first contact with someone from the outside world. Whatever the case, he was hoping the fresh shave and a change of wearing apparel would make him indistinguishable from all the many voyageurs who would descend upon the island with him.

"You will anger the Great Spirit by sneaking around the island like a-se-bou the raccoon," Red Fox warned, as if he'd sensed the direction of Pierre's thoughts.

"I'm just doing my part in the war," Pierre replied. He hadn't wanted to pick up a gun and fight. And because he was an important fur trader, no one had questioned his decision to stay off the battlefield. In fact, because of the relationships he'd already formed with the British over the past several years, none of the British officers had second-guessed his loyalty, even though he was an American citizen.

"The raccoon is nothing but a thief," Red Fox said, puffing out his chest and staring off into the distance. "It is no good to have your feet in two fires. Someday you will get burned."

Red Fox was one of the smartest men Pierre had ever met, but also one of the most superstitious. He believed every legend and lore that had been passed on to him from his people. And while Pierre had tried to speak to him of his God of mercy and love, Red Fox could not understand a God like his. And he certainly couldn't understand Pierre's part in the war, not when he himself didn't know how he'd gotten mixed up with both sides.

"I'm too smooth and quick to get burned," Pierre said, slipping on his shirt. As the damp material slid over his head, his gaze landed on several men poking around his canoes.

Not surprisingly, several other brigades had also stopped at the Straits to bathe before making an appearance on the island. The shore was lined with their birchbark canoes, loaded with the pelts they'd collected all winter, including many of the North West Fur Company voyageurs and their agent.

Pierre stiffened and started toward them.

Red Fox put a steadying hand on Pierre's arm. "You cannot get attention of ladies with cuts and bruises on your face."

Pierre's footsteps faltered. He'd only been jesting with Red Fox about winning the attention of the ladies. The truth was he'd put off his womanizing ways along with his drinking when God had turned him back around.

If he were completely honest with himself, the real reason he wanted to clean himself up was because he wanted to look good when he finally stood before his maman.

But he wouldn't make such a favorable impression on Maman if he showed up with a black eye and busted lip, which was what he'd come away with the last time he'd gotten into a fight with a North West Company agent.

"Stay away from my canoes." Pierre forced himself to stop at the stern of one of his vessels. In the bright morning sun, the strong scent of pine rose up from the white birchbark his men had recently coated with fresh resin so that the canoes would be durable and waterproof for the last leg of their journey.

The agent kept strolling, his thumbs hooked in the waist of his sagging trousers. Like most of the men, he was still shirtless, and his back was the purplish-red of a beet that one too many sunburns had stained over the years.

Pierre quickly took stock of the ninety-pound bundles that had come hundreds of miles, through rapids, over portages, and past many dangerous currents. His brigade had risked their lives to haul the furs out of the wilderness. At the very least they deserved the rewards for the hard labor.

And he was determined to do whatever he could to finish their journey in safety without any further problems from North West Company men who wanted to see free traders like himself put out of business altogether.

"Leave my furs alone." Pierre growled the words. "Don't you think you've done enough to damage my business this year?"

"Nope." A grin turned up the corners of the agent's lips, revealing crooked, tobacco-stained teeth — at least what was left of his teeth. "I figure I still got some time to make you go crying home to your mama, where you belong."

Pierre gripped the closest paddle, decorated with a colorful pattern. The paddle was the arm of every voyageur, his life, safety, and pride, often inherited from a voyageur father, and almost always blessed by a local priest before leaving on a journey.

Of course, his papa hadn't given him *his* paddle.

Red Fox moved next to Pierre, his dark eyes issuing another warning — the warning not to swing the paddle. "Do not fight. One day your belt will be heavy with the scalps of your enemies. But not today."

Pierre struggled against the urge to knock the agent flat on the ground. His men had become his family. The wilderness had become his home. He couldn't — wouldn't — let anyone push him out of doing what he loved. And he couldn't let the North West Company strip his brigade of what was rightfully theirs, not after months of hard work.

The agent ambled along the last of Pierre's canoes as if he were taking a leisurely stroll instead of calculating how he could steal or destroy the cargo of furs.

Pierre started forward, but Red Fox grabbed his shirt from behind and pulled him backward. "Not today," he said, firmer this time.

Pierre strained to break loose from his friend's grip, hoping his shirt would rip and set him free to slam into the agent. But before Pierre could get away, Red Fox had wrenched his arm behind his back and jerked it painfully.

"We need to go now to the Great Turtle," Red Fox said. "Then my people will help keep watch over my brother's furs."

"You're right." Shame slipped a knot around Pierre's heart. "I'm still too quick to pick a fight."

Maybe he was still quick to sin in too many areas. Maybe he hadn't changed enough yet to return home.

He glanced again at the rising hump of Michilimackinac, letting the cool air blowing off the lake soothe him, along with the lingering scent of the whitefish he'd caught and roasted for his men.

Today he had hoped to stand in his childhood home and cook dinner for Maman. He'd seen the near-starvation conditions of the British garrison yesterday during his mission. Even though Maman surely wasn't faring as badly as the soldiers, he'd saved several of his catch, along with the cornmeal and onions he'd purchased from the Chippewa. He wanted to make her a feast of baked stuffed whitefish, and if he had enough of the cornmeal left, he would make her the hasty pudding she so loved.

But maybe he should move on, urge his brigade to St. Joseph's. They had no reason to stop at Michilimackinac. Up until now, they'd always bypassed it. He'd made a point of avoiding home.

Why should he change course now? What made him think Maman would want to see him again?

"We will wait for right time to attack company traders. Then our war clubs will strike like lightning and our arrows will sting like the hornet." Red Fox watched the North West agent slink back to his brigade. His dark eyes glittered as sharp as the edge of his tomahawk. "They have hurt and cheat my people too many times. We will repay them. Someday."

Pierre knew the Indians were getting tired of dealing with the North West Fur Company. Their agents were stealing and encroaching on Indian land. And now many of the natives preferred to work with free traders like Pierre, who were more honest and fair in their dealings.

The Indians had more patience with their enemies than he did. Even so, Pierre knew that when the natives finally had enough of the abuse, their retribution would be swift and brutal.

Pierre was glad Red Fox was his friend and not his enemy.

The young brave's painted face was fierce. "Today is the day of calling to the Corn Spirit so that our bellies will be full when game is scarce. And you must offer the peace pipe to your family. You have withheld the pipe for too long."

Pierre nodded. He'd come this far. He couldn't stop now.

Even if Maman didn't forgive him, at least he'd find peace in apologizing. *Oui.* Red Fox was right. If he faced his fears, he'd finally be able to move on to his future without the past pulling him back.

Pierre rolled his shoulders, easing the tension from them. Then he curled his tongue against the back of his teeth and whistled. The piercing sound rang out over the beach, signaling his men to start packing up.

Red Fox released his arm and nodded at him, his eyes praising him for his self-control this time.

Pierre dropped the paddle.

He wasn't the same reckless youth who'd left the island. He was a changed man.

Hopefully he would be able to prove that to his maman. And eventually prove it to himself too.

CHAPTER 3

Didn't Ebenezer have anything better to do with his life than to spend it controlling every little thing she did?

Angelique turned her back on the man, feigning that she hadn't noticed him poking his balding head out the back door of the tavern to check on her again.

She released a long breath and then sucked another one through her mouth, careful not to breathe in the stench. Cleaning the hen house was the dirtiest job in the world, and she'd thought she would get a break from Ebenezer's constant supervision while doing the spring chore.

"Shoo now," she scolded one of the hens attempting to enter the coop. "I don't need you checking on me too."

The hen squawked and fluttered, then finally strutted — as if seriously offended — outside into the fresh air and the yellowed matted grass that was slowly coming back to life.

Through the open doorway, Angelique counted the dozen hens and the rooster roaming the picketed yard. Beneath the smattering of lusterless feathers, the chickens lacked the plumpness and fullness they needed. The winter had been hard on the few animals left on the island — the few that had escaped butchering.

Thankfully the hens had continued to lay eggs, though not nearly as often as they should. She'd worked hard to ward off frostbite to the chickens' thin bodies, rising early every morning to provide the extra light they needed for egg production in the dark Michigan winters. Yet even on a good day, she'd been lucky to gather ten eggs.

Angelique dug her shovel into the slimy muck that covered the floor beneath her boots. The dried maple leaves she'd laid out last fall had decomposed under the constant droppings of the birds and now only added to the filth and dust coating the hen house.

"If only the war would end soon," she whispered.

She rested the shovel against the wall of the tiny shed Jean had helped her construct and reached for the bucket of muck.

And if only she'd married Jean before he'd had to leave the island.

Jean had been willing, had in fact preferred it so that he wouldn't have to leave his mother on the farm alone.

But at the time she'd only been sixteen. And her stepfather, Ebenezer, had refused and then accused Jean of being a traitor for not signing the Oath of Allegiance to the British. It didn't matter that Ebenezer had already made an agreement with Jean, that Jean had paid the exorbitant bride-price Ebenezer established.

In a matter of one day after the British invasion, Jean had become an enemy because of his unwillingness to compromise his American citizenship. Some of the islanders like Ebenezer had no qualms about switching their loyalty and supporting the British. They'd been allowed to keep their businesses and homes on the island. All the other American men had been deported.

In the two years Jean had been gone, they'd received several letters from him. He'd joined up with the American militia near Detroit and was helping to fight against the British to preserve the American independence that had been won thirty years ago.

Although Angelique didn't really consider herself either British or American since her mother had been French Canadian and her father Scottish, she'd decided to side with the Americans for the sake of Jean and Miriam.

"Oh, why did Jean have to leave?" she whispered, lifting the bucket and lugging it across the hen house, through the door and into the bright sunlight that bathed the afternoon with glorious warmth.

She tried to conjure up the image of Jean — his gentle features and his fair skin and hair, so much like that of Miriam — but she caught only a glimpse of him before Pierre's weather-bronzed face flashed into her mind, along with his handsome grin and the devilish mischief in his eyes.

She couldn't deny that Pierre had always been the more handsome and dashing of the two brothers, that he'd been the one to capture her heart, to make her laugh even when she'd had nothing to laugh about, and to fill her with unexplainable longing.

"Pierre is a louse," she said into the spring air, dragging in a fresh breath. "He's a selfish louse. No, I don't want to see him again. And no, I don't miss him."

But even as the words slipped out, she knew they weren't true. One glimpse of Pierre yesterday had been all it had taken to unleash a swarm of eagerness for her erstwhile friend.

The back door of the inn squeaked open again, this time revealing Betty's thin face. With a furtive glance over her shoulder into the kitchen, Betty opened the door wider and stepped outside.

Angelique hefted the bucket higher and moved toward the necessary.

Had Ebenezer sent Betty outside to check on her?

Out of the corner of her eye, Angelique could see the young woman put one hand on her protruding belly and one on the small of her back. She didn't know how many weeks Betty had left before giving birth, but from the looks of it, the time was growing near.

"Ebenezer left," Betty called after her.

Angelique stopped, surprise charging through her.

Betty's shifting gray eyes kept returning to the open door, as if she expected Ebenezer to barge through at any moment. Not a single strand of Betty's hair hung outside the plain white mobcap she wore. Her unadorned collar stretched high up her neck, and the hem of her skirt covered her feet all the way to the tips of her toes — just the way Ebenezer expected.

Angelique's fingers went involuntarily to

her own high collar.

Even if her life under Ebenezer's care was oppressive, she couldn't complain about his extreme standards for modesty. The plain, unattractive attire kept away unwanted attention on an island populated mostly by men. It also kept her from becoming anything like her mother.

And of course the high collar had kept Ebenezer from seeing the bruises around her neck. She could only imagine his anger if he'd discovered them. As it was, she kept waiting for the quartermaster to pay Ebenezer a visit and tell him that she was doing more than fishing during the early morning hours.

She prayed he'd been too drunk to remember the encounter.

"I saved an extra piece of bread for you," Betty said.

Angelique hesitated, resisting the urge to press her hand against her aching stomach. "Why don't you eat it?" Angelique said. "With the weight of your babe, you have much greater need of it than me."

She didn't think Betty was a day older than sixteen and seemed much too young for a man like Ebenezer. But after his last wife died in childbirth, he'd needed another woman to do his washing and cooking and to tend the customers who stayed at the inn. It was much cheaper to have a wife do those duties than to hire someone.

And it was much more convenient for satisfying his lusts.

Angelique cast her eyes away from Betty to the garden plot, to the rich dark soil she'd recently hoed and readied for planting.

She hated that her tiny dormer room rested above Ebenezer's. And she hated that in the silence of the night she could hear his awful grunts as he sated himself. It had been that way with her own mother, and the next wife, and now with Betty.

If only Ebenezer *could* be completely satisfied with his wife. In the spring and summer after the Indians arrived on the island, she often caught him lurking down by their camps and on more than one occasion sneaking an Indian woman into his room.

Angelique's head shot up.

Indians.

Had they returned to the island? Is that why Ebenezer had left the inn?

She dropped the bucket of muck to the ground and stood on her tiptoes, trying to peer over the cedar fence that surrounded the tavern plot. But the boards were too tall and blocked the view of the beach and the harbor.

"Have the ships come?" she asked.

Betty nodded. "Ebenezer just left for the beach. Now's your chance to eat."

"You have the bread. I insist."

Angelique had given up hope of forming a friendship with Betty when she'd first come to the island as Ebenezer's new bride. From the start, Betty had regarded her with suspicion and most of the time had met her attempts at conversation with silence. Even after Ebenezer had explained that Angelique was his adopted daughter, that he'd sworn to her mother to take care of her until she was married, Betty had still eyed Angelique with mistrust.

During the winter, when they'd both been hungry most of the time, Angelique had done her best to keep Betty's growing belly full. And in return, Betty had often tried to sneak Angelique food, even when she'd had to miss, like that morning when Ebenezer had taken away her bread for arriving home a few minutes late.

But today, Angelique wouldn't need the food, not with the ships arriving. Tonight the islanders would feast on the beach with the Indians. There would finally be enough food to sate their shriveled stomachs.

Unable to contain a smile, Angelique raced toward the back gate, dodging the hens, breathless anticipation giving her feet a new lightness.

As she stepped through the gate and rounded the tavern to Main Street, the air was charged with excitement. Homes and shop doors stood open and men poured out of the distillery and fur warehouse. The workday had come to a complete stop.

The road, which was nothing more than a dirt path along the shoreline, was bustling with townspeople rushing toward the docks, too anxious to take the time to prepare themselves properly. Splattered aprons, smudged cheeks, hatless, and even half dressed, the entire village spilled out onto the wide sandy shore to welcome the arrival of the British supply ships.

A few straggling soldiers were hurrying from the fort on the rise above the town. They tugged on their bedraggled coats and hats as they ran down the sloping path to join the others who'd gathered to greet the first arrivals and give a hand in unloading the long-awaited barrels and bags of provisions.

Angelique stood back a distance, especially when the doctor's wife frowned and pinched her nose as she passed. Angelique knew she should have bathed first and rid herself of the horrid odor that permeated her clothes after spending half the day cleaning the hen house. But she couldn't resist the pull to watch the new arrivals.

Two schooners docked in the bay, their large white sails billowing in the breeze. The sunlight glinted off the water, turning the sails into diamonds and the ships to royal jewels, making them sparkle against the cloudless blue sky.

Behind the schooners, the voyageurs were drawing closer in their canoes, wearing their bright red sashes and caps, wielding their colorful paddles that dipped into the water in unison. Their boisterous songs were faint but grew louder with each stroke.

Angelique's smile widened. She could picture Pierre with his handsome smile and voice raised in a song, as he'd done so often in the past when they'd fished or swam together.

What were the chances Pierre was in one of the canoes?

Every spring she'd watched the canoes, searching for his familiar face, though she'd despised herself for doing so, for missing him, for wishing he'd return.

But how could she keep from missing him when he'd been such a good friend, like the brother she'd never had? Even if he had hurt her — hurt them all — with his leaving, there was no denying the gap his absence had left.

Jean had tried hard to fill the holes left from Pierre's absence. He'd been extra sweet and had done all he could to help her forget about Pierre. It hadn't taken her long to realize that Jean loved her, had probably always adored her in a way Pierre never had.

It had come as no surprise when Jean had finally asked her to marry him. He'd told her he would never leave her. He'd promised to stay on the island with her forever and assured her that she'd fall in love with him someday too.

Eventually she'd known she couldn't resist his attention and his effort to win her any longer. And when he'd asked her to marry him for the fourth time, she'd told him yes.

She squinted against the glare and peered carefully at each canoe. The voyageurs were still too far away for her to distinguish any of them. But after the encounter with Pierre only yesterday, there was the very real chance that this year he'd actually be among the men returning to the island. And if he returned, this time she would make sure he knew who she was.

No. She ripped her attention away from the canoes and tried to focus instead on the silver waves slapping against the beach and the first gulls of spring that had gathered on the rocks, their sharp cries rising above the din of the gathered crowd.

What did she care if Pierre was among the voyageurs?

She'd much rather see what supplies the ships were bringing and get her first glimpse of the civilized visitors that would stay on the island for the summer.

Rowboats began to near the shore, bearing the first of those coming to the island from the schooners. The officer in charge of the fort, Captain Bullock, stood ahead of the other soldiers onshore, still managing to look smart in his uniform despite its hanging too loosely on his skeletal frame.

From her position behind the crowd in the tall sea grass, Angelique spotted the balding head of Ebenezer. He'd forgotten his hat, which meant he'd have to return to the tavern at some point in the afternoon to retrieve it.

But for the present she could take a few moments to watch the festivities without the worry of his censure.

It didn't take long for the rowboats to arrive.

"There's a new captain" came the murmurings. And finally the news filtered back to Angelique that it was Colonel Robert

McDouall, a Scotsman, a veteran of eighteen years' service in the British Army.

A Scotsman? She rose on her toes to get a better look.

Her father had come from Scotland, had talked with a brogue she'd loved and had a face full of bristly auburn hair that had tickled her whenever he hugged her, which hadn't been often.

She didn't remember much about him. But he had given her two things: her hair color and a love of the island.

He'd passionately loved Michilimackinac, had loved every rock formation, every tree, every beach, and every trail. And he'd loved his beautiful wife even more.

He'd adored her.

Only her mother hadn't returned his love with quite the same fervor.

Painful memories still haunted Angelique. Her father's heartbroken, gut-wrenching cries. Her mother's pleading. The slamming of doors and crashing of crockery against the stone hearth.

If only her father hadn't surprised them with a rare visit one winter. If only he'd stayed away until spring like he normally did.

Then he wouldn't have discovered his French beauty in the arms of another man.

Then he wouldn't have rushed blindly away into an approaching winter storm. Then he wouldn't have gotten hopelessly lost. . . .

A farmer near St. Ignace had discovered the body in the spring. Her father hadn't been wearing his snowshoes, almost as if he'd given up, sat down, and decided to die.

Angelique had never been able to make up her mind which had killed her father first — his broken heart or the snowstorm. And she'd never been able to make up her mind who she blamed more for all the problems — her father for being a fur trader and leaving them every fall, or her mother for being so beautiful and unable to resist the attention men paid her.

Angelique pressed her hand over her chest to ward off the pain. She wouldn't let the nightmares of the past trouble her today, not on a day meant for celebration, on a day that brought hope and life to their starving community.

Even though she wanted to stare at the approaching voyageurs, and even though everything within her tightened with the need to look again, to search for Pierre, she forced herself to look away, to find a diversion.

Her attention landed upon the woman standing behind the new captain who'd come ashore. The young lady's features were too young and fresh to be the man's wife. Maybe she was his daughter?

Her gown was much too fancy for the island. There were enough bows and ribbons to sew together and hoist into a sail for one of the ships. She wore a hat with enough feathers to attract a kingfisher looking for its mate. And she held an open parasol that threatened to carry her away with one gust of wind.

The young woman scanned the gathered islanders as if she were looking for someone. She skimmed over Angelique, but then just as rapidly her gaze jumped back. Her delicate eyebrows arched, and she studied Angelique, her eyes alight with interest and something else.

Was it pity? Did the woman feel sorry for her?

A whisper of embarrassment wafted over Angelique. She ducked her head and tried to move out of the line of vision of the newcomer.

She knew she was filthy, especially after her work in the hen house. But she didn't mind. She figured if she kept herself plain and unattractive, that maybe she'd avoid suffering the same fate as her sister Therese.

So far, she'd survived. The townspeople

didn't notice her, except to occasionally acknowledge her as the "fish lass."

She glanced again at the newly arrived young woman and, to her dismay, found herself still the object of the woman's scrutiny. In fact, the lady had leaned toward Father Fontaine, the priest of St. Anne's, and both of them were staring at Angelique. Father Fontaine was nodding in response to whatever the woman was saying.

A trickle of unease wound through Angelique. Just as she was turning to go, the boisterous voices of the voyageurs singing the song of Saint-Malo begged her to stay.

We're going to glide on the water, water away.
On the isle, on the isle to play.
Did come sailing vessels fleet
Laden with oats and laden with wheat.

She hesitated, but then another glimpse over her shoulder at the young woman's pitying gaze sent Angelique scurrying along the sandy path toward the tavern. Her heart thumped out a warning — a warning to avoid the pretty lady, that association with her would only lead to trouble.

Besides, she had no reason to linger on the beach to discover if Pierre had returned.

Jean was enough for her. He was all she needed.

CHAPTER 4

Pierre crossed the open field Papa had cleared many years ago when they'd first settled on Michilimackinac Island. By the full light of afternoon, Pierre was able to assess much more than he had the previous day when he'd rushed past the cabin before dawn.

The mist and darkness of his early morning visit had cloaked the farm, yet now the sun's rays touched every broken fence post, every weed jutting from the unplowed field, every scraggly fruit tree, every piece of crumbling chinking in the cabin wall.

And it glared particularly bright on one side of the roof where several shingles had fallen away, leaving a gaping hole.

If he hadn't seen his maman in the cabin yesterday, he would have assumed the farm was deserted.

He stopped, lifted his heavy haversack, and tried to shrug off the uncomfortable weight of guilt that bore down on him.

Beyond the house, the barn was too quiet. The door hung ajar, and darkness was the only thing that filled the stone building Papa had constructed from all the rocks they'd cleared out of the fields.

Where were the hens that normally strutted around the yard and the pigs that Papa had often let roam freely? He strained to hear the whinny of one of the horses or even the soft bellow of their milk cow. But the farm was deathly silent. Only the drums, music, and songs from the feast on the beach drifted in the air.

The knot that had slipped around his stomach cinched tighter. Why hadn't Maman come down to the shore to see the first ships of spring with everyone else?

He'd helped his men unload the canoes during the past couple of hours. And he'd greeted the Indians when they'd arrived a short while later. Finally he'd worked up enough nerve to begin the mile walk from town.

One of the tall, dry weeds that crowded what had once been Maman's flourishing vegetable garden waved in the breeze as if to warn him to run back to the beach and avoid the meeting that he'd been mentally planning since God had finally gotten his attention.

But he shook his head and pushed aside the temptation.

The island breeze rippled across his freshly shaven face and brought with it the sweetness of lilacs. At least the lilac bushes Maman had planted when he'd been just a boy were still growing on either side of the front door of the cabin. Surprisingly they were trimmed and bursting with hundreds of tiny purple blooms.

At least one thing hadn't changed. She still loved her lilacs.

He dragged in a deep breath and forced his feet to move forward again, and he didn't stop until he stood facing the door.

It was time to ask for her forgiveness. He wouldn't be able to rest until he did. It was what he'd felt God urging him to do since the night a year ago when in one of his drunken stupors he'd almost killed another voyageur during a stupid argument.

Thankfully, Red Fox had pried his fingers away from the man's neck in time. But the incident had scared him, had awakened him to the drunken brute he'd become. He'd realized he hadn't liked who he was, the kind of man Papa had once been — exactly the kind of man Papa had wanted to prevent him from becoming.

He could understand now why Papa had been so angry with him when he'd told him of his plans to join a brigade. He had indeed fallen into the drinking and debauchery that accompanied the life of the voyageur.

But not anymore. Not since he'd repented before God for the despicable man he'd become.

Of course, he wasn't perfect. God was still working to change him. But he'd come a long way in a year's time.

Pierre straightened his shoulders and doffed his cap. He ran his fingers through his hair, combing the wayward curls into submission.

Then slowly he opened the door.

As it swung wide, his attention shifted to Maman, kneeling before the hearth, fumbling with a teakettle and much too close to the small flames scattered among scraps of bark and wood shavings.

At the swish of the door opening, Maman's back stiffened and her hands stilled. From what he could tell, she hadn't changed much in the years he'd been gone. Her hair was still tied in the knot she'd always worn at the back of her neck and was the familiar blond, perhaps a little lighter now with silver threads. She was much thinner, but still had the willowy graceful form he remembered.

For a long, tense moment he held his breath and waited for her to turn. His muscles twitched with the urge to flee.

"Angelique?" she said. "Is that you?"

Angelique?

His mind flashed with the picture of the gangly redheaded girl Maman had loved as a daughter, the sweet girl who had followed him and Jean all over the island and had become the little sister he'd never had. She was apparently still very much a part of Maman's life.

Maman turned slightly.

Pierre's mouth went dry, but he forced himself to speak. "*Non,* Maman. It's not Angelique."

She gasped. The teapot slipped from her fingers and fell with a *clank* into her pitiful fire. She started to rise but in the process brushed her hand against the steaming spout. She uttered a pained cry and struggled to move away from the fire, dragging her sleeve across one of the flames and causing the threadbare material to ignite.

Pierre dropped his bundle and in three strides was across the room and kneeling next to her. With the edge of his leather shirt he smothered the flame on her sleeve and at the same time captured her hand.

"Let's get some cold water on that burn," he said.

But she tugged away and with a cry of joy flung her arms around him and pulled him into a hug. "Oh, Pierre . . ." Her voice wobbled. "My dear, dear son. Is it really you?"

"Oui, Maman. It's really me."

Her fingers came up to his hair, and she smoothed her hand over his curls the way she had whenever he'd come running to her needing her reassurance, especially after he'd done something he'd known he shouldn't, which had been more times than he cared to admit.

His chest tightened and he drew in a breath of the lilac fragrance that surrounded her. He'd hoped and longed for her embrace, but had been afraid he'd never get to experience it again.

"Oh, Pierre," she said again through a broken sob. She pressed her face against his, wetting his cheek with her tears.

He was about to wrap his arms around her when she leaned back and put him at arm's length. Tears trickled down her cheeks. She lifted her fingers to his face and grazed his chin, nose, and cheeks, as if she couldn't get enough of him. A smile lit up her face amidst the tears. "God be praised.

It *is* you."

"Oui, it's me," he said softly.

Her fingers continued to explore his face, almost as if she were seeing him through her sense of touch rather than her eyes.

He looked into her light-blue eyes. They were glassy, like a foggy sky in the early morning. And they didn't look back into his with the directness she'd always used.

Something was wrong. "How are you?" he asked, grasping her arms, studying her, taking in the stains on her tattered apron, the black singes on her sleeves where she'd obviously had further accidents with the fire, and the red blisters on the back of her hand.

"I think I'm in heaven."

Beneath his fingers he felt nothing but her bones. She barely had any flesh left. What had happened to her? To the farm?

"I've been praying for this moment for so long," she said, reaching for him again to draw him into another embrace.

This time he held back, trying to catch her gaze, wanting her to look deep inside him and see the new man he was becoming. But she only stared at his face unseeingly, as if she were . . .

"Yes, Pierre," she said, her smile dimming a little, "I'm almost blind."

"How . . . ?" He cleared the squeakiness out of his voice. "How long have you been unable to see?" Her blindness would account for much of the neglect and disrepair he'd seen around the farm.

"For a while now." She laid her smooth palm against his cheek.

He looked around at the interior of the cabin. On one side of the window hung Papa's paddle, painted in stripes of red and blue. On the other side was Papa's fishing rod. The same hand-hewn table and chairs filled the space of half the room, while a sagging bed occupied the other half. The ladder leading to the attic room that he'd shared with Jean was covered with cobwebs.

Very little had changed about his childhood home except the barrenness. Always before there had been freshly baked bread, soup or stew simmering above the hearth fire, bundles of dried herbs dangling from the ceiling, and some kind of sweet treat for him and Jean and Angelique to share.

But now, as far as he could tell, there wasn't a crumb of food anywhere. Had she been living in the cabin alone all winter with nothing to eat? How had she survived?

With her blindness she wouldn't have been able to plant a garden or plow a field. She wouldn't have been able to hunt for wild berries or nuts. She wouldn't have been able to manage feeding hens or milking a cow — even if she'd had them.

Helplessness poured over him. Someone should have been here to assist her. "Why did Jean leave you here all alone?"

"Jean didn't have a choice."

"He should have stayed."

"He agonized over leaving, Pierre. He really did. He didn't want to go."

Then he shouldn't have, he wanted to say. But he held the words in. He didn't want his reunion with Maman to become clouded with his anger.

"The British learned he was a loyal American," Maman rushed to explain. "If he'd faked his allegiance to them, they wouldn't have trusted him. Eventually they may have accused him of treachery or spying and sent him away anyway."

Pierre sat back on his heels and tried to ignore the guilt that pricked him and reminded him that he'd left the island too, but his reasons hadn't been quite as noble as Jean's.

"Don't blame Jean." Maman caressed his cheek again. "He didn't know I was going blind when he left or I'm sure he wouldn't have gone. And now if word ever reached him of my condition, I know he'd try to return, even though he'd put his life in danger to do so."

Why did Jean have to be the good son, the one who was always doing what was noble?

"My dear, dear son." She pulled him into another hug, wrapping her arms around him and squeezing him with surprising strength.

He slipped his arms around her. He closed his eyes to hold back the urge to weep at her fragile condition.

"I'm so glad you're here." She smoothed his hair. "I've missed you terribly."

"I didn't know if you'd be glad to see me again or not," he said hesitantly. "Especially after all the horrible things I said before I left."

"Pierre, my love for you is unconditional, just as the Lord's is. No matter where you've been or what you've done, both the Lord and I will always be waiting here with open arms."

"I don't deserve your love or forgiveness for the way I treated you and Papa and Jean when I left." A swell of emotion clogged his throat, making him need to clear it before he could continue. "I'm deeply sorry for not respecting you the way I should have. And I pray you'll forgive me, although I know I don't deserve it."

"Of course I forgive you."

"Oh, Maman . . ." He hated that his voice wavered.

A squeak in a floorboard near the door made him jump. He let go of Maman and turned, taking a breath to compose himself. He hoped a tear or two of his own hadn't escaped. His brigade would tease him mercilessly if they ever found out he'd been near to crying in his maman's arms.

Maman let the tears run freely down her cheeks, rising with a smile at the newcomer. "Look who's here."

A young woman stood in the doorway holding a rag-covered bundle. She was frozen in her spot and was staring at him with wide eyes.

Pierre stared back, taking in the mobcap that covered her hair, the pretty face smudged with dirt, the high collar above her bodice, and the ugly gray of her skirt. Where had he seen her?

Accusation flashed through her doe-like brown eyes.

Then he knew. *Yesterday. In the woods.*

The unspoken words hung between them and propelled him to his feet.

She was the same woman he'd come upon during his spying mission on the island, the woman he'd rescued from the hands of the British soldier. And she apparently recognized him even after his shave and bath.

He narrowed his eyes. She wouldn't reveal his secret, would she? With a curt shake of his head he warned her from saying anything.

But she looked away from him, clearly ignoring his admonition, and started across the room toward the table.

Angelique's heart pounded in her chest like the Indians' drums thumping out their rhythm back at the camps along the lakeshore.

Pierre had come.

And he was standing only a few feet away from her.

Now that he'd shaven and cleaned himself, he was more handsome than she'd remembered. From his dark wavy hair to the strength in his features to the ability of his dark brown eyes to melt even the coldest of hearts — everything about his appearance was striking. She stopped in front of the table and leaned against it, trying to calm herself before facing him again.

She flattened her hand against her heart, willing it to slow its crazy banging that she was sure both Pierre and Miriam could hear.

"It's Pierre." Miriam's voice held such joy.

"Yes, I see that," Angelique replied, frustrated at her breathlessness.

She glanced over her shoulder and found him glaring at her. He remembered her from their brief meeting yesterday. And from furrowed brows above his stormy eyes, it was also clear he didn't want her to say anything about their encounter.

But didn't he know that she was Angelique MacKenzie and that she wouldn't purposefully put him in any danger?

She turned away again and placed her bundle on the table. Whatever his trouble, he should have made time to visit Miriam. And even though she'd overheard his plea asking for Miriam's forgiveness, she couldn't stop the bitterness of the past five years from surfacing.

Maybe he'd asked for forgiveness, but that didn't change what had happened, the fact that he'd deserted them and had been gone all these years without sending them a single word. And now that he was back, he didn't remember who she was.

"I've brought you some food from the feast," she said to Miriam, opening the rag to reveal the breast of roasted pigeon and several wedges of potato she'd managed to set aside. The tantalizing smoky aroma of the fowl caused her stomach to quiver.

Although she'd returned to the beach during the feasting, she hadn't wanted to draw any attention to herself again, and had only stayed long enough to gather what she could for Miriam.

"Describe Pierre to me," Miriam said, her voice wistful.

Angelique couldn't resist taking another peek at Pierre. He'd always been strong and sun-browned. But now, after his years of living out of a canoe and hefting the heavy bundles he transported, he had turned into the kind of man who would turn the head of any woman.

He quirked his brow at her, which only made him more irresistible.

Her stomach did a funny flip. If only he didn't have the same effect on her after all these years apart.

She gave herself a shake. He wasn't irresistible to her. She could keep from falling prey to his charm if she worked hard enough. "If he put on his capote and hood and hid in the woods," she said, "you might mistake him for a loup-garou."

He scowled at her. She ignored it, reached for one of the wooden trenchers on Miriam's table, and placed the pigeon and potatoes on it.

After his insensitivity to Miriam, he deserved to squirm for just a few minutes. "I'm guessing — just guessing, mind you — that he'd look even more like a loup-garou, especially with a dark beard and mustache covering his face."

Miriam's smile began to fade, and a flicker of confusion stole over her gentle features.

"But of course now that he's cleaned up," Angelique went on, "I probably wouldn't mistake him for a monster."

"Probably?" he asked.

She paused and gave him a false perusal. "You're right. It still would be a difficult choice."

"Angelique," Miriam said, "you shouldn't tease Pierre today, not on his first day home."

Whatever she knew about teasing, she'd learned from Pierre. Jean was always so much more serious and sensitive, which was something she appreciated about him. He would be a good provider and give her the kind of life she'd always craved.

Even so, she had to admit, she'd missed bantering with Pierre.

"Angelique?" Pierre said slowly, his scowl disappearing and his eyes widening. "My little sister, Angelique?"

"Yes," she said, spinning to face him. Something within her protested his title for her. She wasn't *little* anymore. And she wasn't his *sister* either — although she was almost his sister-in-law.

"I can't believe it." This time he took his time studying her from her face down to one of her bare feet peeking out from beneath her muddy hem.

Her face was unwashed, the muck of the hen house still splattered over her skirt, the stench of it probably in the air. Embarrassment seeped through her. She should have taken more time to clean herself, at the very least change into the other skirt she owned.

But ever since the previous spring when Therese had reached her eighteenth birthday, when Ebenezer had married her off to the trader willing to pay the highest price for her, Angelique had done her best to hide any trace of beauty. She couldn't bear to think that Ebenezer might sell her too, especially now that he no longer considered the marriage agreement with Jean valid.

And since she'd recently turned eighteen, she had no doubt Ebenezer would start looking for a husband for her soon.

Who else would want her — a poor, uneducated woman — if not a trader? The idea of having to marry a fur trader strangled her every time she thought of such a fate. She'd decided the best course of action for the duration of the war was to do the best she could to cooperate with Ebenezer and make herself into the kind of woman no man would want.

And hopefully she'd survive until the end of the war, until Jean came home and she could finally marry him.

"You've grown up," Pierre said.

Gone was the animosity that had filled his eyes. Instead they reflected pity, which seemed to reach across the room and slap her cheeks. Although she'd been the object of pity plenty of times over the past couple of years — like the pretty woman on the beach earlier in the day — none of the pity had stung quite like Pierre's.

"Angelique has developed into a lovely young woman, hasn't she?" Miriam said.

"She's changed so much I didn't recognize her." Pierre avoided eye contact with Angelique just as smoothly as he avoided his mother's question.

Angelique's face burned. Of course she couldn't expect him to agree with Miriam that she was lovely, but deep inside she wished he'd missed her the same way she'd missed him. The truth was he hadn't known who she was and had likely been too busy to think about her even once during all the time he was away.

"Angelique has been a gift from the Lord," Miriam added, smiling in her direction. "I don't know how I would have survived this past winter without her."

At Miriam's words, Pierre looked at her again, this time with new interest.

"She's been such a blessing to me." Miriam shuffled toward her, in slow, halting steps, her hands outstretched. "I thank the Lord for her every day."

Angelique reached for the dear woman's hands and immediately found herself wrapped in Miriam's embrace.

"You've been a blessing to me too," Angelique whispered. "And now I must run home. Before I'm missed."

It didn't matter what Pierre thought of her, she told herself as she released Miriam and backed out of the cabin. It didn't matter in the least.

She'd pledged herself to Jean. And from the letters they'd received from him, she knew he thought of her every day and missed her. When he returned, she'd clean herself up once and for all. She'd marry him, and they'd finally start the life they'd been planning.

Pierre's opinion wasn't important. He'd likely be gone by the week's end anyway.

And this time she'd make sure he didn't carry away another piece of her heart.

CHAPTER 5

Angelique gingerly opened the back door of the tavern, holding her breath and praying Ebenezer was still down on the beach.

She hadn't meant to linger at Miriam's. If only Pierre hadn't been there when she'd arrived. If only he hadn't been kneeling before Miriam, offering the sweetest, most sincere apology she'd ever heard. If only he hadn't returned to the island at all. Then maybe her whole body wouldn't be trembling from the confusion his presence had stirred inside her.

She pushed the door wider, the dark interior of the kitchen devoid of its usual heat. The dining room beyond was alive with the loud laughter and songs of the men who'd claimed a spot at the inn — the first time sleeping in a real bed in a year's time.

Perhaps Ebenezer was busy pilfering his customers, as was his custom. Whatever the case, Angelique released a soft breath, grateful the kitchen was deserted. She closed the door behind her and began to tiptoe past several barrels Ebenezer had purchased from the supplies that had come off the ships.

God had helped them survive another winter. Their days of starvation were over. At least temporarily.

At the beach earlier, everyone had been talking about how an attack from the Americans was imminent, that a fleet of American ships was on the way, and that they would attempt to retake the island.

When she'd heard the news, Angelique didn't know whether to be excited or worried. The last time the Americans had sailed into the northern waters of the Great Lakes, they'd formed a blockade that hadn't allowed the British supply ships to reach Michilimackinac. She just prayed they wouldn't experience another blockade and that this time the Americans would reclaim the island so Jean could return.

She stepped lightly toward the back stairway, but a plank in the floor squeaked. She paused and held her breath, her stomach growling and reminding her that even with the feasting and new food supplies, she hadn't eaten enough to ease the ache in her stomach.

"And where have you been, young lady?" Ebenezer spoke from the doorway that led into the dining room.

Defeat crashed down on Angelique. She'd hoped with the coming of the ships, she'd regain some freedom that came with the busyness of summer.

Her stepfather's bulky frame filled the doorway, and the light from the dining room gleamed off the round bald spot at the top of his head. A ring of black hair surrounded the shining skin of his head, reminding her of the tonsure of the Jesuit priests. His plain gray shirt hung loosely over his fleshy middle, almost like a priestly robe.

"Where have you been?" he repeated louder. "And why are you sneaking in so late?"

"I'm sorry." She hung her head as he would expect. "With all the excitement of the day I lost track of the time."

"You didn't have permission to go any-where."

"I didn't think you'd mind today."

Ebenezer stepped into the kitchen. "Of course I mind." His tone took on the seething angry quality that didn't bode well. "As long as God's given you into my charge, I expect you to obey me and to abide the Ten Commandments."

"I do my best —"

"Not when you steal food right off this very table. Food I forbade you to eat." He brought his hand down as if to slam it against the plank worktable that Betty used for preparing the meals for the guests. But instead of slamming the wood, he stopped himself and thumped it gently with his palm.

"Steal?" She glanced at the table, empty except for several greasy pans. "I haven't stolen anything —"

"Don't talk to me that way, young lady." His tone turned low and menacing. "Betty told me she left the rest of the bread here, but that when she came back into the kitchen, it was gone."

Angelique thought back to her encounter with Betty earlier in the day and the offer of the bread. She knew Betty had eaten it, but she didn't want Betty to get into trouble. "Perhaps one of the guests took it?"

"Stop lying to me!" The words burst out loud and harsh before he caught himself, cleared his throat, and then spoke again in a too-calm voice. "You're only sinning further by lying to me."

"I'm sorry." She quelled her angry retort. She knew it would do no good to argue with him.

"After all this time I'd expected more character growth within you. But instead you are still very much like your sinful mother."

Angelique shook her head. She didn't want to struggle with the longings of her flesh like her mother had, but what if she did have the same wayward tendencies?

Ebenezer crossed the dark room toward her. "Come with me. Apparently you're in need of more discipline." He gripped her forcefully, giving her little choice but to allow him to propel her toward the narrow stairwell.

As he started up the steps, his fingers tightened. With each step they ascended, his breathing grew louder.

When they reached the second floor, a sliver of light met them. Betty stood at the crack in their bedroom door in a lacy nightgown that hung embarrassingly low. Ebenezer stalked past without a glance, dragging Angelique along behind him until they reached the ladder that led to the attic.

"Go to your room." He shoved her away from him toward the ladder. "And you will stay there all day tomorrow, praying and repenting for your sins."

Angelique started up the rungs and couldn't resist glancing through the shadows to where Betty stood. A flicker of remorse crossed the woman's face, but then she quickly closed the bedroom door without saying a word to defend Angelique.

Angelique scrambled the rest of the way up the ladder and crawled into her room, shutting the trapdoor behind her, wishing it were as easy to shut out the sting of Betty's silence.

Though she'd encouraged Betty to eat the food and didn't begrudge her the extra, she wished Betty would have spoken up for her. At the very least, the woman could have deferred the blame on to one of the guests.

The ladder scraped against the wall as Ebenezer pulled it away, trapping her in the cold, windowless room as he'd done many times before.

She sat back on her heels, her head brushing against the low roof rafter. The dark reaches of the attic were crowded with empty crates and a few worthless trinkets left from last fall that Ebenezer would likely sell to the Indians.

What had her mother ever seen in Ebenezer? After all the men her mother had lived with after the death of her father, why had she finally chosen to marry Ebenezer?

That was the question that haunted Angelique during these confrontations. And she didn't want to delve too deeply into the painful memories of the past for fear that blame might rest upon her.

After all, she'd been the one — not Therese — to cry about missing Michilimackinac, to complain about wanting a real family, and to blame their mother for all that had happened to destroy the happy home they'd once had.

Angelique didn't want to think that perhaps her mother had married Ebenezer for her, so that she could return to the only place where she'd ever known happiness, however brief it had been. The thought was too painful to consider.

She sagged against the wall. She couldn't keep from overhearing the click of the door beneath her room, the squeak of the bed frame, and Ebenezer's low voice followed by Betty's higher one.

Quickly she began to hum, and she reached up to the rafter, to the makeshift shelf that doubled as a hiding spot for the only worldly possessions she owned. She skimmed the board until her fingers brushed against the smooth ivory edge of the comb that Jean had once given her. She brought it down and caressed it.

At the sound of Ebenezer's grunt from the room beneath, Angelique squeezed her eyes closed and hummed louder. She wrapped her fingers around the comb.

If only God would hasten the day of Jean's return. Then she'd finally be free. She'd finally be able to have the family and stable life she'd always wanted.

Angelique awoke to the scraping of the ladder against the wall.

"Come down this instant, Angelique" came Ebenezer's call from below.

She sat up and glanced to the far end of the attic, to the light filtering through the cracks in the roof. From the slant of the rays, she could tell it was still early morning.

"You must hurry." Ebenezer's voice held an eagerness that Angelique heard only when he was counting his coins. "You have a visitor."

A visitor? She rose from her sleeping pallet onto her knees, bumping her head against a beam. Who could possibly be calling? And why?

Miriam. Had something happened to Miriam?

She grabbed her mobcap from the dusty floor and pulled it on over her tangle of long curls. Then she scrambled toward the hatch.

Maybe Pierre had come to deliver bad tidings regarding Miriam.

When she lifted the door open, Ebenezer was there, scowling up at her, his all-seeing eyes taking in her disheveled appearance. "You're in no condition to be seen by anyone."

She hastily shoved the curls into her cap out of sight as he required, then straightened her high collar so that it brushed against her chin.

He glanced down at her dirty bare toes before he spun away and hustled down the hallway, clearly expecting her to follow him as quickly as possible.

He didn't stop until he stood in the kitchen by the door leading into the spacious tavern area, where the guests congregated to drink and eat. The mustiness of stale tobacco lingered with the scent of fried fish, making Angelique's stomach rumble, reminding her of how hungry she was.

Ebenezer wiped a hand across his bald spot, polishing it. And then he furrowed his brow so that his ring of hair dipped. "Whatever she wants you to do, you do it."

She?

Ebenezer was already striding into the dining room, a wide smile plastered onto his face.

Angelique knew she had no choice but to

follow him.

"Miss McDouall," Ebenezer said. "Sorry to keep you waiting."

Miss McDouall? Angelique froze halfway through the doorway.

There in the dining room stood the beautiful young woman who'd come ashore yesterday from the ships. She was clothed in a gown just as flouncy and frilly as the one she'd worn previously, with a high waist and lines of ruffles layered over the skirt. Angelique didn't know much about British fashion, but she could tell from the style and embellishments that Miss McDouall was every bit a lady.

Behind her, in the shadows of the doorway, stood a British soldier who'd likely been sent to accompany and protect her.

"No need to apologize, Mr. Whiley. If you would be so kind as to introduce me to your stepdaughter, I would be ever so grateful." She smiled brightly at Angelique, her attention flitting to Angelique's soiled skirt, but then just as rapidly returned to her face, as if she were making an effort not to gape at the filth.

"Ah, yes, Miss McDouall." Ebenezer frowned at Betty, who'd stopped her work of clearing the remains of last night's drinking to stare with open mouth at Miss Mc-

Douall. The mugs and pitchers were drained. The tables glistened with sticky spots, which was all that remained of Ebenezer's overpriced rum.

"This is my stepdaughter, Angelique Mac-Kenzie." Ebenezer waved her forward. "Her poor mother, God rest her soul, gave me charge of the girl and made me vow to take care of her until she's properly wedded. And I've taken my duties very seriously."

"I'm pleased to meet you, Miss Mac-Kenzie," the woman said, her pretty face alight with interest.

What exactly did the woman want? Why had she come?

Angelique's empty stomach cinched. Miss McDouall's presence didn't bode well. Angelique knew she'd be better off staying far away from the woman. But at the warning glint in Ebenezer's eyes, Angelique nodded at Miss McDouall and forced out the greeting expected of her. "Thank you. I'm pleased to meet you too."

"Wonderful." Miss McDouall clasped her gloved hands together. "From the second I saw you, I just knew you would benefit from my help."

Angelique started to shake her head. Everyone on the island looked gaunt and hungry after the winter. They could *all* benefit from Miss McDouall's help. In fact, if Miss McDouall had been on the island all winter she wouldn't have looked quite so fresh herself.

"Perhaps you're just the influence Angelique needs," Ebenezer said before Angelique could formulate a response. "The Lord knows I've tried so often over the years to teach her to be a good Christian. But unfortunately I still have more trouble with her than I'd like."

Protest rose swiftly inside Angelique. How could he say such a thing? She never gave him any trouble. In fact, she always tried to go out of her way to avoid him.

"Then this is indeed a meeting orchestrated by God himself," Miss McDouall said. "My father wasn't quite sure that he wanted a lady like myself to come to this remote and desolate area of the wilderness, but I assured him God had put a call on my life. I've been quite willing to sacrifice my own comfort so that I can be of help to someone less fortunate than myself."

"Someone less fortunate?" Angelique blurted the words before she could stop them. She didn't need Miss McDouall's charity, especially when there were others who would benefit from it much more than her. "I can help you find islanders in need of your generosity. There is one widow in particular who is blind and could use help planting her fields and repairing her roof."

Miss McDouall's smile faltered. "I regret to hear of the widow, Miss MacKenzie." She smoothed her white gloves over the glossy layers of her gown. "But as you can see, I'm not exactly a farmer. I'm afraid I wouldn't do the poor woman any good at all."

"Of course not," Ebenezer said, frowning at Angelique, his narrowed eyes telling her she would pay for her obstinate remark later. "You're much more suited to bestow your kindness upon another young woman, like Angelique."

"I agree, Mr. Whiley. We all do have varying gifts and abilities. I have come to cheer up the soldiers with dances and parties. I hope to form a Soldiers Relief Committee with the purpose of helping provide better clothes and food for our soldiers. And I would like to bestow my personal attention to one of the island's more unfortunate women."

Unfortunate? Angelique wanted to shrink in embarrassment.

"After all," Miss McDouall continued, "I do seem to have a talent for helping less fortunate women better themselves."

"I for one will be grateful for any changes

you can bring about in Angelique."

Miss McDouall clapped her hands together again and her smile returned. "Then I shall start at once. I would like to offer an invitation for Miss MacKenzie to join me for tea this afternoon in the officers' quarters in the fort. Shall we say at half past three?"

Ebenezer spoke hurriedly. "Angelique might be too busy today."

Angelique wanted to laugh at the thought of her being busy — not when she'd be in her dark dormer room doing nothing.

Miss McDouall's smile disappeared altogether, and her expression turned petulant. "I really have no time to waste. My father insists that I leave the island by the end of the summer. If I am to help Miss MacKenzie, then I shall need to take advantage of every opportunity I have."

"Yes, but she must fish. We rely on her fishing —"

"Could she not fish this morning?"

Ebenezer didn't say anything. The silence was filled with the clinking of mugs and clanking of silverware from Betty's table-clearing efforts.

"I'm sure Miss MacKenzie wouldn't mind changing her plans just slightly, would you, dear?" Miss McDouall had turned her sweetest smile upon Angelique.

If only the woman knew just how little control Angelique had over her schedule. "I'm willing, yes, but I must do whatever my stepfather wishes."

The soldier near the door stepped out of the shadows. "Mr. Whiley, I suggest you accommodate Miss McDouall's request as best you can."

Angelique took a quick step backward. It was Lieutenant Steele, the quartermaster, the same soldier that had attacked her two mornings ago.

The lieutenant was dressed in a fresh uniform that had likely been among the items on the supply ships. The red of his new coat was brilliant in the morning sunshine streaming through the doorway. And although his handsome face was still thin, he'd shaven and had lost the wild, ravenous glint.

"Commander McDouall is very supportive of his daughter's charity efforts," the quartermaster continued. "I suggest you do whatever you can to support her efforts as well."

Did Lieutenant Steele remember her?

Angelique resisted the urge to touch her neck and the bruises he'd left.

He didn't bother looking at her. And his

face was stiff and impersonal. If he'd recalled their encounter, he apparently wasn't going to reveal it.

"Well," Ebenezer said slowly, "if you feel it would be best for Angelique to visit you today —"

"I do," Miss McDouall interrupted. "I'd be ever so grateful to you."

Ebenezer looked at Angelique. She could sense he didn't want to release her from her discipline, yet what choice did he have? He couldn't refuse Miss McDouall's request, not with the lieutenant standing by.

"Run along and do your fishing now, dear, if you must." Miss McDouall fanned her hand at Angelique, shooing her away. "Just make sure you're ready at half past three for our tea. I shall send Lieutenant Steele after you to accompany you to the fort."

Angelique stifled a shiver at the thought of having to be alone with Lieutenant Steele again. "Thank you, Miss McDouall. I'll be waiting." And then before anyone could stop her, she turned and sped through the kitchen toward the back door.

She knew she ought to feel grateful for Miss McDouall's invitation. It would mean food and an escape from Ebenezer's overbearing control for part of the day. But she couldn't shake the feeling again, that an association with Miss McDouall would only bring her trouble, especially after she'd worked so hard to stay invisible.

For the moment, though, she was free. Free from the confines of the attic, free to go out in her canoe, and free to savor the beautiful May morning. She would relish the precious moments, no matter the consequences she would face later.

CHAPTER 6

Pierre hoisted the canoe, letting the smooth birchbark rest against the top of his head. He carried the fishing rod inside the canoe — Papa's fishing rod.

He was surprised Maman had suggested he take it. Even though she said she'd forgiven him, he hadn't expected her to allow him to use anything that had once belonged to Papa. It was almost as if she'd not only forgiven him for his mistakes but had forgotten them too.

He wasn't quite sure he could accept that kind of love. It seemed too good to be true. And it made him feel even guiltier that he would need to leave her by the end of the week.

The crunch of twigs under his feet echoed in the crisp morning air. The scent of woodsmoke hung heavy, rising from the Indian campfires along the island's south shore.

He was planning to get done as much

work around the farm as he could before he left. He'd even gotten up early that morning to repair the roof. But a gurgling stomach had prodded him to find the makings of their next meal. Except for the few potatoes left in his pack, Maman had no food anywhere in the house. She hadn't had any food all winter . . .

Except for what Angelique had provided for her.

Angelique.

Pierre tripped over a root buried beneath soggy leaves. The canoe wobbled, and he tightened his grip to steady it.

Gratefulness for Angelique's kindness was quickly replaced by remorse. He hadn't exactly been polite to her since his return to the island.

"It was her fault," he muttered. "Oui. She should have identified herself earlier. The first time she saw me."

It would have saved him the worry about his mission being discovered. His abdomen tensed at the thought of what might have happened to her had he not rescued her from her attacker. The Lord only knew what other trouble she'd experienced during the past two years in her efforts to take care of Maman.

He snagged his boot again, this time on a

rock. He stumbled forward, losing hold of the canoe. It slipped from his head and began to fall. With a lunge he caught the canoe and gently lowered it to the ground. He'd found it in the rafters of the barn, dusty but still solid, the same canoe he'd hewn with Papa's help when he'd been younger — except that Papa had embarked on one of his trips before they could finish.

Pierre had worked on the canoe all winter, attempting to line it with small splits of cedarwood. But he'd only gotten angrier and more frustrated at his ineptness and lack of knowledge, until finally he'd stopped working on the canoe altogether.

He supposed that was when he'd first realized how much he resented Papa having to be gone half the year. When he became a voyageur, he decided he wouldn't have a wife or children. That way he wouldn't have to leave behind a family.

With his sleeve Pierre wiped the perspiration from his forehead. After the hard work of the past couple of hours, he was not only ready to eat but ready to cool off in the pond in the secluded cove where he'd always gone when he was a boy, where he could swim without being disturbed.

He started to heft the canoe again, but then stopped and peered through the newly leafed foliage. A flash of white was followed by the distinct sound of splashing.

Someone was already there. In *his* spot.

Granted, he hadn't been here in over five years. Still, he'd been the one to discover it. His muscles flexed. He once again lowered the canoe to the ground, then crept forward soundlessly. He neared the pond and crouched behind a jagged boulder.

A ball of clothing rested on a fallen log near the swimming hole. He peeked around the boulder.

There in the calm water floated a young woman on her back, the white of her petticoats swirling in the water around her legs, her bare arms paddling. Her long, thick curls fanned around a pretty face, forming a beautiful dark red against the green-blue of the water.

His heart began to race.

Angelique?

He stepped out of his hiding spot, allowing himself a clear view. Her eyes were closed and her expression serene, as if she were relishing every stroke and lap of the water.

He smiled. Yes, it was Angelique. Silently he tugged his shirt out of his breeches and shrugged out of his suspenders. Then he slipped his shirt over his head and shed the boots.

Sunlight bathed her face, kissing the faint freckles sprinkled across her nose. She sighed and kicked her legs, keeping herself afloat.

His grin widened. Before she had time to open her eyes and catch sight of him, he jumped in, letting his entire body hit the water near her, so that his splash crashed over her.

She yelped and flailed her arms and legs.

His body submerged into the pond, and the shock of the cold water took his breath away. When he broke the surface, his teeth were already chattering.

She was sputtering water and wiping tangles of curls out of her eyes, eyes that were wide with fright.

At the sight of him, the fear evaporated into anger.

"Good morning." He grinned, tossing his head and shaking the water from his hair and treading water to keep afloat.

"You scared me." She glared at him, the darks of her eyes wide in contrast to the paleness of her face. Her arms swished back and forth in the water with her own effort to keep from sinking.

"I couldn't resist." He laughed at her

indignation. "For old time's sake."

Her glare wavered. And then, before he could duck, she brought her hand around and sent a wave splashing into his face.

The water filled his mouth and eyes, and for a moment he was the one left sputtering. With a cough he wiped his face clear of water and found that she was watching him, amusement in her eyes.

"For old time's sake," she said dryly.

A burst of laughter welled up, and he let it out. Within seconds he found himself in a splashing war with her, just as they'd done in the days before he'd left. Only she wasn't half his size anymore. And she was much stronger and quicker than he'd anticipated.

Splash after splash knocked into him, until finally he lifted his hands in mock surrender. "You win," he laughed. "I can admit when I'm defeated."

"That's a first." She gave a breathless laugh and swiped at the hair that had fallen into her face. "You used to be such a poor loser. A big crybaby." Her eyes and smile teased him.

"I couldn't have been a poor loser," he teased back. "Since I never lost."

"Oh yes you did. Especially when Jean and I teamed up against you."

His hands and feet were numb from the

cold water, but for some reason his chest pulsed with warmth. "Two against one? *Non.* I don't think that counted as a real victory."

She shrugged. It was almost as if the years hadn't separated them, as if he'd never left. She was still the sweet girl who'd tagged along with him and Jean for all their adventures together.

"I think the only reason you won now was because you were already used to the water." He shuddered. "I'm frozen." It was only mid-May, much too early for swimming.

"So now you're blaming the cold water for losing? Maybe you'd better just accept the fact that I'm all grown up now and can beat you fair and square." At that, she tossed one more splash at him.

Though he was stiff from the cold, he smiled and gave her a nod. "I believe you're right — much has changed since I've been away."

Her gentle brown eyes looked up at him with warm adoration. During those turbulent months of fighting with Papa, amidst all his anger and resentment, amidst the horrible ogre he'd become, she'd followed him everywhere and listened to him. She hadn't condemned him or shut him out like Papa had done.

And now, seeing her again, seeing that

same adoration, an ache grew in his chest. He realized just how much he'd missed her acceptance and friendship.

"It's good to see you again, Angelique," he said softly while treading water near her, brushing her legs with his.

"It's good to see you too." She lowered her head, as if embarrassed by her admission. But then she let out a gasp. "Oh my." Her eyes widened at the sight of his bare chest only inches away.

He shrugged. So what if he was shirtless? As children she'd seen him unclad plenty of times.

She began to back away, and even though the water covered her to her shoulders, he was close enough to see bruises on her neck, and the way the water plastered her chemise to her body and outlined her feminine curves.

Her breathing turned choppy and only served to bring more attention to her wet chemise.

A spurt of heat shot through him, and he couldn't make himself look away as he became aware that she wasn't a little girl anymore. And he was no boy.

She was a woman — a beautiful, full-grown woman.

She glanced up and, seeing where he was

looking, gasped again, kicked her legs frantically and swam a safe distance away from him, toward the shore and the log where she'd left her bundle of clothes.

He ducked underwater and let the cold pressure bring him to his senses. What was he thinking? Angelique was his little sister and nothing more.

He broke the surface and blew out a breath of air and water.

She started to step out of the water, but then stopped and glanced over her shoulder. "Turn around, Pierre. We're not little kids anymore," she called.

"Oui. I can see that," he replied, unable to resist grinning.

She scowled at him, clearly waiting for him to obey her order.

"All right, *ma cherie.* If you insist." He spun in the water so that he was facing the opposite direction. "But you'd better hurry or I might peek."

"You'd better not." Her voice was jagged with her effort to hustle back into her clothes.

"And just why are you swimming without your clothes on anyway?"

"I didn't think I'd have any visitors."

He shook his head at her stupidity. "If I could sneak up on you, then why couldn't one of the other voyageurs?"

"Because they're all still drunk in their beds."

"But there's always the chance that someone might see you."

She didn't say anything.

For some reason her silence fueled the frustration swirling in his chest. "And what about the Indians? They're swarming all over the island."

"I'm fine."

"I suppose you were fine the other morning when I pried that British soldier's fingers from your neck?"

"You have no right to get angry with me, Pierre."

"Why?" He spun to face her, not caring if she was half dressed. But she'd already donned her skirt and bodice, and they stuck to her wet skin and undergarments. "Why aren't you being more careful?"

She reached for her mobcap, pressed a fisted hand onto her hip, and glared at him. "For your information, I was sneaking food to your mother. Without my deliveries every morning, she would have starved to death."

His angry retort died, stabbed by a sword of guilt that had been slicing at him since his return to the island. If he'd been here over the winter, he could have cared for Maman and kept Angelique from having to put herself in danger.

With a breath of frustration, Pierre dove underwater again and swam for the shore. The chilly water stung his cheeks. The muddy scent from the recently thawed snow filled his nostrils. And the taste of guilt lingered on his tongue.

It wasn't his fault Maman had almost starved to death. He hadn't known she was blind and that she couldn't take care of herself anymore. And he hadn't realized the food situation for the islanders had become so desperate.

But would he have been willing to leave the wilderness to return to the island to help her? Would he have sacrificed his brigade, his furs, and the way of life he loved? More important, now that he knew how desperate her situation was, what was he going to do about it? He couldn't very well abandon his brigade or his furs to help her.

Since the fur-bearing animals were nearly extinct in Europe, the British were desperate to keep control of the fur trade in North America. They were paying good prices for each pelt. The past few years of trading had proven to be very profitable for him. He'd amassed four canoes of his own and was an independent, bourgeois headman over nearly fifty men.

If he could trade all his pelts without any further problems, he would accumulate a hefty profit. So long as the North West Company left his furs and men alone.

He needed to stay with his brigade. He *wanted* to stay with them.

Pierre reached the shore and climbed out. Water dripped from his body and formed a puddle at his feet. The spring breeze thrashed against his bare back like a cat-o'-nine-tails.

He couldn't expect Angelique to continue to put herself at risk for Maman, could he?

"I'm sorry the past year was so difficult for you and Maman," he finally said, squeezing water out of the leg of one of his trousers. "It hurts me to think of how much you've suffered."

She didn't say anything.

When he chanced a glance at her, she was staring directly at his chest with her mouth slightly open. Her gaze slid down the length of him and then back up.

A grin tugged at his lips. "We're not little kids anymore," he said, mimicking her tone from only a moment ago.

When her eyes lifted to meet his, his grin widened in expectation of one of her ready smiles. But she didn't smile. She didn't even speak.

Instead a current shot across the distance between them. The intensity of it pierced his gut and charged through his blood.

Her runaway curls tumbled about her face and down her shoulders. Even though her face was thin from hunger, there was no denying that the years apart had shaped Angelique into a beautiful woman.

Again, for a long moment he couldn't make himself look away from her. He felt as though he were riding through a surging rapids with the crashing and swaying of the water pushing on him and threatening to capsize him.

He had the sudden urge to cross the distance between them, grab hold of her, and . . .

And what?

He shook his head, letting his hair flap in the breeze and spray water everywhere. He gave himself a mental shake while he was at it.

Angelique was his friend. She'd always adored him in a brotherly way. That was all she still felt. Wasn't it?

He rubbed his hand through his hair, combing out even more water, and he peeked at her from under his lashes.

She'd turned her head away, and a blush had crept up her cheeks. Non. She felt nothing more than the old friendly affection for him. He'd do best to continue to treat her like a friend just as he always had. He grabbed his shirt and tugged it back on, yanking it over his damp skin.

She didn't say anything but instead busied herself retying her cap and tucking every single strand of her glorious hair out of sight. When she turned to face him again, she'd even shoved her collar up to her chin, hiding the bruises on her neck.

Covered from head to toe in the plainest of garments without a stitch of color, she looked like a nun, which was a shame. Her hair was much too pretty to cover. "I think you should leave your cap off."

She shook her head. "Ebenezer would lock me in my room for a month if he saw me without my head covering."

He forced his foot into one of his boots. "I take it Ebenezer is still giving you a hard time?"

She hesitated, a cloud settling over her features. "Now with Therese gone, he's taken it upon himself to make sure I turn into a saint."

He paused, his other boot in hand. In the distance he could hear the songs of other voyageurs arriving on the island. "I'm sorry about Therese. I heard what happened."

Angelique nodded, her face a solemn mask. "She didn't want to go."

"So Ebenezer forced her to marry Duncan?" He'd suspected as much, but he hadn't known for sure, only that the old trader had boasted he'd won the bid to marry the attractive girl.

Angelique stretched her collar higher. "After mother died, Ebenezer got tired of dealing with Therese. She was too spirited, too independent for him. He warned her if she didn't stop disobeying, he'd marry her off in the spring."

Pierre frowned at the thought of Ebenezer's treatment of Angelique and her sister, the control he'd exerted over them, the harshness, the lack of kindness. He supposed that was why his own maman had opened her home to Angelique. Maman had encouraged Jean and him to include Angelique, even though she'd been just a girl. Maman had tried to reach out to Therese too, but the girl was older and uninterested in fishing or building forts or racing along the island trails.

Angelique started toward the edge of the pond. "I guess Therese wasn't strong enough to make it out in the wilderness."

"The rapids are dangerous for even the toughest voyageur."

She stopped. Her eyes were sad but direct. "She didn't fall out, Pierre."

He nodded, sensing the despair that lay below the surface of Angelique's sadness. Even though she could put on a calm façade, as he'd seen her do many times around her stepfather, she was a passionate girl with a tempest of feelings. He'd always liked that about her. She was genuine and honest.

"Every trader that came in last fall said Therese threw herself out of the canoe. On purpose." Her eyes begged him to contradict her.

But Pierre had heard the same rumor too — the news that Therese had been so miserably unhappy that she'd decided to kill herself rather than live as a fur trader's wife.

"I'm sorry, Angelique." He wished he had better news for her. But the truth was the fur-trading life was not suited to any woman, except maybe an Indian woman.

Pierre shoved his foot into his other boot. After all the problems he'd experienced firsthand over the past five years in the wilderness, he could completely understand why Papa had opposed his decision to follow in his footsteps and enter the fur-trading business. There were long stretches away from home. Even when Papa had come home, he'd been too busy with the farm to have much time for his sons and wife. Not to mention he'd been consumed with drinking and had often let his anger get the best of him.

Pierre couldn't blame Papa for wanting him to go to school in Detroit, for forbidding him to become a voyageur. He'd only wanted to prevent Pierre from making the same mistakes.

He could see Papa's wisdom now. If only he'd realized it at the time he'd left the island. Maybe if he'd understood that Papa had only loved him and wanted to protect him . . .

It might not have changed the fact that he'd become a fur trader. The wilderness and fur trading were in his blood. But maybe he wouldn't have left home spewing such hateful words. Maybe he wouldn't have made so many sinful mistakes.

Angelique bent toward the water. "I've got a couple of fish for Miriam if you'd like to take them back to her."

He whistled under his breath as she lifted a stringful of trout from a shallow pool of water between boulders. "Looks like you've become quite the fisherman."

"I'm all right."

"You better be *all right* considering you had the best fisherman on the island teach you everything you know."

"Best fisherman?" She smiled. "I doubt he'd be the best anymore."

"Is that a challenge?" He returned her smile, glad to put the serious conversation and thoughts behind them.

"You wouldn't want to challenge me." She took three fish off the string and held them out to him. "Because I'd most certainly beat you."

"Tomorrow at dawn. Meet me at the west shore and we'll see who's best."

Her smile stretched into her eyes. "I already know who's best."

"Are you afraid to lose?" He couldn't resist teasing her back.

"Not at all." She pushed the fish at him. "Here. Take these to Miriam."

He took them from her. They were prime-size trout. Their scales glistened in the sunlight, and his stomach growled, reminding him of why he was out in the first place.

She picked up the rest of her fish.

"Maman was asking about you this morning," he said, not ready for their time together to be at an end. "When you didn't come before daylight, she got worried about you."

"Ebenezer detained me." A shadow flitted across her face. "But I knew you'd be there to take care of her."

Take care of her. The words made him squirm.

"I want you to know," he said, "how grateful I am for all you did for Maman this past year."

She started to shake her head. "It was nothing —"

"It was everything. She told me about all you did, coming every morning to bring her food and wood, to start her fire, to cook her fish."

"I only wish I could have done more."

"She said you often gave her your own portion and went hungry."

"We were all hungry." She glanced at the fish she'd given him, and her face pinched with hunger. "If only we hadn't been blockaded. And if only the British hadn't insisted on buying up all our food."

"Stealing sounds like a more accurate way to describe what they did." Pierre spat the words, his frustration with the British mounting more each day that went by. Since arriving he'd learned that when the British supply ships had been cut off from the island by the Americans, the commander had decided to purchase the necessary winter supplies from the locals both on the island and mainland.

Of course, the islanders and local Indians hadn't wanted to part with their precious stores of winter food. But they were given little choice. They either had to hand the food over to the fort commissary and accept a pittance of reimbursement or face having their food confiscated without any payment at all.

Either way, everyone had suffered. They'd had a shortage all winter. And Angelique was obviously still hungry.

His mind returned to the bundle she'd left on the table last night, the small meal she'd brought to Maman. Had she sacrificed for Maman again?

"Come back to the farm and join Maman and me for breakfast," he said. "I'll make you the best fish cakes you've ever eaten."

Her eyebrows shot up. "You? Cook?"

"Oui. You're not going to believe this, but I've turned into an exquisite cook."

"You're right," she teased. "I don't believe it."

"Then I guess you'll have to come back and try my cooking for yourself."

She looked up at the position of the sun

and then peered in the direction of town. "I have to be somewhere at half past three."

"You'll be back in plenty of time." His muscles tensed in anticipation of her answer. More than anything he wanted to make a meal for her, to show her his appreciation for all she'd done for Maman over the winter. And he wanted to feed her, to see the hungry look on her face replaced by satisfaction.

"Please, ma cherie. I haven't killed anyone with my cooking . . . yet."

"That's reassuring."

He grinned.

She hesitated only a moment longer before smiling back. "How can I resist, especially after your promise not to kill me?"

"Good. Let's go then. I'll race you back."

"We can't race anymore."

"Why not? Are you afraid I'm still faster than you?"

"Pierre Durant, you are still as arrogant as ever, aren't you?"

"Just telling the truth, that's all." He loved that she could take his teasing and then give it back to him in full measure.

She lifted the hem of her skirt, giving him a glimpse of her bare feet. He looked down at his boots. She didn't have any shoes? "Maybe we'll have to wait to race for another day —"

She jolted forward and dashed through the brush, leaving him staring after her.

"Last one back has to gut the fish," she called over her shoulder.

He took off running, and as he was chasing her, he realized he was truly glad to be home. Gladder than he'd ever imagined.

CHAPTER 7

Pierre sat back in the kitchen chair, folded his arms across his chest, and let contentment fill his empty belly.

Angelique raised a last forkful of fish cakes to her mouth. With eyes closed she took a long sniff as she had for each bite, and then she closed her lips around the fork. She chewed slowly, savoring every tiny granule of fish and potato that he'd pressed into the patties.

He hadn't been able to resist watching her eat. It had been like gazing upon a beautiful sunset.

"This is so good, Pierre," she said again through her mouthful, as she had at least a dozen times since starting the meal.

Maman's smile was achingly wide, and her eyes brimmed with tears, as if listening to Angelique's enjoyment of the meal was almost as pleasurable as eating it herself.

He'd insisted both the women eat everything he'd cooked. He knew he could always scrounge up some food from his men and eat later. And if need be, he'd buy more supplies from the British.

For now, it was enough to watch Maman and Angelique — especially Angelique — enjoy each bite.

She opened her eyes. The impact of her pretty lips curling into a satisfied smile crushed into him and squeezed his chest.

"You were wrong," she said.

"I'm never wrong."

"You were this time."

Sunlight streamed through the faded curtains and touched the loose curls of her hair, turning them into a lush reddish brown. He was glad that at some point in the race back to the cabin, her mobcap had fallen to the back of her neck, allowing her hair to tumble down around her face again.

"You've almost killed me with your cooking." She set the fork on her empty plate and sat back in her chair.

"What? I almost killed you? Impossible."

"Yes. You killed me with the pleasure of it." Genuine admiration shone from her eyes. "I can't remember a time when I've enjoyed a meal as much as this."

The warmth of her praise spread over him like the sunshine. It filled him and seeped

117

down to his toes. He picked up his coffee cup and took a sip, letting the rich flavor add to the gratification that had settled over him in a way he hadn't experienced in a long time.

"I think I especially enjoyed it because for once I didn't have to gut or fillet the fish." She held her mug of coffee between both hands and inhaled the freshly brewed aroma.

He didn't want to think about the bitter acorn-shell tea he'd thrown out onto the grass or the last time Maman and Angelique had tasted real coffee.

"Of course you only won the race because you cheated," he said.

She smiled at him sweetly. "And here I thought you were learning to accept losing like a big boy."

"You had a head start *and* you took a shortcut."

"Miriam, I think Pierre needs a handker-chief so that he can sop up all his tears."

Maman gave a soft laugh. "It's so good to hear you both teasing each other again. I've missed it."

Already Maman looked less hungry and tired than she had yesterday when he'd kneeled before her and begged her forgive-ness. Her face had lit up when Angelique arrived, breathless and disheveled, after their race home. She'd wrapped her arms around the girl and let go of the worry that had plagued her since Angelique's failure to appear at dawn.

Maman hadn't said anything about being worried, but she'd spent a great deal of time on her knees in prayer that morning. And as he'd worked, he'd lifted his own grateful prayers for a Maman who prayed, for he had no doubt she'd petitioned God on his behalf every day he'd been gone. And he was quite certain those prayers had carried him through many of his rough days and in time brought him back to the Lord.

He reached across the table and captured Maman's hand and squeezed it. He hated to think of how lonely it had been for her living by herself, with her eyesight failing and leaving her stranded in the cabin.

"I'm glad you're home, Pierre," she said, placing her other hand over his and gripping him as if she would never let go.

How could he let go of her now that he was home? How would he ever be able to leave her to fend for herself? But how could he possibly stay?

Angelique was studying his face. Her smile faded, as though she sensed him plotting his departure, and her eyes flashed with accusation — the same that she'd leveled at him last night when she'd first arrived.

Was she angry with him about something? But why would Angelique be upset with him? How could she be, not when she'd always admired him?

She stared at her coffee and forced a smile. "I'll only be glad Pierre is home if he promises to gut the fish every morning."

For some reason he didn't like the thought that she might be disappointed in him, even if just a little. The need to sweep away that disappointment surged through him. "I'll gut the fish forever if it makes you happy," he said softly, wanting to see her eyes light up again.

He hadn't minded gutting the fish. It had given him the chance to watch Angelique without her knowing it. The first thing she'd done was fret over a new burn on Maman's hand. She'd slathered it with salve and then bandaged it using a rag. Afterward she'd emptied and cleaned the chamber pot, swept the floor, and brought in more straw to add to Maman's hat-making supply.

She'd even helped Maman brush and plait her hair and twist it into a knot.

"Gut the fish forever?" Angelique said.

"Oui, and I'll fillet them perfectly and make you fish cakes as often as you'd like."

Some of the light returned to the brown of her eyes, soothing him. "Fish cakes every day would make me very happy."

"If you come for dinner later," he offered, "I'll make you a whitefish stew like nothing you've ever tasted before."

"You're tempting me, Pierre, but perhaps another day."

She glanced out the window at the sun and then pushed away from the table, her chair scraping the floor and signaling the end of their time together.

"You still have plenty of time before you have to go, don't you? I thought for sure you'd like me to regale you with tales of my adventures in the wilderness."

He was only joking with her again, hoping to gain another of her smiles.

But she shook her head, leaned over, and kissed his maman's cheek. "Good-bye."

A shadow passed over Maman's face. She stared hard at Angelique, as if by doing so she could make her eyes work again. "Is everything all right, Angel?"

"Everything's just fine."

But the shadow on Maman's face didn't lift. "Pierre says a battle with the Americans is coming very soon. And when the Americans come, they'll retake the island, and Jean can come home again."

121

Pierre shifted uncomfortably. He hadn't been totally honest with Maman. Oui, the Americans were coming. It was inevitable. But he wasn't sure that they would be able to take back the island, not with the call the British had just put out for more Indians to join up with their forces on Michilimackinac.

Soon, more Indians decked out in war paint would arrive on the island. Along with the hundred fresh soldiers from the Royal Newfoundland Regiment that Colonel McDouall had brought with him, the British forces would be hard to beat.

Somehow he'd have to smuggle a letter off the island to let the Americans know about the increasing odds stacked against them.

"Jean will be home soon," Maman said again. "And then you'll be able to come live here for good."

A flush stole over Angelique's cheeks.

Pierre sat forward. "Why does she need to wait for Jean to come home? Why not just live out here now?"

Angelique made a move toward the door, but Maman held her hand fast. "Ebenezer wouldn't allow Angelique to marry Jean after he refused to sign the Oath —"

"Marry Jean?" Disbelief pushed Pierre to

his feet. "Angelique is going to marry Jean?"

The flush in Angelique's cheeks turned brighter, and she ducked her head.

He gave a short laugh. "Why in the world would Angelique marry Jean?" He couldn't picture Angelique with his younger brother. Jean was much too soft-spoken and serious for a fun girl like Angelique.

"Yes," Maman said with a beaming smile. "Jean and Angelique are betrothed. And just as soon as he returns, they'll be married, even if Ebenezer doesn't agree to it. Right, Angelique?"

Angelique glanced sideways at Pierre.

He could only stare back, confusion eating at his gut. Was Maman serious?

Angelique took a breath, straightened her shoulders, and faced him squarely. "It's true. I'm engaged to Jean."

He forced a grin. "Is this a joke, Angelique?"

"It's not a joke. I'm marrying Jean." Her eyes held the same hint of accusation as earlier. "I'm grateful for his offer of marriage. He's exactly the kind of man I need in my life."

"I suppose he's the kind of man you *need* if you want to be bored all the livelong day."

Angelique glared at him, then managed to break away from Maman and cross toward the door.

"Now, Pierre." Maman's voice held a gentle rebuke. "Jean is a good man."

"I'm not disagreeing that he's a good man. I just don't think he's the right man for Angelique."

With a jerk, Angelique swung open the door. "Good-bye, Miriam." She tossed the words over her shoulder before grabbing her string of fish and darting outside.

Pierre released a pent-up breath. Why should he care that Jean and Angelique were getting married? Shouldn't he be happy for them — even if they weren't right for each other?

"She's doing the best thing for both of them, Pierre," Maman said. "She makes Jean very happy. And Jean will be able to give her a much better and safer life."

Pierre stared at the open doorway. "The news just took me by surprise, that's all."

"Go after her and tell her you're sorry." Maman's plea wasn't necessary. He'd already started across the cabin and out the door.

Angelique stomped across the grassy field toward the footpath that would take her back to town.

What right did Pierre have, bursting back

into their lives after all this time and poking fun at her choice of a marriage partner? What did he know about her life? Or Jean's, for that matter, and what was best for them?

With a huff she tossed her morning catch over her shoulder, not caring that the fish had begun to stink or that their slime was rubbing against her bodice.

"Angelique, wait." Pierre's call came from behind her.

She didn't want to talk to him any further about Jean. She was embarrassed to discuss her marriage plans, though she wasn't sure why. Jean was everything she wanted in a husband. He would be there for her day in and day out. He wouldn't disappear whenever the wilderness called. And he truly loved her. Pierre had no right to insult her decision to marry Jean. Not after he'd deserted her.

"Please, Angelique." Pierre caught up with her. "You know I didn't really mean what I said."

"You meant every word." She lengthened her stride, even though every muscle in her body ached to slow down and be with him.

The entire morning — from the swim in the pond to the race back to the cabin to sharing breakfast together — had filled her with an intense passion for Pierre, the same girlish passion she thought she'd long outgrown.

She'd so carefully patched up her broken heart when he'd left the island. But overnight and in one short morning he'd managed to rip out the seams, and now her heart hung wide open.

"Please stop, Angelique." He easily kept up with her long steps. "Believe it or not, I'm trying to apologize."

Her feet slowed to a halt. She couldn't fool herself. She wanted to be with him too much, and she'd take any excuse she could to spend a little more time with him.

His fingers circled her upper arm, spinning her to face him.

He towered above her, his handsome face lined with worried wrinkles and his dark eyes peering down into hers, so sincere, so hard to resist. His thick, wavy hair fell above his eyebrows.

"I didn't mean to upset you," he said. "I guess I still think of you as my little sister, and it's hard for me to imagine you being grown up enough to get married to anyone, especially my kid brother."

At the earnestness of his words, her resistance melted away. With the lingering taste of his fish cakes on her tongue and the satisfaction of a full stomach — something

she hadn't experienced in many months —
she couldn't stay embarrassed or angry for
long. "I'm not too young to get married.
I'm eighteen, you know."

"I know." He stared at her unbound hair,
and to her surprise he touched one of the
dangling curls by her cheek, tracing the
spiral down to her chin.

She wanted to lean into his hand to feel
his touch against her cheek. But she held
herself still.

"If you love Jean, and he makes you
happy, then who am I to question your
plans?"

Did she love Jean?

In the distance, among the damp thicket,
came the sweet whistle of a yellow warbler.

She turned toward the edge of the woods
and the shadows made by the balsam fir
trees. As much as she liked the heat of the
May sunshine on her bare head, she was
safer within the confines of her bonnet and
hidden among the undergrowth of the
woods.

Maybe she didn't love Jean or even feel
anything for him beyond simple brotherly
affection, but Jean was safe. And that was
all that really mattered. He would protect
her and provide a good home for her.

After Pierre had left, Jean had sought her

out every day. At the time she'd been lonely and needed him. They'd spent countless hours together, working, hiking, talking. Jean had been so kind. He'd been more than willing to help her put her friendship with Pierre into the grave.

"You're right," she said through a tight chest. "You're in no place to question my decision. You haven't been here in five years, and you'll be gone again in five days' time. So please don't say anything more about Jean and me."

With that, she pulled away from his grip and resumed her stride across the open field. When he didn't follow, her footsteps faltered.

"You're angry with me about something else too, aren't you?" he called after a moment.

She took several more steps before finally stopping and spinning to face him across the span of long yellowed grass left from the previous summer, with the shoots of fresh green beginning to break through to take their place.

His shoulders had slumped, and he'd stuck his thumbs into the waistband of his trousers.

She didn't know what to say. Yes, if she was honest with herself, she had to admit that she *was* angry with him. Angry with him for leaving five years ago. Angry that he'd leave again soon. Angry that he could come home and make her care so much again in such a short time.

"What are you mad about?" he asked.

Should she tell him the truth? What good would come of letting him know that when he'd left he'd broken her heart? And that when he left again, he'd break her heart all over again.

"Please tell me what I did, Angelique. I can't stand the thought of you being angry with me." His eyes pleaded with her.

"Why didn't you stop to see Miriam that morning you were on the island?"

"Oh, so that's all?" The wrinkles smoothed from his forehead. "You're mad because I didn't visit Maman?"

If only that were all. She gave a soft sigh. "Don't you think you could have made an effort to see her? If it were me, I wouldn't have been able to wait a single minute longer."

"Believe me, I wanted to see her more than anything. I stopped and watched her through the window, even though I was running late getting off the island." He gave her a pointed look. "Which as it turns out was a good thing."

"Why were you on the island in the first place?"

He hesitated, glancing around to the cabin behind them, then to the scraggly weed-filled garden, to the deserted barn and overgrown fields, and finally to the woods beyond her. He shook his head and lowered his voice. "It would be safer for both our sakes if we pretended I was never here that morning."

She wanted to probe further, to find out his troubles. But she was running out of time. If she didn't leave enough time to clean up before her tea with Miss Mc-Douall, Ebenezer would discipline her. "Just promise me one thing, Pierre."

"Anything."

"Promise me you won't stay away from home for so long next time and hurt Miriam again."

His lips curved into a gentle smile, one that reminded her of Miriam's. "I promise."

The anger swirling through her chest disappeared like a mist chased away by sunshine.

"I was a fool to stay away from my family. I can see that now. But I've changed, Angelique. I'm a different man, and I'm trying to please God with how I live. I'll prove to you that I'm not the same foolish boy anymore."

She wanted to believe him, wanted to believe that maybe he really had grown up in the time he'd been gone. "And just how are you going to prove that you're not a foolish boy anymore?" she teased. "Are you going to stop splashing unsuspecting swimmers and scaring them half to death?"

He grinned. "Of course not. That would require way too much change, and you can't expect miracles."

"Then how are you going to prove you've given up your wild ways?" She'd never tire of bantering with him. She could only pray that the little of him she'd seen and the fun they'd had that morning would be enough to carry her through until he came back to the island again.

His face grew serious, and he peered back at the cabin. His dark eyes filled with something that made her shiver in spite of the sunshine pouring over her.

"I've decided . . ." he started, but then stopped.

Her body tensed, and she wasn't sure that she wanted him to say anything more.

He turned to face her, steeled his shoulders, and seemed to dig deep within himself. "I've decided I'm going to stay for a few more weeks, fix things up around here, and get the fields and garden planted."

For a long moment her heart stopped beating. His words were too good to be true. And she didn't dare move, not even to breathe, for fear that he'd follow up with a jest and she'd discover he was only teasing her again.

"I'll buy some chickens, a milk cow, maybe a hog."

Her pulse started pattering again, this time with a crashing wave of wonder and delight — and a keen longing to run to him and throw her arms around him.

"Why aren't you saying anything?" A shadow of worry flitted across his face. "Am I making a mistake to stay?"

She shook her head. "No." Her words were breathless. "It's a wonderful decision."

His grin returned. "Do you think you can put up with me for a few weeks?"

"Maybe." Her body trembled at the thought that she'd get to be with him longer than she'd hoped possible. "You're a bear to be around, but I think I can handle it for a few weeks."

He laughed, a deep laugh that made her cheeks ache from her uncontainable smile.

"You're a dear girl, ma cherie. I'm glad you haven't changed."

"I have changed," she started to protest.

She didn't want him to think of her as a little girl anymore.

But he'd already turned to head back to the cabin.

"Remember," she blurted, "I've become a master fisherman."

He winked at her over his shoulder. "And you remember. Tomorrow. At dawn. Down at the west shore. We'll see who's best then."

She watched him swagger away, and she wanted to yell out that she wasn't a girl or his sister, that she was a grown woman now. But what good would such a declaration bring? Pierre would only laugh at her and tease her again.

What did it matter anyway what he thought of her?

It didn't matter, did it?

CHAPTER 8

Angelique squirmed in the cushioned chair across the small oval table from Miss Mc-Douall.

"So, then we are agreed," said the young woman, perched on the edge of her chair. She was every bit the lady in another of her beautiful silk gowns, this one robin's-egg blue. "We shall meet for tea in the afternoons for lessons in conduct, as well as lessons in reading and writing."

The panic that had constricted Angelique's chest when she'd stepped inside the fort and into the officers' building cut off her breath again. It wasn't the fort itself that scared her. She'd been inside the walls before when she'd come to sell eggs and fresh produce. The tall, whitewashed stone wall on the south side was imposing, as were the sharp-pointed wooden palisades that surrounded the rest of the hilltop fort.

She was accustomed to the sight of the

structure, since every time she looked up from anywhere in town, it was always there on the cliffs, a serious sentinel looming overhead. But she'd never been inside any of the buildings, much less the large stone house where the officers lived.

As the safest building in the fort, the residence consisted of living quarters for the officers and their families, bedrooms, and offices. There was even room for the kitchen and servants in the building's lower level.

Again Angelique's eyes darted around the grand sitting room. With a lovely carpet at the center, lacy curtains, and brightly cushioned sofas and chairs, it was likely the fanciest room in the fort, perhaps even on the island.

Miss McDouall took a sip of tea from a dainty porcelain cup. Her fingers were delicate and unblemished against the fancy blue pattern of the cup.

Angelique stared at her own fingers, coarse and red and cracked. She'd been afraid during the entire past hour that her cup would slip from her grip and crash to the polished wood floor. Or that she'd spill tea onto the spotless white tablecloth.

Not even the pleasure of real tea with a hint of lemon could take away her discomfort, sitting in close proximity to the elegant Miss McDouall.

"Are you agreeable to the plans, Miss MacKenzie?" Miss McDouall set her cup on the matching saucer, making only the tiniest of clinks. She gave Angelique an encouraging smile like one would to a child.

Angelique smiled back weakly. What need did a poor girl like her have for reading or writing? Or lessons in conduct — whatever that was?

But she knew Ebenezer expected her to be agreeable to the young woman. He'd been giddy to form a connection with the commanding officer, Colonel McDouall, and he'd warned her before she'd left the tavern that she'd better not do anything to jeopardize the position of honor. He'd also reminded her that she would serve her discipline when she returned home — that he'd not forgotten and would still make her pay for her sins.

"I'm not sure that my stepfather will spare me from my work every afternoon," Angelique finally managed.

"He seems like an agreeable man. I shall send him a note and explain our plans." Miss McDouall lifted a linen cloth to her lips and pressed gently. "Surely he will consent once he understands how beneficial

136

such an arrangement will be."

Ebenezer had likely begun calculating how much profit he could make through his association with the important commander. Angelique had the sinking feeling that he wouldn't say no to Miss McDouall's plans, even if he wanted to.

"The very first thing we must do tomorrow," continued Miss McDouall as if the matter were already settled, "is to find more suitable apparel for you to wear when you visit. And I shall show you how to bathe and groom yourself properly."

"This is my best garment." Angelique glanced down at the plain skirt. It was frayed and stained. But it was cleaner than her everyday skirt, which she had changed out of before Lieutenant Steele had arrived to escort her to the fort.

"Then it is a good thing I brought my entire summer wardrobe. My father chastised me for packing six trunks and told me I wouldn't have need for so many gowns. But I had the suspicion I would make good use of them. And I was right."

Angelique eyed the ruffles and lace that adorned Miss McDouall's gown, and she shook her head. She couldn't — wouldn't — ever don one of Miss McDouall's gowns. "I couldn't possibly —"

"Oh, think nothing of it, my dear." Miss McDouall's smile was warm and as sweet as one of the tea cakes Angelique had nibbled with her tea. "I'll look through my trunks this very evening and find something suitable to your station. I believe I included one or two plain gowns from last season with the foresight that I would be in the wilderness and might have use of something old."

A rush of anxiety choked Angelique. How would she stay invisible in one of Miss Mc-Douall's gowns? She'd stand out like a crimson cardinal against freshly fallen snow and make herself a target for some old trapper looking for a wife.

She started to shake her head but stopped. Ebenezer wouldn't make her, not with his strict standards concerning modesty. Perhaps he'd consent to Miss McDoull's daily lessons, but he'd never agree to let her strut about town looking like a loose woman.

Miss McDouall glanced into the front hallway that ran down the middle of the building, separating the commander's living quarters from those of one of the other officers.

During the past hour, various soldiers had been coming and going from the room across the hallway from theirs, where Colonel McDouall was meeting with the previous commander of the fort, Captain Bullock.

Only Lieutenant Steele remained at his post at the entryway of their sitting room, standing erect and waiting for Miss McDouall's beckon.

Angelique had prayed the quartermaster wouldn't have to escort her home. He'd said nothing to her on the climb up the steep path to the fort. She'd almost begun to believe he hadn't remembered their encounter in the woods earlier in the week, until they'd entered the fort and stopped outside the heavy door of the officers' quarters.

His tone had been clipped and filled with warning. "If you say anything at all about me to Miss McDouall, I expect it to be favorable."

She'd hoped he would leave and return to his duties as quartermaster. With all the barrels and crates that had been delivered from the ship, he would certainly have a great deal of work restocking the fort's supplies and distributing them among the soldiers and Indians.

But apparently he'd made time in his busy schedule to dote on Miss McDouall.

"Mr. Durant," Miss McDouall called, rising from her chair, her eyes bright and fixed on a new arrival in the hallway.

Angelique followed the young woman's gaze, and to her surprise she found herself staring at Pierre. He'd changed out of his voyageur attire and wore the garb of any ordinary man on the island. Except Pierre wasn't ordinary at all. He was still as dashing in his corduroy trousers and calico shirt as he'd been in his leather breeches and capote.

At Miss McDouall's call, Pierre paused, and instead of continuing toward the colonel's office, he veered toward the sitting room.

"I'm delighted to see you here, Mr. Durant." Miss McDouall glided gracefully away from the table.

Pierre's attention was focused on the beautiful woman, and he flashed her one of his breathtaking grins. "Lavinia McDouall."

He started into the room, but Lieutenant Steele blocked the doorway with the butt of his rifle.

At the sight of the quartermaster and rifle, Pierre stopped short, and a shadow crossed his face.

Angelique sat frozen in her chair. Did he realize the quartermaster was the one who had attacked her earlier in the week?

"You may let him pass, Lieutenant Steele."

Miss McDouall bestowed a smile on the soldier. "I know Mr. Durant from our association last summer in Montreal."

The quartermaster glared at Pierre before lowering his rifle.

Pierre strode past him, his attention centered on Miss McDouall. "I heard you were here. But nobody told me you were so ravishing."

Her cheeks turned a rosy pink. "I heard you were here too and working for Daddy."

Angelique hadn't had the chance yet to ask Pierre whose side he was on in the war, but she'd assumed he sided with the British like most of the Indians and voyageurs. Otherwise he wouldn't have been welcome on the island.

She was only a little disappointed in his choice, though eased by the thought that he wasn't joining the fighting and wouldn't have to pick up arms against Jean.

Pierre reached for Miss McDouall's hand, brought it to his lips, and pressed a kiss there. Then he bowed gallantly.

Miss McDouall gave a breathy laugh, but at the sight of Lieutenant Steele's scowl, she blushed again and pulled her hand away from Pierre.

For a long moment, Angelique could only stare between Pierre and Miss McDouall.

Then something hot and sharp stabbed her. Did Pierre have feelings of affection toward Miss McDouall?

Angelique sat up straighter and scooted to the edge of her chair. Didn't he see her at all? Was she completely invisible and unworthy of notice in the presence of one as lovely and charming as Miss McDouall?

"When I arrived yesterday to such stark surroundings," Miss McDouall said, "I was worried I might be bored this summer. But now that you're here, I know I shall have a gay time."

"You're right," Pierre replied with a laugh. "You certainly won't be bored with me here."

Angelique had the urge to stand up and slap the silly grin off Pierre's face. He was acting like a besotted fool.

Miss McDouall peeked at Lieutenant Steele from underneath her lashes. "I was very happy to meet the acquaintance of the fort's quartermaster, Lieutenant Steele. He has also assured me that he will do everything he can to make certain my time on the island is entertaining."

The two men again exchanged wary glances.

A smile played at Miss McDouall's lips. She was obviously enjoying the attention and flattery of both the men. When Pierre turned his adoration back upon her, she gave him another bright smile.

Was that what beauty brought? The flattery of handsome men like Pierre? Angelique stared up at Pierre, willing him to look at *her* with adoration.

But the truth was, next to the stunning Miss McDouall, he hadn't noticed her at all. And why would he? Not when she looked the way she did.

She glanced at her roughened hands and then again at Miss McDouall's flawless skin. What would it take to get Pierre to admire her?

She shook her head and pushed to her feet, scolding herself. Why should she care? Let Pierre make a fool of himself with other women. It didn't mean anything to her.

"I don't think you should count on Pierre providing you any entertainment," Angelique said, straightening and facing Pierre. "He's as boring as an old goat."

At the sight of her, surprise widened Pierre's eyes, quickly followed by a spark of mirth. "An old goat?"

Miss McDouall gave a start. "Why, Miss MacKenzie!"

"Besides, he's leaving in a few weeks." An unseen force prodded Angelique, driving her rudeness, along with the need to claim Pierre's attention away from Miss Mc-Douall. "If he does all the work he says he's going to, then I have the feeling he'll be too busy for social calls anyway. Am I right, Mr. Durant?"

Pierre nodded. "I can always make time to socialize, Miss MacKenzie. You should know that all work and no play has never been my motto."

"Do the two of you know each other?" Miss McDouall's delicately shaped eyebrows rose.

"We're childhood friends," Pierre explained. "We were inseparable playmates when we were younger."

"I see," Miss McDouall said. "Then you should be pleased to know that this summer among the charities I'll be heading, I have chosen to bestow my kind attention and help upon Angelique."

The room with its fancy furniture, fine linens, and bookcase of thick books seemed to close in on Angelique. Embarrassed, she felt heat rising beneath her high neckline.

"I didn't know Angelique needed help with anything," Pierre said.

"Why, Mr. Durant, look at her. She needs improvement with just about everything, if I'm to turn her into a lady by the end of the summer."

Angelique wanted to run from the building, out of the fort, and down to the lake, where the cool breezes could soothe the heat on her skin. She didn't dare look into Pierre's eyes and chance seeing pity in them again. She wouldn't be able to bear it.

Pierre was silent for a moment. The loud voices in the hallway, Lieutenant Steele calling a greeting to a newcomer, echoed around them. When Angelique finally dared to peek at Pierre, she was surprised that instead of pity, he offered her a grin.

"I don't think Angelique needs improvement," he said, "except for maybe a few more fishing tips from the master himself."

Gratefulness welled inside Angelique, and she returned his smile.

Miss McDouall slipped her arm into the crook of Pierre's. She fluttered her eyelashes at him. " 'Twould appear I've come to the island at just the right time. Not only to improve Miss MacKenzie, but to give you a few lessons as well."

She started to lead him toward the door. He didn't resist. Instead he placed his hand over hers and tucked it more securely in his grasp. "Then it's a very good thing I'm a willing student."

He flashed Miss McDouall the kind of

smile that made Angelique's chest twist with painful longing. What could she possibly do to make him smile at *her* like that? The kind of smile meant for a beautiful woman, instead of one for an old friend and playmate.

"Good day, Miss MacKenzie." Miss McDouall tossed the words over her shoulder. "I shall expect your visit tomorrow at half past three promptly."

She nodded. What harm would come of letting the commander's daughter teach her a thing or two about how to act more ladylike?

But just as quickly as the thought came, she shoved it aside.

She didn't need Pierre's special smiles. She didn't need to be beautiful, like her mother. She was perfectly happy with the way she was.

CHAPTER 9

Pierre slipped the folded paper into Red Fox's outstretched hand. He glanced around the thickly wooded bluff. The only other sign of life was the breeze blowing through the tall spruce branches overhead and the soft swooshing of the long needles.

"Leave the note with Baxter on Bois Blanc Island," Pierre said quietly. "He'll make sure it gets into the right hands."

He'd gleaned a substantial amount of information regarding the British plans from both the colonel and Lavinia in the short time he'd been back. And now he needed to get that information to the Americans. Although he wanted to take the missive himself, he knew he'd be safer giving it to Red Fox. No one would suspect the Indian of carrying messages to the Americans.

But if anyone caught him leaving the island now that he was back, he'd raise suspicion, maybe even enough that they'd throw him in prison.

As it was, the colonel and Lavinia didn't know anything. In fact, the colonel still believed he was spying on the Americans for him. He'd resumed their friendship right where he'd left off last summer when he mingled with them in Montreal, though he couldn't quite muster the same enthusiasm this time.

He wasn't exactly sure why. Last summer he'd had no problem flirting with Lavinia. He'd considered it one of his more pleasant spying duties.

Maybe he was more uncomfortable now because Angelique had been there watching. What must she think of him? He wished he could confess to her that he had no interest in befriending Lavinia other than what he could gain for the cause.

He didn't want Angelique to think he was a womanizer, because he wasn't. Not anymore.

Red Fox tucked the note into the leather pouch at his side and then gave him a curt nod. The bear grease he'd slathered on his arms, chest, and face made him gleam, even in the shade.

"And if any of the North West agents try anything, you have my full permission to riddle them with arrows."

"You do not need to worry. I have eyes like those of the hawk. Your furs and men will be safe with me."

Pierre took a deep breath, trying to steady the wild thumping of his heart. Was he making a mistake to stay behind on the island? Even though he trusted Red Fox to help bring the furs safely to Montreal, anything could go wrong.

"I'll meet you in Montreal in two moons," Pierre said, hoping he'd have no trouble finding another group heading east in three weeks so that he wouldn't have to travel alone.

"My brother should stay here until I return at end of summer with supplies."

Pierre shook his head. He was only staying three weeks, maybe four, just long enough to plant the fields. Then he'd hire someone to help Maman the rest of the summer, someone who could harvest the crops and help her prepare for winter.

"You must do the right thing." Red Fox's sober black eyes made him look older and wiser than his eighteen years.

"But that's the trouble. I don't know what the right thing is anymore." Pierre didn't know what to do when it came to Maman or with his spying. He supposed he'd never really cared before, had just gone about his business without giving anything much thought.

Was God working on him again?

Pierre peered heavenward through the layers of branches. Why did it have to be so painful every time God began working on turning him into a better man?

"You stay with your mother," Red Fox said. "She needs her son more than her son needs fur."

"I'll stay until I can hire the help."

Red Fox thumped his chest. He was bare except for his breechcloth, leggings, and deer-hide moccasins. "You are my brother." He then pointed a finger to Pierre's chest. "You are my brother in here."

Ever since he'd jumped out of his canoe last spring to rescue Red Fox from drowning in the swollen rapids, the man had been his shadow. No one else had dared to battle the raging river. Everyone else — even Red Fox's own tribe — had given Red Fox up for dead. They'd all known that any rescue attempt would end in two deaths instead of one.

But Pierre hadn't been able to stand by and watch Red Fox drown. He'd never been the kind of man to think before acting. Besides, he'd counted on all his years of swimming in the lake to hold him in good stead. And of course he'd always relied on Maman's prayers.

Thankfully he'd been able to pull Red Fox out of the flooded river. Now the Indian had adopted him as his brother and was willing to do anything for him and go anywhere. Pierre had a feeling the brave wouldn't be satisfied until he had the chance to save Pierre's life in return. Pierre hoped such an occasion would never arise.

"My brother should stay," Red Fox said. "Work hard. Keep out of trouble."

"Now wait a minute." Pierre grinned. "Keep out of trouble? That sounds boring."

"You must keep the Great Spirit happy. Then he will bring me back with many eagle feathers."

"You are a brave man." Pierre's mirth rapidly evaporated at the thought of his brigade leaving without him. "I'll pray that my God keeps you safe."

With the war and the lack of supplies coming into Michilimackinac Island, most of the voyageurs and traders had to travel farther east to sell their pelts and restock before returning to the wilderness for another season of trading.

He could only pray that the North West Company agents would be too busy to pay attention to his small brigade. If not for Red

Fox's willingness to ride the final distance with his men and see them to safety, Pierre wasn't sure he would have been able to keep his rash promise to Angelique to stay for several weeks to help Maman.

He didn't know what had made him blurt out that he would stay, but it had come out before he'd been able to stop it. And now here he was stuck on the island, sending Red Fox away with his smuggled letter to the Americans along with his men and furs.

All he could do was watch helplessly as Red Fox disappeared into the forest as silently as he'd come to their secret meeting spot. Fighting a heavy dejection, Pierre wandered among the woods, until the distant chopping of axes drew him toward the high bluff at the center of the island.

He knew he needed to return to the plowing. The labor to loosen the hard soil had been backbreaking, even with his well-conditioned muscles. He needed to accomplish an overwhelming amount of work if he hoped to leave in three weeks.

But he couldn't resist the draw to take a look at the new fort being built on the highest point of the island. Captain Bullock, the previous commander of the fort, had started the project several weeks ago. But now that Colonel McDouall had arrived, they were apparently pouring their efforts into completing the job.

With an attack from the Americans imminent, Pierre was sure the colonel didn't want the Americans to retake the island with the same tactics the British had used only two years earlier. The British soldiers loved to brag about how they'd arrived on the north side of the island in the early hours of morning under cover of darkness. They'd hauled their two six-pound cannons through the tangled brush and up the steep hills, until they finally reached the top of the island, the hill that towered a half mile above Fort Michilimackinac.

The fort had originally been built to protect the island from a southern attack. But the British had discovered the weakness of the northern side of the fort and had taken advantage of it. With the two cannons pointed down at the fort and with a force of six hundred men, including several hundred Indian warriors, the Americans had been forced to raise the white flag. Everyone had known that any resistance would have incited an Indian massacre.

Fortunately the British had allowed the American troops to retreat unharmed to Detroit. And they'd also given the American citizens who resided on the island one month to either leave or swear allegiance to the British by signing the Oath.

And Jean had left.

Pierre shook his head again, as he did every time he thought about Jean deserting their maman. What had his brother been thinking? Why hadn't he hired someone to do the work? He certainly hadn't expected Maman and Angelique to try to shoulder everything, had he?

"Stay with your mother. She needs her son more than her son needs fur."

Red Fox's caution echoed in Pierre's mind. He wanted to ignore the warning the words sent off, and the guilt. What if he couldn't find hired help either? He doubted he'd stay. How could he?

How then could he judge Jean when he was contemplating leaving Maman too?

Pierre stopped at the base of the hill and peered up the sloping incline to the top, where the blockhouse was slowly taking shape, along with a surrounding picket fence.

Fort George. That was what the British called it, naming it after their king. At least that was what he'd called it in his letter. Pierre had warned the Americans about the new fort and urged them to attack soon, before it was completed and before the

Indian reinforcements arrived.

Now he could only pray the letter reached the Americans in time.

Pierre watched several workers trudge up the incline carrying stones. Only yesterday, Colonel McDouall had issued the order that every islander, including civilians, contribute three days of labor to the construction effort.

He'd heard the grumbling, but the colonel had warned that anyone who didn't cooperate would get to spend three days in the Black Hole instead.

Pierre had assured the colonel that he'd take the evening shift and work as often as he could over the next three weeks. Yet privately he'd been more than a little irritated about the new order. He didn't have the time to spare, and he didn't want to help the British fortify their position.

At this point he was hoping the Americans would be able to take the island back. It would certainly make his life easier if Jean returned to the farm soon. Then he could be on his way again.

With a sigh he turned to go, only to find himself facing another group of civilians carrying the large stones that would be used to construct the bombproof storage building in the new fort. The outline of one young woman caught his attention.

"Angelique?"

She didn't stop.

He followed after her. The overlong, dull gray skirt and formless bodice belonged to only one woman on the island.

"Angelique, wait." He rushed to her side.

She was breathing hard under the heavy weight of the stone she carried. Her face was streaked with dirt and sweat. Her hands were red and chafed.

A burst of fury barreled into him. He reached for the stone and tried to wrest it from her grip as she trudged along. "What are you doing? Give me the rock."

She glanced up at him with weary eyes.

"Let me carry it for you."

She hesitated only a moment longer, then stopped and relinquished the stone.

He hefted it into his arms. It wasn't heavy for him. In fact, he could have carried several. "Why are you carrying stones?"

She wiped her sleeve across her forehead before answering him. "Ebenezer has delegated his three days of work at the new fort to me."

"That lazy old leech," Pierre muttered. He wasn't surprised Ebenezer had gotten out of his work and put the burden on Angelique. The man was a pompous crook.

"I suppose you have to work your own three days after you're done with his?"

She nodded, staring at the hill that stretched before them.

He had the sudden urge to sweep her off her feet and take her someplace where she could rest. "It's a good thing Ebenezer isn't here or I'd teach him a lesson or two with my fist."

"At least I'm free of the attic."

"So that's why you didn't meet me for fishing yesterday morning?"

"He wouldn't let me out."

Fresh anger pumped through Pierre, tightening his muscles. "You need to leave him, Angelique. Why are you still living with him?"

She spun around to face him, her features tight with anger of her own. "And where would I go, Pierre? Where could I possibly go to be safe from him? And even if I could find a place to live, what kind of work would I do?"

Pierre was well aware of the only kind of work available to homeless, single young women. He loathed the thought of any such fate befalling Angelique.

"You could live with Maman." Maman desperately needed the supervision and companionship. Even if he could find hired help for the farm, she'd still be alone in the house all winter. If Angelique came to stay with her, he'd be able to leave with peace of mind.

"There's no place I could go on this island that would be safe for me. If I defied Ebenezer, he'd come get me and marry me off to the first trader to offer him a good deal — just like he did with Therese."

"He doesn't own you."

"My mother gave him guardianship. He can do whatever he wants, and there's no one to stop him." The haunted sadness of her expression spoke of the nightmare she'd lived through with her sister.

"I'll stop him."

She gave a faint smile. "That's sweet of you, Pierre, but you won't be here to help me. You'll be long gone."

He felt helpless. Ebenezer could do anything he wanted to Angelique, and he wouldn't be there — hadn't been there — to protect her. The only thing that could keep her safe was marriage to Jean.

Even though he still scoffed at the idea of Angelique marrying Jean, he was beginning to understand why she'd agreed to the plan, and it was all the more reason to fight for the Americans and help them win the upcoming battle for the island. If Jean could come home and marry Angelique, she'd be safe.

"Maybe I won't be able to protect you from Ebenezer after I leave," he said. "But I can help you now."

She quirked a brow at him.

"Stay here," he said, reaching for her arm and guiding her to the shade of a nearby oak. "I want you to rest while I go talk with the officer in charge of the duties."

"I don't think I should rest."

He gently pushed her down so that she was forced to lower herself. "Promise me you'll stay here and wait for me?" He was relieved when her shoulders relaxed and she allowed herself to sit back. She looked up at him, her eyes warm and trusting. "Promise you'll be waiting for me when I get back?" he asked again.

"I promise." She smiled, and the beauty of it lit her face She was completely guileless and sweet, devoid of the seductive charms and games that women like Lavinia McDouall attempted to use on him.

It was freeing to know that with Angelique he could be himself, that she knew and accepted him for who he was, faults and all — except for his spying. But it was safer for her if she didn't know.

He wasted no time in making his way up

the hill. He spoke with the officer in charge and then returned to Angelique, who was sitting where he'd left her.

He held out his hand to her. "Let's go."

She slipped her hand into his cautiously. "I can't just go, Pierre."

"Yes you can."

"What about the work?"

"I paid so that you can take an hour break." He pulled her to her feet.

"Paid?" She shook her head and started to pull her hand from his. "No, Pierre. I can't let you do that. Besides, isn't that bribery?"

But he wound his fingers through hers and tugged her forward. "It's not bribery. It's simply me getting my way. Don't you know I'm a rich man now?"

"You? Rich?" She gave a soft laugh. "I'd like to see the day when you can hang on to your money. The Pierre I remember was always giving away or spending any pennies he earned."

"I'd give it all away to make sure you didn't have to carry any more heavy stones."

She pulled back. "Are you sure I should leave my work?"

"Oui, ma cherie, I'm sure. The British like me, and they won't care if I take you away to rest for a while."

When finally she fell into step next to him, the tension of the morning eased from his body. Maybe he needed a break just as much as she did. Since coming back to the island and discovering the true state of Maman's situation, stress had been his companion.

For an hour, he wanted to be free — free of guilt and worry and the constant work of the farm. Free to enjoy the beauty of the island, to feel the warm sunshine upon his head and listen to the birdcalls. And he couldn't imagine anyone else he'd rather spend the time with than Angelique.

They made their way to the limestone bluffs east of the island, to the arched rock formation they'd gone to when they were children. They climbed to the center of the rock and situated themselves with legs dangling over the edge.

The long drop below didn't frighten him, not when he'd been climbing onto the ledge for as long as he could remember. And he was glad Angelique was the kind of girl who'd never been afraid to trail after him on his dangerous escapades.

He took a deep breath of the crisp air at the same time she did, and together they smiled at the stretch of beach far below them and the endless blue of the lake beyond.

"Some things never change," he said. "I'll always love this island."

He glanced to the horizon, to the endless possibilities, adventure, and excitement it held. His heart gave an extra beat in anticipation of the places he would go and the things he'd see this fall when he returned with his brigade to the wilderness, the beauty of the land, the thick untouched forests, the clear lakes, and the rivers so clean he could drink from them.

He loved not knowing what he would see around the next bend. He thrived on each new discovery and place, and the people he met. He even loved the grueling work of paddling all day and portaging the long distances between rivers.

"I breathe adventure, Angelique," he said at last. "And as much as I love the island, I don't know how I'd ever be content to live here year-round."

She released a sigh.

For a long moment he wished he could tell her he'd stay. But he knew that would be a lie. Maybe someday he'd be ready to settle down, to have a permanent home, and do something else besides fur trading. For now, though, he couldn't imagine that happening anytime soon.

The wind coming off the lake still had the chill of winter. But the sun's rays poured down upon their heads, warming them. He glanced at Angelique and wished he could pull off her cap, let her hair tumble down around her shoulders.

"Lavinia McDouall is determined to make a lady of you, is she?"

Angelique screwed up her features into a look of disgust. "She won't have much success. I'm not a lady and never will be."

"Good. I like you just the way you are."

She ducked her head and slid her hand over her skirt, covering a large stain. "I suppose I can learn a few things from her."

"I'd hate for you to become too ladylike to sit up here with me or to fish or swim. That wouldn't be any fun at all."

"I'll never be too ladylike for those things."

"Promise?"

"Promise. Besides, Miss McDouall might not be able to give me her lessons anyway. Lieutenant Steele came with a note yesterday explaining that our lessons are postponed since Miss McDouall is ill."

"So I heard."

"The fever and ague?"

"Non. Only a chill that she contracted during the voyage here." He brushed his hand against the loose stones, sending a shower over the edge of the arch. "She should have stayed back in Montreal where she belongs."

He could feel Angelique studying him, but he stared at the solid limestone ridge that jutted out around them. Ladies like Lavinia didn't belong on Michilimackinac Island any more than women belonged out in the wilderness with the fur traders.

"It sounds like you care for Miss Mc-Douall." Her tone carried a hint of accusation.

He grinned. "And it sounds like you're jealous."

"Not in the least."

"Admit it. You're jealous."

"I just can't picture you with a woman like her."

"The same way I can't picture you with Jean." He didn't know why he couldn't just let the issue go. Why did he care so much if Angelique married Jean?

Her eyes flickered with confusion and then with something raw and real. It was partly the admiration for him that she'd always shown, but it was more than that. It was something deeper that went into his blood, pumping it a little faster.

He knew he shouldn't question her choice

of Jean. His brother would give her a better life than any other man could. Jean would treat her kindly and provide for her needs. Pierre should be happy for her and encourage her choice of Jean . . . instead of making her second-guess it all the time.

"I'm sorry." He peered toward the blue of the horizon, willing the American ships to make their appearance and put an end to the war that had been dragging on far too long. "I need to stop teasing you. Jean will be a good match for you."

"Do you think so?"

"Of course he won't be me." Pierre tried to make his voice light. "But he'll have to do."

"No one can be you," she whispered. There was a wistfulness in her tone that made him swivel so that he was facing her.

She looked up at him, revealing such a pure and shining adoration that his pulse sped again.

He couldn't stop himself from reaching for the strings of her mobcap and tugging them loose. He slid it off and freed her beautiful hair, so that her curls spilled around her face and over her shoulders. He let his fingers plunge into the silky thickness.

A tiny warning sounded at the back of his

mind, but the deep, rich red that was softer and more luxurious than the best of his furs was too hard to resist. He intertwined his fingers and brought a fistful to his cheek. The softness caressed his skin. From there it was all too easy to bring the long tresses to his lips, to graze her curls, and to allow them to tantalize him.

He had the sudden desire to pull her into his arms, to hold her, and to bury his face in her hair. And when he locked eyes with her, the intensity of the longing in her expression sent a ripple of warm waves against his chest.

Her breath came in a gasp between her full and pretty lips.

What would it be like to kiss her?

He'd stolen plenty of kisses from women over the past several years, during the summer rendezvous, especially during his years of rebellion against everything Maman had ever taught him.

It would be all too easy to slide his arms around Angelique now and take a kiss from her. He could charm her into responding. He'd done it before to other women. She wouldn't want to resist him. He'd make sure of it.

His fingers in her hair tightened.

Had Jean kissed her?

He shook his head at the vision of Jean pulling Angelique into his arms and laying his lips against hers. He couldn't imagine it — didn't want to even think about it.

Slowly he pried his fingers from her hair. God help him, but he couldn't kiss Angelique — not now, not ever. What was wrong with him? How could he even consider such a thing?

She didn't deserve a fickle man like him toying with her emotions. She didn't need someone using her or taking advantage of her. Non. She needed him to keep her safe from men like himself. She deserved so much more than a few stolen kisses.

He gritted his teeth and wrenched his hand away from her, every muscle protesting the move.

She let out a soft sigh. Was she relieved to have avoided the awkward moment?

With a shaky laugh he said, "I couldn't resist seeing your beautiful hair."

The cries of sea gulls circling over the water below echoed in the air around them, preventing the need for an immediate answer.

Before he knew what she was doing, she'd reached for his hat and swiped it from his head. "I suppose it's only fair if you can bare my head, that I can do the same to you."

"I give you my full permission."

She held his hat out above the ledge. It was one of the hats Maman had woven, perfect for working in the sun. The straw was cooler than felt, and the brim wider, providing protection from the sun.

"If you want your hat back," she said with a smile, "you also have to give me permission to touch your hair."

He was relieved she hadn't taken him too seriously, that she could easily forgive him for his forwardness and make light of it. He shook his head, loosening the strands and letting them flop in disarray. "If you want to touch this awful mess, be my guest."

She tugged playfully at one of the waves that fell across his forehead. Then she combed it back into submission with the rest of his wayward curls.

The gentle touch was innocent enough, but it made him want to lean his head back, close his eyes, and give her the freedom to keep combing.

"Even your hair seems to have a wild streak." She smoothed the hair against his head.

He held himself rigid, hoping she wouldn't realize what effect she was having on him.

Her touch reminded him again that he wasn't a boy anymore, and neither was she a child. He was a man with very manly desires. He'd never expected that he would need to restrain himself with Angelique.

But she'd grown into a desirable woman. And now he would have to try even harder to keep himself from being a fool around her.

He stood and held out a hand to her. "Let's go down and wade in the water and cool our feet before we have to go back."

She readily accepted his hand.

He had three weeks on the island. That wasn't long. If he set his mind to it, he could cherish her as a friend — like he always had — and nothing more.

Chapter 10

Angelique wiped the last bowl with sand, cleaning it of any remaining traces of pigeon pie Pierre had baked for their noon meal. The scent of peppercorn and onion lingered, not only in the grain of the wooden bowl but also on her tongue.

"It's such a treat to have pigeon again," Miriam said from her chair placed in the shade of the lilac bushes outside the cabin.

Miriam's words echoed Angelique's sentiments — except that Miriam was much more positive than Angelique, who couldn't help thinking how glad she was to have a break from the whitefish and trout that had kept them alive during the days of starvation that spring.

She knew she shouldn't complain. She should be grateful for the steady supply of fish she'd been able to catch all winter. But after partaking of Pierre's meals all week, and the fowl he'd shot, she didn't know how she'd be satisfied with plain and simple fish ever again.

Her eyes went to his broad back, the seams of his cotton shirt stretching under the strain of his work repairing the picket fence around the vegetable garden. She'd helped him plant it that week during the noon break that he'd managed to arrange for her every day from her required work on Fort George.

After that first day of sitting together on the rock ledge and then wading in the lake, he'd asked her to come back to the farm and visit with Miriam. He'd mentioned that even though he wanted to run off and play with her again, his mother had longed to spend time with her.

Angelique had been surprised with his request. The Pierre she'd known from childhood wouldn't have considered Miriam's needs, would have rushed off without any thought to anyone but himself and his own pleasure.

Pierre hammered at the new picket, driving it into the ground in place of the rotting piece he'd tossed aside.

He'd changed.

A sense of wonder warmed Angelique as it had all week as she'd watched him. She believed his claim that he wasn't the same foolish boy he'd once been, that he was trying to live to please God.

She glanced over the dark loam of the freshly plowed field. The weeds were gone and the soil ready for sowing. The far fence along the west side of the field had been repaired. The long grass and weeds around the cabin had been cut, the roof repaired, the barn door fixed. Pierre had even purchased a cow and a dozen hens in St. Ignace.

He'd obviously worked tirelessly for long hours. With his own required labor on the new fort, she wondered when he found time to sleep.

A spot of sweat plastered his shirt to his back, defining his chiseled muscles. The June sun was high and hot, but after the long Michigan winter, she never complained about the warm temperatures of summer. They were too fleeting, and she knew she must enjoy every second.

Just like she knew she must savor every second of Pierre's time on the island. He too was as fleeting as the summer.

She could sense the urgency within him to complete the farm tasks so that he could be on his way. He didn't find joy in the farm the way Jean did. He was only pouring out his energy so he could move on to bigger and better things.

With a sigh, Angelique rubbed a fresh handful of sand in the bowl, letting the coarse grains slip between her fingers.

Why must he go?

"I've enjoyed this week of having you here at the noon hour," Miriam said, her hand growing still on the kittens curled in her lap — two fluffy mousers Pierre had brought to his mother only yesterday, more evidence that he was preparing to leave them. "Even though you're done with your work at the fort, will you find a way to come join us for dinner again tomorrow?"

"I'll try." Angelique sat back on her heels. "But you know Ebenezer. He'll be keeping a close watch on all my activities."

"Maybe he'll be too busy with all of his business now."

Ebenezer was always busier in the summer when the inn was full of customers . . . and the beach overflowing with Indian women.

Angelique gave an involuntary shudder at the thought of him slinking out the back door of the tavern last evening. She'd wished she had a place to hide so that she didn't have to witness the angry ripple across Betty's face or listen to her whispered curses. It hadn't taken Betty long to figure out where Ebenezer went and what he did when he left the tavern in the evenings.

"I might be able to sneak over occasionally." Angelique wished her days of work at the fort didn't have to end. After Pierre had asked the officer in charge to give her lighter duties, she'd found her days there almost pleasant. She'd had freedom from Ebenezer's constant control, along with the precious hours at noon to spend with Miriam and Pierre.

Miriam's fingers began their gentle caressing again of the kittens. "Be careful, Angel. I don't want you to get in trouble with Ebenezer."

"Speaking of getting in trouble, I should probably be heading back to Fort George." She pushed up from the ground, brushing the sand from her skirt. Even the walk to and from the fort had been something she'd looked forward to all week. The time alone with Pierre for the short hike had filled her hungry heart, even if they'd done nothing more than chatter and joke.

As if he'd been watching her out of the corner of his eye, Pierre rose and tossed his hammer into the grass. "Ready?"

"Do I have a choice?"

"Oui. I could pay for you to have the

entire afternoon free," he offered with a grin.

"See, I told you that you couldn't hang on to your money."

"Why have money if you can't use it for a good cause?" He started toward her, taking off his hat and wiping his sweaty brow.

Her mind returned to the afternoon when they'd perched on the rock and how she'd dared to take off his hat and touch his hair. Her pulse still lurched every time she remembered the way he'd pressed a handful of her hair to his lips — almost as if he'd wanted to kiss her but had settled on her hair instead.

He hadn't taken her cap off since that day. He'd kept a proper distance between them and had almost seemed to go out of his way to treat her like a friend and nothing more.

She crossed to Miriam and placed a kiss against the woman's head. In the two weeks that Pierre had been back on the island, Miriam had blossomed like one of the spring flowers. Not only was his work around the farm helpful to her, but his sweetness and his smiles were the sunshine that brought everything to life.

How had they lived without him for five years?

"I could use a cool swim right about now,"

he said, scratching his damp hair before replacing his hat. "What do you say we stop by the swimming hole for a dip before heading back to the fort?"

She could only laugh at the impulsiveness of his suggestion. On the one hand, he'd matured. But on the other, he was still the same fun-loving boy he'd always been. "I'm sure the captain would be quite shocked to see me arrive for my afternoon duties soaking wet."

"You can take off your clothes for swimming like you always have."

Miriam gave a soft gasp.

Heat rushed to Angelique's cheeks.

"Now, Pierre," Miriam said, "remember, times have changed — Angelique has changed — from when she went swimming with you and Jean all those years ago."

Angelique couldn't make herself look at Pierre. Was he thinking about the time when he'd found her in the pond and jumped in next to her?

Miriam started. "I almost forgot to tell you, Angelique. We received a letter from Jean today."

"We did?" Letters from anyone were rare — even more so from the men who'd been forced to leave the island. In the past she'd always been excited to get news from Jean.

But now the thought of reading Jean's letter in front of Pierre only made her nervous.

"Pierre, would you get the letter from the Bible?"

Pierre's smile faded, and he hesitated.

"Then you can read it to Angelique," Miriam persisted.

They all knew Angelique couldn't read. Since Miriam had become blind, any time they'd gotten a letter from Jean, they'd had to rely on Father Fontaine of St. Anne's Church to visit and read it for them.

Pierre ducked into the cabin and, a few moments later, returned with a rumpled sheet of paper. He opened it, cleared his throat, and then looked at her over the edge of the paper, as if reluctant to read the letter aloud.

"Please, Pierre," Miriam said quietly.

Angelique nodded. If Jean's letter was like his previous ones, he'd write a line or two for her at the end.

Pierre dragged his attention back to the letter, and he began to read slowly without any enthusiasm. The news was the same. Jean was careful not to reveal anything about the United States Army, knowing full well his letter could fall into the wrong hands.

Instead he spoke of all the things he'd

done during the winter months, mostly studying the books he'd borrowed from one of the local parish priests. He gave the usual instructions about how to care for the animals and the farm in his absence, and he ended with his earnest prayers for them and his hope that they'd soon be together again.

"Give my deepest regards to Angelique," Pierre read in closing, his voice growing taut. "Tell her that I long for our reunion. My absence from her has only solidified my conviction that we are right for each other. And I eagerly await the day when we can begin our life together as man and wife."

Pierre looked at her again, probing her, searching for her reaction to the letter.

She was ashamed to admit Jean's words didn't stir her the same way they had in the past, and she lowered her lashes to hide her reaction from Pierre. She wouldn't give him the satisfaction of knowing maybe he was right in his assumption about her and Jean.

Maybe she wasn't as fond of Jean as he was of her, but no matter what she felt, she would marry him. She'd made her pledge to him, and she wouldn't break it, not for anything.

Jean offered her something steady and certain — something she'd never had be-fore, or at least for a very long time, not since the years her mother and father had lived happily together. Her father claimed to love them, but that hadn't stopped him from leaving every fall for his fur trading.

Which had he loved more, his family or the fur trading? The question had always haunted her.

With Jean, she would never have to wonder if she only had half his heart and devotion. She wouldn't have to take second place to his work. He would be her solid rock, as strong and permanent as the island itself.

She straightened her shoulders. She had nothing to be embarrassed about. "I'm also eagerly awaiting the day when Jean and I can start our lives together," she said with more force than she'd intended.

"Of course you are, Angel." Miriam reached for her hand and squeezed it. "The two of you will be happy together."

"Yes. Very happy."

Pierre folded the letter and returned it to the Bible without a word.

On the walk back to Fort George, he was quieter than usual. He didn't mention swimming again, and she tried to tell herself it didn't matter. She didn't need to worry about what Pierre thought. He was leaving soon. In fact, she'd heard rumors he was looking for a hired hand to do the work on the farm for the rest of the summer so he could be on his way.

The tapping of a drum grew louder as they drew closer to Fort Michilimackinac. When Pierre's stride lengthened and he veered in the woods toward the North Sally Port, Angelique knew his curiosity was as great as hers to learn why the drummer was playing his music at midday.

The red-coated sentinel at the north entrance admitted Pierre with a nod, not questioning him or even stopping to search him.

They passed through the gate, surrounded by the pointed palisades, and entered into what was usually a bustling, crowded interior. Strangely there were no soldiers engaged in the target practice or drilling that had become common since Colonel McDouall's arrival. Instead, the grounds and bunkhouse were silent, except for the steady tapping of the drum.

From the position of the fort on the cliff, they had a perfect view of the bay. The waters were calm and shimmered under the bright June sun. Other than the Indian and voyageur canoes along the shore, and the British sloops anchored in deeper water, the lake was empty of the American ships she'd been hoping would arrive.

Still, she couldn't keep from praying that the drumming meant the Americans had been sighted somewhere.

Pierre led her down the hill past the soldiers' barracks, a large two-story structure. When they rounded the building into the center green of the fort, he stopped abruptly and shoved her behind him. "Don't look, Angelique." His voice was harsh.

His arm held her against his back, but not before she'd caught a glimpse of the lines of British soldiers standing at attention on the green, their long red coats gleaming, their tall black hats standing proud upon their heads.

A slap and then a cry, like that of a wounded animal, echoed in the clearing. It was followed by another tap of the drum.

She didn't have to look to know what was happening. A soldier was being disciplined.

"How many lashes?" Pierre asked under his breath to a nearby woman, one of the laundresses, who stood next to a wooden bucket on a plank table. Her sleeves were rolled up, and she held a dripping shirt in one of her chapped red hands.

"One hundred stripes," the woman replied. Two children sat silently under the table, staring at the whipping post.

Angelique prayed that the man suffering

the whipping wasn't the woman's husband or the children's father. Some of the enlisted men brought their wives, who could earn extra rations by scrubbing clothes. The women and their infants lived with their husbands in the cramped barracks, sharing their room with several other soldiers.

Next to marrying a fur trader, Angelique ranked marrying a soldier as the second worst match. The lack of privacy and the absence of any real home life made the life of a soldier's wife as unappealing as that of a fur trader's.

"What's his crime?" Pierre asked the laundress.

"Drunkenness," the woman said.

"That's a harsh sentence for drunkenness," Pierre muttered.

Everyone knew that overindulgence in rum and whiskey was a common problem among the soldiers, certainly not worthy of a hundred lashes. But Colonel McDouall had arrived on the island with one goal in mind — to prepare for an attack by the Americans. Not only was the colonel driving them to finish Fort George as speedily as possible, but he was also apparently trying to crack down on disorderly conduct among the soldiers.

Another slap of the cat-o'-nine-tails

against flesh rose in the air, along with a hoarse and tortured cry.

Pierre's grip on Angelique was unswerving. But Angelique didn't fight him. She liked the iron of his arm against her body, holding her, shielding her. She relished the warmth of his back so near her cheek she could lean against him if she took but a tiny step closer.

"He broke the curfew last night too," the laundress added.

"Broke curfew?" Angelique slipped from Pierre's hold and glanced at the bloody back of the soldier tied to the whipping post, his arms stretched up, leaving him helplessly exposed. She sucked in a sharp breath at the sight of the mutilated flesh.

With a murmur of disapproval, Pierre wrestled her back behind him.

But she'd already glimpsed enough to see that the culprit wasn't Lieutenant Steele. Thankfully. She didn't want him thinking she'd been the one to reveal his disobedience that early morning he'd attacked her.

"I told you not to look," Pierre said, tossing her a frown.

"I'm a big girl. I can handle it," she said halfheartedly. The sight of the gore didn't turn her stomach, not after gutting fish day after day. But she fell behind Pierre anyway.

She was so accustomed to being strong and carrying so much on her own shoulders that Pierre's concern was a refreshing change.

The drum kept count with the last of the lashes, and when the discipline was finally over and the soldier dragged away, Pierre released her.

His attention shifted to the officers' quarters across the wide lawn. There in the shade of the stone building stood Lavinia McDouall. She wore a green muslin gown, and against the whitewashed wall she stood out like a budding leaf on a bare tree.

And of course Pierre had noticed her.

Angelique's stomach twisted with dismay.

With a new lightness to his step, Pierre started across the yard toward her, past the flagpole where the British colors were raised and flown proudly above the smattering of buildings inside the walls. In good weather the flag was raised faithfully at the beginning of every day. On a clear day she could see it all the way from the Straits when she was out fishing.

Angelique hesitated in crossing the grounds. Should she leave and go back to her duties at Fort George or should she follow Pierre?

"Mr. Durant." Lavinia smiled and stepped away from the building into the sunshine.

Her skin was pale and her cheeks thinner, but she'd obviously survived her illness without diminishing her beauty. "I was beginning to think you had left without saying good-bye."

"I wouldn't dream of it." With a flourish Pierre bowed, reached for her hand, and kissed it.

He wasn't supposed to be so sweet to other women. Or to flirt with them. Or look at them with interest. She was his childhood friend — they were practically best friends, weren't they? His special twinkle, his joking, and his laughter were meant for *her* and her alone.

"You must come see me more often," Lavinia said.

"Now that I know you're recovered, I'll be breaking down the door to see you."

Lavinia gave a tinkling laugh that contained her delight over Pierre's flattery. The sound of it stung Angelique's heart. The young lady tugged at one of her dangling curls playfully. Angelique had a feeling she was communicating with Pierre in a language only men could understand.

Angelique crossed the lawn toward Pierre. Even if he meant nothing by his flirtations, even if he was only bantering with Lavinia, Angelique still didn't like it. She knew she had no right to stop him from having a relationship with another woman. She had no claim on him, not when they were only friends.

Even so, she couldn't stop herself from approaching him. She slipped her hand into the crook of his arm, forcing herself to be bolder than she'd ever needed to be before. Her breath hitched in her chest, and she prayed Pierre wouldn't push her away.

She held herself stiff, not daring to look at either Pierre or Lavinia.

But the solidness of Pierre's arm radiated against her fingers, and he surprised her by not only capturing her hand with his but pulling her closer.

"Miss McDouall, you remember my little friend, Angelique?"

Little friend? She wanted to protest. But when he smiled down at her, there was something warm in his expression.

"Yes, I remember Miss MacKenzie," Lavinia said, turning to Angelique. "It is good to see you again, my dear, although I have to say I'm surprised you're here today."

"I'm with Pierre." The words felt stiff, and Angelique couldn't keep from wishing she knew how to make polite conversation and flirt with Lavinia's ease.

Lavinia didn't seem disturbed by the fact

that Pierre had wrapped his fingers around hers. In fact, her features softened as if with pity. Did she think Pierre was being kind to her out of sympathy?

Angelique glanced up at Pierre, to the chiseled angle of his jaw, to the layer of scruff that gave him a rugged look. Was Pierre being sweet to her because he felt sorry for her? Maybe he'd felt pity for her when she was a scrawny little girl, but he didn't feel that way anymore, did he?

"I'm very sorry my illness postponed your lessons," Lavinia said as she eyed her tattered and dirty skirt. "Perhaps now that I'm on my way to recovery, I can convince my daddy to let me begin my charitable work again."

Angelique hadn't minded missing the lessons. Yet maybe she should try to improve herself, especially before Pierre left the island. Then he would leave with a different picture of her in his mind. Maybe he wouldn't forget about her so easily this time.

"I'll send Lieutenant Steele to retrieve you just as soon as Daddy allows me to have visitors again." Lavinia smiled at the lieutenant, who leaned against the open doorway of the storehouse. His entire focus was on Lavinia, as if he'd been watching her for quite some time, waiting for her to turn and acknowledge him.

He straightened and returned her smile. Over the past couple of weeks, the leanness in his cheeks had disappeared and he'd begun to fill out. In his crisp, clean uniform he was actually quite striking.

Lavinia tilted her head and batted her eyelashes at the quartermaster.

Pierre narrowed his eyes at Lieutenant Steele. Was Pierre jealous that Lavinia was flirting with Lieutenant Steele?

"I'll bring Angelique up to the fort," Pierre said without breaking his attention from the lieutenant. "Just tell me when you want her here."

"Why, Mr. Durant, how kind of you." Lavinia clasped her hands together but continued to make eyes with the quartermaster. "Lieutenant Steele has been so gracious and willing to help me in any way he can, but with his increased responsibilities, I'm sure he will be all too glad to relinquish this duty to you."

"And I'll be happy to relieve him." Pierre's grip on Angelique's fingers tightened.

Angelique couldn't keep from sagging against Pierre. Whatever the case, whether Pierre was jealous of Lieutenant Steele or not, she wouldn't turn down the opportunity to avoid the quartermaster. Even if the bruises on her neck had gone away, she couldn't forget what he was capable of doing.

Besides, she'd take any time she could get with Pierre before he left, even if it was only for a short walk to and from the fort.

He'd be gone all too soon from her life. While everything inside her cautioned against allowing herself to get too close to him, she knew she'd already shoved away the warnings about how he'd broken her heart when he'd left the last time. And now she'd opened herself up to him again.

Maybe if she pretended he wouldn't have to leave . . . maybe if she prayed that he'd change his mind and stay . . . maybe if he decided to give up fur trading . . .

She whispered a desperate prayer — a prayer for a miracle.

CHAPTER 11

Lavinia's lavender perfume was like a thick fog in the air weighing on Angelique. She sat as straight and still as she could on the cushioned bench in front of Lavinia's dressing table. The books Lavinia had placed on her head had already slipped off more times than Angelique could count, and now she hardly dared to breathe for fear of suffocating from the perfume or being battered again by falling books.

The thick ointment on her hands underneath the gloves had begun to itch, and the salve Lavinia had rubbed across the freckles on her nose only added to the torture.

"The ointment will make your skin as smooth as a baby's," Lavinia said, digging through one of the trunks she'd had delivered to her cramped room in the officers' quarters. "You'll need to make more of it at home with lard, honey, rose water, and an egg. Then apply it to your hands every evening before bed, cover with the gloves, and wear it all night."

"Ebenezer won't let me use any eggs —"

"Nonsense. I shall send the instructions along with you. I'm sure your stepfather will be more than agreeable when he realizes the egg is going for a good cause."

Angelique knew it wouldn't do a bit of good to argue with Lavinia, any more than it did to contradict Ebenezer. When they were determined to do something, she'd learned that protesting would only strengthen their resolve.

Of course, Ebenezer had been thrilled when Lavinia's invitation to visit again had finally arrived. He'd admonished Angelique to cooperate with the commander's daughter and to win her favor.

For the past three days, Angelique had subjected herself to what Lavinia called "beauty treatments," but she didn't know how much more she could endure without shriveling up like a worm. Yes, she wanted Pierre to remember her when he left the island. She didn't want him to forget their friendship this time. But was all the discomfort really worth it?

After all, his three weeks were drawing to a close. He would be leaving the island by the week's end, and she wouldn't see him again until next spring — if he remembered his promise that he wouldn't stay away for so long.

"Oh, this is perfect," Lavinia said, rising from the trunk and clapping her hands.

Angelique remained still. Lavinia's enthusiasm didn't bode well.

"Yes, I do believe this is the perfect color to go with your hair." The rustling of satin swooshed in the air, sending more of Lavinia's perfume over Angelique.

Through the reflection in the mirror, Angelique stared in growing dismay at the folds upon folds of satin and lace and ruffles that Lavinia was pulling from the trunk.

"You shall wear it home this very day." Lavinia draped the beautiful gown across her bed.

"I can't." It *was* beautiful. The glossy material was a bright bluish-green, the color of the lake water on a calm and sunny day.

"But it's perfect for you. The turquoise will be stunning with your coloring." Lavinia tilted her head and studied Angelique. "Underneath all your frumpy layers, I do believe we are about the same size."

"It's not the size I doubt." Angelique stared at the bodice, the low square neckline with its ruffled border and the very high waist that formed a tight line at the bosom.

192

She glanced to the bodice on Lavinia's gown, noticing for the first time that it too hugged her chest, outlining her in the most revealing way, leaving far too much skin exposed.

Angelique blushed at the thought of anyone seeing her in such a gown. Even if it was the latest fashion for women, she would feel entirely uncomfortable in it. Not to mention the fact that Ebenezer would never allow it.

She could almost hear the words of sharp rebuke he'd uttered to her mother after they moved into the tavern, the slashing of satin, and the roar of the flames as he burned her gowns, one after another. Her mother had been devastated and had cried for days. And Ebenezer punished her severely until she'd agreed to don the modest, plain apparel of his late wife.

"My stepfather would never allow me to wear such a gown," Angelique insisted. Ebenezer would lock her in her room forever if she dressed in anything but the most austere garments.

"Everyone says he's Quaker." Lavinia's statement was really more of a question, and she paused in her smoothing of the gown, cocking her head at Angelique and waiting for a reply.

"I don't know. He's never said." Ebenezer's past was a mystery to her. He'd been on the island for as long as she could remember, even back during the days when her father had still been alive. But beyond the island, she didn't know where Ebenezer had come from or what had influenced him.

What she did know was that he was a lustful man. At times she wondered if his strict standards, piety, and zeal were his attempts at overcoming his sins. Maybe by making her and Betty wear the modest clothes, he was trying to resist the temptation to sin.

But the truth was he couldn't stop. He'd given in to his desires too many times so that now he was as thirsty for women as voyageurs were for rum. To have an immodestly clad woman in his house, right under his nose, would only remind him of his lust and his sins.

Angelique shook her head at the gown, and the books on her head came tumbling down, hitting her shoulders and arms before landing with a hard thump against the floor. "Thank you for the offer of the dress, Miss McDouall. But I can't wear the gown. I just can't."

It would be too dangerous. Ebenezer would think she was turning into Therese — or worse, her mother.

"I shall talk with your stepfather and convince him of the need."

"How would I work in such a beautiful gown?" Angelique scrambled for any excuse. "I would ruin it within a day."

Lavinia smoothed a hand over the rich satin. "True. You would ruin it with your work. Unless we can convince your stepfather to allow you to partake in the kind of work that befits a true gentlewoman, like embroidery, art, education, and other such skills necessary for managing a home. Perhaps you could participate in charity work, helping me with my newly formed Soldiers Relief Committee."

"It's the busiest time of the year, and he needs my help with the inn and the garden." Angelique knew she had to find a way out of having to wear the gown. It was one thing to learn correct posture and reduce her freckles; it was quite another thing to show up at the inn wearing something that would anger Ebenezer beyond his limits of tolerance.

Lavinia gently spread out the gown until it covered the bed in all its shimmering beauty.

"Perhaps if you have an older, more serviceable gown?" Angelique offered.

"This *is* an old one." Lavinia sighed and

pushed her golden curls off her forehead. "It's outdated and plain, yet I had hoped to be able to give you the opportunity to wear it." She stood back, her lips curved down in a pout.

In the hallway outside the room's closed door, the quick but firm steps of officers passed by as they came and went from the building. Was one of them Pierre? He'd brought her to and from the fort for her visits with Lavinia, and she was always glad for the short time they could be together. But every time they entered the gate past the red-coated soldiers, she expected one of them to swing his bayonet around and point the tip at Pierre's heart and ask him what he, an American, was doing inside the fort.

But no one ever questioned Pierre. They assumed he was as loyal to the British cause as any regular. She wanted to ask him whose side he was really on. The old Pierre wouldn't have cared about betraying his country or his family by fighting with the British. But this Pierre? He couldn't really be working for the British, could he?

She wasn't sure she wanted to know. And Pierre hadn't wanted her to know anything either.

"I have a splendid idea!" Lavinia clapped her hands. "We shall have a dance. Here at the fort. And you shall have the chance to wear the gown then."

Angelique started to shake her head. But Lavinia was already too busy planning to notice her objection to the idea. "It will be wonderful. We shall have the fort musicians play and have plenty of delicious refreshments. We shall invite the officers along with some of the important townspeople. Daddy was just saying he needed to make sure he had the support of the islanders. Would this not be the perfect way to form good relations?"

Angelique didn't have time to think of an answer before Lavinia continued. "The dance will be a time to show everyone just how hard you and I have worked to bring about your improvement."

"What about the war, Miss McDouall?" Angelique rose and stretched her stiff back. "Do you think your father will allow a dance when we're in the middle of a war?"

"Of course he will. My daddy never tells me no." Lavinia gave a soft laugh. "Since Mother died, he's allowed me to do whatever I want. Besides, the dance will be the perfect function for the Soldiers Relief Committee. A dance would take the soldiers' minds off the hardships of this savage place. It will cheer them and remind them of home. What could be more necessary than renewed spirits at a time like this?"

Angelique didn't argue with Lavinia, especially when she indicated they would need at least a month to prepare for the dance. Angelique could only pray that in a month's time the Americans would arrive and retake the fort, and that she and Jean would be happily married. Then she wouldn't have to worry about the shiny gown and what Ebenezer would do to her when he saw her in it.

For now, she would be grateful Lavinia hadn't insisted that she walk out of the officers' quarters in the gown.

"You smell like you took a bath in a perfume bottle." Pierre winked at her as they exited the stone building and rounded the green, where a group of regulars was standing in battle formation, marching and drilling.

Angelique could only shake her head in disgust at the scent that lingered in the homespun linen of her clothes. "She insists on coating me in her perfume every day," Angelique replied. "I think she's trying to rid me of the stench of the hen house."

"That's too bad." Pierre steered her past the low building that served as the commissary. Empty barrels were stacked against the outside walls, and a peek inside the dark interior revealed the stores were already diminished. "For the life of me, I can't understand why Lavinia doesn't like the stench of the hen house. It's so . . ."

"Homey?" She followed after him, enjoying the easy banter, especially after having to be so serious and polite with Lavinia.

"Oui. Definitely homey, in a stinky kind of way."

"I can't understand why she doesn't enjoy it," Angelique teased, ignoring the stares of several soldiers, who were apparently off duty and lounging on the long front porch of the soldiers' barracks, writing letters or mending their socks.

Pierre grinned at her over his shoulder. "Well, ma cherie, even if Lavina managed to drown out your lovely hen smell with her perfume, at least your hair looks pretty."

Angelique lifted her fingers to her hair, to the delicate curls that dangled near her ears. Lavinia had piled her hair high on top of her head in a fashionable style but had left several curls near her ears. "You don't think I look ridiculous?"

"You look ravishing." Even though his words had a hint of playfulness, the look he tossed her was anything but playful. Instead his eyes were dark and sparked with some-

199

thing that heated her belly with pleasure.

"And here I thought you were partial to my wearing my hair down." She couldn't resist the comment as they started up the hill toward the fort's north gate.

"True," he said, nodding at the sentinel, who swung open the door for them. As they stepped outside the tall palisades of the fort, Pierre led her directly toward the woods that didn't pass anywhere near town. "I'm partial to your long hair. But if you must wear it up, then this is perfect."

She didn't know where he was taking her, but as usual she didn't care. She trusted him, loved being with him, and when she was near him, nothing else mattered.

At the edge of the woods he stopped and faced her. "You're perfect, except for one thing." He tugged at her collar, pulling it loose from the bodice, until it hung down, exposing her neck. "There."

Before she could say anything, he spun and started for the thick stand of spruce, weaving through the trees as naturally as if a trail had been blazed there.

She traipsed after him, her heart humming a sweet tune. From behind, she admired his swagger, the proud tilt of his head, and the confidence he exuded. She grew breathless trying to keep up with him, but she was as familiar with the unmarked trails as he was and wanted to prove she was still as strong and agile as she'd always been.

Finally, when they reached the clearing that led to the Dousman farm, Pierre stopped. He peered up into a tall cedar tree — one of the biggest trees on the island — their *thinking tree,* the tree they'd always run to when they needed to be alone.

"Come on. I want to show you something."

"What?" She smiled at his eagerness.

He pulled himself up on the first low branch, then held out a hand to her. "You'll have to wait and see."

He scaled the tree slowly, pausing to wait and help her up each of the stairlike branches. She allowed him to assist her, even though she was capable of climbing any tree on the island without his assistance, just as she had when they were children. The truth was she liked his gentlemanly attention, even if it was unnecessary.

When they'd reached the middle of the tree, he sat on one of the sturdy branches and scooted down to make room for her to sit beside him. It wasn't a wide spot, and she found herself scrunched next to him, her arm against his and his thigh bumping hers. For a moment his heavy breathing mingled with hers, the only sound in the shaded coolness of the towering evergreen.

He glanced up and pointed to several branches above them, to a stick nest with long grass, leaves, and twigs poking out in disarray.

"What is it?" she asked.

"An abandoned squirrel nest, with a family of great horned owls living in it."

"Really?"

He nodded. "I saw the male out hunting last night when I was on my way home from my work on Fort George. I trailed him here to our favorite tree."

They sat quietly, craning their necks and staring at the bottom of the nest.

"Should I climb up and take a better look?"

He shook his head. "If we're quiet, one of the chicks might show itself." The warmth of his breath fanned against her cheek.

Her body tightened with eagerness. She wanted to pretend the feelings came from her anticipation of seeing the baby owl. But she couldn't seem to focus on anything but Pierre's nearness — his body next to hers, the rise and fall of his chest, the heat of his arm.

He tugged his leather pouch out from underneath his shirt, and his work-roughened fingers fumbled at the strap. "Open your apron," he whispered.

She spread out the stained linen, wishing it were clean.

He lifted his pouch and dumped the contents into her lap.

Delight brightened her like one of the shafts of sunlight slanting through the branches. "Wild strawberries," she said.

"I remembered how much you love them and I picked them for you."

"The first of the summer." She lifted one of the red berries, plucked off its green top, and slipped the fruit into her mouth. The mingling of tartness and sweetness was like a taste of heaven, and she closed her eyes to savor each juicy bite.

When she finished and opened her eyes, she quickly picked up another. Though food on the island had been plentiful of late, Ebenezer's stinginess hadn't changed, and her belly was never full enough.

She stuffed another berry into her mouth before she realized Pierre was watching her. She turned to him with a smile. "You'll eat some too, won't you? You can't have picked all these just for me."

But he wasn't smiling. Instead his eyes were dark and unreadable and focused on her lips.

She stopped chewing and held her breath. There was something about the look in his eyes that made her almost believe he was thinking more about tasting her lips than tasting the strawberries.

She didn't move. The world grew strangely silent, and she thought she could hear the wild thumping of Pierre's heartbeat.

He lifted his fingers to her neck, circling them around the back so that his thumb ended near her ear. With exquisite softness he brushed his thumb below her jaw against her pulse, which was throbbing.

She wanted to lean her head back and let his fingers have full access to her skin, but she was too weak, too powerless to do anything but relish the gentle touch.

His gaze lifted and connected with hers. Without breaking the contact, he tilted his head as if to kiss her. He hesitated for the merest instant, a flicker in his eyes seeming to ask her for her permission.

In answer, she could do nothing less than lean toward him. Didn't he know by now that her heart was his for the taking, whether she wanted him to take it or not? It had always been his. She was only fooling herself to think otherwise.

His fingers at the back of her neck tightened and drew her toward him.

She wanted to kiss him, had always dreamed about kissing him. She couldn't deny it any longer.

"Oh," she whispered as he made the barest contact with her mouth, the slight softness teasing her, almost as if he were planning to take his time and enjoy every facet of mingling his lips with hers.

He grazed her lips again, but then pulled back a fraction. Her stomach cinched with longing.

And when his mouth touched hers again, this time lingering a second longer, she moved toward him.

But he held himself just slightly out of her reach, tantalizing her lips with quick feather-like brushes.

"Pierre . . ." she breathed as his mouth grazed hers again. The longing that was growing inside told her there was more, much more to a kiss than this sweet teasing. "Please —"

"Say my name again," he said.

"Pierre," she whispered against him. "Pierre —"

His lips cut her off with a decisiveness that wrapped around her and wouldn't let go. He was a current against her, pulling her in, taking her under with his kiss that kept deepening until she was drowning in it.

A screech from above startled her, and she broke away from him. Her breath came in rasps. Guilt and embarrassment rushed over her, and she quickly covered her mouth with her hand.

Pierre released her, but stared at her with an expression that said he was thinking of pulling her back and kissing her more. The warmth twisting in her insides told her that she would have a hard time resisting if he reached for her again.

He lifted a hand to her hair and touched one of her curls. She shook her head and leaned away from him.

He stopped, and his eyes widened. As much as she wanted his affection, her pulse pounded a warning. She couldn't let him break her heart when he left this time.

Her mind traveled back to the day before he'd departed five years ago, when he'd pulled her along behind him through the woods, just like he had now. And how he'd taken her to one of the cliffs on the shore to show her a broad-winged hawk's nest. They'd sat for several hours watching the nest. She'd listened as he raged about his frustrations with his father and his family for not understanding him. And when he'd finally exhausted himself, he reached for her hand and intertwined his fingers through hers.

"I love you, Angelique," he'd said, and then he laid a gentle kiss against her cheek.

At that moment she'd been the happiest thirteen-year-old girl who had ever lived. It hadn't mattered that he was a man of almost eighteen, that he was angry with the world, that he wanted to leave the island and never come back.

He'd said he loved her.

Her heart had swelled with her own love for him, all the love that had been growing during their childhood. And even though she hadn't told him that day that she loved him in return, she had.

But then he'd left the next morning. He'd gone without telling her where he was going or when he would return. And he'd taken her heart with him.

Over the years he'd been away, she'd learned there were different kinds of love. That Pierre hadn't loved her romantically. He'd loved her as a friend. Nothing more.

But the knowledge had hurt her more than she'd wanted to admit. And it had hurt that in all those five years he'd been gone, he hadn't once thought to write to her or visit or send her even the smallest token of regard.

He'd forgotten all about her. If that had been his definition of love, it hadn't been the kind she'd wanted.

How could she bear the pain again when he left this time?

She shifted so that she wasn't touching him. "I'm sorry, Pierre," she said. "I shouldn't have . . . we shouldn't have . . ."

He took off his hat, jabbed his fingers through his hair, and expelled a long, shaky breath.

She fumbled for something to say that would help ease the tension. "I have to be faithful to Jean."

He jammed his hat back on. "You're right. I wasn't thinking of Jean."

They sat silently for a long moment, a breeze swooshing the pine needles around them, rattling the dry pine cones that lingered in the tree, and stirring the thick scent of resin. Through the branches, the open fields spread out before them. They could see almost all the way to the northern beaches of the island.

"You're leaving soon," she said, not wanting him to be angry with her. "And when the war is over, Jean will come home and I'm going to marry him."

Pierre's shoulders slumped.

Yes, he'd made it clear that he didn't think

Jean was right for her. But did he have deeper reasons for objecting? She fought the flutter of longing. Could his kiss mean he wanted her for himself? Or was he merely charming her like he did most of the women in his life?

After all, she'd seen the way he'd looked at Lavinia. And if he'd been alone with Lavinia in the shadows of a cedar tree, he probably would have kissed her too.

Angelique stifled a shiver. She couldn't make more out of the moment than it contained. This was Pierre. And Pierre was . . . well, selfish. Wasn't he?

She picked up one of the ripest, fullest strawberries he'd gathered for her and held it out to him, hoping he'd sense her peace offering.

He hesitated, then with a nod took it from her, popped the green top, and tossed the berry in his mouth.

She let her fingers linger over the berries in her lap, waiting for him to say something, anything. She didn't want him to leave the island upset at her.

"So I suppose you've kissed Jean?" His question was low, almost teasing.

She breathed a sigh of relief, glad that his good humor was returning. "We kissed once."

"Just once?"

"Just once."

"What's wrong with him?" Pierre laughed.

"He's honorable."

"And dull."

"Pierre!" she chastised, though she knew her tone lacked any conviction.

"If I were him, I wouldn't have been satisfied with one kiss."

"Then it's a good thing you're not him, because that's all I would have given you."

He grinned. "When did he kiss you?"

She knew she should protest Pierre's questions. What had transpired between her and Jean was none of his business. But for some reason she felt as if she must confess the truth. "He kissed me the day the British forced him to leave the island."

"A good-bye kiss?"

She nodded. It had been on the crowded beach, with everyone on the island swarming around them. With tears in his eyes he'd hugged and kissed Miriam, then turned to her. He'd drawn her into a one-armed hug, patting her back awkwardly, and then gave her the briefest of kisses. It had been over before it had begun, leaving no trace of remembrance upon her lips. He then stepped away from her and into the boat that would row him to the ships anchored farther out in the harbor. His sweet smile was all she'd had to store in her heart since he'd been gone.

"A good-bye kiss doesn't count as a real kiss," Pierre said.

"It most certainly does count." It hadn't been anything like Pierre's. Not even close. Her stomach flopped as she thought again about the pressure of Pierre's lips against hers, soft at first and then hard and crushing.

She slipped a strawberry into her mouth and tried to banish the sensation that was embedded on her lips. Even if Jean's kiss hadn't lingered upon her the same way Pierre's had, she wouldn't dismiss Jean's affection or trivialize it.

Pierre was still grinning, but when his eyebrows shot up, he couldn't hide the intensity that lurked amidst the playfulness.

"Any kiss less than fifteen seconds isn't a real kiss." Pierre took another strawberry and stuffed it into his mouth.

"Fifteen seconds?" She gave a short laugh. "I suppose you're the kissing expert now?"

He shrugged. "You've kissed us both. Who's better?"

She couldn't resist glancing up at him, at his lips that had only moments ago taken her to the brink of pleasure.

His smile turned up on one side, as if he'd heard her answer even though she hadn't spoken a word.

She gave him a playful shove. "Oh, stop it, Pierre. You're much too conceited for your own good."

He laughed again, and the warmth of the afternoon wrapped around her, making her grateful for the time she could spend with him.

"If you ever need practice," he said, "I'm here for you."

She pushed him again.

"What?" he asked innocently. "It's obvious Jean needs to learn how to kiss you much more thoroughly. I'd be more than happy to give you a few lessons that you can pass along to him."

With any other person she wouldn't have dared to carry on about something as intimate as kissing. But she'd always had an openness with Pierre that she didn't have with anyone else. "I'm sure, given the right circumstances and setting, Jean will do just fine."

Pierre snorted. "He's about as exciting as a cow chewing his cud."

In her mind's eye she could see Jean standing next to Pierre. Compared to the dashing and handsome Pierre, Jean was fair and plain. He was simpler, down-to-earth, and content with his life. He wasn't constantly dreaming of bigger and better things beyond the horizon.

"Jean may not be exciting like you, Pierre," she finally said, "but he's a good man. And he loves me."

Pierre's smile faded, and a soberness descended over his features.

For the briefest of moments she held her breath and waited for Pierre to tell her that he too loved her, and to promise that he'd always be there for her. But they both knew the truth.

Pierre couldn't promise her what he didn't have to give.

CHAPTER 12

Pierre swung the ax down again. His muscles burned in agony, and his hands stung from the blisters that had formed there hours ago.

The wood split with a crack that jarred him. He bent, picked up the pieces, and tossed them onto the mountainous pile he'd already chopped.

"Take a break, my dear son," Maman called from the cabin. "Please."

Pierre wiped at the sweat that had run into his eyes. His shirt was wet and clung to his skin and did little to keep him dry anymore. And the humidity in the air coated him in a sticky film that was suffocating.

The sky was the color of stormy lake water. If only it would rain and put them out of their misery. He peered toward the west, in the direction of his swimming hole. He wished he could drop everything and sneak away to it. If he'd been with his brigade, he could have jumped into the river to cool off. At the very least he could have splashed himself. The clear river water would have been at his hand, the refreshing wilderness breezes at his back.

"You've worked too hard, Pierre," Maman said. "I think it's time to call it a day."

"I'm almost done," he called. At nine o'clock at night in June, he could probably get in another hour of work before it grew too dark to see. He eyed the pile of logs still waiting for his blade. He wouldn't be done until he split the rest of the wood he'd chopped yesterday. After that he'd need to stack it against the cabin and inside the barn. Even then, he didn't know if Maman would have enough to last her through the winter.

The problem with farm work was that it was never ending. When he finished one job, there were ten others that needed his attention — unlike fur trading, where he could mark his accomplishments by the strokes of the voyageurs. They paddled thirty miles a day, fifty-five strokes per minute, fourteen hours a day.

Even at the portages, he could measure their progress. With two ninety-pound packs strapped to their backs and heads, they could still make the haul overland in ten-minute intervals per half mile.

But farming . . . He shook his head in frustration at all he had left to do.

The three weeks he'd planned on staying had passed, and he was still on the island — without the hired help he'd tried to find for Maman. He'd had several leads, but they'd all fallen through. No one wanted to commit, not with the uncertainty of the war and the inevitable battle that loomed ahead.

And try as he might, he couldn't make himself walk away. He knew he'd feel guilty if he did. He wouldn't be able to paddle to Montreal and find the usual contentment with his brigade knowing he'd left Maman as helpless as he'd found her.

Why was he growing a conscience now after all these years of living the way he wanted?

He glanced to the swirling gray clouds overhead. He knew what was happening. Ever since he'd repented and let God grip him, the fingers of the Holy Spirit had been wrapped around his heart and he could no longer ignore the pressure there, the urging to do what was right.

He had to take care of his maman.

Even though he couldn't audibly hear God, the nudging of the Spirit inside told him the same thing Red Fox had — that

216

Maman needed him more this summer than his brigade did.

Besides, two nights ago under cover of darkness, when he'd paddled to Bois Blanc Island to send another missive to the American forces, he'd picked up a message from Red Fox that the brigade hadn't had any confrontations yet with the North West Company. They were doing fine without him.

Would it really be so terrible to stay on the island for the summer?

He mopped his sweat-drenched eyes again in time to see Angelique step out of the woods and start across the meadow toward the farm. He couldn't stop himself from staring at her, from watching her lovely swaying and the gentle contours of her figure.

His mind flashed to the kiss he'd shared with her in the tree several days ago, the way she'd said his name and the way her lips had melded with his. He couldn't remember wanting to kiss another woman quite as much as he'd wanted to kiss her. Even after she'd pulled away from him, he'd ached with the need to hold her again and keep on kissing her.

What was he thinking? He wasn't supposed to get involved with *any* woman, much less a sweet, innocent girl like Angelique. He'd never had any trouble in the past. He'd always been content to consider her just a friend. What had changed?

Even as the question ricocheted around in his mind, the answer hit the target head-on. *She* had changed. She'd grown up. Not only had she developed into an attractive woman, but she'd become even kinder and sweeter and more fun to be around. He loved the way she wasn't afraid to follow him without any questions wherever he took her, that she wasn't too grown up to climb a tree, and that she still understood him in a way no one else ever had. He had to admit, he was drawn to her the same as when he'd been a boy. Only now he was drawn so much more forcefully.

He shoved another length of wood onto the chopping block, steadied it, and then swung his ax into it. This was supposed to take his mind off Angelique. The pinging of the ax and the splitting of the wood were intended to distract him from her approach. But with each step she drew closer, his muscles hardened with awareness, until he felt like the slightest pressure would split *him* into pieces.

Why did she have to grow up? Why couldn't things have remained the same as always? Out of the corner of his eye he watched her embrace Maman.

Was that why he hadn't left the island yet? Was it because he wasn't ready to leave Angelique?

He lowered the ax and rested the blade against the wood chips scattered around the base of the block. That couldn't be the reason. He wasn't looking for a relationship with a woman right now. He didn't want a woman in his life, did he?

Non. Of course not. He was only concerned about Angelique and Maman because they were alone on the island, having to fend for themselves. And with the danger of the upcoming battle, he wanted to make sure they were safe before he left.

Maybe he would stay through the summer, do as much as he could to prepare for winter, and be there to keep them safe during the battle with the Americans. And then after Red Fox and his brigade returned with fresh trade goods and supplies, he'd take his leave.

He heaved a sigh as he turned to look upon Angelique. He'd seen her earlier in the day when he'd taken her to and from the fort for her lesson with Lavinia. He never tired of being near her.

She glanced at him with a shy smile that

made him want to drop everything, grab her hand, and run off together.

"I see you're shirking your duties at the inn again." He greeted her with a smile.

"And I see you're being lazy around here as usual." She nodded at the enormous pile of split wood.

He was relieved to see she wasn't embarrassed being around him since their kiss and was doing her best to pretend nothing had transpired between them.

But underneath their bantering, he could sense something from her, something more than the usual adoration. Every once in a while he caught her looking at him with an intensity that set his blood on fire. He saw the flush on her cheeks, the intake of her breath, and the desire flitting across her face.

She might have claimed she wanted Jean and that she was waiting to marry him, but a strange need crept into Pierre — the need to prove that she wanted him more than Jean. He could win her affection if he really wanted to. If he worked hard enough to woo her, she wouldn't be able to resist him.

But what about Jean? Pierre had come back to the island to apologize to his family, including Jean. He wanted to repair the broken relationship and gain his brother's forgiveness, not make him angrier.

And yet Angelique had the right to choose anyone she wanted. She wasn't stuck with Jean. She didn't have to marry him out of obligation. If she found someone she loved more, surely she wouldn't feel bound to Jean.

"And how did you manage to sneak here this time?" he asked.

"Ebenezer went out, and Betty is already sleeping. She's heavy with child and tires easily these days."

"So in your rare moment of freedom you decided to come here and see me since I'm so irresistible?" he teased.

"Don't flatter yourself. I came to see Miriam." She tossed him a smile before turning toward Maman. They started to enter the cabin, and he wished he could prevent her from disappearing inside. He wanted to talk with her longer without the time constraints they always faced.

"I'm staying for the rest of the summer." The words came out before he could stop them.

Both women froze, then slowly turned to face him with startled expressions.

"I might as well," he said hesitantly, wondering if he should take back the words, if he really could last all summer. "I can

221

help with the crops and do some hunting so that you're well stocked before winter."

"God be praised," Maman said with a beaming smile. "That would be heavenly, Pierre."

Angelique blinked and then studied his face, her beautiful brown eyes filled with wonder.

"Do you want me to stay for the summer, Angelique?" He needed to know that she wanted him to stay, that she welcomed him in her life.

"Is it what you really want?" she asked.

He searched for a truthful answer. She would expect nothing less. "You know I love my brigade and I'll miss being with them. But I think the right thing — the thing God wants me to do — is to stay here and help."

She nodded. "That's very noble of you. I'm sure the decision wasn't easy to make."

"Knowing you'd be here made it a little easier." He tried to make his words light, but a spark seemed to jump between them.

"I guess now we know who's the irresistible one." Her tone was playful too but had a breathy quality that gave away her reaction to his news.

She was glad he was staying for the summer.

A tiny crease formed between Maman's

eyebrows. She lifted her face toward him. Did she sense that his feelings toward Angelique had turned into something more than friendly affection?

He wanted to tell her that she had no reason to worry, that he wouldn't do anything to hurt Angelique while he was on the island, that he valued Angelique too much to trifle with her like he had other women in the past. But how could he make such a promise? Not when one minute he was telling himself that he couldn't get involved with any woman, but then the next minute thinking about how he could woo Angelique.

"Jean will be grateful for all Pierre's help." Maman grasped at Angelique's hand. "Now he can return to find things just the way he left them."

There was a gentle warning in Maman's words, a reminder that Jean would want to return to find Angelique the way he left her — waiting and ready for marriage.

"Jean will be very happy, won't he, Angel?"

Angelique lowered her head, but not before he caught a flash of guilt. She murmured her agreement and guided Miriam through the door to the dark interior of the cabin.

"Come in and join us, Pierre," Maman

223

called before disappearing inside.

He was surprised at the strength of his desire to follow Angelique and Maman inside. He'd love to make Angelique a meal — roasted duck from the bird he'd shot that afternoon. He'd baste it with a glaze made from fresh parsley and green onions. Then he'd add some of the carrots and turnips that had just started to take root.

She would swoon over the meal. He could guarantee it. And he'd find delight in watching her eat every bite.

The ax handle in his hand seemed to weigh as much as a load of stones. He wanted to let it drop and give in to his impulsiveness. Maybe he didn't have enough time to roast her a duck, but he could make something for her. The light of pleasure would dance to life in her eyes, pleasure with his meal and pleasure with him.

An oil lantern flared inside the cabin, lighting up the interior. From where he stood, Pierre caught a glimpse of Papa's paddle on the wall. The brightly painted red and blue pattern rose up to mock him, to remind him of the day Papa had hung it on the wall and made the declaration that he'd never use it again, that his days of fur trading were over.

It had been the spring after Papa's last

voyage. He'd paddled back to the island, walked away from his brigade on the beach, and the first thing he'd done when he walked in the house was nail the paddle to the wall. Then he'd taken Maman in his arms, kissed her long and hard, and told her he'd never leave her again.

Pierre swallowed a lump that arose at the memory.

Papa had declared he was a changed man, that he'd turned his life over to the Lord, and that he wanted to put his house in order — namely loving his wife and children the way God wanted him to. He claimed that once a man had a wife and family, he couldn't abandon them for nine months of the year for his work.

And Pierre agreed. He'd vowed he would never do that to a wife. He wouldn't marry a woman and leave her behind. And he certainly wouldn't bring her along with him into the wilderness. Living out of a canoe was no kind of life for a wife and children.

Pierre stared hard at the paddle on the wall. The truth was, if he wanted to be with a woman he loved, he'd have to give up his fur-trading ways, like his father had.

Could he ever do that? Could he ever give up the wilderness and his traveling in order to have such a love?

Through the open door he saw Angelique assist Maman into a kitchen chair. She began unraveling the plait Maman wore at the back of her neck until her long hair hung free.

His chest expanded at the thought that Angelique had risked leaving the inn to help Maman with a bath and washing her hair.

Angelique MacKenzie was the sweetest, kindest woman he'd ever met.

If there was a woman who could make him want to give up everything he loved to settle down, she just might be the one.

CHAPTER 13

In the blackness of the hallway, Angelique crept up the ladder to her dormer room, praying the rungs wouldn't squeak. She'd taken too long with Miriam's care.

As she'd slipped into the inn, past the crowded dining room toward the back stairway, she'd held her breath, waiting for Ebenezer to step into the kitchen and stop her. But apparently he'd overstayed his time on the beach with the Indian women and wasn't home to catch her sneaking in.

She fumbled in the dark to find the door latch, but stopped short when her fingers brushed against the metal hook dangling instead of locked snugly the way she'd left it that morning.

Her muscles tensed. Someone had gone into her room.

Though Ebenezer often clamored up and down the ladder into the attic for supplies, he always latched the door. Had one of the voyageurs snuck up into the dark corridor? Was someone waiting even as she climbed, ready to jump out on her as she made her way to her pallet?

She pushed at the trapdoor, then hesitated. She'd never had any trouble with a voyageur sneaking into the private quarters of the inn. Ebenezer insisted the men use the side stairway on the outside of the inn that led to the long bedroom above the dining area.

A sharp cry came from the direction of the room Betty shared with Ebenezer. Was the intruder attacking Betty? Angelique shuddered while slipping back down the ladder. She couldn't let the poor girl suffer, not with the unborn child at risk too.

Angelique stumbled through the dark hallway, skimming her fingers along the wall until she brushed against the door handle. She paused and listened. The usual raucous laughter and loud voices of the men drinking and playing cards came from downstairs. The tobacco smoke from their pipes had filtered through the stickiness of the night and hung heavy in the air. Yet Betty's room remained silent.

If only she had a weapon. Maybe she should return to the kitchen and find a knife. Or she could grab her ivory-handled comb in her room. The prongs were sharp.

She had started to spin toward the ladder when another of Betty's cries stopped her. She didn't have time to go for a weapon. Without another thought, she swung open the door and plunged into the darkened chamber. "Betty?" she called.

The slithering of sheets mingled with strangled panting.

Angelique squinted through the darkness at the bed. Betty lay alone, writhing and gripping her distended abdomen.

"I think it's time to have the baby," the girl moaned.

Angelique crossed the room to the edge of the bed. Her earlier fear was swept away by a new panic. "I'll call for the midwife."

Betty let out another sharp cry. "It . . . it might be too late for that."

"What can I do?" Angelique knew almost nothing about birthing babies, and she dreaded what Ebenezer would do if she didn't go find the midwife. His last wife had died in birthing. He certainly wouldn't want Betty giving birth at Angelique's inexperienced hands.

"I really should call for the midwife," she said, her voice trembling as she searched the darkness for a lantern.

"If you'd been here earlier when I came

looking for you, then you might have had time. Now it's too late."

So Betty had been the one to climb into the attic and had discovered her absence.

"I suppose you're sneaking down to the beach to fornicate too," Betty said bitterly.

"Never!" She'd noticed Betty's growing sullenness over the past month. She'd seen the way Betty watched Ebenezer leave in the evenings, her young face tight with resentment. She could only imagine how difficult it was for the girl to learn about her husband's unfaithfulness.

"Maybe you're the one enticing my husband away from me." Betty's breath came in loud gasps. "I see the way he looks at you."

"He does *not* look at me." The very thought made Angelique shudder.

Betty gave a strangled cry. "I don't know why he doesn't get rid of you. You're older than me. You should be married by now."

"My betrothed was forced to leave the island and is now fighting in the war." Angelique moved closer to the bed. "I'll marry him when he comes back."

"And what if he dies? What will you do then?"

Angelique couldn't bear to think of that happening. She hadn't let herself face such

230

a horrible possibility and the bleak life she might have if Jean didn't make it back. Even though men died in battle all the time, she knew Jean wouldn't. He couldn't.

Betty's tone rose with each breath. "Do you plan to stay here at the inn forever and tempt my husband?"

"I'm not tempting him."

"If you weren't here, then maybe he'd want to stay with me instead of having to leave all the time to avoid temptation."

Angelique could only shake her head. The accusations were ridiculous and completely unfounded. How could Betty believe such a thing? Not when Angelique had tried hard to avoid being alluring like her mother and sister.

The young girl groaned and bent over, hugging her arms to her chest. In the dim light the window afforded, Angelique could see the sheets tangled in Betty's legs and the dark stains from the blood she'd already lost.

Angelique smoothed her hand over the girl's taut back.

"Don't touch me," Betty hissed as another contraction hit her.

"What can I do to help you?"

"You should have been here earlier to go for the midwife."

"I'll go now." Angelique backed slowly toward the door.

Betty shook her head and began wailing.

Angelique stumbled over a discarded shoe and bumped against the edge of a chest. If only she hadn't gone to see Miriam tonight. She'd known she was taking a risk by leaving the inn. But she'd taken risks all winter, and it had been several days since she'd visited Miriam.

As much as she wanted to deny she'd also gone to see Pierre, she knew she'd only be lying to herself. She'd always made excuses to see him or be with him, even as a girl. There was something reassuring about being near him, even if he was outside chopping wood while she cared for Miriam. His strong presence and the occasional glimpses of him comforted her.

And when he'd declared that he was going to stay for the rest of the summer, her chest had expanded with secret relief. She'd have at least two more months with him. Two whole months.

"Don't think that I won't tell my husband about your disobedience tonight," Betty cried out.

Angelique didn't try to defend herself. She was resigned to the fact that Ebenezer would punish her again, lock her in the attic without food, and make her repent of her sins. He'd do it even if it meant he had to get one of the Indian children living on the beach to do her duties. He paid the children with worthless trinkets, which cost him nothing.

"And this time," Betty continued, "maybe he'll finally decide to get rid of you."

Angelique steadied herself and tried to drive away the growing worry over Betty's accusations. Betty was only speaking irrationally out of her pain. She didn't mean what she was saying. Once the birthing was over, surely she'd forget everything she said.

Besides, so long as Pierre was on the island, everything would be just fine. He would keep her safe. Even so, her heart clamored a warning, the warning that she needed to be more careful not to upset Betty or Ebenezer again. She couldn't take any more chances.

CHAPTER 14

"What do you mean you won't let her out of her room?" Pierre's words boomed through the empty tavern. His voice contained all the frustration that had been building, until now his anguish was so intense he couldn't think about anything else except freeing Angelique.

"She has one more day of discipline." Ebenezer rubbed at the shiny bald spot on his head, which was beaded with sweat from the humidity that was plaguing the island and bringing with it the mosquitoes and flies in their ferocious hordes.

"Non. You've had her locked in her room for two days. That's long enough." He wanted to shout that Ebenezer was an idiot, but he forced himself to swallow his anger. He couldn't jeopardize Angelique's situation and make things worse for her.

Ebenezer's eyes narrowed. "I told my stepdaughter she would get three days of discipline this time, and I intend to follow through."

"Miss McDouall told me I wasn't to return to the fort without Angelique today." It wasn't exactly the truth, but Pierre was too frustrated to care.

"I'm sure she'll understand after you explain that my stepdaughter's disobedience nearly cost me the life of my newborn son."

Pierre glanced into the kitchen to Ebenezer's wife, who sat in front of the hearth with a swaddled baby in her arms. The woman averted her eyes, refusing to look anywhere but at her babe.

"From what I heard," Pierre continued, "Angelique returned with the midwife in plenty of time."

"She shouldn't have been out gallivanting about the island in the first place." Ebenezer's voice rose with each word. He cleared his throat and added with forced calmness, "I won't let any member of my household conduct herself like a loose woman."

Gallivanting? Loose woman? Pierre almost snorted. Angelique was the last person anyone could accuse of gallivanting or behaving like a loose woman. She was the purest, most selfless person Pierre had ever met. But obviously she hadn't shared the truth of her whereabouts with Ebenezer, namely that she was risking his punishment to help a poor, widowed blind woman.

Pierre had the feeling if he continued to argue with Ebenezer, he'd only walk away empty-handed as he had the previous afternoons when he'd come to escort Angelique up to the fort. Ebenezer was too controlling. Pierre had come across his type plenty of times in his fur trading. If Pierre applied any amount of force, Ebenezer would cling tighter.

Pierre took a deep breath and uncurled his fists. Red Fox would be proud of him if he could see him now. He wouldn't solve the problem with his strength and punches. No, he'd play on Ebenezer's weakness. At least for the moment.

He reached for the door handle and glanced with what he hoped was nonchalance over the untidy room and the Indian child sweeping the sticky floor. "Then good day to you and your mistress. I'll report back to Miss McDouall your refusal of her request to allow Angelique to visit the fort for her lessons. Miss McDouall will be disappointed you're not cooperating."

Pierre held his breath and prayed Ebenezer hadn't heard that Lavinia was suffering from the fever and ague. With the onslaught of mosquitoes, the poor girl was languishing even with doses of quinine to ease her discomfort. Despite her illness, Lavinia had wanted him to bring Angelique to the fort. But only because she was having her tailor make some adjustments on a gown she wanted Angelique to wear to her big dance.

"Don't say I didn't warn you." Pierre opened the door. "I wouldn't want to be you when Miss McDouall complains to her father. The colonel has been rather tense lately as he's preparing for the upcoming attack, and he won't appreciate having to deal with his daughter's frustration."

He didn't wait for Ebenezer's response. Instead he stepped through the door. Every muscle in his body protested having to walk away. And he resolved that if Ebenezer didn't release Angelique from her attic prison, he'd go back to his old tactics — beat the man senseless, force his way inside, and physically remove her.

As he walked away from the inn, the oppressive humidity weighed on him, drenching him, almost as if the lake and the sky had traded places.

"Wait!"

At Ebenezer's call, Pierre expelled a long breath. He forced himself to count to five before turning around. Ebenezer stood in the open doorway of the two-story whitewashed inn, his shapeless gray shirt clinging to his perspiring body.

"I suppose you're right," Ebenezer said with a frown. "I don't want to cause any further worries for the colonel, especially at a difficult time like this."

Everyone was worried about the coming of the Americans. Most of the townspeople had even begun to store up food and supplies in preparation for whatever awaited them. Some expected the Americans to bomb the island from the harbor. Others suspected an all-out battle with forces landing and taking back the fort. Still others speculated the Americans would set up a blockade and attempt to starve the British off the island.

Pierre didn't know what was going to happen any more than the islanders did. His communication with the Americans had been one-sided, with him delivering updates and not hearing anything in return.

"If I allow Angelique to go with you to the fort," Ebenezer said, "then you must bring her back promptly."

Pierre shrugged as if it didn't matter to him, when in reality he wanted to yell at Ebenezer that he would *never* bring her back. "I don't have anything to do with the time Miss McDouall needs for her lessons.

I'm merely the escort."

"I can always have her make up the discipline tomorrow."

Pierre wished Angelique didn't have to worry about any tomorrows with Ebenezer. "She's a grown woman." He couldn't stop himself from defending her. "You don't need to discipline her as if she were a child."

"I'm her guardian. I promised her mother I'd provide a stable home for her. Someday she'll thank me for taking such good care of her, for teaching her to obey the Commandments and protecting her from the shameful and sinful ways of both her mother and sister."

The last thing Angelique would ever do is thank Ebenezer. But instead of contradicting the man, Pierre peered up at the hazy sun, pretending to check the time. "Since you've delayed Angelique's lesson, you'd better not expect her back on time."

Ebenezer muttered something under his breath before turning back to the tavern. Pierre followed him to the door and waited.

When Ebenezer returned to the dining room several minutes later, with Angelique moving slowly behind him, Pierre released a pent-up breath.

"Just because I'm letting you out of your room doesn't mean you won't finish your discipline when you return," Ebenezer said before he stepped aside to let Angelique pass.

Her face was flushed and a loose tendril of hair stuck to her damp forehead. Her eyes were sunken and glassy, and when she looked at Pierre, she didn't seem to see him.

Pierre's pulse lurched to a halt. Angelique wasn't well. What had Ebenezer done to her?

She took several more steps, but then swayed and grabbed the edge of a table to keep from falling.

Pierre darted toward her and reached for her arm. "Are you unwell?"

She didn't answer except to latch on to him.

"She's fine," Ebenezer said. "She's suffering the effects of her discipline, which is nothing less than what she deserves."

Pierre crossed with her to the door. Angelique dragged her feet, until Pierre was afraid she would collapse. "No one deserves this kind of treatment!" he shouted at Ebenezer, fighting the urge to rush back across the room and use the man's protruding belly as a punching bag.

Instead he swooped Angelique up in his arms and settled her gently against his chest. She gave a soft gasp but didn't protest. He yanked open the door and stepped outside, tossing a glare over his shoulder at Ebenezer. "You can be sure Miss McDouall will hear about your treatment of Angelique. I'm sure she'll be none too pleased when she discovers how cruel you've been."

He took satisfaction at the anxiety that creased Ebenezer's forehead before he slammed the door closed with as much force as he could muster.

"Angelique, ma cherie?" He gazed down at her flushed face. "Tell me what's wrong so that I can help you."

"I need water," she whispered through cracked lips.

Pierre knelt, cradling Angelique in his lap, and fumbled at his side for his leather canteen. He unplugged the spout and brought it to her lips.

She opened her mouth eagerly for the cool water, and he dribbled it in slowly. For several moments he helped her to drink, until finally she nodded. "That's better," she whispered.

"Don't tell me Ebenezer refused you water for the past two days," Pierre said as he situated his canteen back at his side, his fingers brushing against his hunting knife. "Because if you do, you'll force me to walk back in there and stab him."

She didn't say anything, but he could see the truth written in her eyes.

The pompous pig had not only deprived her of food but also water. And in the sweltering heat of her attic room she could have died if Pierre hadn't rescued her when he did.

His muscles tensed, and he uttered a growl. He started to lower her to the ground, knowing he had no choice but to go back to the inn and make sure Ebenezer could never hurt Angelique again.

But her arms snaked around his neck. "No, Pierre. Please don't do anything rash. Please."

He shook his head and tried to pry her arms off him. "I'm going to teach that man a lesson he'll never forget."

"You'll only make things worse for me if you do." Her brown eyes were wide now and the glassy look was gone, replaced with the clarity and openness he loved.

Pierre glowered at the door of the inn.

"I'll be all right, Pierre. Especially now that I'm with you."

He stood again, holding her tighter to his chest, refusing to let her go. His body almost ached with the need for vengeance. But the plea on her face made it impossible to say no. "Fine. Then I'm taking you home and cooking you a decent meal."

She responded with a weak smile.

Angelique rested her cheek against the coarse linen of Pierre's shirt. "I can walk, Pierre," she said, but she knew her tone lacked conviction.

"Oh, so you don't think I'm strong enough to carry you?" His voice had finally lost the fury that had frightened her and made her believe he would stalk back into the inn and kill Ebenezer.

"You're such a weakling, Pierre."

He hefted her higher. "You weigh absolutely nothing." Anger slid back into his tone.

She wound her arms tighter around his neck, trying to block out the torture of the past couple of days when she'd been miserably hot and weak. Her mouth had grown parched, and she'd wavered in and out of consciousness. Of course Ebenezer hadn't given her any food — he never did. But this had been the first time he'd left her without water too.

She'd never seen him as angry as he'd been when he learned she'd snuck out of the inn. Even though he hadn't ranted or raved, the sharp anger in his eyes told her she'd gone too far this time, that putting his wife and newborn baby at risk had been unforgivable.

Had he wanted her to die? Was he ready to do away with her after being shackled with her all these years? Especially after Betty's complaints against her? Angelique had heard every bitter word through the cracks in the floorboards. Betty had begged him to get rid of her, to marry her off as soon as possible.

She shuddered.

"The man's a beast." Pierre hugged her closer. "And a lunatic."

For all Ebenezer's faults, she couldn't begrudge the fact that he'd provided for her since her mother's death. If not for him, she would have been homeless. After mother was gone, Therese had talked about leaving Michilimackinac and going east to live in one of the big cities. But where would they have lived? What kind of work would they have found?

They'd been too young at thirteen and fourteen to make their own way in the world. So Angelique had begged Therese to stay. And she had.

Ebenezer had never once threatened them with having to leave. He'd never once complained about having them live with him, even though they were extra mouths to feed and bodies to clothe. Maybe he hadn't been generous or kind or fatherly, but he'd provided security.

After the past years of sheltering her, she couldn't accept the possibility that Ebenezer would purposefully kill her. It was too sinful. He'd marry her off first, just like he had with Therese.

But she wouldn't let that happen.

Angelique nestled her nose into Pierre's shirt and breathed in his scent — the wood-smoke and the herbs from whatever meal he'd made that morning for Miriam's breakfast.

"Do you need more to drink?" His breath tickled her neck.

"I'm doing better now, thank you." They'd already stopped several times for more water, and she was beginning to revive. She still felt weak and light-headed, but at least her senses were returning. She let her fingers brush against the curls of his hair at the back of his neck. The dark strands were thick and cool beneath her fingers.

Her heart began to race from his nearness. Even more than the fact that she was cradled in his arms was the knowledge that he'd cared enough to rescue her.

"Thanks for saving my life."

"Any time. Don't you know that's my

secret job? To rescue damsels in distress?"

Her fingers seemed to have a will of their own, and they trailed down his neck to his jaw to the scruffiness that always shadowed his face. She traced the strong line of his chin, relishing the tough bristles against her fingers.

His footsteps faltered.

She knew she should stop. She had no right to touch him with such familiarity. But gratefulness flowed through her along with something she couldn't quite name, something sweet and aching at the same time.

"I suppose you require payment for your daring rescues?" she said lightly.

He stopped abruptly and tilted his head back so his eyes met hers with an intensity that sent a burst of warmth swirling around her stomach. The shade of the surrounding woods only added to the darkness in his depths.

For a moment Angelique could almost believe they were the only ones on the island, that they were supposed to be together and that this was their home. The thick moss on the rocks and trunks of the trees, the bed of daisies underfoot, and the tall ferns closed in on them like the walls of a cozy cabin.

His gaze dropped to her lips. "I can think

of a payment I'd like more than anything."

The huskiness of his voice stirred the warmth in her middle. She glanced at his strong mouth. The memory of the kiss they'd shared came back to taunt her, the sweetness and softness of his lips. She couldn't deny that she'd thought of kissing him again.

And written across his face was the desire for another kiss as well. Slowly he bent his head toward hers.

She didn't want to resist. She could feel her body tensing with the keen awareness of what was to come. But a warning blared from her past, the warning that she couldn't allow herself to be hurt again.

"I can't, Pierre," she whispered, then turned her head and buried her face against his neck, needing to get away from the temptation of his kiss. But the salty dampness of his skin tempted her all the more. She pressed softly and realized that was a mistake as soon as her lips made contact.

He sucked in a sharp breath. "Angelique," he said hoarsely, "if you don't want me to kiss you, you sure have a strange way of showing it."

Embarrassment filled her, and she pulled her head away from his neck. For a long moment he stood unmoving, and she hardly dared to breathe for fear she'd lose her self-control all over again.

Finally he dragged in a shaky breath and started forward once more. Within minutes they reached the farm. He didn't say anything as he carried her into the cabin and lowered her into a chair.

Miriam fussed over her as best she could, her gentle fingers soothing her skin and her kind words adding balm to Angelique's confusion.

Although she wanted to ignore Pierre as he put together a salad of dandelion greens, wild mustard, and sorrel while the hominy cakes baked, she couldn't keep from following every move he made. For once, she was glad Miriam couldn't see her. Even so, Miriam grew silent and stared blindly at her from her spot across the table, as if she were trying to see straight into Angelique's soul.

"What kind of man believes he's helping someone by locking her in an attic?" Pierre was saying.

Angelique tore her attention from his back and the curls at his neck where she'd buried her fingers. "I suppose since he had such a hard time controlling Therese, he thinks he's doing the right thing by making sure I don't get into trouble."

"No one can compare you to Therese. She

always was selfish."

Like her mother. The words echoed in Angelique's mind, but she refused to give them voice. Angelique had always done her best to be the exact opposite of her mother. She guessed that was another reason why Ebenezer's strict standards hadn't been as oppressive to her as they'd been to Therese.

But what if she was more like her mother than she realized?

Pierre pulled the Dutch oven out of the glowing embers. "You're not going back to that inn ever again."

While she eagerly awaited the day when she could be away from Ebenezer, she wasn't at liberty to leave him yet. "You know I have to return."

"Non. You're not returning." His words had a finality that pushed Angelique up in her chair.

"And just where am I to go?"

"You can live here."

"I suppose it wouldn't matter to you if your reputation were tainted, but what about mine? What would everyone think if I lived with you?"

"I'll move out. I'll sleep on the beach with the Indians or find lodging at one of the inns."

Could she live with Miriam? But as rapidly

249

as the flicker of hope flamed, she doused it with the reality of her situation. "And when you leave? What will happen then? Ebenezer will find a way to punish me for turning against him."

"I'll make sure he knows he's done with you, that you're no longer his concern." Pierre crossed the cabin with the pan of hominy and placed it at the center of the table. Steam wafted out of the bubbling holes in the golden brown crust.

Angelique breathed in the tantalizing aroma, and her empty stomach gurgled.

Miriam gave a sad sigh. "Pierre, you're very kind to want to protect Angelique, but I'm afraid Ebenezer is more conniving than you realize."

"Not with me."

From the shadows on Miriam's face, Angelique had the feeling her friend was remembering what had happened to Therese the same way she was.

"Therese ran away," Angelique said through a constricted throat. "But Ebenezer gave her to one of the voyageurs staying at the inn anyway. He told the man where to find her and that she was his for the taking — for the right price of course."

Pierre straightened from cutting the hominy into big slices. Furrows formed across his forehead.

"The voyageur found her easily enough. He tied her up, slung her over his shoulder, and tossed her into his canoe. He left the next morning, and I didn't even have the chance to tell her good-bye."

Pierre shook his head, fury beginning to glow in his eyes. "No one made an effort to stop him?"

"Since Ebenezer took care of us all the years after our mother died, how could anyone question his decision?"

"They had every right to stop him. Therese wasn't an animal to barter."

"She was of marriageable age."

Pierre's shoulders stiffened, and his face became a mask of anger.

Angelique held her hands out in surrender. "So you see why I can't afford to earn Ebenezer's disapproval?"

"I should just kill him."

"Please, Pierre," Miriam said softly. "God's kept Angelique safe so far. In fact, it was a blessing, her living at the inn this winter. She had access to food and was able to share it with me."

"He almost killed her today."

"And don't forget," Miriam added, "Jean will be home soon, and they'll be married —"

"Non." The word filled the cabin with its vehemence.

Confusion flickered across Miriam's face. "But you said you think the Americans will be able to retake the island this summer."

Pierre turned away from them and paced to the fireplace. His shoulders slumped, and he was quiet for several long seconds, staring into the flickering flames. At last he said, "I don't know if the Americans will be able to win the battle. Every day they wait to attack, the British forces grow stronger. More Indian allies are arriving at the island, and now that Fort George is almost done . . ."

Miriam sat back in her chair and folded her hands. Angelique recognized it as the sign she was praying.

Pierre leaned against the mantel and bowed his head. From the way he was talking, it almost sounded as if he hoped the Americans would win. Whose side was he on? He hadn't wanted to talk about it with her, and she'd wanted to trust him, like she always had, that he was doing what was best even if she didn't completely understand.

"We'll be fine, Pierre," she said, wanting to offer him a measure of comfort.

He didn't say anything, and the tension radiating from his back was almost as thick as the humidity filling the small cabin.

He spun around and faced her. "Marry me, Angelique."

CHAPTER 15

Angelique froze.

Miriam's silent prayer turned into an urgent whisper.

"Oui," Pierre said as he stepped away from the hearth, the tension easing from his face. "Angelique can marry me."

Angelique stared at Pierre, her mind swirling with disbelief.

Pierre crossed the room toward her, his boots clomping with a confidence that chased away her shock. He dropped to one knee before her. The determination etched in his expression sent a shiver of anticipation through her.

When he reached for her hand and folded it between both of his callused hands, her heart lurched. He wasn't serious, was he?

A grin tugged his lips. "Let's get married."

She studied his face. His smile faded, replaced with a longing so ardent it almost took her breath away. With uncharacteristic seriousness, he lifted her hand to his lips and placed the gentlest of kisses there. "Angelique MacKenzie, will you do me the honor of becoming my wife?"

Everything within her cried out yes, yes, yes. She would marry him this very day and be his forever. But the words stuck in her throat.

"Please say yes." His eyes were filled with such certainty she could almost believe for an instant he really believed everything would work out fine between them.

Would everything work out? Pierre was always so confident about anything he set his mind to doing. And she'd always been willing to follow him wherever he led her. But could she blindly follow his plan this time? Miriam's whispered prayers drifted over Angelique and somehow seemed to urge her to use caution.

If Pierre was willing to marry her, how could she say no? Her whole being yearned for him. In fact, she longed for Pierre with a passion she'd never experienced with Jean. It was a passion that had only grown stronger over the past month of their being together, a passion almost frighteningly like what she'd seen in her mother.

He lifted her hand to his lips again, and this time the heat of his breath, the pressure of his lips, and the spark in his eyes spoke of a longing within him that matched hers.

"Pierre," she said breathlessly, slipping her fingers from his. How could she say no to him? She'd never told him no. She'd never needed to. Yet what he was asking was impossible, wasn't it? "How can we get married?" She finally managed a coherent question through the avalanche of confusion. "I can't — I won't — ever leave the island, and you can't stay."

He sat back on his heels, his eyes pleading with her. "Let's not think about the details right now. Let's marry and figure out everything else later."

She averted her eyes to block out his eagerness. If she looked at him any longer, she wouldn't be able to resist him. The truth was she *had* to resist him this time, even though everything within her shouted not to.

"We can't get married, Pierre." The agony of saying the words wrenched her insides and twisted painfully.

"Oui, we can."

Tears pricked her eyes. "You know as well as I do that our differences are too great. You belong to the wilderness and I belong here on the island." He started to protest again, but she cut him off with a touch of her fingers to his lips. "I'd never be happy living out of a canoe. I know you don't want that kind of life for a wife. And you'd never be happy living year-round on the island."

He didn't contradict her, though a part of her wished he would. The slow droop of his shoulders and the fading light in his eyes told her the reality of the situation was sinking in.

"If one of us sacrificed for the other," she continued, "we'd eventually grow resentful. I could never bear the thought that you'd hate me for taking away something so important to you."

"I'd never hate you, ma cherie."

Maybe he'd never hate her, but he hadn't said he loved her. Yes, he'd spoken those sacred words that long-ago day when she'd been just a girl. But couldn't he say them now too? If he wanted to marry her because he loved her and couldn't live without her, then let him say it.

She willed him to say it. Waited to hear the words.

Jean loved her. In fact, he'd always made it clear he adored her. How could she give that up for such uncertainty with Pierre?

"Oh, Pierre . . ." she whispered through her aching throat.

He was only reacting out of the danger of

the situation today with Ebenezer. Once he had the chance to clear his head and see the situation with more objectivity, he'd realize he didn't need to take such a drastic measure to keep her safe. Marriage was a serious affair, and he couldn't offer it to her so that he could be her hero. He had to think about the long-term consequences. Besides, she'd already promised herself to Jean.

"What about my commitment to Jean?" she asked.

At the mention of Jean's name, Pierre scowled. "Jean isn't the type of man who can make you happy. And even if he was, you can't tell me that you've ever felt with him what you've felt with me."

Angelique couldn't deny it. Jean had never stirred her blood the same way Pierre always had. But that didn't matter. At least that was what she'd been trying to tell herself. Somehow at that moment her inner admonition didn't ring true.

"Pierre, let's be honest with each other," she said, wishing he'd cross the room and put a safe distance between them, because even with Miriam in the room, the scruff on his cheeks seemed to beg her to reach out and caress it.

"Fine. Let's be honest."

"It won't work for me to marry you." She was surprised at how much it hurt to say the words. The pain cut deep inside, down into her soul, and she regretted saying them the instant they were uttered.

He didn't speak. Instead a spectrum of emotions played across his face, until finally resignation settled there. He stood and took a deep breath.

Miriam had grown quiet. Had she been praying for her to marry Pierre or Jean? Had God answered her the way she'd wanted?

"If you must go back to live with Ebenezer," Pierre said quietly, "the least I can do is make sure he won't hurt you again this summer."

She couldn't ask what he had in mind or warn him not to do anything rash that might make things worse. She couldn't speak past the disappointment clogging her throat. It rose swiftly and made her want to bury her face in her hands and sob.

She'd gotten exactly what she wanted. She'd convinced Pierre they weren't meant to be together.

Why then did she feel as though she'd just made the worst mistake of her life?

Pierre stood stiffly in front of Colonel Mc-Douall's desk in the man's office. Across

259

the hallway he could hear the dance instructor chanting the steps for a waltz, the rhythmical one, two, three and the tapping of a cane.

Even though he'd popped his head into the sitting room and smiled at Lavinia and Angelique and pretended to watch the dancing lessons with mirth, his heart was heavy — heavier than it had been in a long time.

He was trying to focus on the discussion between the colonel and his advisors, but his mind kept wandering to Angelique in the other room, to the rosy flush of her cheeks and the sparkle in her eyes, to the beautiful red of her curls and the graceful way her body moved.

His proposal last week had been on a whim. It had slipped out without any thought or planning. He told himself he'd only asked her to marry him for *her* sake, to find a way to protect her when he had to go.

And for a day or two afterward he'd beaten himself up for even suggesting marriage. He felt embarrassed for how rashly he'd behaved. Yet whenever he saw Angelique, he couldn't keep himself from thinking about marrying her, though he knew he shouldn't.

She'd said no. And her reasoning had made sense, hadn't it?

He'd been foolish to bring it up, and he'd been doing his best to put the silly proposal out of his mind. He'd tried to erase all his desire for her and replace it with the friendship they'd always had.

But every time he saw her, his longing for her only increased. He wanted her — wanted to kiss her, wanted to hold her, to run his hands through her hair and over her cheeks. He was surprised at the intensity of his physical reaction to her. But the emotional connection was just as strong too. He loved being with her, loved their laughing together and how they could talk endlessly, how they could do anything and still have fun.

The longer he stayed on the island, the harder it was getting for him to think about leaving her. The only way he'd survived the past week was to make sure he didn't spend time with her. That hadn't been too much trouble since she'd been busy with her lessons with Lavinia, had helped Lavinia distribute invitations for the dance, and was overseeing the cleaning of the government house. The house had a large room, often used for meetings, but now it was being transformed for the dance.

"Perhaps we should set out down Lake Huron and meet the Americans on their way up here," suggested a sergeant sitting in one of the chairs surrounding the imposing desk. The cigar smoke cast a haze over the room. The smoke, the stone walls, the dimness of the room all pressed in on Pierre, suffocating him, making him wish he hadn't come to this meeting.

"We can't keep putting off this confrontation," continued the officer. "Our soldiers are growing weary of waiting."

It was past the midpoint of July and the Americans still hadn't attacked. Pierre couldn't let his frustration show, but it nagged him night and day. He could only assume the American commander hadn't received his messages about the need to attack with all haste.

Now Fort George was done. With the help of the civilians, Colonel McDouall had completed the structure, which was really nothing more than an observation post since the place lacked its own water supply. But it would certainly discourage the Americans from attempting to retake the main fort from the rear.

"Maybe the Americans are trying to wear us down with worry," suggested another officer. "They'll wait long enough until we think we're safe, and then they'll attack."

A number of officers murmured their agreement.

"Durant," the colonel said in his Scottish brogue, narrowing his eyes on Pierre, "how far away is the American fleet? What have your sources told you?"

Pierre leaned against the cold wall, hoping to appear more nonchalant than he felt. "My sources say the Americans aren't anywhere near here yet."

That much was true. His connections had finally told him the American fleet had been delayed because of a disagreement over who was to be in command. At first, Major Holmes had been chosen, but eventually the command had gone to Colonel Croghan, a twenty-two-year-old Kentuckian. Pierre wanted to shake his head every time he thought about such a young man leading seven hundred American soldiers.

The last he'd heard, the fleet was planning to leave Detroit in early July. But he couldn't be sure when or even if they'd set sail. Whatever the case, it could only help the American cause if the British sailed down into Lake Huron for a naval battle. If so, the British would leave the island mostly undefended.

"The Indians are getting restless," he said

carefully. He knew he couldn't sound over-anxious for the British to leave. "I've heard rumors they're planning to depart for their hunting grounds if they don't have the bloodshed they've been waiting for."

The colonel nodded as he steepled his hands beneath his chin. "They are more than ready for a fight," he concurred.

Another officer blew out a great cloud of cigar smoke. "Then I agree. We should set out down the lake and meet the Americans on the way up. It would put an end to all the waiting."

"And it would be an offensive move rather than defensive," said another.

Pierre knew such a move would be completely foolish. If the majority of the British Army left to go off and start a fight, they'd lose the island.

For a long moment the colonel's face was drawn. He was less formal than other British officers Pierre had met, more down-to-earth and likable. He doted on Lavinia, and while he was strict with his regulars, he was also kind, and the men respected him.

The longer Pierre spent with the colonel and Lavinia, the harder the whole spying business was getting. At the start of the war two years ago, when he'd agreed to spy on the Americans for the colonel, he hadn't been walking with the Lord but was living a wild life. He hadn't given a second thought to sharing secret information in exchange for money. He hadn't really cared about the war, had only seen the chance to enrich himself.

After he'd turned his life back around, he'd decided he needed to stop spying. But by that point, the Americans had heard of his friendship with the British and had persuaded him to agent for them instead, to continue the relationship with the colonel but to use it to the Americans' advantage.

After some debate, Pierre had figured spying for the Americans was more noble and acceptable. He'd thought it would be a way to make up for his past, a way to help his family and country. He still was an American citizen, after all.

But now, after being home, after spying on Colonel McDouall, the guilt had piled up like a stone wall. The colonel and Lavinia trusted him, and here he was betraying them.

Pierre took a deep breath, attempting to push the weight off his chest, but it didn't budge. Was God trying to tell him something?

The faint lyrical sound of laughter wafted across the hallway from the sitting room, where Lavinia and Angelique were dancing. His thoughts flashed again to the moment in the tree with Angelique when he'd kissed her. Was that the moment he'd known he couldn't leave the island?

The hard truth was that he couldn't stop spying even if he wanted to. If he stopped, the colonel and other officers would know the truth about who he really was. Immediately they'd put a price on his head, and he'd be forced to flee for his life.

He'd have no choice but to leave Angelique and Maman behind. And how could he do that? What if the British suspected them too and prosecuted them as a result of his spying?

Non, he was stuck in the tangle of lies he'd spun for himself, with no easy way out.

"Would you like my honest opinion, Colonel?" Pierre finally asked.

The colonel nodded. "Of course, Durant."

"I don't think we should leave the island." His conscience prodded him to tell the truth, even if it wouldn't help the American cause. "As strong as we are on the water, we won't be able to win a naval battle against the Americans, primarily because the Indians won't be able to help us in the water from their canoes. They'll just get blown to pieces."

The office grew silent. Lavinia's chatter grew louder from the sitting room.

"Non," Pierre continued. "Since we have the Indians as allies, we'd be smarter to stay on land and use them to our advantage when the Americans attack us here."

The colonel nodded. "I was beginning to wonder about you, Durant. But you've given solid advice this time."

Pierre smiled with what he hoped was a charming grin, yet he had a sinking feeling that it was only a matter of time before the colonel discovered his true loyalties. He prayed the end of the war would come before that happened, or he'd be a dead man.

CHAPTER 16

Angelique flattened herself against the wall
of Lavinia's room, not daring to look in the
mirror to see the finished product — the effect of the hours of labor Lavinia had spent
that afternoon preparing her for the dance.
Instead she placed a hand over her mouth
and kneaded her rolling stomach.

She was going to be sick.

How could she possibly step outside the
door and face the world looking like this?
Her gown cascaded about her in wave after
wave of filmy silk. She slid her fingers
upward over the finest, smoothest material
she'd ever touched, until her fingers came
to the high embroidered waistline that
hugged her bosom.

She drew in a scandalized breath as she
had every time she'd noted the starkly
rounded curves that the drawstring of the
bodice and the stays beneath had thrust
upward until her bosom was fairly bursting

from the broad, square neckline. She didn't want to think about how much her gown resembled those her mother had once worn, but the thought came unbidden anyway.

With shaking fingers she tugged the bodice higher. Even though it wasn't as revealing as the neckline of Lavinia's beautiful golden gown, it was much too immodest for her.

After the years of wearing the shapeless high-collared clothes Ebenezer had required her to don, she felt almost naked.

"I can't go out there like this," she whispered to the empty room, to the discarded clothes strewn about among the ribbons, pins, and assortment of toiletries Lavinia had used to prepare them both.

If only she'd had the courage to tell Lavinia no. But over the past several weeks, as Lavinia had planned the dance and had the gown tailored just for her, Angelique had let the woman have her way. She'd gone along with the dance lessons, the instructions on how to hold herself like a lady, how to walk gracefully, how to eat properly, how to greet others, and even how to hold a fan.

Angelique hadn't believed the day of the dance would actually arrive. She'd hoped the Americans would come first and put an end to the British presence on the island once and for all — in spite of Pierre's reservations.

But no one had spotted even the slightest trace of the American forces. After nearly a month of preparing and laying up stores for a siege, both the British and the islanders had started to relax. As the hot days of July came to a close, some of the islanders had even begun to put aside the idea of an attack altogether. The summer would be ending all too soon on Michilimackinac. Why would the Americans attempt to take over the island and then leave themselves so little time to prepare for the long northern winter?

In fact, the mood at the fort that whole day had been festive, as if the British were already celebrating a victory. And Lavinia had been a flutter of excitement, declaring the dance to be the first civilized event of the summer. Even Ebenezer had been invited and had allowed Angelique to leave her duties early so she could ready herself for the dance at the fort with Lavinia.

Angelique lifted her hand to the curls next to her ears. Her head was bare of a cap, and Lavinia had piled Angelique's hair on top of her head, leaving a few loose curls dangling. "To tease the men," she'd said.

What would Ebenezer say when she showed up at the government house looking like a loose woman? Would he force her to return to the inn? Or would he bide his time and punish her later, when Lavinia left at the summer's end, when he no longer had the pressure of trying to keep her from complaining to her father?

Pierre had followed through on his promise to talk with Ebenezer and had warned him that neither he, Lavinia, nor the colonel would tolerate any more cruelty. But what would happen when they were all gone? Who would protect her from Ebenezer's anger then?

Angelique expelled a pent-up breath.

Why hadn't she just married Pierre when he'd asked? She had mentally slapped herself a thousand times since the day she'd turned down his proposal. Maybe he'd been right not to worry about the details of the future. If they were married, surely they'd figure out a way to work things out so that both of them would be happy.

But he hadn't brought up marriage again. Instead he seemed to be going out of his way to treat her like a friend. And she'd done her best to resume their friendly way of relating, especially since he'd obviously put thoughts of marrying her out of his mind. The ease with which he could do that startled her, even hurt just a little.

A soft rap on the door made Angelique jump. She reached for the gloves Lavinia had left for her on the bed and pushed a hand through the tight satin, wrestling the glove upward until it reached her elbow. With the short puffy sleeves of the gown, there was still too much skin on her arms showing. But what could she do about that now?

"Miss McDouall is waiting in the sitting room" came the voice of the girl who had been assisting them with their preparations. "She'd like you to join her so that you can walk over to the dance."

"Thank you. Please let Miss McDouall know I'll be right there." Angelique's fingers trembled as she worked the other glove over the stickiness of her palm.

She took in several deep breaths of the sugary-sweet perfume in the air and recalled the words Miriam had spoken many times over the past couple of years whenever her circumstances had grown unbearable. " 'He only is my rock and my salvation; he is my defense; I shall not be greatly moved.' "

Angelique wanted to believe God was as solid as a rock, as reliable as the limestone bluffs that hedged the island, and that He was a fortress as safe and secure as Fort George up on the highest hill. But after she'd been forsaken so many times in her life, how could she trust that He wouldn't leave her eventually too?

With a final tug on each glove, she spun to face the door, opened it before she could change her mind, and stepped into the hallway.

Voices and laughter came from one of the rooms down the long hallway that ran through the center of the officers' building.

Her heart quavered, but she forced one foot in front of the other until finally she reached the open doorway of the sitting room.

Lavinia, in all her golden glory, was perched on the edge of the settee. She smiled at Lieutenant Steele, who sat on one of the wing chairs next to her. He was dressed in his best uniform, his white pantaloons spotless, the buttons on his red jacket gleaming, the felt of his black hat brushed until it shone.

Another man stood on the other side of the settee with his back to the door. A navy tailcoat stretched taut across his wide shoulders, its long tails falling over gray pantaloons. His dark wavy hair had been combed into submission, although a curl here and there had revolted.

Pierre?

As if she'd spoken his name aloud, he turned. His ebony eyes rounded with first surprise, then wonder.

She smiled at him shyly.

At the sight of her, Lavinia stopped speaking mid-sentence and smiled. "There you are, Miss MacKenzie. I was beginning to think I would have to come after you myself."

Lieutenant Steele rose but gave her only the briefest of glances before he held out a hand to Lavinia.

"Does she not look wonderful?" Lavinia asked as she accepted the quartermaster's assistance to her feet.

"No one can compare with you tonight," Lieutenant Steele replied. "I don't believe I'll be able to take my eyes off you to look at anyone else."

Lavinia's laughter tinkled through the elegant room, her delight in his compliment bringing a flush to her cheeks.

"You must at least look at Miss Mac-Kenzie," she insisted. "Especially after all my hard work and the weeks of grueling effort to transform her into a lady."

The lieutenant glanced at Angelique and made a show of perusing her before turning his attention back to Lavinia. "You've outdone yourself, Miss McDouall. I do believe you've effectively erased all trace of the fish lass, even the smell."

Lavinia gave another laugh. "Pierre, what do you think of all my hard work in transforming Miss MacKenzie?"

Pierre's attention hadn't budged from Angelique. A silky white cravat tied about his neck couldn't hide the motion of his hard swallow. "She's stunning."

Angelique's lips trembled into what she hoped was a semblance of a grateful smile.

"I knew it." Lavinia clapped her hands together and stared at Angelique as if she were a masterpiece she'd finished painting. "I just knew I could do it."

"She's as beautiful as always," Pierre said, finally seeming to find his voice. "I don't think you've transformed her, Lavinia. You've only helped to uncover the beauty that's been there all along."

Lavinia's lips turned into a playful pout. "Why, Pierre, you are always the charmer, aren't you?"

The sourness in Angelique's stomach welled up. She'd known she was only a summer project for Lavinia, one of her many charity efforts. Is this what she was to face all evening? Would everyone see her only as Lavinia's project and offer compliments on

Lavinia's behalf while secretly harboring pity?

She started to back into the hallway. How could she endure the dance? It was all wrong. *She* was all wrong. She didn't belong in the gown, in the gloves, with her hair sitting atop her head like a jeweled crown. It was all just one step down the hill to becoming too much like her mother.

At her movement Pierre started toward her with quick steps. "You're right, Lavinia. I can be a charmer when I want to be. But I'm always honest. I never say anything I don't mean."

His eyes beckoned Angelique to stay. In his gentleman's attire he was more dashing than she'd ever seen him. And yet, even though he was clean-shaven and wearing the latest fashion, an air of ruggedness hovered about him that he couldn't shed. It was the same dark wildness that she'd always loved about him.

Her footsteps faltered.

"The truth is I've never met anyone as beautiful as Angelique." He continued toward her. "And she's even lovelier on the inside."

His words were as powerful as the adoration brimming from his eyes. They reached across the distance and soothed her. The

276

sweetness of them overpowered the uncertainty roiling inside. He was a good and loyal friend, and she was grateful for him.

Lavinia glanced between her and Pierre. "You are rather savage and uncivilized yourself, Pierre," she said with a forced laugh. "With your breeding and background, we certainly cannot rely on you to be the expert in beauty."

Pierre came to a stop only inches away from Angelique. "I know real beauty when I see it."

"Thank you, Pierre," she whispered, drawing hope from his kindness. Even if he was a charmer and had said the same thing to a hundred other young women, at least he was doing his best to ease her discomfort. And she loved him for it.

She loved him.

The truth sank deep inside like a precious gemstone.

Yes, she truly loved Pierre. And not just for his kindness at that moment, but for everything. She loved everything about him.

Her chest swelled with the knowledge, and it brought a smile to her lips. The love rolled around, warming her insides. She'd let herself fall in love with him that summer even though she'd warned herself to guard her heart.

Or maybe she had always loved him but had just been too afraid to admit it.

But she couldn't deny it any longer. She could only stare up at him, sure that he could see the glow of her love. How could she hide it? Did she even want to?

"Well, gentlemen," Lavinia said, starting across the plush rug at the center of the sitting room, "shall we depart?"

"I'm ready." Pierre's eyes warmed to the color of coffee, and his attention shifted to Angelique's lips.

"Lieutenant Steele, you may escort me to the dance." Lavinia's voice contained a petulance that Angelique hadn't heard there before. "I am apparently not beautiful enough for Pierre."

Pierre tossed a grin over his shoulder at the young woman. "Since I'm such an uncivilized savage, Lieutenant Steele is the better choice anyway."

Lavinia gave him a coy sideways look as she slipped her hand into the crook of Lieutenant Steele's arm.

The lieutenant's brows had furrowed together in a dark line, and he glanced at Pierre as if he were a pesky fly he'd like to squash.

Pierre bowed with an exaggerated flourish and waved for the couple to precede him into the hallway. Then he offered his arm to Angelique.

She slipped her gloved hand into the curve of his muscles. His solidness seeped into her and gave her fresh courage. With him at her side, maybe she could find the strength to survive the night.

Their clipped footsteps echoed in the empty hallway. The normally busy house was silent of the usual commotion, as most of the servants and officers were already at the dance. As they stepped out of the officers' quarters and into the warm summer evening, the peacefulness of the fort made Angelique almost forget they were at war.

There were still plenty of soldiers lounging around the soldiers' barracks, the unlucky men who hadn't been invited to the dance. Several groups were playing cards and stopped to stare as Lieutenant Steele escorted Lavinia past the center green toward the South Sally Port.

Angelique followed behind the couple with Pierre, who tucked her closer so that her arm brushed against his. He leaned in to her. "You're so beautiful you take my breath away."

His voice was husky near her ear. It unleashed a flutter in her stomach like waves lapping against a beach. "Lavinia's right. I'm sure you say that to all the women."

He pulled her to a stop, heedless of Lavinia and Lieutenant Steele strolling ahead.

The warmth left over from the summer day chased away the chill on her bare skin. Overhead, only the wisps of a few clouds tinged the clear blue sky. It was a perfect summer evening, and whether she was at the dance or not, she knew she needed to savor the all-too-fleeting beauty.

"I don't say that to all the women, ma cherie," he said softly, earnestness tightening the strong lines in his face.

"Well, maybe not all," she said.

"The way I feel with you . . ." he started, leaning even closer. "I've tried to deny my feelings over the past few weeks, tried to just be friends with you, but I can't. I've never felt this way about anyone else."

Her breath caught in her throat. His confession was everything she'd secretly wanted to hear but never thought possible. "I think you just like seeing me half unclothed."

His gaze dropped to the exposed skin above the neckline of her bodice, then to her neck and down to one of her arms. "I admit. I like seeing you in something other than the bag-like apparel Ebenezer forces on you. But it doesn't matter to me what you wear. You're always beautiful."

She couldn't keep from thinking back to that day he'd proposed to her, how sincere he'd been. Like now . . .

And once again she wanted to cry out at herself for turning him down. If he really cared about her, if his feelings for her were growing like hers, then why couldn't they make a marriage work?

Intense longing wrestled with reality, just as it had over the past weeks whenever she'd thought about him. Standing with him now, dressed in their finest, with his dark eyes glimmering with something she didn't understand but that sent shivers to her belly, she wanted to throw caution away. She wanted to turn back the time and pretend they were in Miriam's kitchen again, with him down on one knee in front of her.

"Pierre . . . I . . ." She couldn't just blurt out that she'd changed her mind about marrying him. What if he hadn't really meant it? Or what if he'd decided it was a stupid idea after all?

He waited, watching her face.

What if it was still a bad idea like it had been before?

"Miss Mackenzie and Mr. Durant," La-

281

vinia called from near the arched entrance of the fort. "You mustn't lag. Everyone will be waiting for our arrival."

"Are you sure you want to go to the dance?" Pierre asked without moving forward.

From the fort's position on the bluffs, the lake stretched out as far as the eye could see. She drew in a breath of air that hinted at the cooler days that would soon be upon them. "Where would we go instead?"

"Fishing?" The beginning of a grin played at his lips. "We still haven't had that contest to see who is really the master fisher."

"Fishing? Dressed like this?"

"True. You'd probably have an unfair advantage. When the fish see how pretty you look, they'll jump into your net just to be with you."

She laughed. "You can't admit I'd beat you fair and square, can you?"

His grin broke free.

"Miss MacKenzie," Lavinia said again more sharply, next to the sentinel on duty. "I really must insist that you stop dawdling."

Angelique wavered. Part of her longed to run off with Pierre. The very thought of being alone with him sent tingles all over her skin. But another part of her warned her against such rashness. Lavinia had gone to a great deal of trouble to prepare her for the event. She didn't want to think about the problems she might bring upon herself and Pierre if she defied the young woman.

Pierre cocked an eyebrow.

"I have to go to the dance," she said. "Besides, after spending the past two weeks learning how to waltz, I'd like to dance with you since you look so dashing."

"I do look dashing tonight, don't I?"

"Don't let it go to your head."

"Too late for that," he said, starting forward down the dirt path with more spring to his step.

She wouldn't tell him she thought he was handsome *all* the time, or that the real reason she wanted to dance with him wasn't because of how he looked. The real reason was because she wanted him to pull her close. She wanted to be in his arms, to feel his tender touch, and to hear the soft rasp of his breath near her ear. Such thoughts shamed her, yet she couldn't deny them.

They exited the fort through the front gate and made their way down the steep path cut into the side of the bluff until they reached the bottom, where the government building was located. The big brick house sat on the edge of town, surrounded by the vegetable gardens the British Army had

283

planted with hopes of providing fresh food to the troops.

The double doors stood wide open, the numerous windows as well. The spacious first-floor room was already crowded. All the furniture had been removed, except for a few chairs along the side and a long table laden with refreshments. A group of soldiers with a variety of instruments had formed a makeshift orchestra at one end of the room.

Angelique wanted to hide in a corner, especially when she saw Ebenezer filling a cup with spiced cider. Of course he hadn't allowed Betty to participate in "the lewdness," his description of the dance. He never let the girl go anywhere, especially now that she needed to take care of the son she'd borne him.

Lavinia pulled her away from Pierre and circled around the room with Angelique in tow, apparently determined to show her off to everyone. Angelique tried to ignore the openmouthed astonishment of many of the islanders who'd always scoffed at her. And she forced herself not to shiver when Lavinia paraded her in front of the officers, including the colonel.

The interest and lust that flared in the eyes of some of the men reminded her too much of the way men had looked at her mother. Her mother, however, had flaunted her beauty, enjoyed the attention of the men, and hadn't been able to resist the flattery. Surely Angelique would never sink so low. At least that was what she told herself as she tried to ignore the warning bells that sounded in the back of her mind.

Angelique was grateful when Pierre came over to her, linked his hand with hers, and glared at any man who stared at her too long.

She began to despair that Lavinia would never tire of the praise for her charitable efforts. Then when the orchestra started to play, Lavinia finally left her in peace. Angelique stumbled through the first waltz with Pierre, feeling exposed and awkward, aware of all the attention upon her. It came as no surprise to discover that Pierre was a graceful dancer, and he was good about smoothing over her mistakes.

Ebenezer stood next to the refreshment table talking with the island doctor. Although he kept himself busy tasting the delicacies on the table, she could sense his disapproval.

After several dances, she began to relax a little and enjoy being near Pierre. She focused on his lapel as he guided her around the floor. "Please don't let anyone else dance with me, Pierre."

Pierre's fingers lingered possessively on her waist. "Don't worry. I've spread the word among the men that you're mine. No one else gets to dance with you tonight."

"You did?" She relished the closeness of his body, the feeling of being protected by him.

"They're grumbling, but I promised a fist into the face of anyone who tried to take you away from me."

She smiled, not quite sure if he was teasing or being serious. "It's a good thing you scared them all away, because I don't want to be in anyone else's arms but yours."

"Not even Jean's?" Though he spoke the words lightly, they fell between them like a wall.

Jean. Dear, sweet, safe Jean.

"Pierre . . ." She paused. Why did Pierre have to show up after all these years and make her feel things that she'd never experienced with Jean?

"I'm sorry, ma cherie," he said, as if sensing the conflict warring within her. "I shouldn't have mentioned him. That was insensitive of me."

She nodded and pulled away from him. "I think I could use a breath of fresh air."

"Please forgive me." His fingers tightened

on her waist.

"I just need a minute to clear my head." Even with all the windows open and the breeze blowing in off the lake, the room felt stuffy. She needed to get away from the crowds, Ebenezer's glare, and the whispers and glances slanted at her. She needed a moment to think, to try to make sense of what was going on inside and the tumble of confusion over Pierre and Jean.

Pierre began gently guiding her through the dancing couples. "There's a grove of fruit trees behind the building."

"I'll be fine by myself for a few minutes," she said after they'd slipped out the back exit into one of the bigger vegetable gardens. She moved ahead of him toward the shade of the trees that bordered the large plot.

When he started to follow her, she held up a hand to stop him.

"I'm not leaving you out here unattended." He reached for her hand and captured it in his, as if it were the most natural thing in the world for them to hold hands.

"I won't be able to think with you here." She tiptoed past the winding vines of the bean plants, bunching a fistful of her gown to keep it from brushing the soil.

"What do you need to think about?" he asked.

"Everything."

"Please, let me help you."

"You can't help me when you're part of the *everything* I need to think about." Reaching the shade of a large apple tree, she spun to face him. She knew she should send him back into the building, that she'd never be able to think straight with him standing before her.

His head brushed against a low branch, and the twigs poked into his hair, finishing the job of tousling the locks he'd groomed. "Give me a try," he said. "I might be able to help you more than you realize."

She didn't dare look into his eyes, but instead peered at the calm, blue bay.

He stared at the water too. Then he slipped his arm around her and drew her to his side.

She held herself stiff only for an instant before leaning into him and laying her head against his shoulder.

"This place is magnificent, isn't it?" he said as a loon circled in the cloudless sky before dropping down and landing with ease on the water's surface.

"This island's the best place in the whole world."

"You're right."

"I'm right?" She'd been expecting his usual contradiction about how much he loved the island, but how he loved his adventures in the wilderness more.

He turned to face her. The seriousness of his expression brought her pulse to a stop. "This is the best place in the whole world," he whispered, "because you're here."

"Pierre, please don't —"

"Let me finish before you tell me no again. If after hearing me out you still say no, then I promise to paddle away from the island at the end of summer and I won't say anything about it again." He reached for her hands and grasped them between his. "I can't stop thinking about marrying you."

She began to tremble, and her knees grew weak.

"I can't sleep, I can't eat, I can't even work without thinking about wanting to be with you, Angelique."

She knew exactly how he felt, because it had been the same for her. As much as she'd tried to be normal with him over the past few weeks, she couldn't pretend any longer.

"I know you don't believe I could ever give up my fur trading. I know you think that eventually I'd be unhappy here on the island."

"It's true —"

"No. Maybe it would have been true once upon a time with the old Pierre, the man I used to be. But it's not true anymore, not since I repented and made peace with God. I'm trying to follow His plans for my life now. And maybe my papa was right about fur trading, that it only leads to the worst sins, that any godly man should stay as far away from it as possible."

She longed to agree with him. But every part of her resisted, because she knew she'd be lying to him. As much as she wanted him to stay, she knew she couldn't make him stay by being untruthful. "Your father wasn't right. Just because he let the fur trading corrupt him doesn't mean you have to let it do the same to you."

Pierre started to shake his head, but Angelique went on, "You don't have to give in to the temptations that come with fur trading. Your work doesn't have to lead you into sin. In fact, you can be a good example to the other men and show them what it means to live for God."

He was quiet with a faraway look in his eyes. Was he picturing his brigade and all the voyageurs he led?

"You're a natural leader, Pierre. If anyone can go out there and make a difference, it's you." She didn't want to convince him to return to the wilderness, but she couldn't let him believe anything other than the truth about himself. "God gives us all different passions, and you love what you do. You don't have to give it up, because He can use you wherever you are."

The music coming from the open windows of the government building drifted around them, blending with the gentle lake breeze that waltzed through the leaves overhead.

At last Pierre faced her again and brought one of her gloved hands to his lips. Through the thin silk the warmth of his kiss sent a tingle up her arm. "Thank you for your honesty, Angelique. You've always encouraged me and believed in me. Since coming home, I realize just how much I've always needed it and loved it."

The wind teased one of his wayward curls, and she couldn't resist reaching up and touching it. She wanted to peel off the constricting gloves and let her fingers slide through his hair with abandon. But she forced herself to do nothing more than smooth down the errant strand.

At the soft pressure of her fingers, his gaze collided with hers, sending a spark across the short distance between them.

"I know you understand how much I love fur trading." He fingered one of the curls next to her ear, his knuckles grazing her cheek.

"Fur trading is in your blood," she whispered.

"I won't deny it." He let his knuckles make a trail down her cheek to her chin. "But I've found something I love more than fur trading."

She held her breath and waited for him to speak the words she'd desperately wanted to hear from him.

"I love you, Angelique." The words became a caress as soft as his fingers on her face.

The tenderness in his eyes told her that he desired her as a woman, that he wasn't professing the love of a friend as he had the last time he'd spoken those words to her. Even so, she couldn't allow herself to be mistaken again.

"We're friends," she said slowly. "And I love you too."

"Friends?" His lips twitched into a smile. "Is that all I am to you?"

She waited, dared him to prove that his love was more than that of friends.

With a growing smile he circled one hand behind her neck and laid the other against the small of her back. He drew her in closer until she was leaning into him.

He dipped his head toward hers. With his cocky grin he teased his lips against hers with an agonizingly soft graze. He brushed first her bottom lip and then moved to her upper one. Her stomach quivered with each slow stroke until it fanned the fire within her, and she knew she couldn't go another second without a kiss from him.

She slid her arms around his neck, rose to her tiptoes, and shamelessly pressed into him so that he had no choice but to stop teasing her and give her a real kiss.

He chuckled softly, as if he'd gotten the reaction he wanted. He then delivered what she'd longed for. His lips crashed against hers, meeting her passion with his own. He took her captive, letting his kiss linger until she could hardly breathe.

He broke away from her all too soon and tilted his head back. Her knees buckled, but his strong arms held her against him.

He smiled. "If you ask me, that seemed just a tad more than a friendly kiss."

"Only a tad more," she managed to say.

"Admit it. You love me too."

She gazed up into his eyes. "I love you, Pierre. I love you more than life itself."

"Then let's get married," he whispered. "There's nothing stopping us. I want to stay with you on the island."

"What about your fur trading?"

"Maybe it was once in my blood. But you're all I want now."

With the truth of his words reflected in his eyes, she couldn't think of a single reason to say no to him. She pushed aside all the nagging doubts. She didn't want to say no to him ever again.

"Say you'll marry me," he begged as he nuzzled his nose against her cheek.

"Yes. Yes, I'll marry you, Pierre."

At her declaration, he pulled back. "You will?"

The surprise and delight in his eyes brought a smile to her lips. "I will."

"You're not just saying yes because I'm such a good kisser, are you?"

She laughed. "Of course that's why I want to marry you. What other reason could there possibly be?"

"Oh, let's see. Because you think I'm incredibly handsome, and sweet, and fun. And because I can cook the best stuffed whitefish in the world."

"And because you're very conceited," she teased.

"That too."

His gaze held hers for a long moment, filled with longing. When he moved for another kiss, her lips quivered with the anticipation of it. He bent his head, and she parted her lips with a sigh, hungry for more of him.

A flurry of shouts from the direction of the government house stopped Pierre short. He pulled back and glanced toward the back door, his brow crinkling.

The music had ceased, replaced by harsh barking commands. The loud blast of the trumpet sounded from the fort and echoed over the town and bay. They looked to the bluffs and the cannons pointed over the front stone wall of the fort in perpetual readiness for an attack.

Pierre's countenance turned grave, and he reached for Angelique's hand. "Come on. Something's wrong."

As they hurried through the garden, her mind scrambled to make sense of the commotion and the shouts. By the time they made their way through the kitchen and back into the big room where everyone had gathered for the dance, Angelique was breathless.

She ran into Pierre's back when he halted in the nearly deserted room. Through the open front door they could make out the red coats of the British rushing up the path that led to the fort. Lavinia hurried away on the arm of Lieutenant Steele, the gold of her gown glinting in the evening sunlight.

The musicians were hastily packing their instruments, while the remaining townspeople were busy gathering their belongings, their faces reflecting alarm. Ebenezer stood by the dessert table. He was filling his pockets with jam tarts.

"What happened?" Pierre demanded.

Ebenezer took a quick step away from the table and hid his hands behind his back. "The Americans are on the way."

"How do you know?"

"An Indian messenger arrived with the news that the American fleet burned the British fort at St. Joseph's to the ground and also seized and destroyed a North West Company ship full of trade goods over at Johnson's Sault Sainte Marie post."

Pierre began to remove his tailcoat, his face contorted into a scowl. Angelique wished she could drag him back out under the apple tree and pretend that none of this was happening.

He tossed his coat aside onto an empty chair and went to work on the cravat around his neck, yanking it as if it were choking him. "That means they'll likely be here within a day or two."

"That's what the colonel thinks," Ebenezer said.

"How many ships?" The hardness of Pierre's tone sent a tremor of fear through Angelique.

"Five schooners."

Pierre threw his necktie on top of his coat. He turned to Angelique, his eyes as steely as his voice. "I want you to go up to the fort and stay there with Lavinia in the officers' quarters."

Everyone knew the building would be the safest place on the island during an attack.

She started to nod, but Ebenezer shot her a look that silenced her. "She's not going anywhere but back to the inn with me."

"She belongs in the fort."

"I'm in charge of her," Ebenezer said. "I'll say where she goes, not you. Especially when she's dressed like a harlot."

Angelique gasped at the insult. Pierre growled and in two long strides crossed toward Ebenezer. He grabbed the man's shirt at his chest, half lifting and half shoving him back into the dessert table. Several serving platters crashed to the floor.

Pierre raised his fist and aimed it at Ebenezer's face. His arms stretched the seams of his shirt, revealing the bulk of taut muscles beneath.

Ebenezer cowered, as if waiting for the first strike.

"Pierre, no!" Angelique called.

But Pierre had already swung. His fist came in contact with Ebenezer's nose with a sickening crack.

Ebenezer cried out as blood spurted from his nose. Pierre pushed him up against the table harder and swung again. And again. With each punch Ebenezer wailed in pain.

"Stop!" Angelique screamed at Pierre.

But he pounded Ebenezer with unrelenting strength. Fear slithered into Angelique's throat and constricted her breathing. He was going to kill Ebenezer if she didn't stop him.

She threw herself at Pierre's back. "Stop, Pierre. Please stop!" She latched on to his arm, wrestling him, heedless of the fact that she might get hurt in the process.

At the contact of her body against his arm, he froze. He sucked in a breath and tore his attention from Ebenezer. It took several seconds for his eyes to clear and to focus on her instead.

"Pierre, please . . ." she whispered, the desperation in her voice finally penetrating through his anger. "Let Ebenezer go. You won't solve anything by hurting him."

He glanced again at Ebenezer, who had crumpled to the floor. He was clutching the edge of his sleeve to his nose.

At the sight of the blood, Pierre staggered back and groaned. "What have I done?"

Angelique released her hold on his arm and found that she was shaking. "It's all right," she said, hoping to reassure him. But the truth was, the force of his violence had frightened her.

He wiped his arm across his eyes as if he could wipe away the sight of his brutality.

Angelique went to Ebenezer and knelt beside him. "I'll walk him back to the inn and take care of his injuries."

With a moan Ebenezer let her help him to his feet. Pierre didn't make a move to stop her.

Ebenezer leaned heavily against her as she shuffled with him toward the door. The blood from his nose ran down his fingers into a rivulet on his arm, dripping onto her blue-green gown and streaking it.

As she stepped out the door, she waited for Pierre to say something — anything — but he'd hung his head and was letting them go.

Their beautiful moment alone in the garden already seemed like a dream. Had it really happened? Had he really told her that he loved her? Or had it all been just a mist that would soon disappear with the first rays of the morning sun?

CHAPTER 17

Pierre couldn't see where he was going in the early morning fog as he paddled his canoe through the grayness. Instead he let instinct guide him. His innate sense of direction and intimate knowledge of the lake and island had always held him in good stead.

After days of storms, the rain had finally ended last night. He'd told the American Colonel Croghan if he wanted to attack, that morning would be the best time.

The mist still hung heavy, but it would burn away once the sun rose high enough. The British knew little about the island, and they wouldn't realize the fog was lifting until it was too late and the American forces had already landed. At least that was what he'd planned with Colonel Croghan during his midnight trip off the island. It hadn't been the first sleepless night over the past week and a half since the American fleet had shown up. In fact, he'd had too many to count.

Pierre was beginning to think Colonel Croghan and Captain Sinclair didn't know what they were doing. They'd spent the first several days of their so-called frontal attack of the island exchanging harmless fire with the British. During the process, Captain Sinclair had learned that the American ships' guns couldn't be elevated high enough to enable them to hit the fort. The eighteen cannons on the *Lawrence* and the *Niagara* were practically useless.

If the gunfire could have reached the fort to bombard it, the Americans might have been able to retake the island within a day or two. Instead, the useless fire had fallen against the cliffs and gardens below. Thankfully no one had been hurt, since most of the residents had taken refuge inside the fort.

The morning after Lavinia's ill-fated dance, when the British sentinels had sighted the American fleet moving toward Michilimackinac, Colonel McDouall had issued the orders for everyone to move up to the fort, and by sunset the village had been deserted.

Pierre let his paddle drag in the water, turning his canoe toward his usual hiding spot in the secluded area of the coast, where none of the British soldiers on patrol would be able to discover his treachery.

If anyone stopped him, he could always explain that he'd gone out to spy on the Americans. Colonel McDouall still believed he was working for the British. But since the dance, his friendliness had cooled considerably. Pierre hoped it had more to do with Lavinia than the colonel suspecting anything about him.

Of course Lavina had been upset that he'd danced with Angelique the whole time, that he hadn't let any of the other men have a chance with her. And she'd probably complained to her father about him. He suspected the real reason she was offended was because he hadn't made *her* the center of his attention at the dance. It hadn't mattered that she'd had the undivided attention of Lieutenant Steele and nearly every other man on the island; she wanted his too.

At least she'd allowed Angelique and Maman to stay with her in the officers' quarters. She might be a bit arrogant like many of her class, but overall she had a kind heart. She wouldn't turn away anyone in need. He could rest easy on his missions knowing Angelique and Maman were both tucked away in the safest place on the island.

Pierre pulled the paddle up, rested it on the edge, and let the waves carry him toward the shore. The lake was much calmer this morning than it had been the other times he'd gone out. He was grateful for the easy trip back to the island.

He wiped his hand across his eyes, fighting a heavy weariness. The mist had soaked into his clothes, making him shiver in the cool morning air. What he really needed was to go back to the farm, do the chores, and then sleep for a couple of hours. But there was no time for any of that. The Americans would be arriving on the north end of the island as soon as the fog burned away. Hopefully they'd be able to take the British by surprise.

He had to make sure the landing went according to plan.

With a breath that drew from his last reserves, he plunged the paddle back into the lake and began the steady rhythm he'd practiced over the years, first one side of the canoe and then the other.

The bow scraped against something.

He rammed the paddle deeper, pushing backward. Had he hit a boulder, and if so, how? He knew the island so well that he could navigate the shoreline blind and still not have trouble.

He strained to see through the mist that blocked even the hand he raised in front of his face. For an instant the fog thinned and he caught a glimpse of the side of another birchbark canoe . . . and a tumble of red curls.

"Angelique?" he called.

"Pierre!" came her surprised reply.

He steered in the direction of her voice, bringing his canoe alongside hers. He fumbled blindly, found the edge and latched on, holding the vessels together.

"What are you doing out here?" Her question came at the same time as his.

"You shouldn't be out here," he answered, dodging the truth. "You should be back in the fort where it's safe." The thought of her being outside the walls of the fort, with the imminent threat of a battle with the Americans, turned his blood cold.

"The colonel wanted me to fish this morning. He's worried they'll have another shortage of food."

"I don't care if every soldier in the fort is starving, you shouldn't be out here." How dare the colonel let a young woman venture out alone? He knew the colonel was growing more concerned every day that the American fleet was sitting in the harbor and blocking supply ships from reaching the island. Not only was the colonel needing to feed the soldiers but he was providing for the Indian allies as well. With so many mouths to feed, the supplies never lasted long enough.

Even so, the colonel shouldn't have allowed Angelique to leave the fort. "Why didn't he send a couple of his men to fish instead?"

She didn't answer. She didn't need to. They both knew why Colonel McDouall had sent her. She could make a catch. And the British didn't know the first thing about fishing in the lake. Even if they had attempted it, they didn't know the island or how to navigate through the dense fog.

"You shouldn't have come." He had the urge to march up to the fort and yell at the colonel for sending a girl out, no matter how well she could fish. "I'm taking you back to the fort right now."

"I'm fine, Pierre." She sounded almost amused at his concern. "Besides, I needed a break from Lavinia's perfume."

He couldn't seem to muster any amusement at her attempt at a joke. The situation was too grave. He didn't want to think about what would happen if she got caught outside the fort during the battle. "Lavinia's perfume is much better than the stench of blood."

"Blood?" Alarm tinged her voice. "Whose blood? Are you hurt?"

"I'm just cold and tired." He bit back the revelation of the upcoming attack and his part in it. She didn't need to know about his secretive dealings. If something happened to him and he was implicated for spying, he didn't want anyone to turn around and try to hurt her.

"How's Maman?" he asked, hoping to divert her attention to another subject.

"She's as well as always."

"She's not too mad at me for forcing her to go to the fort?"

"No one can stay mad at you for long."

He leaned across the distance between them. It seemed like ages ago that he'd held her and kissed her in the garden at the dance and proposed to her again. Had she really said yes or had he only dreamt it?

"Then you're not mad at me any more for beating up Ebenezer?"

"I was never mad at you."

"Disappointed in me?" He was disappointed in himself. He'd thought he was changing, becoming a better man, pleasing God with how he lived. But he'd let his temper get the best of him. Even if Ebenezer

306

had insulted Angelique in the most debasing way, he shouldn't have hit him.

Angelique's fingers found his on the edge of the canoe. She squeezed his hand. "You're a good man, Pierre. You want to do what's right. But sometimes we struggle to do the good we know we ought to."

He nodded. "I seem to have a war raging inside me. I tell myself I'm going to do the right thing, but then I end up doing the opposite."

"Don't be too hard on yourself. At least you're learning from your mistakes, and you have your whole life to practice doing what's right."

The mist swirling between them parted for a moment so that he could clearly see her pretty face. He reached out and caressed her cheek. "I've missed you this week."

She leaned into his hand. "I've missed you too."

"Have you told Maman about us?"

"No," she said slowly. "We're never alone. Lavinia's always there, and she invited some of the other island women to take refuge in the building as well."

He hadn't told Maman yet either. He'd been so panicked to secure her safety in the fort that he hadn't taken the time to inform her of his plans to give up fur trading and

307

marry Angelique. Maman would likely be happy he was doing what his father had wanted — staying home and helping with the farm. But he wasn't so sure she'd be happy he'd won Angelique's affection away from Jean.

He'd reasoned that Angelique had the right to choose between them, that if Jean had loved her enough, she wouldn't have fallen so easily into Pierre's arms.

"We'll tell Maman soon," he said, forcing more confidence than he felt. "Once we get through all the danger."

And what about Jean? How would they tell him? The unasked question hung between them.

Although he hadn't seen Jean in any of his visits to the American fleet, he'd heard there were several former island residents who were part of the United States Army. If the American attack succeeded, there was the very real possibility they would get to see Jean soon, maybe even by the day's end.

"Speaking of danger, we need to get you back to the fort as soon as possible." He gave her canoe a gentle push to get her started.

She didn't protest. She knew as well as he did that the sun would soon burn the fog away. Even now the air was lightening and growing warmer. It would only be a matter of thirty minutes or so before it would disappear altogether, replaced by bright summer sunshine.

They paddled swiftly the short span to the shore, hid their canoes among the tangle of overgrown reeds and silverweed grass, and then started through the woods. Pierre carried the two dozen fish she'd caught. With each long stride he took, his sense of urgency grew until he was practically jogging. Angelique's long skirt and bare feet slowed her down, and she began to fall behind.

A sudden boom like that of cannon fire stopped him. He froze, stifling his heavy breathing, straining to listen. Another boom soon followed. Were the British shooting off their cannons?

Even as he prayed that was the case, frustration burst through him. The cannon fire was too far away and was coming from the north side of the island. It couldn't be the British. It had to be the American fleet, already having dropped anchor where he'd instructed them to.

But why in the world were they firing? Especially when they'd planned on a surprise landing.

Angelique's labored breathing filled the air behind him. "What is it?" she asked.

"Are the Americans attacking?"

He could only shake his head at the idiocy of Colonel Croghan. If Angelique could figure out what the bombing meant, then the British troops and their Indian allies would be entrenched in fighting position in no time. So much for taking advantage of the mist and launching a surprise attack.

His body tensed with the need to sprint to the northern shore and discover what had happened to their carefully laid plans. He glanced through the dense woods that lay between them and the fort. Angelique would be safe for the last two hundred yards on her own, wouldn't she?

She looked up at him, still attempting to catch her breath, her eyes as trusting as always. Angelique was a smart girl. If she hurried, she'd be fine. He knew that.

Even so, he hesitated. "Promise me you'll go straight to the fort and lock yourself away with Lavinia in the officers' quarters until this is all over?"

"Where are you going?"

"I need to find out what's happening."

"Can't you come back to the fort with me?"

He shook his head, draping the strings of her fish over her shoulders. "I have to do my duty, Angelique."

"Duty to whom?"

There wasn't a hint of condemnation in her tone, only curiosity. But the question stirred guilt within him anyway. "It's better for you not to know." He spun away before she could see the truth in his eyes. He didn't like all the guilt that had been eating at him lately, first in how he'd handled his anger toward Ebenezer, and now for his duplicity in the war. "Hurry back to the fort," he said over his shoulder as he started running.

For a long moment he could sense that she hadn't budged, that she stood watching him dodge the low-hanging branches and leap over windfall. He was tempted to turn around, to rush back to her. He could think of nothing he wanted to do more than to kiss her and hold her tightly in his arms. Yet he forced himself to keep running. Tomorrow he would kiss her.

If he lived through today.

Angelique stood rooted to the same spot long after Pierre had disappeared through the thick woods.

The booming continued to echo in the northern part of the island. Her heart thudded at the thought that Pierre was running into the line of danger.

A long bugle call sounded from the fort.

She was sure it was a call to action, which meant the British soldiers would soon be marching out to meet the Americans. The Indians would likely join in the fight.

Pierre was right. She'd be safest inside the fort.

Was that why he'd been in such a hurry to get her back to the fort? Had he known about the impending battle? She hadn't thought to question why he'd been out on the lake in the mist or why his face had been lined with exhaustion.

He'd been out communicating with the Americans. She was certain of it. Although she'd suspected he was spying and had figured that was why he'd been on the island that first morning he'd come back, he hadn't made any mention of his allegiance to the Americans.

He'd played his role as a friend to the British flawlessly. She'd almost begun to believe he really was an ally with the British, especially after seeing the kind of relationship he had with Colonel McDouall and Lavinia.

Angelique took several steps toward the fort, trying to ignore the unease rolling around her stomach. She wasn't sure she liked the idea that Pierre had been deceptive with the colonel and Lavinia.

While she knew those kinds of things happened in war, she didn't want to believe Pierre would resort to lying, not now when he was attempting to live for God. And she didn't want to think of the potential danger if the British learned of his treachery.

She let the lines of fish drop from her shoulders to the ground. With dread tapping a warning, she swung around and began to race after him. She didn't know what she could possibly do to keep him from getting into trouble, but she couldn't hide away in the fort.

When she reached the edge of the forest that bordered the Dousman farm, she stopped and listened, her breath coming in short gasps. The cannon fire had ceased and an eerie silence had descended over the island. To the east she heard the neighing of a horse and caught sight of a contingent of Redcoats near a ridge that overlooked the farm.

She hesitated. She didn't dare cross the open field ahead. With a glance around, she spotted their thinking tree, the home to the great horned owls, the same cedar she'd climbed with Pierre earlier in the summer when he'd kissed her for the first time.

She made her way through the brush to the tree and began to climb it. The tree's high branches would make the perfect hiding spot and also provide her with a lookout. She'd be able to see the distant northern shore and perhaps even be able to glimpse Pierre.

A whisper of caution urged her to retreat to the fort, where Pierre expected her to be. "I didn't promise him I'd go," she muttered to herself. "I'll only stay for a little while, just until I make sure he's not in danger."

It didn't take long for Colonel McDouall to arrive with more soldiers. They dug in on the higher ground, making quick work of chopping several trees and angling them against boulders to form a protective wall.

As the additional soldiers moved into view, Angelique shuddered. Almost every British soldier on the island had assembled for the battle. The colonel had obviously not left many to guard the fort.

On the opposite side of the farm in the woods that edged it, she caught sight of the United States Army moving among the trees, the sun glinting off their polished swords. When the soldiers finally began to move out into the open fields near Dousman's farmhouse, Angelique released a pent-up breath.

The United States Army was at least double the size, if not triple. They would hopefully be able to outmaneuver the British. She strained to see Pierre. Would he be with the Americans or would he return to the British side and continue his charade?

As the Americans moved into two long battle lines, the British Royal Artillery opened fire. Angelique cringed into the trunk of the tree, covering her ears against the deafening noise. Smoke and dust clouded the air around the field, preventing her from taking stock of how the American forces were faring against the fire.

Her body tensed during the long minutes of waiting, until finally the haze cleared enough for her to see that except for creating some confusion among the American ranks, the fire had fallen short of the target. For a while the American artillerists returned the fire, but they were well off their intended targets too, and finally the cannons on both sides became silent.

Again Angelique peered through the smoke, studying both sides, praying for a glimpse of Pierre. Her stomach gave a low rumble from having skipped breakfast, and her backside was numb from sitting in one position for so long. While the evergreen branches fanned around her, providing cool shade, the stickiness of the summer day penetrated her hiding spot. It wouldn't be long before she was hot and thirsty. Should she go now, while she still had a chance?

Her eyes swept over both sides one more time and came to rest on the broad shoulders of a man approaching Colonel McDouall, who was mounted on a horse well behind his soldiers.

She sat forward. The swaggering steps belonged to only one man. Pierre.

He halted before the colonel and spoke at length, motioning with an arm to the south, to the rear of the British position. Within seconds of their conversation the colonel shouted orders to one of the regiments and pulled part of his force away from the oncoming threat of the United States Army. He charged off with his men through the woods in the direction of the fort, leaving one of his captains in charge of the troops that remained.

What had happened? Had Pierre given the British troops information that would help or harm the Americans?

She wanted to believe he was helping the Americans, but she didn't know what to think anymore. Pierre began to edge his way back into the woods, slinking away while the British were busy regrouping the remaining troops. Angelique watched his every move until he disappeared.

Her heart urged her to follow him, but at the snap of a branch below, she froze. There in the shadows of the trees she saw Indians, squatting among the trunks and hiding behind boulders.

With a hushed gasp she flattened her back against the cedar, gripping the sticky bark with shaky fingers. Had they seen her? She closed her eyes and waited, prayed they wouldn't spot her and climb up after her. After holding her breath until her lungs burned, she finally exhaled and dared to peer through the branches to the surrounding woods.

She counted at least two dozen Indians hiding around her. They were painted for war and brandishing clubs, hatchets, and even a few muskets. Angelique's initial assurance in the strength of the Americans quickly faded. She had no doubt the entire woods surrounding the farm field were full of the Indian allies.

They were silent, their bronzed bodies taut, their attention focused on the American soldiers who had begun to march forward.

One of the American officers and his bodyguard moved out in front of the rest. The Americans were obviously hoping to take advantage of the smaller number of

British troops that were left. If only they knew the danger that lurked in the shadows.

Angelique wanted to scream, to warn the approaching troops of the ambush, but she found she couldn't move and couldn't make her voice work. No matter how hard she tried to speak, fear clamped its hand around her throat and squeezed tight.

The remaining British forces marched toward the Americans and pushed their artillery with them. One of the Indians arose and lifted his musket, aiming it directly at the American officer at the front of the company. The Indian next to him stood and aimed his gun at another officer.

At the bang of the gunfire, the rest of the Indians jumped up and released piercing war cries. They poured from their positions, leaping toward the American troops with raised clubs and hatchets.

The bullet from one of the Indians hit the officer who'd been in the front, killing him instantly. He crumpled forward, his sword and cap flying in front of him as his body struck the earth.

More shots pounded the air. A bullet tore through the arm of one soldier at the same time an Indian hatchet embedded in the chest of another. Horror paralyzed Angelique, forcing her to watch even though she wanted to run as far away as she could and never look back.

For long agonizing moments the United States Army was in disarray and began to fall back, leaving behind their wounded and dead. In the chaos, only one man attempted to drag off one of the wounded soldiers. He moved with speed and agility, blending in so that she hardly would have noticed him, except that he wasn't in uniform and his hat had been knocked off, revealing dark curls . . .

Pierre! Her mind shouted his name, yet nothing came forth from her mouth. With growing terror she watched him scramble backward toward the woods, dragging the wounded American soldier by both arms. Bullets whizzed around him even as the Indians continued to strike with fierceness.

Her body tensed as she waited for the first bullet to hit Pierre. And sure enough, the next instant he fell backward, disappearing with a crash into the tall brush. All she could think about was that he'd been hit by a stray bullet. That he would end up lying there wounded and bleeding to death. And that he needed her.

Angelique climbed down the branches until she half fell, half jumped to the ground beneath. She didn't stop to brush off her hands or to see if anyone had noticed her. She couldn't think of anything but finding Pierre and helping him.

Her heart raced as she ran in the direction where he'd disappeared. When she reached the area, he was no longer in sight. But all she had to do was follow the trail he'd made dragging the body, the blood from the man's wounds smearing the leaves with bright crimson. And she prayed that Pierre's blood wasn't mingled in.

The war whoops and steady gunfire raged behind her. She refused to think about what would happen if the Indians retreated into the woods and found her there.

Instead she forced herself to use every skill Pierre had ever taught her about tracking. When she lost the trail of blood, she decided that Pierre had slung the wounded soldier over his shoulder and had started carrying him. His heavier footsteps were easier to follow, along with the trail of broken stems and crushed wildflowers and only a few smears of blood.

She whispered a desperate prayer that Pierre wasn't injured too badly. Eventually she figured out where he was headed and picked up her pace.

Her labored breathing drowned out the battle noises in the distance. She didn't care what else was happening on the island anymore. She didn't care if the Americans won or lost. All that mattered was making sure Pierre was safe.

She ducked under a fallen tree and then crawled on her hands and knees up an incline until she reached the dark open mouth of a small cave, the cave they'd dubbed Pirate's Cove when they'd been younger — playing that they were pirates hiding their treasure. She paused, sat back on her heels, and brushed her loose hair off her sticky forehead.

Below, the lake spread out clear and blue. She could see all the way to St. Ignace and could almost pretend the day was just like any other summer day, that the gunfire was only the usual target practice coming from the fort.

But then the blood and carnage she'd witnessed on the battlefield flashed before her mind. No. This was no ordinary day. It was as if the gates of hell had opened and revealed the horrors there.

With a fresh shudder she ducked her head and crawled beneath the overhanging vines and branches that hid the gaping cavern. A cool mustiness greeted her. She started to whisper Pierre's name when a hand slid across her mouth and cut off her breath.

Then an arm wound around her neck, strangling her.

CHAPTER 18

The hand at her mouth was slimy with the metallic scent of blood. "Don't move" came a harsh whisper.

It was Pierre. She sagged back against him and let the solidness of his chest hold her up. It didn't matter that he didn't know it was her. She pressed a kiss against his palm, tasting the saltiness of blood, and she prayed it wasn't his.

His grip fell away and he spun her around, lifting his hands to her face, caressing her cheeks. "Angelique?" His whisper was an echo of surprise.

"Yes." Her hands moved to his arms, to his chest, searching for a wound. "Are you injured?"

"Non, ma cherie. I'm fine."

She expelled a long sigh, then jerked away at the realization of her forwardness. "I thought maybe you'd been shot."

"What are you doing here?" The surprise

evaporated, and his voice became hard. "You're supposed to be in the fort."

"I couldn't make myself go back, not without knowing you were safe."

"How did you know I was here?"

"I saw you pull the wounded soldier from the battle and I tracked you here."

He released her and groaned. The coldness of the cavern slinked around her, and she hugged her arms across her chest.

"Then you were at the battle?"

"No one followed me," she said quickly. "They're all still fighting."

"I'm not worried about being followed. I'm worried about you getting hurt."

"What about the soldier?" she asked, glancing at the prostrate form of the wounded man. Finally her eyes began to adjust to the light coming from the shaded opening of the cave.

"You shouldn't have come. I can't do anything else now until I take you back and make sure you're safe inside the fort."

"Don't worry about me. I'll be fine. I was fine all winter —"

He grabbed her arms, cutting off her words. "Don't tell me not to worry, that you'll be fine. Not when I'm scared to death that something will happen to you."

"You didn't tell me you'd found yourself

a woman, Pierre" came a weak voice from deeper in the cave. "Sounds like you're having a lovers' quarrel."

Pierre didn't respond, though his grip on her arms tightened. She didn't budge. Something in the soldier's voice drew her attention.

"Who is it, Pierre?" The question from the soldier was stronger this time, and his voice sounded familiar.

She gasped. "Jean? You pulled Jean from the battle?"

Pierre nodded.

Jean. Her Jean was there. And he was injured. A fresh burst of anxiety broke through her chest. Before Pierre could say anything more, she wrenched away from him and hurried across the cave toward Jean.

Once she was beside him, her pulse thudded with nervousness. "Jean, it's me. Angelique."

"Angelique?" He pushed himself to his elbows. Through the faint light she could see the outline of his face. The beard and mustache were new since he'd left the island. His dusty blond hair was longer. But otherwise he seemed unchanged.

She knelt next to him, willing herself to feel some enthusiasm for seeing him again, even the tiniest amount of joy. Yet besides concern over his injury, all she felt was a strange emptiness.

He let himself fall back to the dirt floor, as if the effort to raise himself had completely exhausted him. He held out a hand. "Angelique, is it really you?"

"Yes," she whispered, putting her hand in his. "It's really me."

A smile lit his grime-streaked face, and for a long moment the tight lines of pain eased. He brought her hand to his chest and laid it near his heart. "Angelique, my sweet girl."

Pierre edged next to her, and she could feel the heat and strength of his body. He had to crouch low under the slanted ceiling of the cave. He let his shoulder brush against hers with a familiarity that made her cringe with shame. She couldn't let Jean see them together. Not here, not when he was wounded.

"Where are you hurt?" She scanned his uniform through the darkness.

"It's not too serious." He pointed toward his lower body. He grimaced and was obviously fighting back a contortion of pain. "Took a bullet in my leg. That's all."

Pierre leaned against her again. To break the contact with Pierre, she bent over Jean and searched for his wound. Her fingers found the wet spot in his trousers below his knee. The fabric was saturated. He'd lost a lot of blood.

She brushed against a length of ripped linen tied tightly above the wound. At least Pierre had attempted to stem the flow. Even so, the ball needed to be removed from his flesh before infection set in.

At her slight touch, he hissed. "Are you in a lot of pain?" she asked.

"I've forgotten about it now that you're here." Jean's voice was pinched, but he held her hand against his heart as if that were the healing touch he needed. And he smiled again at her. Even through the darkness she could see his eyes glimmering with happiness. "You look so beautiful. Just the sight of you is enough."

She returned his smile and let him stare at her. In her usual plain garments she knew she was nothing special to look at. She wished she wanted to stare at him in return, but his presence, his lanky body, his scruffy face, his kind eyes didn't stir anything in her the way the sight of Pierre did.

He shifted and his features contorted in pain. His hold on her hand tightened, his breath coming in gasps. "I'm sorry we have to meet like this, Angelique," he said haltingly. "This wasn't the reunion I'd dreamed about."

"Shhh," she whispered, smoothing his hair off his forehead. "Just rest now."

He closed his eyes and didn't move. Had he passed out?

"We need to get the doctor, Pierre."

"I've already considered it." Pierre's answer was close to her ear. "But it's too risky. Dr. Henderson's leanings are with the British."

"He's known Jean since he was a boy. He wouldn't turn his back on him now."

"This is war, Angelique. We can't trust anyone."

"That's ridiculous." She pulled her hand away from Jean and sat back. "Jean needs a doctor right away. If you won't go get him, I will."

"Even if the doctor wants to help Jean, it would still be too risky. We can't chance word getting out that there's a wounded American on the island."

"What's wrong with that?"

"The British would find him, haul him up to prison, and leave him there to die."

She paused, letting the truth of his words sink in. "But the Americans will retake the island today, won't they?"

"Not a chance in the world." Pierre spat

the words. "Not after the way Colonel Croghan bungled the whole landing."

With a weary sigh he sat back next to her.
For a moment the steady dripping of water
somewhere farther back in the cave filled
the silence, along with Jean's heavy breathing.

They couldn't just sit there and do nothing. "Jean needs help." She started crawling
on her hands and knees backward toward
the entrance. "And I'm going for it."

"You're not going anywhere." Pierre followed after her, grabbing her around the
waist and hoisting her until she was practically sitting on his lap.

She pushed against him. "Let me go."

But he clamped his arms around her, and
the steel of his muscles trapped her.

"Pierre's right," Jean said, his voice surprising her. "We can't let anyone else know
I'm here."

She held herself tense against Pierre.

"I'm just grateful Pierre got me off Dousman's field when he did," Jean said. "I've
seen what the Indians do to the injured who
are left behind."

"We can't just leave that bullet in your
leg," Angelique said.

"Pierre will sneak me off the island tonight
and take me back to my ship." Jean's voice

grew weaker. "I'll be under the care of an American surgeon eventually."

Would it be soon enough to prevent infection? She didn't ask the question, but instead the desperation of the situation fell over her, as if crushing her under its weight. She buried her face against Pierre's chest and sucked in a breath. She couldn't keep from wrapping her arms around him, drawing strength from his presence.

He relaxed his grip. One of his hands splayed across her back while the other slid up into the waves of hair that tumbled about her head.

She rested her cheek against his shirt, and the rapid thumping of his heart pulsed through the linen. At the same time she could feel the heat of his breath against her hair, and the kiss he pressed on the top of her head. She was glad for the darkness of the cave that hid them from Jean.

"Pierre asked for my forgiveness for his past and told me he was a changed man," Jean said.

She stiffened, dislodged herself from Pierre, and was relieved when he didn't try to hang on to her.

"Of course I told him I forgave him." There was something strained in Jean's voice that sliced into her.

"You'd be proud of him," she said. "Once he saw the condition of the farm, he let his brigade go on without him so that he could stay and help Miriam for the summer."

She moved closer to Jean again, praying he hadn't suspected anything between her and Pierre, and hoping that Pierre hadn't mentioned anything about their relationship and their plan to get married. They couldn't break the news to Jean this way, not when he was wounded and in pain.

"It looks like you and Pierre are still close." Jean's breathing became more labored, the pain more pronounced.

She could feel his attention bouncing back and forth between them, and panic rushed through her. "We've always been the best of friends. You know that."

"I'm sure you told him we're engaged, that we're getting married just as soon as the war is over?"

"Of course I did."

Pierre cleared his throat. She held her breath. She had to stop Pierre from saying anything about their plans to Jean. They couldn't hurt him like this.

Before Pierre could get a word out, Jean spoke again. "Then I guess Pierre really has changed. Because the Pierre I used to know would have taken one look at you, saw what a beautiful woman you'd become, and decided he needed to have you for himself, regardless of anyone else's feelings or previous commitments."

The hard truth of Jean's words pummeled into her chest. And whatever Pierre was planning to say fizzled into a sigh.

Jean reached for her hand again. This time he brought it to his lips with uncharacteristic passion and kissed the back of her fingers. "I've missed you, Angelique."

"I've missed you too," she replied, hating that Jean's lips against her skin elicited nothing, not even the tiniest of tingles.

"I've thought about you every day, every hour." He tugged on her hand, giving her little choice but to lean closer to him. "It was the thought of marrying you that carried me through every horrible battle."

Each of his words stabbed her tender heart again and again, until she didn't think she could breathe through the pain in her chest. It was obvious he adored her.

"Jean . . ." Pierre began.

But then Jean pulled her down, captured her face between his hands, and guided her lips to his. For a long moment he moved his mouth against hers, and even though she tried to muster the response he would be expecting, the kiss felt stiff and forced.

When he finally released her, she had to resist the urge to wipe her sleeve across her mouth to remove the cold wetness he'd left there.

"I love you, Angelique," he said, placing one more kiss in her palm. "And the next time I set foot on this island, I'm going to marry you."

She rested her hand against his cheek, knowing she should tell him she loved him too and that she couldn't wait until he returned. Yet the words stuck in her throat.

When Jean had asked her to marry him two summers ago, before the war had started, she'd respected him and even cared deeply for him. She'd been so young, and it hadn't mattered that she didn't love him. Jean had even said as much. He'd told her he loved her enough for the both of them. She'd figured that kind of marriage would be more than satisfying, especially compared to the life she had with Ebenezer . . .

Until Pierre returned and made her feel things she'd never known were possible.

"Come on, Angelique." Pierre yanked her away from Jean almost roughly. "We've wasted enough time already. I need to get you back to the fort."

"Tell me you'll be waiting for me." Jean clung to her hand with a desperation that hadn't been there before.

She squeezed his hand but couldn't make the words come out.

"Promise me." His voice shook. "I don't know how I can survive without knowing you'll be there for me when I return."

How could she refuse him now? He needed her. He needed to hope in their relationship. She couldn't bear to think he might give up the will to live if she broke his heart now.

"I'll be there," she promised, trying to keep the misery from her tone.

Pierre pulled on one arm, and Jean held her fast with the other. She wavered between the two men, her heart wrenching into pieces. But Jean's grip was weakening, and one last tug from Pierre was all it took for Jean to lose his hold and for her to fall against Pierre.

"There's no time to waste." Pierre dragged her toward the cave entrance. "We've got to get you back inside the fort before the battle ends or you'll come under suspicion too."

She didn't argue with Pierre. She followed him out of the cave, into the woods, and ran silently after him as he led her in the direction of the fort. She tried to think of some excuse she could offer the sentinel for why she was so late in returning from her

334

fishing, but all she could think about was Jean lying in the darkness, in pain, and how he'd be in greater agony if he learned she'd broken her commitment to him.

Could she really break it?

The question pounded louder with each step she took away from the cave until it drowned everything else out.

When they were within sight of the walls of the fort, Pierre halted. He pulled her down to a crouch next to him so that they were hidden in the shrubs.

His chest heaved with his breathing, much the same as hers.

"My fish?" she asked.

"No time to go back for them."

She nodded. In the sticky heat of the morning, the fish would likely be covered with flies and starting to turn putrid anyway.

"This is as far as I can go." He peered toward the west blockhouse and the North Sally Port beyond. "Tell the sentinel you got caught in the path of the battle. He'll believe you."

In the distance the popping of gunfire continued to echo with the occasional blast of a cannon. The Indian war shrieks had faded, and she could only pray that Pierre had been wrong, that the tide of the battle had changed to favor the American troops.

She started to rise, but then stopped and grabbed Pierre's arm before he could slip away. "Don't tell Jean about us yet, Pierre. Please. Promise me."

His brows came together in a stormy furrow. "We need to tell him sooner or later. Why wait?"

"He's hurt, and I can't stand the thought of causing him more pain."

"I suppose that's why you lied to him — why you told him you'd be there for him?"

"I don't know," she said, wanting to block out the anger flashing in Pierre's eyes. "I didn't know what to tell him. I don't know what to do anymore."

"You don't know what to do?" Pierre gripped her shoulders and made her face him. "How can there even be a choice? You love me. Not him."

"I care about him too. He loves me and he was there for me all those years when you weren't."

"But you don't love him," Pierre insisted. "You couldn't say the words to him. I saw it."

The high morning sun beat down on her bare head, pounding with unrelenting pressure. "Maybe that doesn't matter."

With a growl Pierre jerked her against his chest, so that his face was only a breath away. His face was smeared with the dirt of battle and lined with weariness. But something powerful filled his eyes.

When he leaned into her, closing the gap between them, she didn't have the strength or the will to resist him. He bent his face against hers, and she met his lips with eagerness. She was hungry for him and let his lips demand from her a response that she was all too willing to give.

Then he groaned and cut off the kiss, dragging his mouth away and leaving her lips bruised but wanting more.

"Don't tell me that Jean's kiss was anything like that." Pierre's chest heaved, his face once again a mask of frustration. "Don't tell me you kissed him back the way you just kissed me."

She couldn't deny Pierre's words. She shared a passion with Pierre that she'd never once felt with Jean. But could their passion and love survive the challenges they would face in the days to come? Yes, Pierre had claimed he'd give up his voyaging ways. But could he? Could they really be happy together?

She couldn't bear the thought that Pierre would grow miserable on the island. And if she forced him to stay, she knew it was only a matter of time before he'd grow restless.

Besides, she'd just promised that she'd wait for Jean's return. How could she break her word?

Her mind spun with the memory of the winter morning her father had surprised them with his visit, of the joy that had spread across his face when he'd picked her up and embraced her with his big arms. His nose had been icy against hers, and the snow in his beard had tickled her cheeks.

But only moments later, his limbs had stiffened, and his expression had clouded with a confusion and pain that had ripped her little-girl heart, when her mother, wrapped only in a blanket, had swung open the bedroom door. The bare man-sized feet poking out from the end of the bed had been all her father had needed to see before he'd moaned in agony.

And his moan had ricocheted through the depths of Angelique's soul. There were times in the quiet of the early morning before dawn that she could still hear it.

It was the groan of betrayal.

How could she ever bear to hear it come from Jean's lips? And it would come eventually — if he learned she'd been cheating on him. Cheating just the way her mother had done with her father.

Angelique lifted trembling fingers to her

lips to stifle a cry at the realization of what she'd been doing. She'd been unfaithful to Jean. She'd neglected her promise to him at the slightest attention from Pierre. She'd allowed Pierre's flattery, his kisses, and his declarations of love to turn her head from doing the right thing, honoring her commitment to the man who adored her.

As much as she'd tried to prevent it, she'd become as brazen and forward as her mother. She'd reveled in forbidden kisses and touches. She'd let her flesh dictate the situation. What was to prevent it from happening again when the next man came along who turned her head? An anguished cry slipped from her lips, and tears sprang to her eyes. What kind of woman had she become?

She shouldn't have let herself care about Pierre and make plans with him, at least not until she'd had the chance to talk honestly with Jean. She and Pierre should have waited, should have used restraint until Jean returned. If their love was strong enough and meant to be, wouldn't it have lasted until after they'd done the honorable thing?

Instead she'd spurned all that Jean had offered her, his sweetness and goodness to her over the years. She'd gone behind his back, deceived him, and trampled his kindness in the dirt as if it meant nothing, just as her mother had done to her father, time and time again.

"Pierre, I'm sorry," she whispered, yanking away from him, panic giving her new strength. "I can't hurt Jean any further."

Pierre fumbled for her, but she slipped out of his grasp and tumbled out into the open grass, where the soldiers in the blockhouse would be able to see her.

"Come back, Angelique," Pierre hissed from his hiding spot in the brush.

She darted across the distance that separated her from the walls of the fort. She knew Pierre couldn't follow her, not without putting himself in great danger.

"Angelique, ma cherie," he called in a raspy whisper, "please come back."

She forced her legs to run away from him, putting as much distance between them as she could.

The shout of a soldier came from one of the square firing holes in the blockhouse. They'd spotted her.

She couldn't turn around now even if she wanted to. With a sob she forced her feet forward, even though she wanted to do nothing more than fling herself back into Pierre's arms.

"I'm back," Pierre said as he climbed through the narrow opening of the cavern.

"I'm surprised you returned," Jean said weakly, "and didn't leave me here to die."

Pierre made his way across the incline to the back of the cave, to the dark recess where he'd hidden his brother. He didn't reply. He was too angry, and ashamed to admit that he'd considered abandoning Jean.

Part of him wanted to let Jean fend for himself. After all, he was the one who'd gotten himself into trouble. If Jean was gone, then he wouldn't have to fight for Angelique's affection anymore. He'd have her without any worry of Jean. But the other part of him knew he couldn't abandon his brother, that his anger was irrational, and that he was only upset because of Angelique's stubbornness.

Why did she have to feel so strongly about her commitment to Jean anyway. Why did it matter?

It wasn't as if she'd married him yet. She had every right to change her mind about who she wanted to be with. And she clearly didn't love Jean the way she loved him. Did she?

His muscles rippled in protest at the thought that she might harbor affection for Jean.

"Here. I've brought you fresh water." Pierre held up Jean's head and lifted the canteen to his lips.

Jean took a long sip before falling back with a groan.

Pierre skimmed his fingers across Jean's wound, then trickled water over it. If only he had something from Dr. Henderson that would allow him to tend the wound. He'd contemplated finding the doctor and begging him for medicine — anything that could help ease Jean's discomfort during the long wait ahead of them.

But he couldn't risk being seen by anyone. Not until he'd gotten Jean safely off the island.

"She's mine," Jean said.

Pierre wanted to pretend he didn't know what Jean was talking about. But what good would that do? Jean had obviously sensed the attraction between him and Angelique. "Angelique's a grown woman and can make up her own mind about who she wants."

"Not with you around whispering sweet nothings in her ear every time she comes around." Jean's pained voice held an unfamiliar bitterness.

"I don't have to whisper sweet nothings for a woman to like me."

"Stay away from her, Pierre."

It's too late! he wanted to shout. He then remembered how Angelique had begged him not to say anything to Jean about their plans. As much as he wanted to tell Jean that he was marrying Angelique, he knew he couldn't break her trust. If he said anything to Jean now, he'd only push Angelique further away.

Non. He needed to let her share the news with Jean in her own time and in her own way. Maybe she could write him a letter to inform him that she wasn't planning to marry him anymore.

"You wouldn't make her happy anyway," Jean said.

"And what makes you think *you* would?"

"Because I can give her everything she wants, a home and a family on the island. I'll give her plenty of children, and someday I'll even be able to build her a bigger house."

"Who says I can't give her that too?" Once he sold his equipment and his brigade, he'd have more than enough money to build Angelique a big house and give her everything she wanted.

Jean gave a short laugh. "You'd never be happy here on the island. You'd go crazy, just as crazy as you did that spring before you blew up at Dad and all of us."

"I've changed."

Jean didn't say anything.

Was Jean right? Would he go crazy if he had to stay on the island? He thought back to the long hours he'd worked in the fields that summer, to the monotony of the plowing, the sowing, and the weeding. He was already tired of working the land day after day, and he still had the harvesting to do, the hardest work of all.

Even so, there were plenty of other things he loved doing on the island, and he'd be able to do them with Angelique. Maybe he could open his own business. Maybe together they could build a fishing business. After all, the fur trade in the Great Lakes region wouldn't last forever, just like it hadn't lasted out East. Eventually the islanders would have to find another means to survive out in the wilderness, without relying upon fur. Maybe he could forge the way into developing the fishing industry for the island.

He unfolded his stiff limbs and sat back against the cold dampness of the cave wall. The uneven rocks jutted into him, and he shifted, trying to find a comfortable spot for the long day of waiting. He stretched out his legs and leaned his head back. He was exhausted, but his mind spun with a thousand questions about Angelique and Jean and him and the future.

Jean's labored breathing softened, and Pierre could only pray his brother would sleep or fall into unconsciousness so that he wouldn't have to feel the burning agony from his wound. For all the frustration he felt about Jean and Angelique, he didn't want to see his brother suffer.

"I used to be angry that you'd rejected us and run off." Jean's hoarse voice came out of the silence and startled Pierre. "I was angry that you thought you were too good for the island and for farming. I resented you for thinking you were better than me."

"As I told you earlier, I'm sorry for all that. I was wrong —"

"Your pride was wrong," Jean said with surprising strength. "But when I think back to that last argument you had with Papa before leaving the island, I can see now that Papa was wrong."

Pierre's mind flashed with images of Papa standing in the horse stall in the barn, his wide stance and his broad shoulders blocking his escape. His black eyes had been hot with anger, and he'd brandished a shovel in his hands. He shouted at Pierre, called him stubborn and foolish for wanting to join a brigade and for refusing his offer to pay for school in Detroit.

He swung the shovel in the air. And even though he'd never hit Pierre before, for once Pierre believed Papa was angry enough to knock him down.

"Go ahead," Pierre taunted, stepping away from the wall. "Hit me."

Papa glared at him.

"If you want to hit me, I won't stop you." Pierre straightened his shoulders and puffed out his chest, preparing for the first swing. He'd seen Papa come to blows with plenty of other men. Though Papa had claimed to be a changed man, his temper still flared all too often.

At almost eighteen, Pierre was as tall as Papa and just as broad-shouldered, but he knew he wasn't a match for Papa's strength. Even so, he stood without flinching as Papa lifted the shovel above his head.

In the loft, Jean's glare matched that of Papa's. He remembered thinking, *If they all hate me so much, why should I bother staying?*

"I hate you." He ground the words out and flung them at Papa.

Papa rocked backward almost as if the hate had knocked him in the stomach.

346

Slowly he lowered the shovel and then let it fall from his fingers into the soiled hay. His shoulders slumped, and his eyes filled with an incredible sadness that still pierced Pierre whenever he thought about it.

His declaration of hate was the last thing he ever said to Papa. He shoved his way past the big man, stuffed a bag with his belongings, and left the farm without looking back.

Papa was right. He was a stubborn fool.

If only he'd had the chance to tell Papa the truth before he died, the truth that he'd never stopped loving him, that he'd respected him, and that now he understood.

"Papa wasn't wrong," Pierre said into the cavern. "He was just trying to keep me from making the mistakes he did."

"But he was wrong to try to force you to do what *he* wanted," Jean replied. "We each have to forge our own way in this world, and that includes making a few mistakes along the way."

"And I've made plenty."

"That doesn't mean you should give up doing something you love."

Pierre's soul burned with the remorse of all his sins, even though he'd long ago confessed them to God and pleaded for forgiveness. He'd been as guilty as Papa for all the drunkenness and debauchery that came with the voyageur life. He'd fallen into the trap of living for the next beach and the next night of drinking.

But he'd tried to turn his ways around. "I haven't had a drop of rum in a whole year."

"You've got the best qualities of both Maman and Papa in you," Jean said, his voice growing weak again. "You've got Papa's physical abilities and Maman's spiritual strength. If anyone can live a godly life in the wilderness, it's you."

At Jean's words, Pierre's chest grew tight. "Thanks, Jean."

Silence fell between them. He imagined themselves as if boys again, that they were merely resting in the cave after playing all morning. He wanted to forget that a bloody battle was still being fought only a few miles away. He wanted to pretend that he and Jean weren't fighting over Angelique.

"Go back to the wilderness, Pierre," Jean said. "It's where you belong."

He wanted to deny Jean's words, yet his heart beat faster at the truth of them. "You're just trying to get rid of me, aren't you?" His words were meant as a joke, but somehow they lacked the mirth he'd intended.

"I'd be lying if I said I wasn't afraid of you tempting Angelique away from me. I realize the friendship you've always had with her. She always followed after you first, always sought you out more than me."

"True." Pierre forced a laugh, hoping to cover his discomfort at Jean's words. If his brother knew Pierre had already tempted Angelique away, he'd want nothing more to do with him. Maybe Jean hadn't really hated him the way he'd rationalized that day in the barn, but when Jean learned Angelique was going to marry him, this time the hatred would be real.

"Besides keeping you away from my bride-to-be," Jean continued, his voice falling to a whisper, "I know you need to go. The fur trade is part of who you are. It's what you love most."

"Someone has to stay and take care of Maman now that she's blind."

"Blind?" Jean groaned. "What do you mean? How? When?"

At the agony in Jean's questions, Pierre wished he could take back his words. But Jean demanded to know everything. And by the time Pierre had finished telling him about the blindness and the condition of the farm that spring when he'd returned, Jean was thrashing in agitation.

"I'll stay until you return," Pierre assured, reaching out a steadying hand to Jean's shaking one. "I won't leave Maman here alone. I promise." He wasn't deserting Angelique either. No matter what Jean said about him needing to go, he loved and wanted to be with Angelique more. He wouldn't think about leaving her, especially not at the mercy of Ebenezer.

"I guess then I'll have to trust you." Jean's whole body was shaking now. From pain, cold, or fear, Pierre didn't know. He squeezed his brother's shoulder, wishing he could comfort him and tell him he had nothing to worry about.

He wouldn't lie, though. Not any more than he already had. "I'll take good care of everything."

He refused to think about what would happen to him on the morrow, when he returned to the island after delivering Jean to safety. He had no doubt he'd raise the suspicion of some of the officers, since he'd deceived the colonel into moving part of the army away from the battle.

Just the thought of his lies burned his soul. And he knew he had to be done with the spying. He couldn't betray the colonel anymore. At the same time he'd have to find a way to cover up what he'd done so that he could stay on the island. He couldn't leave Maman and Angelique.

He'd lay on the charm like he usually did, and he'd be fine.

He had a feeling the real trouble would be getting Angelique to lay aside her guilt about Jean. He'd have his work cut out for him in making her see she wasn't bound to Jean anymore. He could do it if he tried hard enough. He'd just have to charm her too.

CHAPTER 19

The morning sunshine couldn't warm the chill that filled every corner of Angelique's heart. "Are you ready?" She linked one arm through Miriam's, and with the other she slung the grain sack containing Miriam's clothes over her shoulder.

"More than ready," Miriam said, moving away from the officers' quarters, where they'd lived for nearly two weeks.

Early that morning, Colonel McDouall had given the islanders permission to return to their neglected homes and businesses. And now the wide open commons that had been filled with the makeshift tents and supplies of the villagers taking refuge inside the fort lay empty. The spots of flattened yellowing grass were the only reminders of the noisy, crowded mass that had gathered there.

Word had come pouring back to the fort all day yesterday, first that the Americans had been forced to withdraw from their position, and then that they'd fallen back to the shore and to their ships waiting for them off the northern end of the island.

Angelique had heard reports that the British hadn't lost any lives but had sustained several injuries, and that the Americans had suffered many casualties and countless injuries. She could only pray that the jubilant British soldiers returning from battle were exaggerating. Yet if the bloodshed she'd witnessed was any indication of how the fighting had gone the rest of day, then she suspected the Americans had fared just as poorly as the British were bragging.

Of course, Angelique wasn't celebrating with Lavinia and the other women who shared British loyalties. Instead she'd been sick with worry all day thinking about Jean in the cave with a bullet in his leg. And she'd been equally worried about Pierre attempting to sneak Jean off the island in the dark of the night. What if someone spotted them?

She'd heard reports that two of the injured Americans had been captured and thrown into the fort's guardhouse, and that one of them hadn't made it through the night. She didn't want to believe that the two had been Pierre and Jean, that somehow they'd been discovered in the cave and thrown in prison.

During her fishing trip that morning, she'd gone to Pirate's Cove. But there hadn't been a trace of their presence, not even a drop of blood. She'd searched along the shore and had gone farther out into the lake than she normally did, hoping to find Pierre. But she hadn't caught sight of his canoe anywhere.

"Time for us to be going," she said to Miriam, trying to quell the anxiety that had grown with each passing hour of Pierre's absence. Maybe he was waiting for them back at the farm.

She hadn't told Miriam about Jean or Pierre. They hadn't had the opportunity to be alone for her to mention anything. Still, with the constant whispers of prayer coming from Miriam's lips, Angelique suspected her dear friend knew something was wrong. And her solution to every problem was prayer and plenty of it.

Miriam reached for Lavinia in the doorway of the building and squeezed the young woman's hand. "Thank you for your gracious hospitality over the past days. You've been a sweet blessing to us."

"It's been a pleasure to get to know you." In a gown the color of lilacs, Lavinia was as fresh and pretty as always, as if she'd been entertaining them for afternoon tea instead of two weeks of tense, hot seclusion. "I'm certainly glad I could be of such help to so many during these difficult days."

Angelique couldn't fault Lavinia's kindness during the time when the fort had been crowded with islanders. She'd opened her quarters, shared her food, and distributed supplies among those camping on the commons.

She'd even honored Angelique's request to find lodging for Ebenezer, Betty, and their newborn in a deserted room in the storehouse. She was hoping it would soften Ebenezer's anger toward her. He hadn't forgotten about Pierre's beating after the dance and still wore a yellowish bruise around his eye from it. From the sharp glances he gave her from time to time, she suspected he was just biding his time until he could punish her.

Maybe she deserved his punishment. Maybe he'd seen the fickleness in her long before she had. He'd tried to warn her, but she hadn't listened. In the end she'd followed too closely in her mother's footsteps.

She shivered and readjusted Miriam's sack on her shoulder.

Not anymore. She'd make a new path for herself. She didn't know exactly what she was going to do, but she knew she couldn't go behind Jean's back any longer.

"I would like to continue our lessons, my dear," Lavinia said, smiling at Angelique. "I only have a few more weeks left before Father will send me back to civilized society. And I'm determined to have some success with you before I leave."

At least during the confinement over the past couple of weeks, Lavinia had stopped focusing so much on her appearance and had turned instead to her education. Angelique was surprised to find how much she enjoyed Lavinia's lessons on reading and writing.

A shout and two soldiers stiffening and cocking their rifles by the North Sally Port drew their attention.

"Take me to the colonel" came a familiar voice, followed by the sight of Pierre's swarthy frame swaggering between the two British sentinels.

Pierre was safe.

Angelique released a breath and sagged against Miriam.

Miriam squeezed her arm. "God be praised," she whispered so quietly that Angelique almost missed it.

Pierre shrugged off the grip of one of the soldiers as they made their way down the steep hill toward the soldiers' barracks. The soldiers lounging on the porch were polishing their guns. Several wore bandages from wounds sustained in the battle. They grew silent, and their expressions darkened at the sight of Pierre.

Angelique had the overwhelming urge to run to him, throw herself against him, and tell him she'd been wrong yesterday, that the only place in the world she wanted to be was in his arms.

But agony held her back. It was the same anguish that had been tearing through her since she'd realized she'd been unfaithful toward Jean, that she was becoming the kind of woman she'd been trying so hard not to be.

The British sentinel regained his grip on Pierre's arm, but Pierre yanked away from him. "We've got orders to bring you in," the young man said as he reached for his sword.

"I insist that you take me to Colonel McDouall first." Pierre's voice rose in anger.

"I've got orders to take you straight to the guardhouse." The soldier unsheathed the sword and pointed the blade at Pierre.

With one swift kick Pierre sent the soldier and the sword tumbling away from him down the hill.

An instant later the other soldier raised

his musket, aiming the barrel at Pierre's head. "Don't move," the soldier yelled, "or you're a dead man."

Angelique started forward, but Miriam's grip on her arm stopped her from recklessly charging toward Pierre in a foolish attempt to come to his aid.

"What's the problem?" came the strong voice of Lieutenant Steele from the doorway of the storehouse. More empty barrels and crates had been stacked outside the house, a sign the British were running dangerously low on supplies again.

"I've got Durant," the soldier replied, the gun against Pierre's temple wobbling a little.

The lieutenant leaned against the doorframe and seemed to casually observe the situation, although he'd pushed aside his coat and his fingers had strayed to the pistol holstered at his side.

When Lavinia walked out of the officers' quarters and shielded her eyes from the glaring sun to peer at Pierre, Angelique let herself breathe. If anyone could help Pierre, Lavinia could. "Let Mr. Durant go," Lavinia commanded the soldier. "There is no reason to treat him like a common criminal."

"I beg your pardon, Miss McDouall," the soldier said, "but I have orders to bring in Mr. Durant if he makes an appearance."

"Orders from whom?" Lavinia asked.

The soldier glanced at Lieutenant Steele.

The lieutenant shoved away from the doorframe and sauntered toward Lavinia.

"I can explain everything if you take me to the colonel," Pierre said, glancing sideways at the gun.

The hard glare in Pierre's eyes sent a shiver through Angelique, and she prayed he wouldn't try to break free from the soldier. He'd only get himself shot in the process.

Lieutenant Steele halted in front of Lavinia. "I sincerely apologize, Miss McDouall." He then turned to Miriam. "I'm sorry, Mrs. Durant."

Miriam's face paled, and her fingers dug into Angelique's arm.

"What is this all about?" Lavinia demanded, glancing from the lieutenant to Pierre and back.

Pierre's attention shifted to the women, as if noticing them for the first time. He looked first at Miriam, then at Angelique.

Dismay chased away his bravado, sending a chill to Angelique's heart. They both knew what was happening and there was no use pretending otherwise. The British had figured out Pierre was a spy.

Lieutenant Steele spoke quietly, almost

gently to Miriam. "I regret to inform you that we have reason to suspect your son is guilty of espionage."

Miriam didn't say anything. The pain that lined her face did all the talking.

"Well of course he's guilty of espionage," Lavinia said testily. "Everyone knows he's been spying on the Americans and reporting back to Daddy."

"Maybe he *was* spying on the Americans." Lieutenant Steele threw a glance at Pierre, one that revealed his disgust. "But who knows if what he was reporting to the colonel was the truth or only what the Americans wanted us to believe was the truth."

"Pierre has been a good friend to both Daddy and me," Lavinia said. "He would never be dishonest with us. Would you, Pierre?"

Pierre didn't look at Lavina. Instead he focused on Lieutenant Steele. "If you let me speak with the colonel, I'm sure I can clear up any misunderstanding."

"Maybe you can explain why at the outset of the attack you told Colonel McDouall a contingency of Americans was planning a surprise attack farther south on the island in an attempt to take back the fort, when really the entire bulk of the United States

Army was on the north end."

Pierre didn't say anything.

Lietuenant Steele only nodded. "Admit it. You thought to deceive the colonel into moving some of the army so that the forces were weaker and unable to repel the American attack."

Pierre shrugged. Angelique could see the battle raging across his face over whether to confess his part in spying or whether to talk his way out of trouble.

She wanted to shout at him that he needed to deny any connection to the spying. He needed to make any excuse he could. She didn't want to think about what they would do to him if he admitted to his deception.

But hadn't she talked with Pierre just yesterday morning, when they'd been out in their canoes about the struggle to do what was right even when it was hard? How could she demand anything less of him now?

"We also have evidence that you assisted a wounded American soldier from the battlefield," Lieutenant Steele continued.

"In the confusion of the battle," Pierre replied, "how could anyone possibly find evidence for such a thing?"

"I found evidence." The lieutenant moved closer to Pierre, and his expression spoke of victory. "I saw you pull the enemy solider from the field with my very own eyes."

Lavinia gasped. Her face drained of color and took the same pallor as Miriam's.

A crowd of regulars had been growing during the discussion. Men poked their heads out of windows in the barracks. Others had gathered outside of doorways. The glares they leveled at Pierre sent a tremor through Angelique.

"We're guessing that's why you disappeared," Lieutenant Steele said louder, apparently for the sake of those who were gathering near. "You were returning the wounded soldier to the Americans."

Pierre glared at Lieutenant Steele with a fierceness that sparked a flicker of hope in Angelique. He wouldn't give in without fighting. He couldn't just hand himself over to them.

"You have no proof of any of this. And I think we all know why you're leveling these accusations at me." Pierre puffed out his chest and batted the barrel of the gun away from his head. "Because you're jealous. You want me out of the way so that you can have Lavinia's attention all to yourself."

The lieutenant's lips curved into a tight grin. "Don't flatter yourself, Durant. There's never been any competition."

Lavinia stared at Pierre, her eyes and lips

drooping. "Pierre, please deny all of this. Please."

"I want Lieutenant Steele to take me to the colonel as I've requested." Pierre's words were clipped. "I'll be able to set everything straight."

"The only place Colonel McDouall wants to see you is in front of a firing squad."

Miriam swayed, and Angelique slipped an arm around her waist, even though she was trembling herself. She needed to get Miriam away from the fort and the accusations against Pierre. It was too much for her. She shouldn't have to hear such claims leveled against her son — even if they were true.

The lieutenant motioned to a couple of burly soldiers standing nearby, and they started up the incline toward Pierre.

"You have no proof of anything," Pierre said, eyeing the approaching soldiers.

"The current evidence piled against you is quite enough for the colonel." Lieutenant Steele's fingers stroked his pistol. "And we can certainly find more if need be. I have a knack for extracting information from prisoners. I'm sure with a little persuasion the American soldier we captured yesterday will be more than happy to tell us what he knows about you."

"I don't want anyone to get hurt on account of me," Pierre said.

The lieutenant nodded. "I thought you'd see it that way."

Pierre didn't resist when the two soldiers reached him and each took one of his arms.

A cry of protest rose inside Angelique. "Lavinia — Miss McDouall — you must do something! You have to help Pierre."

But Lavinia was already stepping backward through the entrance of the officers' quarters, her trembling fingers reaching for the support of her servant who stood behind her.

Lieutenant Steele turned to the servant girl. "Take Miss McDouall inside, away from all this unpleasantness."

Lavinia didn't resist as the girl led her away, taking the last remnants of Angelique's hope with her.

The lieutenant spoke to the soldiers holding Pierre. "Search him for weapons and then tie him up."

As the soldiers frisked Pierre, the lieutenant disappeared into the officers' quarters.

Pierre didn't resist the soldiers, though Angelique had no doubt he could have overpowered them if he'd wanted to. His shoulders had gradually slumped, and his eyes reflected a resignation to whatever was to come.

For a long moment he refused to glance to where she stood. But then once the soldiers had bound his hands in front of him, he lifted his head and looked at her. "Take Maman home."

Angelique nodded, her throat tight.

He studied every inch of her face as if he were memorizing it. "Looks as though you won't have to worry about breaking your commitment to Jean after all."

On the one hand, his words were reassurance that somehow he'd been able to deliver Jean back to the American ships. But on the other, his statement slipped around her neck like a hangman's noose.

He'd given up. He knew he was a dead man.

She started to shake her head. There had to be some way to save him.

"Sound the call to assemble," Lieutenant Steele said to one of the soldiers as he stepped out of the stone building and let the door close with a loud bang behind him.

Pierre glanced at the lieutenant and then spoke to Angelique in an unnaturally soft voice, "You need to take Maman home. Now."

Angelique followed his gaze, but then jerked back. There, dangling from the lieutenant's hand, was the cat-o'-nine-tails.

Its knotted cords hung stiffly, brown and dry from the blood of the last soldier who'd been flogged.

The lieutenant started toward Pierre.

"Go on," Pierre said more urgently to Angelique. "Take Maman out of here."

With halting steps, Angelique pulled Miriam forward, a cry of protest burning in her chest. She didn't want to leave him.

"I love you, my dear son," Miriam cried out over her shoulder, tears streaming down her cheeks. "No matter what, I'll never stop loving you."

Angelique choked back a swell of anguish. Miriam knew as well as she did that she was losing Pierre. After finally having him back in their lives, he was being torn from them forever.

The blast of the trumpet sounded in the morning air, calling the soldiers to congregate in front of the whipping post. Each shrill note clawed Angelique's back, as if the thin knotted strips of the whip were lashing her instead of Pierre.

Miriam dragged her feet as Angelique urged her away from the fort. She had to get Miriam out of there so that she couldn't hear the slap of the cat-o'-nine-tails against Pierre's bare flesh or his agonized moans.

She almost wished they'd shoot him first,

yet she knew they wouldn't let him get off that easily. They'd flog him until he was half dead to make an example of him to any other soldiers who were tempted to spy. And then after they'd made him suffer, they would lead him out in front of the firing squad and kill him.

As far as she could tell, there was no way he'd be able to escape his fate.

A deep sob rose in her throat, and she gulped hard to keep it down. She knew with certainty that she wasn't ready to lose Pierre. Not now. Not ever.

Chapter 20

Angelique paced in the hallway outside Lavinia's bedchamber. The silky skirt swished with each step. She'd donned the blue-green gown Lavinia had given her for the dance, had combed her hair, and had even washed the dust from her face. She'd taken as much care as she could to do all the things Lavinia had taught her during their lessons that summer.

She'd made sure that Ebenezer hadn't seen her leave the inn dressed in the ridiculous gown. But now she was so desperate, she no longer cared if he caught her in it.

Lavinia had claimed illness for over a week, since the morning Pierre had been arrested. With each passing day that Lavinia canceled their lessons, Angelique had grown more impatient and worried, until she'd decided she couldn't wait another moment to see Lavinia.

Angelique had decided the gown was her

only hope, that if Lavinia knew she was wearing it, then maybe she'd allow her a visit. She prayed that when Lavinia saw her in it, she'd be pleased enough to listen to her plea to save Pierre's life.

Angelique paused in her pacing and listened to the voices inside the bedchamber. The servant girl had gone in to announce Angelique's presence. She'd instructed the girl to tell Lavinia she was wearing the gown. Angelique tried to still the trembling in her limbs. If Lavinia refused to see her, what other hope did she have?

Every morning over the past week, when she'd delivered her catch of fish to the fort, she'd begged for news of Pierre. And each morning it had been the same. He was still in the Black Hole.

The deep, damp hole in the ground was reserved for the worst of prisoners, especially those sentenced to die. The dirt cell wasn't big enough for a grown man to sit in comfortably and was devoid of light.

Angelique shuddered at the thought of Pierre languishing in the blackness, the gashes on his back from the whipping likely festering.

She rubbed her gloved hands over her bare arms to ward off a chill. Even though mid-August was still warm, the sky was stormy that morning and had brought a cooler breeze, taunting her that fall was fast approaching. There wouldn't be many days left before the voyageurs and Indians left the island for their winter hunting grounds in the west.

And it wouldn't be long before Lavinia left the island too.

Angelique glanced at the closed door to the young woman's chamber and then resumed her pacing. After the past week of agony, she'd finally begged one of the sentinels to allow her in to see Lavinia. At first he'd refused, but when she'd offered him several eggs, his eyes had lit up.

It was no secret the food and other supplies within the fort were almost gone and that the situation was growing more desperate every day. In fact, word had reached them only yesterday that the Americans had destroyed a British blockhouse on Nottawasaga Bay, along with the schooner *Nancy* that had been bound for Michilimackinac and loaded with shoes, leather, candles, flour, pork, and salt.

Now that the last of the British storehouses in the area had been destroyed, the Americans had set up a blockade to the east, cutting off the lines for any further British ships to reach the island. Apparently the Americans had decided that if they couldn't bombard the British off Michili-mackinac, they'd starve them into sur-rendering.

Even before the battle, the provisions on the island had been low, but now the garri-son was on half rations. The gardens down by the government house had been picked over, everything edible gone. Once their stores were empty, would the British de-mand that the islanders sell the food they were storing up for the winter?

If the British didn't find a way to break the blockade and restock before the winter, Angelique dreaded what might happen. Last winter had been bad enough. It would be even worse if they were already starving before winter set in.

She slid her hands up and down her arms again. If only she could find a way to sneak food to Pierre. If the soldiers were hungry, Pierre would be the last person in the fort they would be willing to feed out of their precious remaining supplies. Why would they bother feeding a man condemned to die?

The door to Lavinia's room opened a crack. Angelique stopped, her heart patter-ing at twice the speed.

The servant girl squeezed through and

closed the door behind her. "Miss Mc-Douall doesn't wish to be disturbed."

Angelique eyed the door. Maybe she should force herself past the servant and barge into the room regardless of what the servant said. She would throw herself upon Lavinia and weep and plead and beg. As hopeless as the situation was, she was still determined to do whatever she could to save Pierre's life.

"I'm sorry, miss," the servant whispered.

"Did you tell her I was wearing the gown?"

"Yes, and she said you may keep it. That she wishes to give it to you as a gift."

Angelique shook her head. "But I don't want the gown. I just want to see *her*."

"She's too ill to do any further lessons with you."

"Would you let her know I don't need a lesson? I'm here because I need her help freeing my . . . my friend from the Black Hole."

She couldn't very well call Pierre the man she loved, although that was exactly what he was. As much as she wanted to deny the fact, she couldn't. No matter how much she blamed herself for becoming too much like her mother, and no matter that she'd determined to do better in the future, she still loved Pierre. And she always would. Even

372

after he was executed.

The servant hesitated. "She mentioned you might be here for that purpose, and she told me to tell you it's time for you to forget about him, that after what he did you need to focus your attention on someone more worthy."

Forget about Pierre? That was like asking the moon to forget about the sun. He brightened her life. He brought her laughter. And he turned the shadows into sunshine.

Besides, Pierre *was* worthy. Maybe he'd made some poor choices in his involvement in the war. Maybe he'd been careless with his spying. But he was steadily growing into a godly man.

She couldn't abandon him.

The servant began to back away.

Angelique reached out a hand to stop her. "Please tell Lavinia that I'll do whatever she wants me to do. Anything."

The servant hesitated.

"Please," Angelique pleaded, "if she's unwilling to ask for his pardon, then maybe she can ask that he be moved out of the Black Hole into the guardhouse. And maybe she can help me gain permission to bring him food."

The young girl started to shake her head.

"The Black Hole is no place for anyone to

die." Everyone knew the Black Hole was a death trap. It had such little air, a prisoner had once died of suffocation there.

"I'm helpless to change Miss McDouall's mind," the servant said, glancing at the door. "But she did talk of getting out of bed tomorrow. Perhaps you can try again then?"

Angelique thanked the servant and then took her leave, clinging to the slim hope that she might still have the chance of gaining Lavinia's help, somehow on the morrow.

When she slipped through the back door of the inn, Betty was standing in front of the hearth, stirring a large kettle. With the storm clouds forming over the island, the room was only faintly lit by the flames flickering under the pot.

The fishy scent of soup mingled with that of onion, making Angelique's stomach ache with hunger. But her own pain only served to remind her that Pierre was wasting away in the Black Hole. If his wounds or the lack of air didn't kill him, he would die of starvation. She must find a way to help him, at least to ease his suffering in his last days.

Betty didn't glance up. "My husband has been looking for you."

Angelique picked up her pace as she crossed the room, dodging the baskets of cucumbers, green beans, and beets she had picked that morning and intended to preserve and pickle, if the British didn't confiscate them first.

"I was at the fort with Miss McDouall," Angelique said. She prayed she could get out of the gown before Ebenezer discovered her in it.

Betty had been in her bedchamber and nursing the baby when Angelique had left. Angelique had purposefully timed her leaving during a nursing so that Betty wouldn't see her in the gown.

"If I were you, I'd just confess the truth right away," Betty said, her voice tinged with warning.

"What truth?" Angelique asked.

"The truth about what you were doing," Ebenezer said from a corner of the room.

A sharp crack of thunder was followed by a flash of lightning that brightened the room, revealing Ebenezer perched on the edge of one of the barrels of rum.

Angelique froze.

He rose slowly, each motion deliberate and calm. "Where have you been for the past hour in that revoltingly immodest gown?"

"I went to the fort to meet with Miss McDouall. That's all."

"You're lying!" His words burst out like a

roar, and he slammed his hand against the barrel.

"I'm not lying. Ask the sentinel at the South Sally Port. He'll tell you I was at the fort."

"Cavorting with all of the soldiers, no doubt."

"No —"

"Don't deny it, young lady!" He brought his fist down again. But then he straightened, cleared his throat, and continued in a low, placid tone, "It's become clear to me that you've been paying far too much attention to your outward appearance."

"This is the first time I've put on the gown since the dance."

Another crash of thunder was followed by a deluge of rain pounding against the window. Ebenezer moved toward her. "Then how do you explain the presence of this among your possessions?" He stretched out his arm, and in his palm was the ivory-handled comb Jean had given her upon their engagement.

She lunged for it, but he jerked it out of reach. "That's mine," she cried, desperate to keep the one beautiful thing she owned. "Give it back to me."

But Ebenezer tucked it into the folds of his long, shapeless shirt. "So you're admitting to your sin of vanity?"

"There's nothing vain about owning a comb." She trembled. "Jean gave it to me as a pledge of our commitment to each other."

"Then it's fitting I should take this comb away." He patted the pocket at his side. "Since you've broken your commitment to him with all your fornicating."

Betty had stopped stirring and was watching the scene unfold between her and Ebenezer. Over the past few weeks, Betty had continued to send her withering glances. She supposed Betty needed someone to blame for Ebenezer's lust with the Indians, and somehow she'd convinced herself that Angelique was the problem.

"I haven't been fornicating," Angelique said. "You must believe me."

"What I believe is what I see." Again his voice rose in anger, and he waved his hand toward her gown with its low neckline. Through the dimness of the room the lust in his eyes flashed.

Revulsion forced her back, and she covered her chest with her hands. Maybe Betty hadn't been wrong. Maybe she had caught Ebenezer staring at her with lust on other occasions. What if the woman's concerns were justified?

Ebenezer tore his attention away. "Young

lady, such a gown is the tool of the devil, intended to lead men astray. There's no other reason for it."

"I'd only hoped to please Miss McDouall after all our lessons this summer."

"You'd only hoped to please the soldiers!" he shouted, clenching his arms stiffly at his sides. "How many men did you let inside your skirt today?"

The crassness of his words took her breath away. He approached her with a raised hand as if he would strike her across the cheek. He held it above her for a long moment, and she tried not to cower.

No matter what he said, she'd done nothing today for which she need be ashamed.

"You're an ungrateful, disobedient girl," he said. With measured restraint, he lowered his hand and instead grasped the bare skin on her arm above her glove. "I'm disappointed that you've spurned all my efforts to help you. The Lord knows how hard I've tried to shepherd you into becoming a pure young woman, and how hard I've worked to protect you from your own sinfulness."

He yanked her toward the steps, his fingers pinching into her flesh. She wanted to say something to defend herself, to remind him of how carefully she'd obeyed him, of how submissive she'd been to his rules. But she knew he was too angry to listen.

He'd lock her in the attic for a couple of days, and then he'd release her after he'd had the chance to calm down. At least she prayed that was what he'd do.

"I had the feeling you'd end up just like your mother and sister," he said, then shoved her more roughly than usual toward the stairway.

"I'm trying not to be like them," she said, but the guilt of the summer came rushing back to haunt her, the pleasure she'd found in Pierre's arms, the sweetness of their stolen kisses, the passion one look from him could arouse. They shouldn't have shared intimacies, not while she was pledged to another. How easily she'd thrown away her loyalty to Jean, how quickly she'd forgotten about her commitment to him. Angelique hung her head.

"I'm beginning to think Betty has been right," Ebenezer said. "It's time to find you a husband."

"No!" Panic poured into her, and she struggled against him. "I'm waiting for Jean to return."

"I suppose that's why you had your body pressed all over Pierre's at the dance."

"I was wrong —"

"Yes, you were." His fingernails dug into her arm as he pushed her ahead of him up the stairs. "You were very wrong."

"But I'm still waiting for Jean."

"It appears to me that you gave up that right when you decided to fornicate with his brother and half the other men on the island."

Shame slapped Angelique in the face, the same shame that had lurked in her heart over the past couple of weeks. She wanted the dark stairwell to swallow her and put an end to her misery.

Ebenezer forced her over to the ladder that led to the dormer room. "It's time I found you a husband."

She groped for the rungs. "Please don't make me marry someone else. I've repented and I promise I'll be better. I promise I won't sin again."

In the darkness between them, his breathing was heavy with the odor of rum. The heat of his mouth came near her. Then in one sweeping motion he wrenched away from her. "Get to your room."

She scrambled up, knowing she needed to get away from him before he grabbed her again.

"And stay there!" he shouted after her.

"You'll stay there until I find you a husband."

CHAPTER 21

Pierre wiggled his toes, and sharp tingles like a hundred porcupine quills shot through his legs. It was all the movement he could manage.

The first week that he'd been in the Black Hole, he'd tried to keep moving. At times he'd made himself stand and stomp from one foot to the other, to keep the blood flowing and bring warmth into his limbs. Even though he'd had to stoop in the oddly shaped hole, at least he'd been able to move from the cramped sitting position.

But as the days had passed with only a crust or two of bread, and with only a scant amount of water — just enough to keep him alive — he became too weak to muster the energy needed to raise himself off the dirt floor and out of his own filth.

In the complete blackness he'd lost track of time. He guessed that at least two weeks had elapsed since he'd been arrested. The last time the hatch had been opened, going by the weakening of the sun's rays, he figured it was nearing the end of August.

He hadn't expected to languish in the pit quite so long. But apparently Lieutenant Steele wanted to kill him slowly and painfully. And after the torture of the past days, every time the chain on the trapdoor rattled, he prayed it would finally be time to face the execution squad.

He was ready to put an end to the hunger, the stench, the pain in his cramped limbs, and the struggle for every breath in the diminished oxygen of the pit. He was ready to meet his Maker.

He'd had little else to do in the Black Hole except pray. He'd begged God to forgive him for his stupidity in how he'd handled his part in the war. He'd played both sides. He'd had his feet in two fires, and as Red Fox had once warned, he'd gotten burned.

With a groan he shifted his back against the cold dirt wall. Thankfully, the bloody gashes had dried and begun to heal. But they'd caused him agony for many days.

A jangle on the lock above brought his head up. He peered through the blackness, but couldn't see anything but the thin cracks around the door that offered only the scantest of light.

Was it time?

His weak heartbeat sputtered with hope.

The chains clinked together until finally the trapdoor creaked open, letting in a sliver of light and fresh air.

For a moment the faint light blinded him, and he could only blink. At last he could make out the outline of a face above him.

"Good. I see you're still alive" came Lieutenant Steele's voice.

"You'll have to shoot me if you want to kill me," Pierre said weakly.

Through watering eyes, Pierre stared beyond the lieutenant's head, soaking in the clear evening sky that was turning into the deeper blue that came before sunset. He took a gulp of the fresh air that surged down into the pit, giving him blessed relief from the stench for an instant.

"Thirsty?" the lieutenant said.

Pierre didn't respond.

The lieutenant dangled a bucket down toward him.

Pierre wanted to reach for it, but before he could get his arms to work, the lieutenant tipped it and dumped the water, letting it pour over Pierre's head. It ran in rivulets down Pierre's face, and he opened his cracked lips to catch every drop he could.

The lieutenant laughed. Pierre was too

thirsty to care. In the distance came faint shouts of laughter and celebrating.

"Do you hear that?" the lieutenant asked. "That's the sound of victory."

"Congratulations," Pierre said sarcastically.

"We've broken the American blockade. Our troops managed to sneak up on the *Tigress* and overpower her. And once they were in control of the *Tigress,* it was only a matter of time before they were able to capture the *Scorpion* too."

The news hit Pierre like an avalanche of boulders. Captain Croghan and Sinclair had returned to Detroit in the *Niagara* along with the wounded, including Jean. But Pierre had placed hope in the remaining American ships to bring an end to the British domination in the Great Lakes. He hadn't wanted the islanders to suffer, yet he'd hoped the British would get hungry enough to give the island back to the Americans.

He'd wanted Jean to be able to return and take care of Maman and Angelique before winter set in. Especially since he'd be dead and wouldn't be there to help them.

Now the chances of Jean's return had vanished. There would be no way for Jean to come back to Michilimackinac with the

British still in command. And that meant Angelique and Maman would have to suffer through another winter on their own.

The very thought made him groan.

"You're in luck," Lieutenant Steele said, then tossed down a crust of bread. "Several *bateaux* from Georgian Bay have arrived with food."

Pierre eyed the dried piece of bread next to his foot in the muck. He didn't have the strength to reach for it. His own brigade would likely be returning any day now too, the canoes loaded with fresh trade goods. They'd be eager to be on their way west before the weather turned cold. What would become of them now?

"Since we have plenty of food to go around now, I thought maybe I'd share some with you . . . for your final meal."

Pierre glanced up.

The lieutenant grinned. "That's right. Your last meal. I've decided as part of the celebratory festivities tomorrow that we'll line up the firing squad and give the soldiers the target practice they've been longing for."

It's about time, Pierre thought, though he didn't say anything for fear the lieutenant would change his mind and keep him in the Black Hole until he was nothing more than a pile of bones. If he had to die, he wanted to get it over with quickly.

The lieutenant started to back away.

Pierre greedily drank in the faint streaks of orange and pink in the wisps of clouds far overhead, and he dragged in a final breath of the cool air before the staleness of the Black Hole could settle back around him.

"Oh, and by the way," Lieutenant Steele said, spitting and aiming so that the glob fell against Pierre's head. "I've heard rumors that Ebenezer Whiley is looking for a husband for Miss MacKenzie."

Pierre pushed himself up. "A husband?"

The lieutenant gave a hollow laugh. "Thought that might interest you."

It didn't just interest him. It carved a path of alarm through his battered body.

"Now with the return of commerce to the island, seems he's determined to marry her off to any man willing to pay the right price."

Please, God, no! he screamed silently as he struggled to rise from his cramped position, his arms and legs protesting every movement with sharp pain ricocheting through his body.

"Let me out, Lieutenant." Pierre clawed at the dirt wall in front of him, sending a shower of crumbling stones and dirt down upon his head. "I beg you to let me out."

He didn't care that he was begging now. He didn't care if he had to get out and kiss the lieutenant's boots. He'd do anything to keep Angelique from the fate she'd feared more than anything else.

Lieutenant Steele reached for the trapdoor.

"Please, Lieutenant, I'll do anything you want. Anything. Just let me out so that I can help Angelique."

"It's nice to see you so cooperative, Durant. Finally." He began to lower the trapdoor.

"No!" Pierre shouted. "Let me out!" Laughter mingled with the creaking of hinges until a final bang cut off all light and sound. All that remained was the echo of his protest. "No!" he yelled again.

His breath came in gasps, and he tore at the sides of the pit. He needed to get to Angelique and help her before it was too late.

"Let me out!" he screamed, even though he knew it wouldn't do any good.

He was as trapped now as he'd been the day he walked into the fort and was arrested by the sentinels. No one was coming to rescue him. No one was going to bail him out of trouble. He'd brought this upon himself and was determined to face the consequences of his actions. He'd decided to take the punishment for his foolish spying so long as he knew Angelique would be taken care of with Jean.

If he couldn't have Angelique for himself, then he would gladly give her up for his brother. Jean would love her and provide her with a good life. In fact, he couldn't think of a better man than Jean.

But now . . .

He loathed the thought that Ebenezer was selling her off to any old fur trader willing to pay him a bride price. He had no doubt that if Ebenezer set his mind to do it, he would. Look what he'd done to Therese.

Panic seized him at the idea of some dirty trapper touching Angelique. "Help!" he called again toward the heavy slats.

With the little strength he had left, he dug into the dirt wall and tried to climb up the incline. He managed only a few small steps upward before the dirt crumbled and he lost his hold. He fell backward awkwardly. A cry of frustration slipped from his lips, filling the pit with all the agony welling inside him.

For once in his life he was completely helpless, unable to do anything in his own power or charm. He couldn't save his own life, much less Angelique's. He pounded his knees with his fists, then hunched into a quivering and exhausted mass.

He knew he'd always thought too much of himself, put too much stock in his own abilities. Was this God's way of showing him how prideful he'd been?

"I admit it, God!" he cried out. "I've been arrogant and stubborn. I can't get myself out of this situation on my own."

Maybe he shouldn't have relied so much upon himself in the first place and should have been turning to God for help.

It wasn't too late to start doing that, was it?

Angelique huddled against the attic wall, her arms wrapped around her knees, her cheek against the smooth fabric of the gown Lavinia had given her.

The early morning slants of sunshine coming in through the cracks in the roof marked the eighth morning of her captivity in the attic and one more day that she was safe from marriage.

At least during this discipline, Ebenezer hadn't starved her. He'd sent Betty with food and water twice a day. Surprisingly, Betty had been friendlier than she had since she'd arrived last fall. She'd kept her updated on the news, telling her about the end of the blockade, that starvation had been avoided, that companies of voyageurs were returning to the island, and the Indians were coming for their last gifts before returning home.

Angelique had no doubt Ebenezer was making sure all the returning men knew about her. It would only be a matter of days before one of the men decided he wanted a wife to take with him into the wilderness.

"I won't go," Angelique whispered into the darkness. "I'll run away first."

But she despaired every time she thought about Therese trying to run, only to be captured and forced to leave the island anyway.

Angelique buried her face in her arms. Once out in the wilderness, where could she possibly run? If she tried to sneak away from her husband, she'd only face the harsh elements and wild animals. She'd be trapped again.

Had Therese found the only true escape?

The ladder creaked, the signal of Betty's morning ascent. Within seconds the lock scraped open.

"I have news," Betty said, lifting the door and popping her head into the dormer room. Her head was covered in her usual mobcap and long collar pulled up to her chin. "Ebenezer has found you a husband." Rather than a bowl of soup and bread, Betty came with a washbasin and towel. "My husband says you're to make yourself presentable before you come down."

"Very well," Angelique said, waiting for Betty to leave. She wasn't washing for anyone. If Ebenezer hadn't taken away her everyday skirts, she would have changed into one first. She knew what he was doing. He'd left her in Lavinia's gown because he wanted her to look appealing so that he could earn as much money from her as possible.

"He told me I wasn't to leave you until I saw the job done."

For a long moment, Angelique refused to budge.

"When Ebenezer decided to marry me, I didn't have a choice either, you know," Betty said, sliding the basin of water across the floor toward Angelique.

"I know." Angelique sighed and reached for the tin bowl.

"I've had to learn to make the best of it."

Why was Betty willing to be pleasant to her now on the morning she was being forced to marry and leave the island?

"Truth be told," Betty continued, "I've

grown to have affection for Ebenezer . . . even though he's far from perfect."

Angelique splashed the water on her face, wiping away the many tears she'd shed over the past week. Mostly tears at knowing she'd failed to save Pierre. She'd missed the chance to plead with Lavinia one last time for his life. At the thought of his death, her heart had broken over and over until there was nothing left.

It was too late for her to do anything. And now she was the one who needed saving.

"Maybe in time you'll grow to love your new husband too," Betty said.

Angelique started to shake her head, but Betty slid something across the floor toward her. A comb. The comb Jean had given to her.

She sucked in a breath. Was this some kind of trick? Was Betty tempting her to take it only to make her pay later?

"Go on. You can have it." Betty crossed her arms.

Angelique hesitated.

"I want you to take everything with you so that there aren't any reminders to tempt Ebenezer."

The pain in Betty's eyes reached across to Angelique. Did the young woman think Angelique's leaving would end her problems with Ebenezer's unfaithfulness? Was that why Betty was being so kind to her — now that she was no longer a threat?

"Thank you, Betty." Angelique picked up the comb with its smooth ivory handle. With the comb as a peace offering between them, Angelique didn't have the will to defy Betty's instructions to clean herself up. She took pains to comb the tangles from her hair, but then stretched her cap across her head.

As she descended the ladder behind Betty, her legs shook with the need to retreat and hide. But there was no place left for her to go, and no one who could help her.

She followed Betty into the dining room, and at the sight before her, she shrank in horror. Standing near the doorway were two Indians, a fierce-looking man with his hair shaved on either side of his head with a strip running down the middle. Next to him stood an old Indian with stooped shoulders and a long gray braid. They weren't covered in the war paint the Indians had worn on the day of the battle against the Americans. Even so, their dark eyes were cold, their expressions as unrelenting as stone.

"This can't be right," she whispered through a burst of panic.

"Oh, it's right," Ebenezer said from his

spot at one of the long tables still slick with spilled rum and piled with dirty dishes. He didn't bother looking up from the coins he was stacking in front of him. But his greedy smile spoke loud enough. He'd gained all he wanted and more out of the exchange, and there was no way he'd change his mind now.

Betty stared at the Indians with widening eyes. "I thought you said you'd made a deal with a fur trader."

"Then you heard wrong."

Angelique was surprised when Betty's fingers made contact with hers. The young girl squeezed her hand and offered her a look of sympathy that only filled Angelique with more dread.

With a scowl the younger brave scrutinized Angelique from her head down to the tips of her shoes. He shook his head and then turned and spoke to the older Indian. The tone suggested they were arguing, and Angelique hoped they didn't like what they saw and that they would refuse her.

The younger one lifted angry eyes to her once again. "Come." He motioned her forward with a jerk of his hand.

Angelique's body stuck to the wall. Her fingers intertwined with Betty's.

The Indian motioned to her again, this

time more impatiently. "Come. We go now."

The older Indian nodded at her. There was something kind about his face, almost encouraging, as if he were trying to reassure her that everything would be all right.

Still, she couldn't make her legs move, not even when Ebenezer glared at her. "What are you waiting for? It's time for you to go."

The brave gave a curt shake of his head, the feathers in his hair swirling and the metal discs around his neck clinking. He took several long strides toward her. When he stopped in front of her, she flattened herself against the wall.

His bronzed skin glistened with bear grease and emanated a powerful odor. Was he to be her husband, or had the older Indian paid for her?

The young Indian studied her face and then, before she could stop him, yanked on her mobcap and tore it from her head. Her curls tumbled down her shoulders and about her face in wild disarray.

His eyes rounded, and he fingered a strand of her hair reverently.

She tugged her head away, pulling her hair out of his grasp.

But he reached for a handful this time and tugged it hard. A pained cry slipped from her lips.

He turned and grinned at the old Indian. He then spoke something in his native tongue, something that made them both nod and smile, as if sharing a private joke.

The desperation that had been rising inside her finally burst. "Please," she called to Ebenezer. "Don't make me go with them."

She tried to scramble away from the Indian back to the kitchen, back to her attic room, but he was too quick. He captured her arm in a grip that told her she wouldn't be going anywhere but with him.

"You have nothing to fear," he said, surprising her with his good English and his almost gentle tone. "I will keep you safe."

But everything about the brave spoke of danger, hardship, and a way of life that was completely foreign to her. She had *everything* to fear.

His ebony eyes implored her. And when she still didn't move, he jerked her, giving her little choice but to move away from the wall. Her legs shook with each step she took, and she willed herself to go with him bravely, without further struggle. She didn't want him to tie her up and sling her over his shoulders. She couldn't go the way Therese had.

If she cooperated, maybe she could figure out a way to get away from them before they took her too far from the island. If she could steal a canoe, she might be able to paddle back to the island and take refuge with Miriam. She could hide on the farm, help Miriam through the coming winter, and wait for the day when the war ended and Jean could finally come home.

A tiny flicker of hope fanned to life. Even if the plan was nearly impossible, she had to cling to something.

As she approached the door, the older Indian nodded at her. She tried to muster a return nod, but her muscles were wooden. When she stepped outside and cast a glance over her shoulder to say good-bye, Ebenezer was too busy counting his coins, and Betty was staring at the floor.

Angelique stiffened her shoulders, lifted her chin, and tried to quell the thought that no one was there to say good-bye to her.

No one would know or care she was gone — no one except Miriam. But what could her dear blind friend do to save her? If the war ever ended and Jean made it home to learn the news of her marriage to the Indian, he'd never be able to find her out in the miles and miles of wilderness. She would be as good as dead to him.

And with Pierre gone, what reason did she have for living anyway?

CHAPTER 22

Angelique huddled under the wool blanket the older Indian had given her, but after hours of exposure to the cold drizzle, the blanket no longer kept her dry or warm. She stared over the side of the canoe at the endless churning of Lake Michigan. The stormy gray of the water reflected the low clouds overhead.

They'd been paddling for three days. And with each passing day, she'd lost hope that she'd ever see Michilimackinac Island again. Her slim chance of escape had vanished. The young Indian never let her out of his sight, and even if she had managed to steal the canoe, she didn't know how she'd be able to return that far by herself.

As it was, the older Indian was struggling. The waters had grown choppy, and the cold wind had become stronger. Lines of weariness had settled on the man's face.

She glared at the straight back of the

young Indian in front of her. He was pushing the old man from dawn until well after dark every day. Couldn't he see his friend was almost as miserable as she was?

But the silence stretched between them as wide and long as the lake itself. He'd spoken only a few sentences to her since they'd met. She still didn't know where they were going or which of the men was to be her husband.

She'd guessed the younger one since every time he looked at her, his eyes were more intense and filled with an interest the older one didn't seem to share. She was grateful neither one had attempted to touch her or hurt her in any way, at least not yet.

She couldn't imagine spending the rest of her life with either one. The thought brought another wave of misery crashing over her. She let her hand hang over the side of the canoe and dragged her fingers through the cold water. Down below the waves, far in the depths where the fish swam, the lake was calm and peaceful. It was a place without trouble, a place where she'd be free of pain, where she'd finally be rid of the lonely ache that had pierced her.

Pierre was dead, Jean was lost to her, and she was being taken from the one spot on earth she loved, the only place she'd ever wanted to live. It would be easy to put an end to her misery. All she had to do was stand and lean over. The jolting motion of the canoe would send her into the open arms of the waves. The water would embrace her and pull her down to its bosom, to a warm place where no one would be able to hurt her ever again.

Surely God didn't expect her to go on living this kind of life — a life without hope or a future. Her numb fingers dipped deeper into the water, and the icy spray splashed her bare arm. Her long tangles of hair clung to her damp face.

Was this how Therese had felt? Had the deep waters called to her too?

Angelique squeezed her eyes closed against the image of her sister shivering in the middle of a canoe, leaning ever closer to the water and peering into it with hopelessness in her heart.

She hadn't wanted to become like her mother or sister. But was she destined to repeat their sins whether she wanted to or not?

"No," she whispered through trembling lips and jerked her hand from the water. She wanted to be like Miriam — sweet and prayerful Miriam. When Miriam had been captured by Indians as a child, she'd survived.

Angelique tucked her stiff fingers beneath the folds of the soggy blanket. Miriam's captivity had been worse than hers. Even though the dear woman rarely spoke of the time, she'd shared enough that Angelique had been able to piece together the story. Miriam had been just a young girl when Indians had broken into her family home and taken the entire family captive. They'd forced them to march through the wilderness for weeks, giving them very little to eat.

Along the way, Miriam's mother had prayed and reminded them of their blessings, that they were alive and together. She'd encouraged Miriam to remember that no matter what happened in the days to come, the Lord would be her refuge and strength.

When Miriam's family had finally reached an Indian village, the Indians had split them up and forced them to work as slaves. Under the harsh conditions, Miriam's mother had died along with her two younger siblings. But Miriam's father had persuaded the Indians to take the rest of the family to Montreal, where the Indians traded them to the French as servants.

Even though her father had tried to raise enough money to redeem all her family, he'd fallen short. Miriam never was able to return home. She'd eventually met Pierre's father and married him.

Angelique hugged her arms across her chest. If only she could have the kind of faith Miriam had. Was it possible to find hope to keep going, no matter her situation? If Miriam had been able to do it, couldn't she?

"Oh, God," she whispered, "help me believe you are my refuge and strength. Help me believe."

Behind her, the old Indian gave a weak shout. She turned to see his paddle floating in the water away from them. With a deftness and strength that Angelique couldn't keep from admiring, the young Indian dug deeply through the waves to retrieve the paddle.

"Let me help for a while." She grabbed the handle as the brave held the paddle out to the older Indian. "He's tired."

The brave glanced at his friend, to the slumped shoulders and the weariness in his face, then gave a curt nod to Angelique before turning and resuming his quick but deep strokes.

Angelique shrugged out of her blanket

404

and handed it to the old Indian, who took it with a grateful nod. She plunged the paddle into the water and fell into an easy rhythm with the brave.

She didn't stop even when her shoulders and back burned from the need to rest. For some reason she wanted to prove herself to the young Indian. From the disdain she'd noticed in his eyes from time to time, she'd gotten the impression he thought she was fairly worthless.

If she was going to have to marry him, then she didn't want him believing she was weak and helpless. She could do more than he realized.

As the darkness of evening began to fall, he guided the canoe to a sheltered area of the shore. Though her body ached more than it ever had before, she took the young Indian's fishing pole, dug up several worms as bait, and waded out to her waist to fish.

She didn't like fishing from the shore as well as from her canoe, but she could still make the catch. By the time the young Indian had collected wood and started a fire, she had two trout. The older Indian smiled at her and held out his hunting knife.

She helped him move closer to the fire and spread out the wool blanket to dry before she gutted and filleted the fish. She could sense the brave's careful scrutiny of her while he patched a leaky seam of their canoe with a gum-like mixture of beeswax and pitch.

By the time she'd roasted the fish and divided it between them, giving her portion to the older Indian, the brave's mistrust had dissipated. He broke his own piece in half and shoved it toward her. "For you."

"You need it more than I do." She fanned out the folds of her skirt near the flames, attempting to dry the silky material and trying to ignore her rumbling stomach.

He placed it in the sand next to her feet and nodded at it. "Eat it."

She glanced at him in surprise.

"You are kind to Yellow Beaver, my grandfather." He glanced at the older man, who was already curled up asleep on the opposite side of the fire.

She rounded the fire and tugged the dry half of the wool blanket over the older man. The young Indian's eyes followed her every move. And when she returned to the fire and rubbed her hands in front of it for warmth, the brave spoke again. "Thank you."

His voice was kind. She could almost begin to believe there was something likable about him. She nodded at him and then picked up the warm piece of fish and brushed the sand from it. "And thank you."

After taking a bite of the trout, she moved out of the cold sand that squished between her toes and found a spot of grass. A gentle voice whispered that even though she'd left her island, she could still find a solid place to stand, that whatever she faced in the days to come, God would be her rock and hold her up.

Maybe she had to give up hope in everything she'd ever wanted, the things that faded and could easily slip through her fingers, so that she could finally put her hope in God, who would never change or leave her.

The next morning the sun came out for the first time since they'd started their journey away from Michilimackinac. Angelique took turns paddling with Yellow Beaver, who was content to sit back and watch the changing landscape and let her help his grandson.

When she finally allowed herself a glimpse of the shoreline, she drew in a deep breath of the cool morning air and for a brief moment had a stirring of peace. The lake was clear and glassy, reflecting the yellows and oranges of the trees that were gaining their fall colors. Several mallards swam along the shore, and she caught a glimpse of a doe drinking at the edge of the lake.

Perhaps she could begin to understand some of why Pierre had fallen in love with the wilderness, why it had been so important to him. Maybe over time she would grow to appreciate it too, although she doubted she'd ever be able to love it more than Michilimackinac. But if she had to leave her beloved island and make a home somewhere else, the wilderness was beautiful.

The brave said something in his native tongue and then pointed westward. Yellow Beaver sat up, squinting as he stared into the distance.

Angelique let her paddle grow idle and peered ahead at the wisp of smoke rising in the air from a peninsula jutting into the lake.

With a nod, Yellow Beaver replied to the brave, then took the paddle from Angelique. A new eagerness chased away the tired lines in his face, and he plunged the paddle into the water with fresh energy.

As they drew nearer, Angelique stared at the peninsula with unease. Was this where she would find her new home? Once they reached the rest of the Indian's tribe, would he make her his wife? Her insides twisted at the idea of sharing intimacies with him.

The brave said something over his shoulder in his native tongue. Her pulse thumped with rising panic, and she glanced at the water and the ripples made by the smooth gliding of the canoe. Was it too late to jump?

"They are waiting for us," the brave said. "That is why we reach them today."

Along the shore were half a dozen large voyageur canoes pulled up into the sand with stacks of trade cargo piled on the beach under tarpaulins. Shirts and capotes were strewn in the brush, apparently drying in the warm morning sunshine. A couple campfires were burning with men lounging beside them, some playing cards, others sleeping. Several men were busy patching canoes while one knelt at the shore, shaving his cheeks.

"What is this place?" she muttered.

The young Indian let out a shrill cry that resembled the war cries the Indians had used on the day of battle. She half expected a tribe of Indians with hatchets and clubs to jump out of the woods and descend upon the peaceful camp of voyageurs. Instead, the men sat up and stared at their canoe, which was drawing closer by the second.

The man kneeling at the shore splashed water on his face and then rose to his feet, shaking his head and his dark curls, letting the water cascade down his wide shoulders and broad bare chest.

"Pierre . . . ?" she whispered, knowing that in her desperation for him she was turning some other man into his likeness. Pierre was dead. He couldn't possibly be standing on some remote peninsula on the shore of Lake Michigan.

But with each paddle closer, his chiseled features grew clearer, until she was sure it was his midnight eyes that peered across the lake at her.

"Angelique!" he called.

Her heart stopped altogether, and she felt herself collapsing at the realization.

A grin spread over his features as he splashed into the lake toward them. Within seconds the canoe glided into shallower water, and Pierre waded up to his thighs in his eagerness to reach them.

A rush of joy broke through her shock. She waved to him. His face was thinner but was still just as darkly handsome as before, if not more so.

He grabbed on to the edge of the canoe and dragged it toward him, his eyes catching with hers and shining with excitement.

"Pierre!" she said, hardly able to believe he was really standing before her, breathing and moving and whole.

He reached for her and lifted her out of the canoe in one easy motion. The solidness of his chest and arms, the warmth of his skin, the heat of his breath all confirmed what her mind couldn't grasp.

"It *is* you." The joy inside clogged in her throat, making her want to weep.

"Of course it is." He took several giant steps toward the shore, and the movement forced her to wrap her arms around his neck.

She lifted her hand to his smooth freshly shaven cheek, needing to feel him and make sure he was real.

"Angelique," he whispered, lowering his head, his eyes taking her in like a starving man. "I missed you." Then before she could say anything more, his lips crashed against hers, and he took possession of her with the force of his kiss.

She could do nothing less than respond with the same fervor. The mingling of their lips contained all the desperation that had built during the weeks they'd been apart, the uncertainty, the longing, and the relief of being alive and together again.

With each swirling second she grew weaker until she was as soft and helpless as a wilted flower. She didn't want to break away from him, but the cheering and hooting coming from the men on the shore finally penetrated her consciousness.

And out of the corner of her eyes she could see the brave staring at them stoically from the canoe.

With a gasping breath she dragged her lips away from Pierre's. "You're alive," she said, still unable to comprehend his presence.

"I couldn't die," he said with another grin that sent her heartbeat into a wild tumble, "not without one more kiss from you."

She couldn't contain her smile. "Oh, Pierre, I thought you were dead."

"And leave you, ma cherie?" He kissed the tip of her nose. "Never."

She let her fingers skim his cheeks and his chin. "How did you possibly survive the Black Hole? And how did you get here?"

He nodded at the young Indian, who'd jumped from the canoe and was lugging it onto the shore with Yellow Beaver still inside. "My brother Red Fox came after me."

Angelique glanced at the proud stiff back of the brave. "Your brother?"

"He isn't called 'fox' without a reason."

For the first time, the brave smiled at her.

"Red Fox climbed over the stone wall section of the fort, broke the lock on the Black Hole, and pulled me out."

"All without alerting the guards on duty?" She looked again at the Indian she'd sat behind in the canoe for the past several days. She was more than a little relieved she didn't have to marry him, but a new respect bloomed inside her. He'd saved Pierre's life.

"Most of the soldiers were too busy celebrating their defeat of the American blockade. Lieutenant Steele had come earlier to taunt me, had seen how weak I'd become, and knew I couldn't escape. So he hadn't left a guard at the Hole."

Pierre looked again at Red Fox. "But little did he know that my brother was back on the island and that he was determined to save my life, the same way I once saved his."

Angelique's chest swelled with uncontainable relief.

"It was the perfect night for an escape." Pierre sloshed to the shore, carrying her as if he never planned to let her go. "I couldn't have planned it better myself."

"So you sent Red Fox to rescue me too?"

He nodded, his eyes flashing with anger. "I heard Ebenezer had put out a bride price for you. So I sent Red Fox back for you with my profit from the furs."

"Then you're the one who paid for me?"

"Of course, Ebenezer has no idea it was me. But oui, I was the one who bought you."

She wiped a damp strand of his hair off his forehead. "Thank you."

"I couldn't let anyone else have you. You're mine." He nuzzled his nose against the tangles of her hair and then pressed a kiss on her head.

She ignored the tiny warning that whispered in the back of her mind that she wasn't Pierre's, that she still belonged to Jean. "You're my hero."

"That I am." He swaggered forward.

She laughed, overflowing with thankfulness that God had spared his life and had given her another opportunity to be with him. She wanted to savor the moment, and for just a little while forget about everything else except them.

He climbed out of the water and onto the stretch of rocky shoreline. She wiggled to free herself from his hold, but his grip on her didn't budge.

"I'm not letting you go," he said, his breath warm against her temple. "I'm holding you forever."

She laughed again. "I won't protest." His arms, his smile, his strength surrounded her like the warmest sunshine on a summer day. She wanted to bask in it.

He laid a tender kiss on her forehead, lingering against her skin, making her wish he'd move his lips down to hers and give her another one of his passionate kisses.

"The bourgeois needs time alone with his girl," one of the voyageurs nearby called with a laugh. "I think we should pack up and head out and give the bourgeois some privacy."

The guffaws and suggestive calls of the other voyageurs burned Angelique's ears. This time she broke free of Pierre's grasp and forced him to release her. When her feet touched the ground, she ducked her face with the pretense of smoothing down her skirt.

Pierre spun to face his friends, falling into an easy banter with them, cajoling them with the same measure they gave him.

Angelique straightened and, at the sight before her, gasped. There, crisscrossing Pierre's back, were at least a hundred red welts, some of them wide scabs where his skin had been ripped open.

With trembling fingers she reached out and grazed his mangled flesh. He stiffened and slowly turned. His mirth was gone. In its place was a deadly seriousness, an acknowledgment of how close he'd come to dying.

"How did you bear it?" she whispered, her lips quivering at the thought of the pain he'd endured.

"I'm tough," he said with a gentle smile. "And I deserved it. I shouldn't have been playing both sides or been so deceptive."

He grabbed his shirt from a nearby boulder where he'd spread it to dry. He jerked it over his head as if anxious to hide the marred skin.

"Don't worry," she teased, "you're still just as handsome as you've always been."

He paused, the shirt only half on. Then with a grin he flexed one of his arms, showing off the muscles there.

Red Fox leveled a censuring glare at Pierre. "His head is already as big as a moose's. You should not make it bigger."

"That's why Pierre likes me so much," Angelique said, smiling. "I supply him with plenty of praise for his oversized pride."

Red Fox didn't smile back. Instead his eyes narrowed on her.

Pierre tugged his shirt down his chest and then slid his arm around Angelique's waist, drawing her to his side. "Admit it," he said to Red Fox. "She's perfect for me."

Even though Pierre's tone was playful, there was a hint of something serious and expectant as he watched Red Fox.

The sun glinted off Red Fox's strip of hair and the grease he slathered over his body on a regular basis. His expression was sharp, and Angelique had to resist the urge to cower against Pierre.

The brave turned back to the canoe, retrieving the grain sack that contained all the possessions Angelique owned. He held it out to her with a nod. "She is good for my brother."

Angelique sensed that Red Fox wasn't the type of man to give praise lightly, and she nodded at him with her thanks, hoping he could see that her gratitude went much deeper than his kind words.

"She's mine now," Pierre said, his arm tightening possessively. "Forever and always mine."

Her heart expanded with a love so fierce, she was helpless to do anything but hug him in return. Although the warning in her head clanged louder, for now all she wanted to do was enjoy being in his arms again, she was too happy to think about anything but their being together. Later she would sort through how she needed to do the right thing this time.

CHAPTER 23

The brigade teased him mercilessly about Angelique, for he couldn't take his eyes off of her. After the past several days of waiting for Red Fox to catch up to them, he'd nearly driven his men crazy with his worry.

He hadn't wanted to stop and wait for Red Fox. He knew he needed to put as much distance between himself and Michilimackinac as possible. He had no doubt Lieutenant Steele and Colonel McDouall would send out an Indian war party to hunt him down. And when they found him, they'd kill him on the spot. In fact, he expected they'd cut him up limb by limb and completely destroy every trace that he'd ever existed.

The officers would be desperate to make sure he was silenced. They couldn't risk any word spreading that he was alive. Such news would only make them look inept. After all, no prisoner had ever escaped from the Black

Hole or the fort before, and they wouldn't want anyone to think it had happened under their command.

But after three days of paddling hard with his crew, Pierre hadn't been able to shake the worry that something had happened to Red Fox and Angelique. So he'd stopped. And they'd waited all morning, until he'd been as tense as a bowstring.

When he'd finally heard Red Fox's war cry and caught sight of Angelique's stunning red curls, his relief had swelled in his chest, almost choking him. He'd wanted to linger on the beach with Angelique, had wished he could send his brigade ahead so that he could have a whole afternoon alone with her to fish and hike and talk for endless hours. But one grave nod from Red Fox toward the east told him that a war party was on their trail.

They loaded their canoes with their usual speed. Then he tucked Angelique securely behind him in his spot at the head canoe, and they pushed off from the shore.

They paddled swiftly, and he prayed their speed as experienced voyageurs would give them an advantage over the band of Indians on his trail.

Even with the threat of danger creeping up on him, he relished every moment of the day spent with Angelique so near. They managed to talk more than he'd expected. She was full of questions about all that she saw.

As the day wore on, he could almost believe Angelique belonged in the canoe behind him, that she could fit into his life as a fur trader. Even in Lavinia's fancy gown, she maneuvered with a naturalness that had likely developed over the years from all her fishing. She wasn't afraid, didn't complain, and seemed to enjoy the ride. With each passing mile she'd observed the landscape with an eagerness that fueled his own love of the land.

Had he been wrong to think he couldn't bring a wife along during his voyages?

He urged the brigade onward until well past dark, using the excuse that he wanted to get as far away from Michilimackinac as he could. He didn't have the will to tell them that he was being hunted. He wanted to deny the truth for as long as possible — the truth that eventually he would have to leave his brigade and strike out on his own. It was the only way to keep his men and Angelique safe.

Long after nightfall they finally stopped and made camp. After a meal of hominy and salted pork, he sat against a boulder near his fire and pulled Angelique in front of him so that she had little choice but to lean back against him.

The September air was cool, and he wrapped his arms around her like a blanket, telling himself he was only trying to keep her warm and comfortable. But the truth was he couldn't get enough of her.

She folded her arms across his and laid her head against his shoulder so that her curls tickled his chin. The popping flames and the sparks rising into the black night mingled with the low voices of his men at their campfires. The sky was clear with a magnificent display of stars fanning out over the lake all the way to the horizon.

"It's beautiful, Pierre," she whispered. "I'm beginning to understand why you love the wilderness."

He drew in a breath of the pristine air broken only by woodsmoke. "Do you think you could ever be happy out here?"

She hesitated. "I'm not sure. I'd like to think I could be happy anywhere. I'm learning to trust God to be my rock through every situation. But I love the island, Pierre. I think I love it as much as you love this." She glanced to the waves lapping against the rocky shore, to the sliver of moon reflected in the water.

Even though he didn't want her words to bother him, disappointment sliced into him.

"You belong here," she said softly. "After watching you today, I can see it in a way I couldn't before."

He shrugged. After Red Fox's update on the ongoing struggle with the North West Fur Company that summer and their continued efforts to put the free traders like himself out of business, he wasn't sure how much longer he'd be able to protect his brigade and trade for furs anyway. He had a feeling his fur-trading days were numbered. "It doesn't matter where I am —"

"This brings you to life in a way the farm never did."

"That's not true . . ."

"I always tell you the truth, Pierre."

He swallowed the words of rebuttal, knowing he couldn't deny what his heart had already told him. He lowered his head, wanting to kiss her, wanting to forget about everything that stood between them.

Why did it have to be so complicated? They loved each other. Couldn't that be enough?

He nestled his lips against her hair, dragging in a deep breath of her. Lifting his fingers to her chin, he tilted her head so that he could kiss her.

"Pierre . . ."

He could sense the trust in her voice, the desire, and the same need to be with him that he felt for her. But when he bent to capture her mouth, she turned away.

"Pierre, we can't."

He gently nudged her head back, wanting to silence her protest.

She resisted again, this time pulling out of his arms altogether. "I'm not free to love you yet."

He released a ragged sigh. "Don't tell me you're going to let Jean stand between us again."

She shifted positions and knelt in front of him. "He still believes we're to be married when he returns. I gave him my promise I'd be waiting."

"People change, Angelique."

"Not like this. I can't do it this way, not by deceiving him." Her words caught on a sob. "I can't kiss you and find comfort in your arms, not when I pledged myself to Jean."

His body tightened with a rush of frustration, the same frustration he'd experienced since the day he'd pulled Jean from the battle.

"I don't want to become like my mother." She grasped his hands. "You've got to understand that. She cheated on my father and broke his heart. I can't do that to Jean."

"You're nothing like your mother. And besides, you're not married to Jean yet."

"But if I can so easily throw aside my commitment and cheat on Jean now before marriage, it's only the first step down the path to being unfaithful in other things."

"Then write to my brother and tell him you can't marry him."

"I can't end things with a letter. He's a good man, and he deserves better than that."

Deep inside, he knew she was right, that he was being selfish again, as he had so many times in the past. But his desire for her and the helplessness of not being able to have her dueled within him, slashing his heart wide open.

"I paid the bride price to Ebenezer," he said, unable to keep the rumble of anger from his voice. "You're mine now."

"Jean paid it too."

He shook his head. "When he left he gave up his right to have you."

"Just because he left, he shouldn't have to worry about me pushing him aside for someone else when he's gone. How would you feel if the situation were reversed? You wouldn't want me to do that to you, would you?"

He jumped to his feet. He didn't want to think about what was right. He'd almost died, almost lost his opportunity to ever hold her again. And he wasn't going to give her up now that he had her. How could he?

"I had Red Fox bring you out here so that we could be together," he said hoarsely. "Are you telling me you want to just throw that away?"

She shook her head, the firelight reflecting the wretchedness in every line of her pretty face.

He wasn't being fair to her. He would have rescued her from Ebenezer no matter what the outcome was for himself. He didn't want Angelique to suffer, forced into marriage with just any man. He wanted her to be happy. And if he coerced her into marrying him and staying in the wilderness, wouldn't he be relegating her to the kind of life she'd always dreaded?

"I want you to know I'm grateful you rescued me," she whispered. "I wish I could just forget about Jean and my promise to him, but I can't. I have to be a woman of honor."

"What do you want me to do? Do you want me to take you back so that you can be with him?"

He willed her to contradict him, to tell him she wanted to stay with him, that she loved him more than Jean, but she just hung her head instead.

"So just like that you're giving up on us and shoving my love back in my face?" He hated that his voice was harsh. He didn't want to lash out at her, but he couldn't stop himself.

"I don't want to give up on us," she said, lifting her face. In the firelight the tears on her cheeks glistened. "I don't want to think that this is the end, but don't you see that even if Jean didn't stand between us, I could never ask you to give up your fur trading for me?"

He couldn't find the words to respond to the discussion they'd already had too often. He knew that she was right. And he hated it. All he could do was growl and spin away. He stood stiff and unmoving with his back facing her.

"And I can't leave Miriam alone for the winter," she added. "You won't be able to return to the island without risking your life again. Jean won't be there. Who will take care of her if I'm not there?"

He closed his eyes against the impossibility of their situation. Why had he ever

426

thought they could make things work? Why had he believed their love could overcome such odds? That maybe she'd want to stay in the wilderness with him?

"I want to offer you my love," she said behind him. "But love without honor is worthless."

He didn't turn.

"I have to do the right thing." Her words were broken and filled with pain. "Maybe someday, if we do what's right, we'll find a way to be together."

"I'm not waiting for *someday*, Angelique." He spun on her with all the anguish pumping through his blood. "You've made your choice. So let's not make this any worse than it already is with false hopes and dreams."

Tears streamed down her cheeks.

And before he fell to his knees before her, begging her not to leave him and making an even bigger fool of himself, he forced his feet to move away from her. He strode into the darkness of the forest and let himself mourn silently where no one could see him.

At the barest hint of dawn, Red Fox touched Pierre's shoulder. "You must go now."

Pierre sat against the tree at the edge of the camp, where he'd positioned himself for the night. He'd closed his eyes for only a moment, knowing he had to rest, that he would need all the energy he could muster in the days to come.

"Menominee warriors will be here at first light. They will kill my brother."

Pierre nodded and rose, adrenaline surging through him.

Red Fox shoved a bag into his arms. From the contents within the bag, Pierre could tell his friend had packed everything he would need to survive the coming days of running.

"I will pray to the Great Spirit to give you the swiftness of the hare, that your feet will fly and carry you to my people. They will keep you safe."

That was *if* he made it across the miles to the Chippewa winter camp without being caught by the Menominee, but neither of them spoke the words. Pierre stared at the shore, to the fire where Angelique lay sleeping under a thick blanket.

"I will keep her safe," Red Fox said.

Pierre swallowed the bitter lump in his throat. He wanted to go to her and kiss her good-bye and tell her he was sorry for the argument they'd had. He didn't want to part with her like this. But what more could he say? She'd chosen Jean and the island.

"Take her back to Michilimackinac, to my maman." He gripped Red Fox's arm. "Please."

Pierre didn't want to think about what Ebenezer would do with her once she was back on the island. He had to believe the money he'd paid would prevent the corrupt man from trying to hurt her again. He attempted to block out the warning that Jean's payment of the bride price hadn't stopped Ebenezer from giving her away to him.

"I will ask Yellow Beaver to stay with her," Red Fox said as if reading his mind.

"Would he do that?"

Red Fox nodded. "She is kind to him, like a daughter."

Relief weakened Pierre's legs. "I'd be indebted to him and will pay him handsomely."

"You will not need to pay. He will sacrifice for my family."

The breeze rattled the branches overhead and sent a chill up Pierre's back. He glanced to the dark shadows moving in the woods behind him. He needed to go now before the shapes became the warriors the British had sent to kill him.

He didn't know how he'd outrun them or how far he'd make it, not without a canoe.

But somehow he had to distract the warriors from attacking his brigade and hurting Angelique.

"Please, take Angelique away from here."

Red Fox nodded, his expression somber. "I will take her now."

"If possible, bring my canoe back to this place and hide it." Pierre didn't know how or when he'd be able to return. Although he had a slim chance of surviving the chase, he knew he'd have a much better chance if he had his canoe.

Pierre took one final look at Angelique's sleeping form, then said farewell to Red Fox and turned toward the forest. Whether he lived or not, he had the feeling it was the last time he'd ever see her.

CHAPTER 24

Angelique fell into Miriam's arms, and she sobbed against the woman's shoulder, her breath coming in deep, wrenching heaves. After three days of hard paddling back to the island and containing her sorrow, she couldn't hold it in any longer.

Each stroke away from Pierre, every league between them made the parting more painful and more permanent. It hadn't helped that Red Fox had driven them with a relentless urgency, constantly looking over his shoulder to the lake behind them and to the shore, with fear creasing his weathered forehead.

"Angel, Angel . . ." Miriam murmured, her gentle hands caressing Angelique's hair, combing it back from her forehead.

Angelique knew she ought to be happy to return to her beloved island. She should be overjoyed to see Miriam after the weeks apart. But she couldn't pretend any longer how utterly wretched she was.

She hadn't known just how wretched she'd been until she arrived at the farm and Miriam pulled her into an embrace. She knew then that nothing mattered to her as much as Pierre. And now he was gone. In fact, he'd left her without even saying good-bye. When Red Fox had awoken her in the early morning darkness with instructions to pack the canoe, there hadn't been a trace of Pierre anywhere.

Red Fox had answered her questions about Pierre's absence with grunts. She'd only been able to assume that Pierre had been too hurt and angry and hadn't wanted to say good-bye.

"Oh, Miriam," Angelique said as she wiped the tears from her cheeks, "it's good to see you again."

"God be praised." Miriam's cheeks were wet with tears too. Her beautiful, unseeing eyes shone with both joy and sorrow. "I never stopped praying for your safe return."

Angelique took quick stock of the farm, the tall weeds, the untended garden with its yellow withered leaves, the fields that were ripe for harvest. All of Pierre's hard work from the summer was wasting away. Would they be able to harvest enough to last them through the winter?

Yellow Beaver had already entered the enclosed garden and had started picking some of the vegetables that hadn't rotted. Red Fox had disappeared inside the barn. He'd explained that Pierre had made arrangements for Yellow Beaver to stay with her and Miriam for the winter.

Even so, Angelique couldn't shake the despair or the fear that had assaulted her the moment she'd stepped onto the beach near Main Street. When she'd walked the sandy path past Ebenezer's Inn, she'd tried not to think about what he would do to her once he discovered she was back.

She wouldn't be able to rely on him to help feed her and Miriam in the coming months. Although they'd have Yellow Beaver's help, would it be enough?

Miriam lifted a hand to Angelique's cheek after she'd explained all that had transpired during the time she'd been gone. "You've changed," Miriam said, letting her fingers trail over Angelique's features to do the seeing for her.

Angelique nodded. She felt as though she'd somehow passed a test. As excruciating as it had been to withhold herself from Pierre, she'd done it. She'd done something her mother had never had the strength or willpower to do. She'd done what was right, even though it had been the hardest thing she'd ever accomplished.

Out of the corner of her eye, she caught sight of the ugly red marks on Miriam's hand. "Miriam, what happened to your hand?" But she didn't need to ask. She already knew that Miriam had burned herself over the fire, just as she'd done too many times since her eyesight had failed.

Miriam tried to pull her hand away, but Angelique wouldn't let go. "Do you have any salve left?"

"I don't know."

Miriam's confession twisted Angelique's heart.

As she entered the cabin to look for the salve, one glance confirmed Miriam's plight. There were flies hovering above a piece of molding squash on the table next to the skeletal remains of a fish, the floor was littered with refuse, and the woodbox sat empty. The scent of charred food permeated the stale air, along with the smell of a chamber pot in need of cleaning.

Her friend needed her. No matter what the future held, for the time being she was where she needed to be.

She was smoothing the ointment over Miriam's burns when Red Fox exited the barn with Pierre's boyhood canoe slung over his shoulders. He strode toward her with the same confident walk Pierre always had. "Get me a paddle," he commanded.

Angelique stared at Pierre's canoe with unease. "Why do you have Pierre's canoe?" He would be with his brigade in the long vessels crafted to carry pounds and pounds of trade goods out to the Indian winter camps. Once he arrived he'd trade the beads, guns, ammunition, coats and other items to the Indians in exchange for the fur pelts the natives had trapped. He wouldn't need the little canoe. It was in need of patching anyway.

Red Fox shook his head to her question and then addressed Miriam, "You get Pierre's paddle. He needs it."

Miriam's unseeing eyes seemed to take in everything. Her expression turned serious. "I don't know where Pierre's paddle is. But I have one you can give him."

When Miriam disappeared into the cabin, Angelique glared at Red Fox. "Tell me what's going on. Why do you need Pierre's canoe and paddle?"

Red Fox scrunched his brows with a fierceness that may have once frightened her but no longer did. The darkness in his eyes wavered, and he jutted out his chin. "He runs from the Menominee. They hunt him for the Redcoats."

The news penetrated Angelique like the first hard frost of the fall. Pierre was a wanted man. Why hadn't she thought of it before?

She could only imagine how angry Colonel McDouall and Lieutenant Steele had been when they'd discovered the empty Black Hole. Such an impossible escape would embarrass them and undermine their authority. She had no doubt they were anxious to get him back and had likely put a price on his head.

"He is fast and smart," Red Fox said, eyeing the door. "He will come back to you."

She shook her head. "We aren't meant to be together."

"You are good for my brother."

"But I'm pledged to another —"

"You are pledged to another here." He tapped his head. "But you are pledged to my brother here." He pounded a fist against his heart. "One pledge can be broken and repaired. The other cannot."

Miriam's reappearance silenced any further protest. Angelique sucked in a sharp breath when she saw the paddle Miriam carried, the bright red and blue one that had been hanging above the kitchen table. Angelique had never imagined she'd see it

436

anywhere but on the wall.

Miriam hesitated in the doorway, her fingers caressing the smooth wood of the handle. Then she thrust it toward Red Fox. "Give this to Pierre."

Red Fox pried it out of Miriam's stiff grasp.

"I should have given it to him long ago," she said.

The brave gave the slender piece of brightly painted wood nothing more than a cursory glance. To him it was simply a means for moving a canoe. But Angelique knew it represented much more than that. Maybe Pierre's father hadn't given him the paddle like so many voyageur fathers did to their sons. But she could imagine that if Mr. Durant had been there at that moment, if he'd seen the kind of man Pierre had become, a man of faith and integrity, he would have gladly given Pierre the paddle.

But now Miriam was bestowing the heirloom upon Pierre in her husband's place. And even though Miriam was doing the right thing, Angelique had the urge to grab it out of Red Fox's hands and return it to the wall.

She didn't want Miriam to give Pierre her blessing on his fur trading. She didn't want Miriam to believe Pierre belonged in the wilderness. She wanted Miriam to pray that Pierre would come home and settle down.

But Angelique could only stand back as Red Fox strode away, the paddle under one arm and the canoe on his shoulder.

A tear slipped down Miriam's cheek, and Angelique reached for her hand.

Miriam tried to smile. "I should have told Pierre I was proud of him."

"He'll know that now."

If he lived. But she bit back the words and squeezed Miriam's hand.

Somehow Miriam's acceptance of Pierre's wandering ways made his choice of fur trading all the more final. Even if he outsmarted those who were searching for him, he would be forever lost to them now.

Pierre huddled in the shallow, crumbling mound. Sticks poked into his wet shirt and scraped his back. His feet dangled in the icy water at the opening of the abandoned beaver lodge. He'd hunched inside the dome as tightly as he could, and now he prayed the decaying structure wouldn't topple down around him. At least until his pursuers passed by.

Outside, the splashing of footsteps going against the current alerted him to the approach of one brave who had been steadily trailing him.

Pierre held his breath and hoped the brave wouldn't notice the pile of sticks hidden along the edge of the riverbank beneath a tangle of dead leaves. Of course Pierre had spotted it. Over the years of trading he'd become an expert in locating beaver lodges. Hopefully the brave wasn't an expert too.

The brave's sloshing slowed. Pierre's stomach rumbled, and he pushed his fist into his belly to silence it. He'd been running for days, hardly sleeping and rarely eating, always trying to stay one step ahead of his enemies. He didn't know how much longer he could keep going.

From the shortening days he knew that September would soon pass into October. And if he hoped to make it to the Chippewa winter camp, he had to set out for it soon.

He closed his eyes, exhaustion crashing over him like the rapids he'd just swum across. His body was numb, his hands cracked. His boots were in shreds, and his feet were now bruised and bleeding, leaving him no choice but to stay in the river so that he could wash away any trace of his blood.

He'd been praying ceaselessly. He'd decided that even if the Menominee captured him, he was trusting in God's strength this time. Whether God gave him life or death, he wasn't relying on his own efforts alone.

Perhaps God had given him another trial to drive him back to his knees and turn him into a man of prayer. Maman had always prayed for him. Maybe it was time to start praying for himself. Over the past days of running, he'd prayed about everything, including his angry parting with Angelique. Every time he remembered the way they'd left each other, he wanted to go back in time and redo it.

He'd only been thinking about himself. And when he thought back over his life, he'd come to the conclusion that he'd spent most of his life focused on doing what he wanted without much consideration for anyone else. He'd made the majority of his decisions to please himself.

He was ashamed to admit that even his decision last summer to give up fur trading and stay on the island had been all about his need for Angelique. He hadn't thought much of what Maman had needed, or even what Angelique needed. He hadn't thought about what would be best for her, that maybe she wanted someone in her life more reliable, like Jean, and that maybe he *had* tempted her into cheating on Jean.

The honorable thing would have been to wait to pursue her until after she'd called off her engagement with Jean. He hadn't been fair to her or Jean.

Jean hadn't deserved to have him come onto the island and woo Angelique into his arms. Why had it taken him so long to see that?

The splashing outside the beaver lodge grew faint, and he allowed himself to breathe again, sucking in gulping breaths saturated with molding leaves and damp moss. He closed his eyes again, unable to fight the exhaustion any longer. The dark coldness of the hovel closed in around him.

Angelique didn't need someone like him, someone who was constantly facing danger and death. Look at him now, curled up inside a beaver lodge, trying to outwit his pursuers.

He would have laughed at himself if he hadn't been so cold and tired. Instead, for the first time in days, he allowed himself to fall into a deep sleep. And his last thought before weariness claimed him was that Angelique would be better off with Jean.

He only wished he'd realized that sooner, before he'd broken her heart.

CHAPTER 25

May 1815 — eight months later

Angelique wriggled her toes in the warm sand and gazed out over the harbor crowded with schooners, canoes, and rowboats transporting cargo between the ships and the shore.

The gulls flew low and circled above the recently thawed water, their sharp cries welcome after the long winter of isolation from the rest of the world. The voyageur songs mixed with laughter and swirled around her, turning her insides into a frenzy of nervousness and excitement.

She wasn't looking for Pierre. She'd told herself she wouldn't. She'd only come to watch the arrival of the Americans and to take news back to Miriam and Yellow Beaver.

Even though Angelique had promised herself that she wouldn't look for Pierre, that she wouldn't get her hopes up, she found herself narrowing her eyes upon several canoes moving across the lake from the mainland to the island. She held her breath, waiting for them to draw closer so that she could carefully study each form.

At a rough shove against her arm, Angelique lurched sideways into the crowds bustling along the waterfront.

"Ah, the fish lass" came the clipped voice that belonged to Lieutenant Steele.

Angelique's stomach curdled at the sight of the loup-garou coming to a halt next to her. Of course the past winter hadn't been overly harsh, and the lieutenant wasn't skin and bones like he'd been last spring. Still, he'd been the one to torture and almost kill Pierre in the Black Hole. And because of that he'd always be a loup-garou.

His uniform was frayed, the red faded, and his body thin, as were those of the regulars following behind him carrying crates that the British were loading into the waiting tenders.

"Are you watching for someone, fish lass?" the lieutenant asked, his sharp eyes roaming over the docked boats. "Perhaps a tall, broad-shouldered voyageur with dark unruly hair."

Was it that obvious she was searching for Pierre?

The sunlight blazed upon the lieutenant's battered black hat, likely the same hat he'd worn the night of the dance last summer when the hat had been new and buffed and immaculate.

"I'm here for the same reason as everybody else," she replied, pulling herself up. "Watching the arrival of the Americans."

When the first ships of the spring had arrived at Michilimackinac two weeks ago, they'd brought joyous tidings that the Treaty of Ghent had been signed in December.

The war was over, had been over for the past five months. But because of their remote location and the ice that prevented communication with the outside world, the residents of Michilimackinac were some of the last to hear the good news.

The treaty provided that the Americans and British give up the territory that had been conquered during the war. After three years of inhabiting the fort and controlling the island, the British would finally have to leave.

The American ships had arrived yesterday. Miriam had sent Angelique repeatedly down to the harbor to find out if Jean was returning with the other islanders who'd been forced to leave at the beginning of the war.

One boat of civilians had already come

ashore that morning, among them a young graceful lady whose beauty reminded Angelique of Lavinia. Only this woman had been dressed much simpler, as if she had the intention of adjusting to island life rather than trying to make it adjust to her. Eventually rumors had sifted toward Angelique that the lady was the daughter of the American surgeon who would be stationed at the fort.

Amidst the unloading of American troops and goods, the British were retreating to their awaiting ships and readying to depart. As fort commissary, Lieutenant Steele was likely in charge of making sure all the British supplies were transported onto the ships. The British wouldn't want to leave anything for their American enemies.

Lieutenant Steele stepped aside and let his two soldiers pass by. They struggled under the weight of the crate, their boots sinking into the sand as they staggered toward a waiting rowboat. After they'd passed out of hearing distance, the lieutenant leaned toward Angelique, close enough for her to get a whiff of the sourness of rum on his breath.

"You might as well stop looking for Pierre Durant," the lieutenant said with a gleam in his eyes. "He's dead."

The blunt words slammed against Angelique, nearly sending her toppling again.

As if seeing that he was getting the reaction he'd hoped for, the lieutenant's lips quirked into a half smile. "I got reports last week from the Menominee warriors that I sent after him. They found his body. All that remained was a heap of bones. And his paddle. A red-and-blue-striped paddle."

Please, God, no. Desperation swelled inside her chest. A strangled cry rose in her throat. If they'd found his paddle and his bones, that meant he hadn't made it to the Indian winter camp in time.

It was too painful to consider that Pierre was dead, even though she'd known it was a very real possibility. She'd tried to prepare herself for it. At the beginning of the winter, she'd attempted to forget about Pierre and focus her thoughts on Jean. But Red Fox's words had haunted her until the truth of them had wrapped their cords around her and held her captive.

Her pledge to Jean was in her head and was one she could eventually set aside after she had the chance to honestly speak with Jean. For although she'd tried to resist Pierre's charm, she'd fallen prey anyway. No matter how hard she'd tried that winter, she hadn't been able to unravel his presence from deep inside. It was almost as if his essence had woven threads through her heart that she couldn't pluck out without destroying herself in the process.

Through the long days of winter, while ice fishing with Yellow Beaver, during the hunting trips she'd taken with him, and in the evenings sitting beside the fire, she hadn't once stopped thinking about Pierre.

While she'd been learning to sew on the pretty calico skirt Miriam had given her to make over, she'd thought about Pierre's eyes full of laughter. When she'd been whittling with Yellow Beaver, she thought about Pierre's disarming grin. When she'd curled up with Miriam and the kittens in the corner bed during the endless nights, she'd prayed for Pierre.

She should have been thinking about Jean and praying for him, but she hadn't given him more than a passing thought.

She'd been consumed with missing Pierre and hadn't left room for anyone else.

But now he was dead.

Her knees weakened, and her body trembled. Just then all she wanted was to fall down and die too.

The lieutenant continued in a low voice, "No captain, British or American, will let any man live to tell about escaping from the

Black Hole. Such news would only encourage future prisoners to attempt the same thing."

She pressed a hand against the pain radiating from her chest. Tears stung her eyes. She needed to run, to get far away from the crowds, where she could let herself grieve in private.

The lieutenant's news made perfect sense. That was why Pierre hadn't returned to the island two weeks ago with the first round of voyageurs and ships. That was why he hadn't come any other day in between, and why he would never come back again.

He was gone. Forever.

"Go back home, lass," the lieutenant said. "You won't find Pierre Durant here today or any day."

She didn't wait to listen to anything else the lieutenant had to say. She didn't care anymore who was coming ashore. All she could think about was getting away from the crowd, somewhere she could let the sobs and pain have release.

Heedless of where she was going, she raced away from the shore, tears blinding her. She ran until she couldn't breathe, and then she crumpled to the forest floor, laying her head against the thick moss, burying her face in damp leaves.

She wept until there was nothing left inside. Nothing but a painful emptiness.

Pierre was gone.

After a winter of harboring hope, she had to let go. Finally.

She supposed she'd clung to the possibility that if he'd lived, he would return for her, even though he had absolutely no reason to do so. She'd told herself she would let go of her need to marry Jean and all the security he offered. She'd clung to the safety of a marriage with Jean rather than trusting that God would take care of her completely no matter where she was or who she was with.

It was the same lesson God had been teaching her when Red Fox had bought her from Ebenezer last summer, when she thought he was forcing her into marriage and away from the island.

She'd even resolved to speak honestly to Jean, to tell him that she couldn't marry him, to give him back his comb. She'd wanted to do the right thing by ending her relationship with Jean first so that she could be free to accept Pierre and the life he offered her — if he ever offered it to her again.

It was why she'd returned to the island in the first place. She realized that now. To end her relationship with Jean.

She wiped the tears from her eyes, sat up, and took a deep breath. She peered past the tall tamaracks and pine that surrounded her to the sky overhead.

But now what did it matter?

With heavy steps she started down the rocky path that led back to the farm. She knew she should be filled with gratefulness for the life God had given her, for the freedom to come and go as she pleased, to dress any way she wished, to be within the folds of Miriam's loving care. It had been so long since she'd had such love and freedom that it had taken weeks for her to lose her fear of Ebenezer's control.

Yellow Beaver's presence on the farm that winter had kept Ebenezer far away. She'd spoken with Betty only once at St. Anne's for Christmas Mass and had learned that Ebenezer didn't care where she lived with her new Indian husband so long as he had his money. She hadn't corrected Betty's assumption about Yellow Beaver being her husband. She'd figured that if it kept her safe, then that was all that mattered.

Yellow Beaver had become like a grandfather to her, teaching her many things over the winter, and she would miss him when he left.

When Angelique reached the edge of the

meadow, she stopped. The door of the cabin stood wide open and a haversack like the one Pierre carried had been discarded beside it. Standing by the barn next to Yellow Beaver was another Indian with a black Mohawk much like the one Red Fox wore.

She couldn't see the Indian's face, but she knew it was Red Fox. It had to be. And if Red Fox had come back, maybe he'd brought Pierre. Her heart gave a lurch, and her feet sped into action. She ran as fast as she could across the long grass, her legs snagging in the bright calico skirt she'd recently finished. She stumbled and caught herself, eagerness urging her forward until finally she reached the door, breathless, frantic expectation tightening every muscle.

But as she ducked inside and squinted into the dim interior, her breathing came to a halt at the sight of Miriam embracing . . . Jean.

Of course it was Jean. Pierre was dead.

At the abruptness of her entrance, he pulled back from Miriam and brushed a hand against his cheek, wiping away the wetness there. His skin was shaven, the scraggly beard that he'd had during the battle gone. His fair hair had the neatness of a recent trim, and his face had a healthy glow.

"Angelique?" The joy in his voice, the beauty of his smile, the longing in his gentle expression made her tremble.

As much as she wanted to smile, she couldn't. Her lips quivered. The disappointment was too great to hide.

The light in his eyes dimmed, and wariness sprang to life in its place.

"Jean?" She forced cheerfulness to her tone. "Welcome home."

"Isn't this wonderful?" Miriam asked, tears streaking her cheeks the same way they had last spring when she'd been reunited with Pierre. "Jean's home. God be praised."

"It *is* wonderful." Angelique meant it. She only wanted the best for Jean. He was a noble, kind, and dear man.

"I came as soon as I could," he said. "I only wish I could have returned in December after the peace treaty was signed."

"We didn't even know the war was over until a couple of weeks ago," Miriam said, holding on to Jean's arm. "God has been good to us. He sent Yellow Beaver to help us over the winter. We never once went hungry."

Jean nodded to the old Indian, who had come into the cabin behind Angelique. "I can't thank you enough for helping them through the winter."

Yellow Beaver nodded in return. "Angel is a daughter to me."

He'd picked up more English during their time together and had begun to teach her the Chippewa language. If Pierre had been there, he would have been proud of her. Angelique strained to see behind Yellow Beaver, hoping for a glimpse of Red Fox. But he was nowhere in sight.

Disappointment surged through her again. She'd wanted to speak with him, to see if he had any more news of Pierre's death, anything that could put her at ease.

Smiling hopefully, Jean said, "I was most anxious to return so that I could finally marry Angelique."

She was afraid he would cross the room, take her in his arms, and kiss her. She wasn't sure she would be able to bear it. She'd probably burst out into sobs.

"I missed you, Angelique," he said softly. "And I've dreamed of this day for the past three years, the day when I could come home and make you my wife. Some days, thoughts of you were all that kept me alive."

Her throat constricted. What should she say? What reason did she have for saying no to him now?

He took a step forward, and for the first time she noticed he was holding a cane. She glanced to his leg, the one that had taken a bullet during the battle for the island. He looked down too. "The surgeon saved my leg, but just barely. It was his daughter who nursed me back to health these past months."

"I saw her come ashore this morning. She's beautiful."

"We'll have to thank her," Miriam interjected. "And thank her father too. They must have cared about you a great deal to give you so much attention."

Jean shrugged. "They were both kind to me."

"I'd like to meet her," Miriam insisted, her expression serious. Her lips stalled. She wanted to say more but didn't know what.

Jean took another halting step, and his cane thumped against the wood floor. "I'm grateful for their help in keeping me alive, and I'm thankful to still have my leg. But the fact is I'm a cripple. And I'll always be a cripple."

"You're a good man," Angelique said, "and the condition of your body doesn't change that."

"Then you're still willing to marry me? Even though I'm less of a man now?"

"You're not less of a man," she said at the same time Miriam gave a murmur of protest. "You could never be less of a man."

Even so, he would never be able to manage the farm by himself. How would he do the hard physical labor of plowing and sowing and harvesting alone?

Jean smiled hesitantly. "I didn't think you would turn me away and refuse to marry me because I'm a cripple now. But I wasn't sure. I wouldn't blame you if you did."

"Of course I wouldn't refuse to marry you for that." What was she saying? Her mind stumbled over the words that could explain how she really felt.

"Let's get married as soon as possible," he said, his face flushed and his eyes bright. "Today. After I have the chance to clean up."

Could she really marry him, especially when she didn't love him?

She hadn't loved him before the war either. He'd told her it hadn't mattered, that his love would be enough. But would it? After all she'd experienced with Pierre, would a loveless marriage ever be truly enough?

"Please say yes." His eyes regarded her with all the adoration he'd always had.

She didn't want him to believe she was refusing him because of his injury. But if she told him no, he'd think that she didn't care for him anymore because of his condition.

How could she do that to him? And if she didn't marry him, who would help him with the farm? He would need her now more than ever to work the land and help take care of Miriam.

"Please, Angelique . . ." He limped across the cabin. The swish of his dragging foot and the tap of his cane pressured her, shouted at her to give in.

Miriam didn't say anything more. And Angelique wanted to yell out in frustration. She wished her friend would voice her opinion for once, share her wisdom and reveal God's will in the matter.

But Miriam's lips moved in silent prayer, her answer to every problem.

Angelique stifled a sigh. Couldn't her friend try something else today?

Behind her, Angelique sensed Yellow Beaver's confusion. He'd watched her with Pierre. He'd seen the love they'd shared. Would he step in and help her?

Jean reached for her hand. "I promise I'll always love you and give you everything you've ever wanted." His eyes pleaded with her. There was a desperation there she hadn't seen before. It tore at her.

She couldn't refuse Jean. She wouldn't be

able to live with herself if she did. There was no reason to put off marrying Jean. No reason at all. Not now that Pierre was dead.

Jean, Miriam, and the farm all meant too much for her to just turn her back on them and walk away. Where would she go anyway? Now that she'd been free from Ebenezer, she would never be able to return.

She swallowed hard, then nodded at Jean. Yes, she would marry him. She would have to put her love for Pierre behind her and pray that God would help her care about Jean, help her be the kind of wife he deserved.

And at some point she would have to break the news to Miriam that Pierre was dead.

Chapter 26

Pierre crunched through the woods. The branches swung back and swatted him, and the vines snagged his feet and tripped him. "Even you are telling me I shouldn't have come home," he said to the island.

When he'd stared at Michilimackinac earlier that morning from the mainland, every nerve in his body had keened with the longing to jump in his canoe and go to Angelique. But he'd told himself that he wouldn't, that it would be too hard to see her again and know he couldn't have her.

All winter long he'd held fast to his decision to sacrifice his own selfish need to be with her and do what was best for both her and Jean. And if he had any hope of keeping his vow, he knew he couldn't return to the island. He didn't trust himself. Even though he'd grown a great deal through his trials over the past year, he was far from being a perfect man. Some days he lost his battle with his sinful nature. He was afraid if he saw her, he'd resort to his old selfish ways.

But Red Fox had prodded him all morning while he'd shaven and cleaned himself up, until finally he'd given in to his friend's pressure.

Now that the Americans were back on the island, he supposed he was relatively safe, as long as he kept away from the British, especially Lieutenant Steele. He didn't want to risk the lieutenant seeing him, to discover that he was still alive. There was no telling what the man might do, even if the war was over.

Now that he'd paddled to the island, he hadn't worked up the courage to return to the farm. He had a strong feeling Jean would be there. Could he really face Jean and Angelique and then walk away and let them be happy together?

"You'll have to help me through this one," he prayed with a sigh. "Even with your help, I'm still going to have a rough time."

His feet had veered from the path that led to the farm, and he found himself heading to the spot where he could always find solace. He knew he was putting off the inevitable, but a cold swim would steel his muscles to fight the coming temptation.

The splash of water and a flash of white through the brush halted him. He crouched and peered through the branches, past the long grass and boulders surrounding the swimming hole.

There, kneeling at the water's edge, was Angelique. She was dressed in a shift that outlined every curve of her body. Her beautiful red hair hung in a wet mass about her, and she was lathering some soap into it.

He couldn't move. He was helpless to do anything but watch her.

She was obviously bathing, and he knew he should back away and give her privacy. But his heart ached too much to do anything but take in every detail about her, from the bare skin of her arms to the dainty toes poking out from under the fabric.

Oh, God, help, he pleaded. He wrenched his attention away and forced himself to look at the moss-covered stone by his knee. He needed to run. Run away as fast as he could.

He started to retreat, but at a splash he lifted his gaze again. She'd jumped into the water and disappeared below the surface.

He stood and waited for her to come up.

Long agonizing seconds ticked by, and when she still didn't break through the water, he jolted forward, crashed through the thick brush, and sprinted toward the shadows of her sinking under the water.

He managed to shed his capote as he ran but didn't take the time to slip out of his boots before he hit the pond at a running jump. He sank into the frigid depths. The biting cold took away his breath. Water filled his mouth and nose and dragged him down with the weight of his clothes and boots.

Arms and legs flailed near him, and he grasped her.

She fought him, squirming against his hold, pulling away from him. But he was quicker and stronger and was able to grab her arms, giving her no choice but to rise upward with him.

They broke through the surface, each gasping for air. She choked, spitting out the water she'd swallowed. When she could finally breathe again, she swiped the tangles from her face.

At the sight of him, the irritation in her eyes evaporated and was replaced with wide-eyed shock. "Pierre!" Her voice shook and her face paled.

"Are you all right, ma cherie?" He searched her face.

"Is it really you?" She lifted a hand, hesitated with her fingers outstretched before grazing his cheek. "You're alive!"

He grinned. "Oui. Of course it's me. Who else is this handsome and charming?"

She didn't smile, but her eyes lit with wonder. "I don't believe it. Lieutenant Steele told me you were dead. The Menominee found your paddle next to a pile of bones."

His thoughts went back to the torturous weeks of avoiding capture and how he'd finally outsmarted the warriors who'd been trailing him. "I located the grave of a voyageur we'd buried the previous year, dug up the bones, and then smeared them with blood from a wild turkey I killed. I had to leave most of my belongings behind to deceive the Menominee, including my paddle."

He'd hated to leave his papa's paddle behind, knowing how much it must have cost Maman to give it to him. But the deception had worked. They'd finally stopped their relentless hunt after assuming he'd been devoured by a pack of wolves that had left a bloody heap of bones.

It was a good thing he'd lost the warriors when he did because he'd barely made it to the Chippewa winter camp before the lake had frozen. He didn't want to think about how he'd nearly died during the canoe trip across the waters that were freezing even as he paddled.

Only the thought of seeing Angelique again had kept him going, when he'd been weak from hunger and cold, when the ice forming on the lake had begun to trap him, and his body had urged him to give up — to lay back in his canoe and fall asleep forever.

"Why did the lieutenant tell me you were dead?" she asked.

"That's what I need him to believe."

She touched his smooth-shaven cheek again as if unable to believe he was really there. "If Lieutenant Steele sees you and realizes you're still alive, won't he throw you back in the Hole?"

"I won't let him see me," he reassured her. He wouldn't tell her that he was leaving in a couple of hours. That he'd hug and kiss Maman, make sure Jean was safe, and then he would leave the island for good.

Facing her now, he knew he'd have to leave sooner rather than later or he'd do something very foolish, like kiss her, and then he wouldn't be able to tear himself away.

"I came back because I knew you'd need rescuing," he teased, trying to lighten the moment.

"What do you mean?" Underneath the surface her feet and legs bumped his as she kicked them to stay afloat.

"You were drowning and I saved your life."

"I was rinsing the soap out of my hair."

"You disappeared under the water and didn't resurface." He couldn't relinquish his hold on her arms.

She cocked her head, and a smile twitched her lips. "Do you really think I'd drown, Pierre? You know I can swim as well as a fish."

"Oui. You're right. What was I thinking?" He knew he hadn't been thinking of anything but how beautiful she'd looked. But he couldn't tell her that.

Treat her like a friend, he commanded himself, forcing his eyes not to look anywhere but at her face — her sweet, lovely face.

Her smile widened, and it was as welcoming as the blue sky overhead. Her eyes lit with joy and wonder and . . . desire. Water dripped from her hair and ran in rivulets down her face, meeting at her lips and drawing his attention there, irresistibly.

A sudden and powerful urge shot through him. He needed to kiss her more than anything, even more than taking another breath.

Treat her like a friend. The words shook him, breaking his thoughts and demanding he do the noble thing.

He let go of her and pushed a wave of water at her.

She sputtered at the cascade of water in her face. "What was that for?"

He made himself grin, trying hard to appear carefree when everything within him protested. "That was for scaring me half to death."

She wiped her face, clearing the water away. And then before he could duck, she sent a wall of water splashing into his face. "And that was for scaring *me* half to death."

It was his turn to sputter. He lunged for her, but with a laugh she darted away from him. He swam after her, but she was slippery and quick, always evading his grasp. Laughing with her, he chased and splashed her until finally he snagged her shift.

When he pulled her against the flow of water toward him, this time she didn't resist.

"I let you catch me," she said, her legs treading water near his. She looked up at him with all the adoration she'd always had.

"Oh, no you didn't. I'm still faster than you." Even though his limbs were numb from the frigid water, all it took was one look into her doe-like brown eyes to heat

465

his insides thoroughly and completely.

"You just can't admit defeat, can you?" Her smile was glorious and touched a place deep inside him with such bittersweet pain he wanted to cry out at the unfairness of everything.

Bantering with her and seeing her in all her beauty made him realize once again how much he wanted her. Desperately.

His hold on her arms tightened. His grin slipped away. He could see by the reflection in her eyes that his desire was etched into every line of his face.

Her smile vanished too, and her eyes widened, revealing the love he'd hoped to see there. She tilted her head just slightly, but it was enough of an invitation.

The soft intake of her breath, and the tiny nibble she gave to her lower lip sent fire racing through him.

He was going to kiss her. He was going to lose the battle, and part of him didn't care. He wanted to be with her too much. But another part of him screamed for him to stop, to flee from the temptation.

He groaned, let go of her, and submerged his body under the water, letting the iciness crash against his face. He forced himself to swim toward the shore. And he didn't stop until he'd climbed out and moved a safe distance away.

She followed him out of the water slowly, until she stood in her wet shift shivering, dejection dripping from every fiber of her body.

He grabbed his capote where he'd discarded it and held it out to her.

She wrapped it around herself, yet her teeth chattered and her body shook uncontrollably. "I'm sorry for hurting you last fall, Pierre."

"You were right to reject me." He set his shoulders, preparing for battle against his selfishness. "During all the running I had to do, I realized I was only thinking about myself and what I wanted. I didn't take into consideration you or Jean and what would be best for the two of you."

She reached out a hand to him.

He forced himself not to take it. "I'm sorry for pushing you to be unfaithful to Jean. And I'm sorry for making you feel like your mother. I loathe myself for how I hurt you."

"I've done some thinking over the winter too," she began.

"Let me finish, Angelique." He had to get everything out before he lost his courage. She shook her head, but he continued anyway. "You belong here on the island, and

467

I don't. At least not at this point in my life."

Tears escaped from the corners of her eyes, and the sight of them squeezed his chest until he could barely breathe. "Please don't cry, ma cherie." He wanted to go to her and comfort her, but if he allowed himself to be near her again, he wouldn't be able to tear himself away this time.

"I love you with all my heart," she whispered. "I realized that I don't care where we are so long as we're together."

A tiny waft of hope fluttered in his chest.

"I'd planned to tell Jean I wouldn't marry him. That I couldn't. I wanted to be honest with him. Finally. But then after I heard you were dead and when I saw Jean this morning, I couldn't tell him no. I promised him again that I'd marry him." The words came out strangled. "With his injury he needs me now more than ever."

The hope vanished, leaving him with an overwhelming sorrow.

"We're getting married at St. Anne's at noon." Her shoulders slumped. "I came here to wash up and prepare for my wedding."

He couldn't move or speak. The gentle lapping of the water, and the song of a warbler in the surrounding woodlands echoed in the silence that settled between them. He wanted to yell out his protest, wanted to grab her and take her away with him, far from Jean and the island. But he was strangely empty.

He took a half step back. "You're doing the right thing."

She nodded.

"I want you to know," he said, his voice cracking with the effort it took to restrain himself, "I love you even more for your sacrifice."

"And I love you more for yours."

He held her gaze, knowing it was the last time he would look into her eyes. He let himself feast on her love for one final moment before he spun away from her and disappeared back into the forest. His unshed tears blinded him, and he tripped over a long, smooth stick. He would have ignored it, except the perfectness of the wood stopped him.

He reached down and picked it up. It wasn't just any stick. It was carved and oiled and rounded at the top, obviously fashioned with great care by someone.

He tucked the stick under his arm and ran. His chest ached with too much pain to think about anything but losing Angelique again. His chest was an open wound, as if a Menominee warrior had chopped through his skin and bones, dug inside, and wrenched out his heart.

CHAPTER 27

Angelique twisted the last strand of curls up into the loop she'd fashioned at the back of her head, then stood back and examined herself in Miriam's tarnished silver mirror. Her hair didn't look quite as fancy as it had the night Lavinia had styled it for the dance, but it would have to do.

She swished the skirt of the shiny gown Lavinia had given her. She'd long ago repaired the rips and stains gained during the canoe voyage last fall and had packed it away carefully inside a trunk.

"Thank you," she said, handing the mirror back to Miriam. She took a deep breath, letting in the scent of lilacs from the bouquet she'd arranged that morning and placed on the table.

The faded yellow curtains fluttered in the open window, bringing in a hint of smoke from the Indian campfires on the beach and the faint sound of drums, the signal that spring had finally arrived. This year, unlike the last, the walls on either side of the table were bare. The paddle and fishing pole were both gone, and Angelique knew now they'd never return. It was time for something new to go in those spots, something that belonged to Jean.

Angelique had done the best she could to be the beautiful bride that Jean deserved. If Lavinia could have seen her, she would have been pleased with the outcome.

"It's time." She reached for Miriam's arm and hooked it through hers.

Strangely, over the past hour of preparations, a sense of peace had settled over Angelique, replacing her need for Pierre. She had a calmness for what she was about to do. She wasn't sure if the peace came from knowing Pierre was alive and well or if perhaps it was God's way of assuring her that she was being faithful. She'd resisted temptation, and she'd come out stronger as a result.

Miriam shuffled toward the door, feeling her way forward. She'd changed into her best skirt for the wedding and looked as lovely as the blooming lilacs.

Angelique started to open the door, but Miriam stopped her with a gentle tug. "Wait, Angel."

She turned to Miriam. She'd expected her dear friend to be happier now that both her sons were home. Of course she'd been overjoyed at the first sight of Pierre, had shed tears when she'd hugged him, but her gentle features were grave now. Was she sad that he had to leave again so soon? He'd declared his intent to sneak off the island before noon, even though Miriam had pleaded with him to stay for the whole day.

Angelique could see that he wanted to be gone by the time she stood next to Jean at St. Anne's. As it was, Pierre lingered outside near the barn, waiting to talk with Jean.

"You know I've loved you like you were my own daughter," Miriam said.

"And you've been a mother to me more than my own mother ever was."

"I haven't wanted to meddle in all that's gone on with you and Pierre and Jean. I've done the best thing for you that I could, and that is to pray God would direct each of you into His plans for you."

Angelique wasn't surprised Miriam had guessed their struggles. She may be blind, yet she still saw many things clearly.

"I promise I won't start meddling today," Miriam continued, "but I couldn't help noticing you're preparing to marry a man you don't love."

"I'm just trying to do the right thing."

"I can't imagine the right thing is marrying someone because you feel obligated to him while throwing away your chance to spend your life with the man you love."

Miriam's words were quiet, but the power of them knocked into Angelique with a strength that took her breath away.

Miriam squeezed her arm. "Like I said, I don't want to meddle, so I promise I won't say anything else."

Angelique didn't know how to respond. She'd already decided she must marry Jean and help him with the farm. Pierre had agreed she was doing the right thing. What should she do with Miriam's advice now?

Fighting a wave of confusion, she opened the door and stepped outside the cabin. Instantly the May sunshine and warmth enveloped her.

Next to the barn, Red Fox and Yellow Beaver shifted their attention to her from where they stood talking with Pierre, who was busy cleaning his musket. Yellow Beaver grinned, and Red Fox stopped mid-sentence.

Pierre didn't look up but instead continued polishing the rifle. Several wayward curls clung to his forehead. He'd changed into a pair of clean trousers and a dry shirt since she'd seen him at the swimming hole.

Even across the span of the yard he looked as ruggedly appealing and handsome as always. The mere sight of him sent her pulse racing and chased away the last remnants of peace.

She was marrying Jean. She needed a glimpse of him, his joy, and his desire for her. That would restore her peace.

Red Fox shoved Pierre and grunted something harsh. But Pierre kept his eyes focused on the rifle barrel in his hands.

"Where's Jean?" Angelique glanced around the farmyard that Yellow Beaver had kept in immaculate condition. "We're done readying ourselves."

Earlier she'd laid out Jean's Sunday best. Even though the clothes had been wrinkled and musty when Miriam pulled them out of the trunk, Angelique made quick work of pressing them with the hot iron.

"Jean?" she called, expecting him to emerge from the barn.

"I'm still waiting for him," Pierre said, working on his musket as if it were the most important job in the world at that moment. "I haven't seen him since I got here."

Angelique searched the freshly plowed fields and then the line of evergreens beyond. "Does anyone know where he went?"

"The last I knew," Miriam said, "he was heading to your swimming hole to take a bath. He said he wanted to clean up before he went to St. Anne's."

"Did he ever come back from the pond?" Angelique asked, a knot of worry cinching her belly. Had he fallen and been unable to get up?

"Swimming hole?" Pierre slapped his forehead and groaned. "Oh no . . ."

"What?" Angelique pressed her hand against her middle, fighting against the growing anxiety.

Pierre pointed to a smooth stick in the grass by his feet. The rounded top gleamed in the sunshine.

Angelique stared at it. Was it Jean's cane? If so, why had he left it behind?

Shaking his head, Pierre handed Red Fox the musket. He picked up the cane. "I'm guessing he was on his way to the swimming hole to wash up . . . but then he got distracted."

Angelique wanted to ask Pierre what he meant by Jean being distracted, yet the sadness in his eyes told her the answer. Jean had overheard them as they'd played in the water and then made their declarations of love to each other.

"He must have been in such a hurry to

476

get away," Pierre said, "that he left his cane behind."

"After he left the swimming hole, where would he have gone?" She could only imagine how their passionate pleas of love had shocked him and wounded him to his core.

Pierre stared at the woods, his brow furrowed. "I think I know where he went." He didn't wait to explain but sprinted across the open field toward the forest.

Angelique picked up her skirts, kicked off her satin slippers, and started after him. He was much faster, and she soon lost him. But she could easily track his progress through the woods, and it didn't take her long to figure out where he was headed.

She arrived at the edge of Dousman's field hot and breathless. Her hair had come loose from the pins she'd used with such care, and the soles of her feet were pricked and sore from the run.

She tiptoed toward the big cedar tree, their thinking tree, and she could see the bottom of Pierre's boots dangling from where he perched on a lower branch. Farther up the tree, she caught a glimpse of Jean's shoes.

She hesitated at the base of the tree. The long branches covered with needles swayed gently in the breeze and shielded them from her sight, though she could hear them talking.

Jean's voice was raised. "You stole her from me, Pierre."

"It was selfish of me, I admit."

"Yes, it was. What kind of brother would do such a thing?"

"Oui. I've not been a very good brother to you."

"You knew she would be better off with me." The pain in Jean's voice stabbed Angelique. "Why couldn't you leave her alone? Why did you have to win her affection?"

"It was wrong of me, Jean. I see that now." Pierre's words were laced with anguish. "I shouldn't have gone behind your back. She didn't want to, but I pursued her anyway."

A long silence followed, filled only by the sound of the wind rustling the branches around them.

"I know I don't deserve your forgiveness," Pierre finally said. "But I beg you for it. And once I have it, I promise I'll leave this island and leave you both alone."

A silent cry arose in Angelique, but she cupped her hand against her mouth. For endless moments she didn't dare to breathe for fear of crying.

At last, Jean let out a sigh. "Honestly, you

didn't steal her from me. You were only claiming what has been yours all along."

"What do you mean?"

"She's always loved you." The anger in Jean's voice had changed to frustration. "Always, even when we'd climb this tree, she'd chase after you, sit on the branch next to you. You were always the one she watched with those beautiful eyes of hers."

Pierre remained silent.

"She never looked at me like that. She didn't notice me until you were gone."

"I don't know —"

"But I'm not you," Jean interrupted. "And she wants you. She's always wanted you . . . not me."

Angelique pressed her hand tighter over her mouth to keep another cry from escaping, a cry that would acknowledge the truth of Jean's words.

"When she walked into the cabin this morning, I could tell she'd been expecting you, Pierre. And when she saw it was me, she tried to hide her disappointment. But I knew it was you she wanted."

"Jean, I —"

"And last summer in the cave, I knew then too. How much you cared for each other, and that you'd fallen in love with her."

Angelique looked past the cedar tree to

the yellow grass of the field with its shoots of new green growth popping up everywhere. It was hard to imagine it was the same spot of the bloody battle that brought Jean back to the island.

"I tried so hard to hold on to her," Jean said. "I wanted to cling to the hope that she would still have me, that maybe you'd realize she'd be happier with me here on the island."

"And I have realized that. I want her to be with you, here, the place she loves most in the world."

"She *won't* be happy. You know that, brother."

"But she loves it here," Pierre said.

"No. She won't be happy anywhere unless it's by your side."

Tears pricked Angelique's eyes. She couldn't believe what she was hearing, but she knew it was the truth, the truth that God had been wanting her to know all along. She shouldn't look to a place or circumstances for her happiness. If God was her rock, then she could be content anywhere.

"I wanted her to marry me anyway," Jean admitted, "even though I knew how much she loved you. I tried to justify to myself that I'd make her happy eventually. That I'd do everything I could to make her forget about you, and that she'd come to love me someday." His voice cracked. "Then when I saw you both at the swimming hole, having fun and laughing together, I realized I've never made her laugh. I can rarely get her to smile."

He grew silent for a few moments, then added, "I realized that if I force her to marry me, I'll only make her miserable. I'll never see her smiles or hear her laughter, no matter how hard I try."

The tears in Angelique's eyes brimmed over. She knew she shouldn't eavesdrop any longer, and yet she couldn't make herself walk away.

"Don't you see?" Jean went on. "I've been selfish too. I wanted her for myself, and I didn't care about what was best for her."

"No one is as selfish as me," Pierre said. "I'm the worst."

"And the most boastful," Jean said dryly. "Even when it comes to the negative."

Angelique couldn't keep from smiling. She could picture the two men exchanging grins. Her tears spilled over once again, this time in gratefulness that she hadn't destroyed their brotherly love for each other.

"Does this mean you forgive me?" Pierre asked.

"If you forgive me."

"Deal."

"And if you promise you'll marry Angelique and make her happy every day of your life."

Pierre hesitated.

Angelique stiffened.

"I don't know if she'll have me now. She was determined to marry you."

"You'll marry him," Jean called down toward her. "Won't you, Angelique?"

She gasped and stepped backward. How long had they known she was standing there listening?

Within seconds Jean appeared on the branch above her as he made an awkward descent, favoring his injured leg. When he hopped to the ground, he landed on his good leg but still gave a grunt of pain.

She wanted to rush to help him, but when he straightened, the sadness etching his face stopped her. He took halting steps toward her, holding the cane Pierre had brought to him, dragging his injured leg. He reached for her hand, brought it to his lips, and placed a tender kiss on the back of it.

"I'm sorry for breaking our commitment, Jean," she began. "I was wrong to give way to my affection for Pierre when I was bound to you."

He shook his head. "You were never mine to begin with. And now I release you to be with the one you've belonged to all along."

She fought back tears. "You're a good man, Jean. You deserve a woman who will love you with all her heart."

"I don't think there are too many women who will want me now, not like this." He cocked his head toward his leg.

"I have no doubt God will bring the right woman into your life, a woman who will see the wonderful, godly man you've become and love you exactly the way you are." She thought of the woman who'd come ashore earlier, the surgeon's daughter. "In fact, maybe you've met her already."

He smiled sadly. "Whatever happens, you'll always have a special place in my heart, Angelique." He kissed her hand again. After giving a nod upward toward Pierre, Jean squared his shoulders and limped away.

She watched him go, fighting the urge to run after him. But the proud way he held his head told her that to chase after him would only wound him further. She needed to let him go with a measure of his pride still intact.

She watched him silently until he disappeared, and afterward she turned and stared up at the cedar tree. She wanted to wait for Pierre to climb down to her, but something told her that this time she needed to be the one to go to him.

With a shaky breath she bunched her skirt into one hand and ducked under the canopy of branches. She placed her bare foot on the lowest branch, the bark scratchy against her tender sole. Then she looked up.

Pierre was leaning back against the trunk and peering down at her. "It's about time."

Heat flamed into her cheeks. "You knew I was listening?"

He grinned. "In that gown I think I'd be able to notice you even if you were a mile away."

Gingerly she started to climb, her feet not yet having developed the calluses that would come after a summer of going barefoot. "I suppose that's why you noticed me when you were talking with Red Fox and Yellow Beaver by the barn?"

He reached out a hand to help her up the last several steps the branches provided. "I didn't dare look at you," he said as she lowered herself on the branch next to him. "If I'd allowed myself even one glance, I would have marched over to you, slung you over my shoulder, and carried you to St. Anne's to marry you myself."

"And I don't think I would have resisted."

"Of course you wouldn't have." His tone was warm and playful. "Since when have you been able to resist me? I'm irresistible, you know."

"I can resist you if I want to," she teased, pivoting so that she faced him.

"I'd like to see that." His dark eyes sparkled and matched his smile. The shadows from the branches above only made his face more handsome.

"Very well." She lifted her fingers to his lips and traced the edges, skimming the fullness of his mouth.

His smile faded, and the spark in his eyes changed to a flash of desire.

She let her fingers make a trail to his smooth chin, then to his neck, giving herself the liberty to taunt him.

He leaned toward her, determination etching his features.

Her middle fluttered in anticipation of his kiss. But when he lowered his head near hers, she placed her hands on his cheeks to slow his descent. She forced his head back and instead rose so that she was leaning into him, so that her lips were near his but not quite touching.

She grazed lightly against his mouth, taking a soft nibble of his lower lip.

He gave a low moan.

She leaned in closer, but then pulled back so only her breath touched him. His mouth chased hers, but she quickly turned and all he found was her cheek.

"You're teasing me." His whisper against her ear sent a shiver through her.

"I'm resisting you."

He pressed a kiss against her ear, the heat of his breath making her tremble. "I admit," he whispered, "you're the irresistible one. I can't stop myself from wanting to kiss you every time I see you."

She smiled. "Every time?"

"I've had to use way too much restraint around you," he said quietly, "more than humanly possible for any one man. I'm thinking it's about time to cut the chains holding me back. But first you have to answer Jean's question."

"What question?"

"You will marry me, won't you, Angelique?"

At the worry that flickered in his eyes, she caressed his cheek. "Jean was right. You're the only one I've ever loved. And no matter where you go or what you do, I want to be by your side for the rest of my life."

"You know I can't stay on the island. I have to leave this afternoon. I can't take any chances that the British might see me alive."

"I don't have much to pack. I can be ready whenever you are."

"Are you sure?"

She nodded. "I'm going with you, Pierre, as your wife. I want to be with you the rest of my days, whether that's in a canoe in the wilderness or sitting up in this tree on our island."

He studied her face as if testing her words. "I guess it's settled then, because I won't go anywhere either unless you're there with me."

Joy bubbled deep inside her. "And if I climb down this tree and go to St. Anne's for a wedding at noon?"

"I'll be right by your side." He smiled. "In fact, I'll race you there."

She smiled back. "What are we waiting for?"

"For this." He leaned in to her, his breath warm and eager. And when his lips met hers, she knew she was right where she belonged, that no matter where they went she was where she wanted to be for the rest of her life.

AUTHOR'S NOTE

Michilimackinac Island is known to most of the world as Mackinac Island, a popular tourist and vacation destination in northern Michigan. But long ago, before the island became famous for its horse-drawn carriages, fudge, and Grand Hotel, the island was important for its strategic location in the fur-trading business.

Fur trading in the early 1800s dominated the Northwest. Great Britain, France, and the new country of the United States of America all had holdings in the Great Lakes region. Michilimackinac was in a pivotal location and of great importance to the fur industry.

In their efforts to gain the upper hand in the profitable trade in beaver, fox, mink, otter, and other pelts, the nations fought for control over the tiny Mackinac Island and even built an army fort on the bluffs of the island for its protection.

By the time of the War of 1812, the Americans had been in control of the island for close to fifteen years. So it was with great disappointment and fear that the American captain in charge of Fort Michilimackinac lost the island at the beginning of the war after the British invaded and pointed their cannons at the fort.

As portrayed in *Captured by Love,* the American men who refused to sign the Oath of Allegiance to the invading British Army had to leave Mackinac. Those who remained had to swear allegiance to King George.

The British had a decided advantage over the Americans during the war because they had cultivated friendships with the area's Indian tribes. The British plied the Indians with presents in order to win their loyalty. And so with the help of their Indian allies, the British regained control of the upper Great Lakes for the duration of the war.

Most of the events surrounding the War of 1812 on Mackinac Island happened the way I've portrayed them in *Captured by Love.* The British Army and the islanders faced starvation from blockades on several occasions. The Americans really did attempt to reclaim the island by invasion at one point and bungled the entire effort. I tried to retell the battle the way it occurred, along with an odd diversion in which the British left the battlefield supposing an attack was happening elsewhere on the island. When the war ended in December 1814, the people on the island didn't receive the news until spring, when the first ships began to arrive.

While the main characters of this novel are fictional, I used the names of real war heroes, captains, and colonels, as well as the names of places that exist on the island today. The fort still sits today on the bluffs of the island, with the stone officers' quarters, soldiers' barracks, and storehouse. In fact, you can even peer down into the infamous Black Hole.

The voyaging and fur-trading era played an important role on Mackinac Island for many years. The term *voyageur* is associated with the men who paddled the canoes, the freight haulers of the fur trade. The canoes would leave from eastern ports loaded with trade goods, food, and other supplies. The hardy voyageurs would paddle the canoes out into the wilderness, where they would trade the goods to the Indians for the profitable pelts that were in high demand, especially back in England.

After the War of 1812, Jacob Astor took control of the Great Lakes fur trading with his post on Mackinac Island, and free traders like Pierre struggled to survive against the growing businesses of fur magnets like Astor's American Fur Trading Company. Astor made his millions in the fur trade, though by the early 1820s the region had been harvested of most of the pelts, while the demand for beaver was on a steady decline. It wasn't long before he pulled his company out of the area.

After the fur-trading era, it's a wonder that life on Mackinac Island continued. Yet despite the harsh winters and isolation, the determined islanders continued to persist, turning instead to fishing for their survival. And then as steamboats came into use, the island became a tourist destination for the millionaires of the Midwest due to the scenery, interesting geology, and pleasant summer climate. It continues to be a favorite tourist destination to this day.

It's my hope that through *Captured by Love,* you will come to appreciate the history behind this popular island. But more than that, I pray you will seek your refuge in the Solid Rock, the One who is there for us no matter where we go or what we experience. He is the constant presence and help amidst the shifting sands of our lives. May you look to Him to see you through your most difficult days.

ACKNOWLEDGMENTS

Numerous talented people had input into the making of this book. First, I must thank my dedicated and fabulous editors at Bethany House. I'm forever grateful for your help, encouragement, and challenges that continually push me to become a better writer.

Thank you to all the Bethany House staff who read, edit, and put hours into designing my books and covers. I'm so thankful for your dedication time and time again.

I also appreciate the marketing and sales staff, who do a remarkable job of promoting my books both in stores and online. Thank you for your innovativeness and hard work.

A special thanks to my mom for listening and brainstorming with me during the initial stages of this book's development. Thanks for coming with me on my research trip to Mackinac Island and putting up with all my note-taking during our sight-seeing. I appreciate your letting me talk on and on about the characters and their histories as if they were real people. And thank you too for reading the manuscript in first-draft format and giving me your excellent feedback.

I'd like to thank my friend Karen Lehman and her children for educating me on the art of raising chickens in Michigan, which I learned isn't as easy as it appears! Thanks for letting me experience the chickens *up close and personal,* including the dust, dirt, and all. The information was invaluable to a city girl like me whose idea of raising chickens has been limited to "raising" eggs off the shelf and putting them into a grocery cart.

A huge thank-you to my fellow Bethany House historical author, Regina Jennings, for critiquing *Captured by Love.* It's truly a labor of love to provide feedback on a full-length novel. I appreciate each and every suggestion you made that pushed me to make this story better.

I want to thank my many writing friends for always being an encouragement to me. Thank you for cheering me on, standing by my side, and always being there to listen.

Finally, I thank you, dear reader, for taking the time to read this book. One of the best things about being an author is knowing that readers are enjoying my stories. I love hearing from you! So always feel free to visit my website, jodyhedlund.com, and drop me a line at jodyhedlund@ jodyhedlund.com.

ABOUT THE AUTHOR

Jody Hedlund is an award-winning historical romance novelist and author of the bestselling *Rebellious Heart, A Noble Groom,* and *The Preacher's Bride.* She holds a bachelor's degree from Taylor University and a master's degree from the University of Wisconsin, both in social work. Jody lives in Michigan with her husband and five busy children. Learn more at jodyhedlund.com.